LAST TRAM TO LIME STREET

Molly Bennett and Nellie McDonough have been neighbours since they were both newly-weds. Their friendship has helped them through good and bad times and they have shared tears, heartache and laughter. When Steve McDonough proposes to Molly's daughter, Jill, Molly and Nellie plan a knees-up party to celebrate.

A cloud hangs over their plans when a new family, the Bradleys, disrupt the community, and an elderly widow is robbed. Molly's teenage daughter Doreen, meets Philip at a dance, and can't wait to bring him home. But she's in for a shock when she finds out who his family are...

To my sons Philip and Paul,
my grandsons Mark and David,
and all of my family and friends.

LAST TRAM TO LIME STREET

by
Joan Jonker

Magna Large Print Books
Long Preston, North Yorkshire,
England.

British Library Cataloguing in Publication Data.

Jonker, Joan
   Last tram to Lime Street.

A catalogue record for this book is
available from the British Library

ISBN 0-7505-1118-4

First published in Great Britain by Headline Book Publishing, 1995

Cover illustration Gwynneth Jones by arrangement with Headline
Book Publishing

The right of Joan Jonker to be identified as the author of this
work has been asserted by her in accordance with the Copyright,
Designs and Patents Act, 1988

Published in Large Print 1998 by arrangement with Headline Book
Publishing Limited

Magna Large Print is an imprint of
Library Magna Books Ltd.
Printed and bound in Great Britain by
T.J. International Ltd., Cornwall, PL28 8RW.

Acknowledgement

To the many people who, have written to say how much they have enjoyed my books I send my sincere gratitude.

I get a lot of pleasure from writing, and to know that my books are read and appreciated by so many is an added bonus. All the letters I receive have one thing in common: their warmth and friendliness—just like the characters I love to write about.

Thank you, once again, for writing to me and I hope you will continue to enjoy my books.

Chapter One

'Ma, will yer stop fussin' around, yer gettin' on me nerves.' Molly Bennett clicked her tongue. 'The house 'as been done from top to bottom, yer can eat yer dinner off the flamin' floor, but yer still not satisfied.'

'Isn't it natural, now, that I'd want the place lookin' nice for yer da comin' out of hospital?' Bridie Jackson's Irish accent always became more pronounced when she was excited. 'After ten weeks, yerself wouldn't want him comin' home to a midden, would yer now?'

'A midden!' Molly gazed around the living room of the small two-up two-down terraced house and smiled. It was like a little palace, with the furniture shining so bright you could see your face in it, the grate blackleaded and gleaming, and a glowing fire roaring up the chimney. And with the walls newly decorated in a light beige paper patterned with small sprigs of leaves and flowers, the room looked light and airy. It had been a rush for her husband, Jack, to get the room finished in time, because they'd only had three days' notice that her da would be coming home. But over the weekend the whole family had got stuck in, scraping the walls, trimming the paper and helping with the pasting. It was midnight last night when they'd finished and stood back to admire their handiwork.

'A midden, did yer say?' Molly stood with her hands on her hips. 'We've worked our fingers to the bone for the last three days, washing curtains and windows, scrubbing everything it's possible to scrub, an' yer still not happy. A flamin' midden indeed!'

Bridie walked to the sideboard, moved the vase of flowers a couple of inches, then changed her mind and moved it back again. 'I'm so nervous and excited, yer'll have to make allowances for me, so yer will.' She touched her daughter's arm. 'Molly, me darlin', I don't know what I'd have done without you over the last few months. You, Jack, and the children, yer've kept me going, so yer have. I'd have been lost without you, and don't I give thanks to the good Lord every night for blessing me with such a marvellous family?'

'Oh, come on, Ma, don't go all soppy on me.' Molly was trying hard to keep her emotions in check. 'With Da comin' out of hospital, we should be singin', not cryin' our eyes out.'

Bridie straightened her shoulders. She was a fine-looking woman, with a face that was still beautiful, even with the worry lines that had grown deeper each day since her beloved husband, Bob, had had a heart attack. She had a slim, almost girlish figure, and her hair, snow white now, was combed straight back from her face and rolled into a bun at the nape of her neck. 'Will we have time for a cuppa an' a sandwich before the ambulance comes?'

Molly glanced at the clock on the mantelpiece. 'They said sometime in the afternoon, an' it's only twelve o'clock, so there's plenty of time.'

There was a hissing noise from the fire before a piece of coal fell on to the hearth. Bridie moved as though she'd been shot from a gun. She grabbed the shovel and brush from the brass companion set and swept up the offending piece of coal to throw it back on the fire. 'Will yer look at that now?' She viewed with disgust the black sooty mark left on the hearth. 'Just when yer think everything's right, something always comes along to prove yer wrong, so it does.'

With a resigned shrug of her shoulders, Molly made her way to the kitchen for the floor-cloth. When she came back there was a cheeky grin on her face. 'Here yer are, Ma.'

Bridie, on her knees in front of the grate, turned to take the cloth from her daughter's outstretched hand and noticed the grin. 'What's tickling yer fancy now, lass?'

'Nothing!' Molly let the smile slip from her face. 'I was just wondering if yer'd like me to take me tea an' sarnies down the yard to the lavvy to eat, save makin' any crumbs?'

Bridie threw the cloth down and fell back on her heels. 'Sure now, wouldn't that be a pretty sight for sore eyes?'

The sound of a motor outside brought Bridie scrambling to her feet and rushing to the window. 'He's here, Molly!' She let the curtain fall back into place. 'Bob's home!'

'All right, Ma, just calm down!' Molly held on to her mother's arm and wagged a finger in her face. 'Remember what the doctor said, no upset or excitement.'

Bridie nodded as she wrenched her arm free and bolted down the hall to open the front door. She was waiting by the kerb when the back doors of the ambulance opened and Bob stepped out. Her arms outstretched, she flew to him. 'Welcome home, me darling.'

Bob held her close while the ambulance men looked on. One of them, a man with sandy hair and laughing blue eyes, said, 'It looks as though someone's glad to see you, Mr Jackson.'

Bridie beamed at him. ''Tis more than glad I am, son.'

Molly had been watching the scene with a lump in her throat. Now she moved forward and touched her mother on the shoulder. 'Move over, missus, an' let someone else get a look in.'

Too full of emotion to speak, Bob smiled as Molly rained kisses on his face. There'd been times in the hospital when he thought he wasn't going to pull through, so the sight of his beloved wife standing outside the little house that held so many happy memories, brought tears to sting the back of his eyes.

'I think we'd better move out of the way so these men can get about their business.' Molly winked at the two men who were waiting patiently to close the doors of the ambulance. 'Make yer sick, wouldn't it? Married over forty years and still love struck.'

The man with the sandy hair called, 'Take care of yourself, Mr Jackson.'

'Huh!' Molly watched her parents disappear into the house. 'No need to worry about me da lookin' after himself, she won't let the wind blow on him. Anyway, thanks, lads.'

When Molly walked into the living room, Bridie was helping Bob out of his coat. 'Now sit yourself by the fire while I make yer a nice cup of tea. The kettle's been on the boil for an hour, so it'll not take long.'

Molly took the overcoat from her mother. 'I'll hang it up, you see to the tea.'

Bob fell back in his favourite chair, pleasure and relief on his face. 'You've no idea how good it is to be home, lass, these ten weeks have seemed like a lifetime.' He gazed around the room. 'Been busy, I see.'

Molly could hear her mother pottering around in the kitchen. 'She's had everyone up the wall, rushin' around like blue-arsed flies to make sure everythin' was perfect for yer coming home.' She patted his knee and smiled. 'Anyone would think she was expectin' the King himself.'

'It looks nice, lass, and I'm grateful for everythin' yer've done for Ma while I've been away. You and Jack, and the children, have all been marvellous.' He swallowed hard. 'It can't have been easy for her, the first time we've been parted since the day we got married.'

'I know that, Da, an' I know yez love the bones of each other. But don't let her kill yer with kindness. If Ma has her way, yer'll be sittin' in that chair all day while she waits on yer hand an' foot. An' that's not goin' to do yer any good. I know what the doctor said, that yer can't go back to work and yer've got to take things easy. But he also said that if yer were

11

sensible, there was no reason why yer couldn't live a normal life. So don't let Ma molly-coddle yer too much.'

Bridie bustled in, carrying a wooden tray covered with a hand-embroidered cloth and set with a china tea pot, milk jug and sugar basin. 'You'll enjoy this, me darlin', so yer will. A nice cup of strong tea, just the way yer like it.'

'I won't stay, Ma.' Molly stood up. 'Mary from over the road said she'd pick Ruthie up from school when she went for Bella, but I don't want to play on her goodness. Besides, I've got dinner to see to.'

'Will Jack an' the children be coming round tonight?' Bob asked. 'It seems ages since I saw the kids.'

'Not tonight, Da.' Molly shook her head. 'They wanted to, but I said they'd have to wait a day or two, till yer got settled in, like.'

Bob looked disappointed. 'I was looking forward to seeing them.'

'Yer've only just come out of hospital, Da, yer don't want to be tiring yerself out.' Molly bent to kiss him. 'I'll come in the morning, see how yer are. If me ma thinks it's okay, the whole gang can come tomorrow night, but just for half an hour, mind yer! Yer still an invalid, so there'll be no knees-up or jars out.' Her eyes twinkled. 'We'll wait till next week for that.'

Bridie was about to object when she realised her daughter was only joking. 'Will I ever get used to your humour?' She tutted. 'Sure, I nearly fell for that one, right enough.' She busied herself with the cups on the tray. 'Now will yer .be on yer way before the tea gets cold.'

Molly winked at her father. 'Did yer hear that, Da? She's worked me to a standstill, but now she doesn't need me any more it's a case of "on yer bike, pal"!'

Bob chuckled. 'Now I know I'm home.'

'Has she behaved herself?' Molly clutched her daughter's hand. 'Not been givin' yer any lip?'

'No, she's been as good as gold.' Mary Watson leaned against the door jamb. Her house was right opposite Molly's, and their seven-year-old daughters were the best of mates. 'How's yer dad?'

'He looks well,' Molly answered, tightening her grip on Ruthie, who was pulling to get away. 'But yer can never tell with a heart complaint, can yer? He looked the picture of health five minutes before he had the heart attack, so as I say, yer can never tell. Looks can be deceiving.'

'Mam, let go, yer hurtin' me,' Ruthie cried, stamping her foot. 'I want to go 'ome and get me hoop.'

'Molly, why don't yer leave her here till yer get the dinner on?' Mary offered. 'She can play upstairs with Bella.'

Molly looked down into her daughter's pixie-like face, and when she noted the petulant droop to the rosebud mouth, Mary's offer was too tempting to resist. 'Are yer sure yer don't mind? I've been at it since early this mornin' and I'm not in any mood for her shenanigans.'

'Come on, Ruthie.' Mary held her hand out. 'You and Bella can play tiddly-winks.'

Molly turned to cross the road. 'Yer a pal, Mary. I'll give her a shout when the dinner's ready.'

The gas plopped when Molly put a match to it, and she quickly put the pan of potatoes on the ring. There was meat and cabbage over from yesterday, so she only had to warm it up to have with the potatoes. She was bending down to get the frying pan out of a cupboard when there was a loud ran-tan on the knocker. 'Ye gods and little fishes!' Molly said aloud, closing her eyes. 'Is there no flamin' peace for the wicked?'

'Hiya, Molly, I've been lookin' out for yer.'

'Oh, thank God it's only you. Come on in.' Molly pressed herself back against the wall to let her eighteen-stone neighbour pass. Nellie McDonough lived three doors away, and she was Molly's oldest and best friend.

Nellie waddled down the hall, her hips brushing the wall either side. 'How's yer dad?'

'He looks fine, just the same as when yer saw him in hospital last week. I'm slippin' round in the mornin', if yer'd like to come an' see him.'

'Ooh, yeah, I'd like that, girl!' A smile crossed Nellie's chubby face. 'I've got some news for yer.'

Molly pulled two chairs away from the table. 'Take the weight off yer feet, but I haven't got long, mind, 'cos I've been out since early this mornin' and I'll have to tidy up before the family get in.'

The chair creaked ominously as Nellie sat down and Molly held her breath. One of these days her friend would end up on the floor on her backside, a broken chair beneath her. 'Well, what's the news?'

Nellie adjusted the turban on her head before folding her arms under her mountainous bosom. 'D'yer know that empty house at the top of the street, the one the Culshaws did a midnight flit from on Christmas Eve?'

'Yeah, what about it?'

'A family moved in there this mornin'.' Nellie was rewarded by Molly's look of surprise. 'The cart came just after you'd left to go to yer ma's.'

'Go 'way!' Molly's fingers were making patterns in the plush of the chenille tablecloth. 'It's a wonder the rent man didn't say anythin'. Mind you, I haven't seen Mr Henry for weeks, you've been payin' me rent.' Molly's eyes narrowed. 'You're losin' yer grip, aren't yer? Fancy not gettin' that news out of him!'

'Humph!' Nellie jerked her head back, sending her layers of chins swaying in all directions. 'I don't 'ave time to stand gossipin' to the flamin' rent man! Got more to do with me time.'

'Ah, well, yer see, look what yer've missed by not spendin' a few minutes gossipin' with him! If yer'd known they were moving in, yer could have taken a chair up an' sat outside, makin' a note of what furniture went in, an' how many were in the family. Then yer could 'ave passed the information on to me.' Molly could picture the scene in her mind and her

15

tummy started to rumble with laughter. 'Fine mate you are, Nellie McDonough! Now we'll never know what they've got in their 'ouse.' The movement of the floorboards beneath her feet warned Molly that laughter was going to erupt from her friend's mouth any second. And when Nellie laughed, the whole house would shake. She stood up quickly and rounded the table. 'Come on, missus, off that chair before yer break the bloody thing.'

Nellie was pulled to her feet just as the laughter came, and her whole body shook. The two friends clung to each other as tears rolled down their cheeks. Neighbours for nineteen years, they'd grown so close they were like sisters. Nellie had had three children one after the other, just a year apart. And Molly had followed suit, each of hers a year younger than Nellie's. But Molly had broken the mould when seven years after Tommy, her youngest, was born, she became pregnant with Ruthie.

'D'yer know, that's the best laugh I've had for months.' Molly ran the back of her hand across her eyes. 'Thinkin' of you sittin' outside the new people's house, takin' a note of what went in, well, can yer imagine it?'

Nellie's chins were doing a quickstep as she tried to control her mirth. 'What I could do, if yer like,' she spluttered, 'I could knock on their door an' ask to borrow a cup of sugar. With a bit of luck they might ask me in.'

'I'd better come with yer, then, so I can pick yer up after they've belted yer one.' Molly sniffed. 'D'yer know, that laugh's done me

16

a power of good. Better than six bottles of stout.'

Nellie was wiping her nose on the corner of her wraparound floral pinny. 'Cheaper, too! Anyway, the day wasn't wasted, I did see the man an' his wife. About our age, I should think. And I saw two teenagers, but whether they're the only kids they've got, I wouldn't know. An' from what I saw of the furniture, well, it was just so-so, nothin' to write home about.'

Molly's eyes were wide. 'How the 'ell did yer see all that from down this end?'

Nellie tapped her nose. 'Ah, well, I mightn't gossip with the rent man, but I do spend some time in the corner shop talkin' to Maisie an' Alec. And as luck would 'ave it, I was there when the cart rolled up. An' from the shop window yer can see right over to that house.'

'You nosy beggar!' Molly pressed her hands to her waist. 'Don't yer dare make me laugh again, Nellie McDonough, 'cos I've got a stitch in me side now. But tell me, did yer just stand lookin' out of the shop window, watchin' everythin' that was goin' on?'

'Yeah!' Nellie rolled her eyes. 'Look, if yer goin' to get a cob on 'cos I make yer laugh, I'm not goin' to tell yer any more.'

Now she had Molly filled with curiosity. 'Nellie McDonough, if yer think yer gettin' out of this 'ouse without tellin' me everythin', then yer've got another think comin'. So come on, spit it out.'

Nellie took a deep breath, wondering how she could possibly stop herself from laughing. 'I was

17

in the shop when the cart came past loaded with furniture. Naturally me and Maisie, and Alec, were interested to see where it was goin' so we went to the window. Then a customer came in, you know Mrs Barrow from the next street, and she told Alec she wasn't in a hurry, so she stood watching with us. Pretty soon the shop was full, and we all had our noses pressed against the three windows.' It was no good, Nellie couldn't keep her face straight. Her chubby cheeks moved upwards to cover her eyes as she bent double. 'Honest, girl, there must have been about twenty people in that little shop, an' every one of them swore they weren't in a hurry.'

'An' how long did that go on for?'

Nellie's loud guffaw filled the room. 'Until the cart was empty and the peep show was over. I told Maisie afterwards she should 'ave sold tickets, her an' Alec would 'ave made a fortune.'

Once again the two women clung to each other. Molly could feel her shoulder damp from the tears that rolled unchecked from Nellie's eyes. 'I'll tell yer somethin' for nothin', Nellie, I don't like the new people, they're not a bit considerate,' Molly wheezed. 'Why the 'ell didn't they leave it until tomorrow to move in? I could 'ave had a seat right in the front of Maisie's window.'

'It was better than goin' to the pictures, girl,' Nellie said. 'Funniest thing I've seen in years.'

Molly's eyes lighted on the clock on the mantelpiece and she broke away. 'Holy sufferin' ducks, look at the time! I'll be laughin' the other side of me face if the dinner's not ready when Jack an' the kids get in.' She turned Nellie to face the door. 'On yer way, kiddo! I might slip up later when I've got Ruthie to bed. Ta-ra for now.'

'No, none of yez can go to see Grandad.' Molly let her eyes stay for a second on each of the faces around the table. Only Ruthie was missing. She'd been tired so Molly had given her her dinner early and put her to bed. Jill, her eldest, was sixteen. A lovely-looking girl with a slim figure, long blonde hair, vivid blue eyes and a peaches-and-cream complexion. Next to Jill sat Doreen, who was a year younger. Doreen was very like her sister in looks, but their natures were completely different. Jill was shy and gentle, while Doreen was a livewire, outgoing and outspoken.

'Just for five minutes, Mam, please?' Tommy pleaded. 'I'm dyin' to see me grandad.'

Molly's gaze landed on her fourteen-year-old son. He'd left school at Christmas and now worked in the same factory as his dad. Like the rest of the family, he idolised his grandad, and after ten weeks it was only natural he wanted to see him. 'Perhaps tomorrow night, son.' Molly had a soft spot for her only son, who was the spitting image of his dad, tall, dark and good-looking. 'When I see him in the mornin', if he looks well enough, we'll all nip around for half an hour.'

'Five minutes wouldn't hurt,' Tommy growled.

'Yer heard what me mam said, so stop yer

19

moaning.' Doreen aimed a kick at him under the table, but it was her father's shin her foot came into contact with.

'We'll have less of that, young lady.' Jack pointed a fork at his daughter. 'We sit around the table to eat, so mind yer manners.'

'Oh, here we go again, not in the 'ouse five minutes an' fightin' already.' Molly leaned towards Jill. 'It's a good job you an' me haven't got bad tempers, isn't it, sunshine? Life wouldn't be worth livin'.'

Jill smiled. She never got involved in family squabbles, but they didn't upset her because they were soon over and nobody sulked or held grudges. 'I have my moments.'

Jill was the clever one of the family. She could have gone on to high school when she was fourteen, but Molly needed her working and bringing in a wage. With six mouths to feed, clothes to buy and all the bills to pay, she was hard pressed to make ends meet on Jack's meagre earnings. For years she'd had to scrimp and save, robbing Peter to pay Paul, and although it broke her heart, she had to deny her daughter the chance of a better education for the sake of all the family. Jill never complained. Instead she got herself a job behind the counter in Allerton's cake shop, and did a two-year course at night school learning shorthand and typing. Now she was working in Castle Street, in the offices of Pearson, Sedgewick and Brown, a firm of solicitors.

'D'yer want to hear somethin' funny?' Molly now asked her. 'These lot needn't listen if they don't want to.' With a smile already on her face, she began to relate Nellie's story, mimicking her friend down to the last detail. She was looking at Jill, but out of the corner of her eye she could see smiles appearing on the faces of the others. By the time she was halfway through the story, the room was ringing with loud laughter.

'Ay, Mam, that's not 'alf funny,' Tommy chuckled. 'I can just imagine Auntie Nellie, she looks like Norman Evans, doin' his "Over the garden wall" thing.'

'Don't yer dare tell her that, she'll 'ave yer life.'

'I think the funniest part is all the customers crowded round the windows in that little shop,' Doreen giggled, her face flushed. 'I'd love to 'ave seen it.'

'What's tickled my fancy,' Jack said, 'was you pulling Nellie off the chair in case she broke it. The size of her, yer could have broken yer back, never mind the chair!'

'I laughed that much, I nearly wet me knickers,' Molly said. 'She's a real case when she gets goin', is Nellie.'

'You know, Mam, I bet if you'd dared her to go up to the new people and ask to borrow a cup of sugar, she'd have gone.' Jill was courting Nellie's son, Steve, and she knew the tricks her boyfriend's mother could get up to. 'I wouldn't put anything past her.'

'No, yer can always expect the unexpected with Nellie.' There was a twinkle in Molly's eyes as she gazed around the table. 'Yer all in such a happy frame of mind, it seems a shame

21

to wipe the smiles off yer faces. But yez can all get stuck in an' get the dishes washed, cos I ain't doin' them, I'm worn out.'

'Ah, ray, Mam! I'm goin' out!' Doreen and Tommy cried in unison, dismay on their faces.

'When the dishes are done yez can go to Timbuctoo for all I care, but not before,' Molly told them. 'I've been on the go the whole flamin' day, an' I've had it up to here.' She patted the top of her head. 'So, no moans, just get crackin'. The sooner yer start, the sooner yer finished.'

'I'll do the dishes,' Jill said. 'Steve's not coming until half seven.'

'I'll give a hand,' Tommy grunted, pushing his chair back. 'It won't take long.'

'We'll all get stuck in.' Doreen started to stack the dirty plates on top of each other. 'Many hands make light work.'

Molly smiled at Jack across the table. 'Not bad kids, are they?'

Jack smiled back. 'If they're all going out, we'll have the house to ourselves. Just think, a couple of hours' peace an' quiet.'

'Yer'll have it all to yerself, sunshine, 'cos I promised to go up to Nellie's for half an hour.'

Jack moved his head from side to side. 'Haven't you seen enough of each other for one day? Beats me what yez find to talk about.'

'I won't be out long, just half an hour. I'll be back before yer've finished readin' the *Echo*.' Molly stood up and pushed her chair back under the table before going into the kitchen. She put her fingers to her lips, and winked, her eyes

22

telling the children to make less noise and listen. Then she went back to Jack. 'Besides, we won't be doin' much talkin'. We're goin' for a little walk, just up the street. We want to see what kind of curtains the new people have got up.' The look of bewilderment on Jack's face egged her on. 'Yer can always tell what kind of folk they are by their curtains. Dead giveaway, they are.'

'Molly, have yer lost the run of yer senses? Yer can't just walk up to a person's house and stand gawping at their curtains! They'll wonder what sort of a neighbourhood they've moved into.'

'Well, it's like this, yer see, Jack. Me an' Nellie agree that because we've lived 'ere for nearly twenty years, it's our territory, like, isn't it? We reckon we're entitled to vet any new people that move in.' The startled look on her husband's face was too much for Molly. She leaned her elbows on the sideboard and gave way to the laughter that had been building up inside her.

When Jack saw the three grinning faces appear round the kitchen door, he cursed himself for being taken in so easily. He should know, after all these years, to take everything his wife said with a pinch of salt. 'Okay, I give in.' He held his hands up in surrender. 'You caught me out again, Molly Bennett.'

'That's why I love yer, Jack Bennett, yer so easy to manage.' Molly plonked herself on his knee and put her arms around his neck. 'I wouldn't 'ave yer any different for all the money in the world.' She was about to kiss him when she remembered they had an audience. 'Back to work, you lot. There's some things not meant for your eyes.'

Holding Molly's body close, and listening to the happy giggling in the kitchen, Jack thought how lucky he was to have a wife who could turn tears to laughter. And when her soft lips covered his, he told himself there wasn't another bloke alive who had what he had.

Chapter Two

'Good news, Jill!' Miles Sedgewick's smile as he waltzed into the office was as wide as his face. Without taking his eyes off Jill he put his briefcase on the floor and sat on the corner of his desk. 'A letter came in this morning's post from the Ministry of Defence to say I'd been accepted for the post.'

Jill's fingers hovered over the typewriter keys as she gazed across the office she shared with Miles, the son of one of the partners in the firm of solicitors. She tried to feel some enthusiasm but it wasn't easy. She really didn't care one way or the other about Miles leaving, it was his reason for getting another job that galled her. Mr. Sedgewick senior thought a war with Germany was on the cards, and because he knew people in the right places, he'd wangled a job for his son in a reserved occupation. Which meant, if there was a war, while all the eligible men were being called up, Miles would be sitting pretty. And Jill didn't think that was fair. As her mam said, it just showed what money could do.

'That's nice for you.' Jill flicked the arm at the end of the typewriter to start a new line. 'I bet your father's pleased.'

'He and Mother are delighted,' Miles told her, smugly. He was twenty-one, tall, and quite good-looking, with a thick mop of dark hair and hazel eyes. 'Father said I can leave on Friday, so I'll be starting my new job next Monday.' He rounded his desk and sat down. 'I feel very pleased with myself.'

'Will you still be studying, the same as you are here?' Jill asked.

'Oh, yes! It'll be a few years before I'm a fully fledged solicitor. If there is a war, and Father seems to think it's inevitable, it won't last long, probably only a year or so, then I'll be back here to join the firm as a junior partner.' Miles took a fountain pen from the top pocket of his suit and tapped it on the desk. 'This calls for a celebration, don't you think? A leaving party to send me on my way.'

'I'm sure your father will arrange something.'

'Oh, I don't want to celebrate with Father! I was thinking you and I could go out together for a meal and a drink. How are you fixed for Friday night?'

He's got a nerve, Jill thought. Doesn't even bother asking if I'd like to go, just takes it for granted. 'No thanks, Miles, I'll be going out with Steve on Friday.'

'Surely he can take your chains off for one night? After all, it's only to bid me a fond farewell.'

Jill shook her head. Miles had talked her into going with him and his parents to a Christmas function in the Adelphi, and it had been the cause of a split between her and Steve. Her boyfriend had begged her not to go, couldn't understand why she wanted to go out with another bloke. But Jill had already promised Miles, and because she thought it would sound childish if she said her boyfriend objected, she'd gone. In her mind she'd felt sure Steve would come round when he'd got over his fit of the sulks, but he hadn't. For three weeks he'd stayed away from her and although Jill had kept her sadness to herself, it had been the longest three weeks of her life. Miles had persuaded her to go out with him a few times during those weeks when she was at a loose end, and he'd gone out of his way to win her affection, but it hadn't worked. Jill's heart belonged to Steve, and all she could feel for Miles was friendship. Now she was back with the boy she loved, she had no intention of doing anything else to jeopardise their relationship. 'No, Miles! I bet you wouldn't like it if you had a girlfriend and she went out with somebody else.'

'If I had a girlfriend, I wouldn't be so possessive.' The expression on Miles' face reminded Jill of a petulant child who couldn't get his own way. 'Steve must be very unsure of himself if he's afraid to let you out of his sight.' The tapping of his pen became louder.

26

'I think he's very immature, and you are very silly to give in to him. Surely you're capable of thinking for yourself, having a mind of your own?'

'Oh, I do have a mind of my own, Miles.' Jill tried to cool her temper by reminding herself that this was her boss's son. But her pride wouldn't let him get away with what he'd said. 'Nobody twists my arm, makes me do anything I don't want to do. Steve is my boyfriend because I want him to be my boyfriend. He always has been, always will be, and that's the way I want it.'

'Then let me wish you all the luck in the world,' Miles said, his voice thick with sarcasm, 'because, believe me, you'll need it.' Throwing his pen down, he swivelled in his chair and pulled at the handle of the top drawer in his desk. In his temper he forgot it opened at a mere touch, and before he could stop it the drawer slid completely out of the desk, scattering its contents all over the floor. 'Damn and blast!'

Under normal circumstances Jill would have rushed across the office to help pick up the papers and sort them back into the appropriate files. But not today. Miles was behaving like a spoilt child, so she let him get on with it. She watched him get down on his hands and knees to retrieve the scattered papers and knew it would take him ages to file them away in the correct order, whereas she would have had it done in half the time.

But when guilt started to niggle at Jill's conscience she quickly banished it. Miles was a grown man, but he'd been so molly-coddled all his life he thought he could have everything he wanted, including her. He'd never known what it was like to be poor, never known hunger. His clothes were the best money could buy and he owned a big posh car. Jill had never begrudged him these things, she wasn't jealous or envious because she was satisfied with her own life. But it rankled that he'd been wangled into a nice cushy job where he'd be safe if a war started. There'd be no exemption for other blokes his age, like Steve, or their Tommy when he was old enough, and it seemed so unfair.

'I'd give you a hand, Miles,' Jill could only see the top of his head above the desk, 'but Mr Brown wants this letter urgently.'

'I'm quite capable of managing on my own, thank you.'

Jill rolled her eyes. The atmosphere in the office was going to be decidedly cooler now. Never mind, she could put up with it for a week. She checked the dictation on her pad and started to type.

'Stop gobblin' yer dinner down.' Molly glared across the table at Doreen. 'Anyone would think yer hadn't seen food for a month.'

'I'm meeting Maureen in an hour.' Doreen spoke with her mouth half full. 'We're goin' to Millington's.' She chewed for a while, then swallowed. 'Why don't you an' Steve come with us, Jill? Connie promised to teach us the tango tonight.'

'No, I'll never make a dancer.' Jill smiled as

28

she tossed her head. 'I'm like a block of wood, no rhythm.'

'That's 'cos yer won't let yerself go,' Doreen said, repeating what she'd heard at the Constance Millington Dancing Academy. 'If yer let yer body go loose and learn to sway with the music, it'll soon come to yer.'

'No, I don't feel like going. Besides, me and Steve are going round to see Grandad.'

'He looks fine,' Molly told them. 'He was dryin' the dishes when I got there this mornin', an' me ma was smilin' that much yer'd think she'd won the pools.'

'Oh, I nearly forgot!' Jack laid his knife and fork down and leaned his elbows on the table. 'Me an' the lads 'ave come up this week, three draws we got.' He was in a syndicate with six of his workmates, each paying fourpence ha'penny a week towards the three-bob stake. There were only four draws on the coupon, so we're bound to get something. But don't go breaking eggs with a big stick, it might only be a few bob.'

'Don't knock it, Jack Bennett, a few bob's a few bob!' Molly rubbed her hands in glee. 'Might be enough to get meself a new pair of shoes.'

'Will yer mug us, Dad?' Doreen coaxed. 'I could do with a new pair of shoes too!'

Jack smiled, thinking how lovely it would be if the winnings were enough to treat the whole family. Could be, if the lads in work were right. He didn't understand about permutations and things, he left that to the bloke who filled the coupon in, but apparently they had about

29

five lines up. He was feeling pretty excited himself, but he wasn't going to tell Molly in case she built her hopes up. It was only a second dividend and if there were a lot of winners they could end up getting paid out in peanuts. Better to be cautious than have to dash everyone's hopes. 'Let's wait and see, eh? Don't bank on anythin' till we know for sure what they're paying out on.'

There was a bang overhead and all eyes went to the ceiling. 'Oh my God, Ruthie's fallen out of bed.' Molly scraped her chair back but Jack motioned for her to stay where she was. 'I'll go up.'

He was back seconds later, clutching Ruthie's well-loved doll. 'She must have turned in her sleep and knocked the doll off the pillow.'

Molly put a hand to her heart. 'Gave me the fright of me flamin' life! I had visions of her lyin' on the floor with a broken arm or summat.'

'That's daft, tha' is.' Tommy had been quiet, considering how he could join the football pools syndicate. But it was no good, he couldn't afford it. Fourpence a week out of his pocket money would mean he wouldn't have enough left to go to the pictures. 'She'd be screamin' her head off it she'd hurt 'erself, wouldn't she?'

'Oh, aye, hard clock, yer there, are yer?' Molly tutted. 'Fancy silly old me not thinkin' of that!'

'I'd better get me skates on,' Doreen said. 'I've got to get washed and changed and be down at Bedford Road by eight o'clock.' She picked her plate up and kicked her chair backwards, sending it crashing into the sideboard.

'In the name of God, are yer tryin' to wreck the place?' Molly glared. 'The furniture's fallin' to pieces as it is, it doesn't need any help from you.'

'Sorry, Mam!' Doreen rushed to the kitchen with her plate and they heard her bang it down on the draining board. When she came back into the room she dropped a kiss on her mother's forehead and whispered, 'Yer might be able to buy yerself a new suite out of me dad's winnings.'

'Aye, an' pigs might fly,' Molly called as her daughter took the stairs two at a time. 'If I ever do get new furniture, an' it's a ruddy big if, there'll be some changes in this 'ouse, believe me! Yez won't be able to lay a finger on anythin', or sit down. Dinner will be served in the kitchen and yez can eat it standin' up.'

'Let's hope I don't win a fortune then,' Jack chuckled. 'Life wouldn't be worth living.'

'Oh, I didn't mean you, light of my life.' Molly leaned forward to pat his arm, speaking in her posh accent. 'If you come into money, it would only be right and proper for you to be waited on hand and foot. Your every wish would be my command.'

'Now that is something I'd have to see with me own eyes before I'd believe it.' Jack put his knife and fork down and pushed his plate away. 'Now for a nice cup of tea, a ciggie, a read of the *Echo* and a chance to unwind.'

'Are you goin' out, Tommy?' Molly asked, watching Jack move to his favourite chair at

31

the side of the fireplace.

'Only up to Ginger's. There's nowhere else to go 'cos we're both skint.' Tommy eyed his mother hopefully. 'Yer wouldn't lend us a tanner to go to the flicks, would yer?'

Molly turned her head away. How could she refuse him when he looked so much like Jack had at his age? But once she started lending him money he'd always be in debt. When he had to pay it back at the weekend, he'd be skint again and on the scrounge. The girls had always managed on their pocket money, so Tommy had to learn to do the same. 'I'm sorry, sunshine, but I've only got enough to see me through the week.'

'I'll give you sixpence,' Jill said, seeing the disappointment on her brother's face. She got much more pocket money because she was on a decent wage, and most weeks she didn't spend it all. 'You needn't pay me back, I'll treat you.'

'Ooh, the gear!' Tommy's face lit up. 'Yer a pal, our Jill!'

'She's too soft-hearted, yer mean,' Molly said, but she wasn't displeased. Jill's generosity meant she wouldn't have to spend the night feeling guilty.

There was a knock on the front door and Jill jumped to her feet. 'This is probably Steve.'

'Keep him talkin' a minute till I get this table cleared.' Molly hastily gathered the plates together. 'It looks a mess for anyone to walk in to.'

Jill and Steve came in hand in hand, their pleasure at being together written on their faces.

'Hi, Mr Bennett.' Steve McDonough was a handsome lad. Six feet tall, shoulders on him like an ox, and a glowing, healthy complexion. He had a mop of dark brown hair, eyes that were constantly changing from hazel to green, strong white teeth and dimples in his cheeks.

'Hello, son.' There was warmth in Jack's smile as he pointed to the couch. 'Sit yerself down.'

'I'll give me mam a hand with the dishes,' Jill said. 'I won't be a minute.'

Molly's head appeared around the kitchen door. 'No need, I'll 'ave them done in no time.' She winked at Steve. 'All right, sunshine?'

'Yeah, fine, Mrs B.' When Steve grinned the dimples in his cheeks deepened. 'How's yerself?'

'Can't complain.' Molly chuckled, smoothing down the blonde hair that had once been as bright and shining as her daughter's but was now peppered with strands of grey. 'At least I could complain, but what's the use when no one will listen?'

'Me mam's expecting yer.'

'Yes, I said I'd go up for a natter.' Molly came further into the room to lean on the sideboard. 'I've been so busy the last couple of weeks, what with going round to me ma's every day I've lost track of everythin'. Apart from sayin' "hello" to the neighbours as I've been passing, I've missed all the news and gossip.'

'Can you understand women, son, 'cos I'm blowed if I can.' Jack turned his head to wink at Steve. 'They're never happy unless they've got someone to pull to pieces.'

'Oh, aye!' Molly stood to attention. 'And tell me, pray, whose ears come out on sticks when I've got a juicy bit of gossip to tell? The only reason men don't gossip is because they never bloody do anythin' worth gossipin' about!'

'I'm goin' out before yez come to blows,' Tommy said. 'I'll see yer, Steve.'

'Yeah, ta-ra, Tommy.'

Jill held her hand out to Steve. 'Come on, I'll get me coat on the way out.'

Molly walked to the door with them. 'Don't stay long, will yer? Grandad goes to bed early.' She watched them stroll up the street, their heads close, their arms around each other's waists. Molly loved Steve like a son and she'd been upset when he and Jill had fallen out. But they were back together again, and this time, please God, it was for keeps.

'Can yer get in, girl?' Nellie pressed back against the wall to let Molly pass. 'Tight squeeze, isn't it?'

'Nah, yer tummy's like a feather pillow, it squashes in.'

'Give us yer coat, I'll hang it up.'

Molly undid one button on her coat, then paused. 'D'yer feel like comin' to Ellen's? I've seen nothin' of her for months, don't think we've exchanged more than half a dozen words.'

Nellie nodded. 'I'll just tell George where we're goin'.'

'I'd better pop me head in as well, otherwise George will think I've fallen out with him.'

'Hello, Molly!' George McDonough ran his fingers through his thinning, steel-grey hair. 'Yer quite a stranger these days.'

'Well, things should be back to normal from now on.' Molly grinned. 'I'll be back tormentin' yer, as usual.'

'I'll only be gone an hour,' Nellie told him, pushing Molly back into the hall. 'When the fire goes low, get off yer backside an' put a shovel of coal on. If it's out when I get back, I'll flatten yer.'

Nellie banged the door behind her and they walked the few yards to Molly's next-door neighbour, Ellen Clarke. As Nellie's hand lifted the knocker, Molly's mind wandered back over the last twelve months. If anyone had told her last year that one day she'd be visiting Ellen as a friend, she'd never have believed them. Nobby Clarke, Ellen's husband, had been a violent bully, who spent all his money in the pubs or on the horses. Whenever you saw him, he was either too drunk to walk straight or in a violent rage, so everyone in the street gave him a wide berth. It was obvious he kept his wife short of money because she and their four children never had a decent stitch on their backs. Downtrodden was the word that came into Molly's mind whenever she saw Ellen walking down the street with her head bowed, never passing the time of day with even her closest neighbours.

Molly had felt sorry for Ellen and the kids, with their pinched, unhappy faces, but because of Nobby she'd kept her distance. He wasn't a man you could take to, unless you were in the mood for a fight. The one thing Nobby was good at was using his fists and shouting obscenities. Molly could do her share of swearing, but she drew the line at some of the things that came out of Nobby's mouth.

But one day last year circumstances had brought Molly closer to the Clarkes, and she was horrified when she found out exactly how bad life was for Ellen and the kids. Twenty-five shillings a week was all Nobby gave his wife to live on. Out of that she was expected to pay the rent and gas, and buy food, coal and clothes for six of them. The rest of Nobby's wages he kept in his pocket to spend on drink, horses and ciggies. Ellen was so frightened of him she went without herself to make sure there was a decent meal on the table for him every night. If there wasn't, it was woe betide her. She'd be beaten and kicked until her thin body was covered in bruises. She and the children never knew what it was like to have a full tummy or decent clothes on their backs. No fire ever burned in their grate, and in bed at night they had to cuddle together under their coats for warmth. Their home was cold and cheerless, their sticks of furniture only fit for a bonfire.

It was Nobby's drinking that had finally freed Ellen from the nightmare she'd suffered for years. He got so drunk one day he walked in front of a moving tram. His legs were so badly mangled they had to be amputated, and his brain was affected. After a period in Walton Hospital, he was classified as being mentally insane and transferred to Winwick Hospital in Warrington.

Molly was so deep in thought she jumped when Nellie touched her arm. 'She must be flamin' well deaf!' the big woman growled. 'I've knocked loud enough to wake the dead!'

'I'll give a tap on the window.'

Within seconds they heard a shuffling, then the door opened. 'I was in the kitchen an' wasn't sure whether I was hearin' things.' Ellen stood aside. 'Come in. It's nice to see yer again, Molly.'

'I'm glad to be back in the fold, Ellen.' Molly slipped her coat off. 'I've got a lot of catching up to do.' She gazed around the newly decorated room and at the bright fire burning in the gleaming grate. What a difference a year could make. 'The room looks nice, Ellen, Corker did a good job.'

Ellen blushed as she always did when Corker's name was mentioned. 'It looks smashin', doesn't it? Wouldn't think it was the same room.'

Jimmy Corkhill, when he wasn't away at sea, lived with his widowed mother at the top of the street. Until Nobby's accident, no one realised he'd known Ellen since they were teenagers, because he never went near the Clarkes' house. Knowing Nobby from old as a drunken bully, always on the lookout for a fight, Corker had steered clear. But in the last year he'd been a good friend to Ellen and the kids. In fact, everyone in the street had rallied around to help, especially Molly and Nellie, who had talked the local butcher into giving Ellen a job so she could keep a roof over her head.

'When's Corker due home?' Molly asked. 'Should be this week, shouldn't it?'

'Thursday or Friday.' Ellen realised she'd given the game away and turned her head from their knowing smiles. 'At least I think so.'

Molly winked at Nellie. They both thought Corker's feelings for Ellen went beyond the bounds of friendship. But they also knew he wouldn't get anywhere, not with Ellen being so straight-laced. As far as she was concerned she was still a married woman, even if her husband was locked up in an asylum and hadn't recognised her on the few occasions she'd been able to afford the fare to visit him.

'Nellie tells me there's new people in the Culshaws' old house,' Molly said, leaning forward to rest her elbows on her lap. 'Have yer seen anythin' of them?'

Ellen pulled a face. 'If the wife is anythin' to go by, they're a right lot! She came in the shop one day, the first time she'd been in, mind you, an' she was as sweet as honey. Told us how she'd just moved in, an' that she'd be buyin' her meat off Tony from now on. Then she had the nerve to ask him for tick!'

'Go 'way!' The expression on Nellie's chubby face was comical. 'Well, how's that for ruddy cheek? That's the best yet, that is!'

Ellen giggled. 'That's what Tony told 'er to 'er face. An' yer should have seen the way she changed! Called 'im fit to burn, and I've never heard anythin' like the language she came out with. He got called everythin' under the sun

38

'cos he wouldn't give her tick. She was yelling
'er head off, her arms flyin' here, there an'
everywhere. I thought she was goin' to come
around the counter and belt him one. I'm glad
Tony was there, 'cos if I'd been on me own I'd
have died of fright. She's a hard case, all right,
an' as common as muck.'

'Of all the cheek!' Molly said. 'I don't like the
sound of her! Good job she lives at the top of the
street, I wouldn't want them for neighbours.'

'If the rest of the family are like the mother,
it's God help the people livin' next to them,'
Ellen said. 'She's as tough as old, boots.'

'Well I never!' Molly sat back in the chair.
'Some people would buy an' sell yer, wouldn't
they? First time in the shop an' asking for tick!
I'd never 'ave the cheek to do that, even if I
was starvin'.'

The corners of Nellie's mouth moved upwards
as a huge grin covered her face. 'Yer certainly
see life in the shop, don't yer, Ellen? I bet yer
could write a book on the goings-on.'

Ellen nodded. 'Me an' Tony have a good
laugh at some of them. But he's very good to
his customers. There's one old lady comes in
and she'll stand for ages sayin' she can't make
up her mind what to have for a change, when
we both know she'll end up with half a pound
of mince 'cos that's all she can afford.'

'Poor bugger,' Nellie huffed, 'it must be
lousy to live on yer own an' have to count
yer coppers.'

'Don't worry,' Ellen said, 'Tony looks after
her. Most days he'll stick a chop in with her

mince, or some neck ends.'

'This is nice, isn't it?' Molly crossed her legs, pulling her dress down over her knees. 'I haven't half missed our little chats.'

'Be honest, girl, it's not us yer've missed, it's all the juicy bits of gossip!' Nellie laughed. 'But I'll tell yer somethin', an' Ellen will bear me out, there's nothin' happened while you haven't been around. I'm beginnin' to think it's you that starts it all!'

'Uh, uh! Don't be givin' me that, Nellie McDonough! You don't hear it 'cos yer don't keep yer ear to the ground. Ellen knows about the new people up the street, but you're here all day an' wouldn't know them from Adam! It strikes me yer slippin', Nellie, losing yer touch.'

'Aye, well, I haven't 'ad you around to egg me on.' Nellie pressed her tummy in to lean forward and gaze into Molly's eyes. 'But I've no doubt yer'll soon have me up to scratch. By this time next week I bet yer'll be able to tell me everythin' that's goin' on in all the houses this end of the street.'

'Why stop at this end?' Molly looked innocent. 'Those new people live opposite Corker's mam, don't they? An' didn't I always tell Corker I'd keep an eye out for his mam when he was away?' She clicked her tongue on the roof of her mouth. 'There's no need to look at me like that, Nellie McDonough, 'cos honest to God, I'd made up me mind to go an' see Mrs Corkhill long before Ellen said anythin'.'

'I believe yer where thousands wouldn't.'

Nellie winked at Ellen. 'Give us a knock when yer goin', girl, an' I'll come with yer. I don't see why you should 'ave all the fun.'

'I'd stay clear of that family if I were you,' Ellen warned. 'I wouldn't go near them to save me life.'

'Don't worry, I've no intention of goin' near them,' Molly answered. 'I'm just goin' to visit Mrs Corkhill, see how she is. Mind you, if she mentions them of 'er own free will, I won't stop her. Wouldn't be polite, would it?'

Ellen started to titter. 'Never a dull moment with you two, is there?'

'No!' Molly grinned. 'We've got no money but we do see life, eh, Nellie me old mate?'

'We see it because you go lookin' for it,' Nellie said. 'That's why I'm comin' with yer tomorrow, to keep yer out of trouble.'

'Me very own bodyguard.' Molly blew her a kiss. 'Don't know what I'd do without yer.'

Chapter Three

Molly rapped on Mrs Corkhill's door before turning sideways to view with curiosity the house opposite. The downstairs curtains were still closed, dragged across any old way to give the house an unkempt appearance, while the upstairs window had no curtains at all, just a piece of newspaper covering the bottom panes of glass. There were two girls outside playing with a rubber ball, and Molly thought they looked about eight and ten years of age.

'Looks a bit of a mess, doesn't it, Nellie? How would yer like them for neighbours?'

'Huh! I'd do me flamin' nut! Look at the houses either side of it, all spick an' span, an' that one stickin' out like a sore thumb!'

'Who is it and what d'yer want?'

The voice from behind the door sounded abrupt, not a bit like the welcome they usually got from Corker's mother. Surprised at having to communicate through the door, Molly called, 'It's only me, Mrs Corkhill.'

There came the sound of a heavy bolt being drawn back, then the door opened. 'This is a surprise, I wasn't expectin' anyone.'

'Just got up, have yer, Mrs Corkhill?'

'Nah, I've been up since six o'clock.' The old lady shuffled down the hall in her carpet slippers, leaving Molly to close the door behind her. Fancy being caught like this, with her mob cap on and her false teeth in a cup of water in the kitchen. 'When yer get to my age yer don't need much sleep.' Corker's mother was small and slight, with pure white hair and deep lines etched on her face. But she was a wiry little soul and fiercely independent. Did all her own shopping and housework, and kept the place spotlessly clean.

'Go 'way with yer, yer just a spring chicken!' Molly gave her a hug. 'I thought with the bolt still bein' on yer must have just got up.'

Mrs Corkhill bent and pushed the poker

42

between the bars of the grate, lifting the coals to let a draught in. 'The fire's a bit low, but it won't take long to burn up.' She turned to face them, a hand covering her toothless mouth. 'I wasn't expectin' visitors an' yer've caught me on the hop. Me hair's a mess an' I've got no teeth in.'

'We're not visitors, we're mates!' Molly and Nellie sat side by side on the couch. 'If it makes yer feel better, though, sunshine, go an' comb yer hair an' put yer teeth in.'

A veined hand hid Mrs Corkhill's smile. 'Even at my age a woman's got to have some pride, an' there's nowt worse than being caught with no teeth in.'

'Go an' see to yerself, then, girl,' Nellie said, nodding knowingly. 'Me an' Molly aren't in no hurry.'

'I'll only be five minutes.'

When Mrs Corkhill had disappeared into the kitchen, Molly's hand swept around the room, which was filled with ornaments and pictures that Corker had brought home from his trips at sea. 'I bet there's somethin' here from every country in the world. Corker never comes home without a present for his ma.' She pointed to the rug in front of the fireplace. 'He brought that from India.'

'They're very nice and all that, but I'd hate the job of dustin' this lot. Just look at all the brass ornaments on the sideboard and the mantelpiece, there's a full day's work just polishin' that lot!' Nellie's chins wobbled. 'No, I'll stick to me Whistlin' Boy, thank you very much! A quick flick of the duster an' he's done.'

Molly lifted a warning finger. 'Sshh! I thought I heard the door. Yeah, there it is again.' Molly pushed herself up. 'There's someone knockin', Mrs Corkhill, shall I go?'

'Wait a minute.' Mrs Corkhill came in, drying her hands, the mob cap gone and her teeth in place. 'Tell them I'm not in, will yer, Molly?'

Molly turned, her hand on the door knob. 'I can't say that or they'll wonder what I'm doin' here. Anyway, yer don't know who it is, it might just be someone canvassing, tryin' to sell something.'

Mrs Corkhill shook her head. 'It'll be them from over the road, on the borrow, as usual. She sends the kids over a few times a day on the cadge. Either a cup of sugar, some marg or a few rounds of bread. They've got me moth-eaten.'

'Don't tell me yer give them what they ask for?' Molly saw the telltale blush and huffed with temper. 'The bloody cheek! They've only been here five minutes!'

'I don't like refusing.'

'If yer'd refused in the first place they wouldn't keep comin' back! Now they've got yer taped, they'll never leave yer alone.' Molly was beside herself with indignation. Fancy borrowing from an old lady! She looked at Nellie. 'They certainly know who to pick on, don't they?'

The knock on the door was loud enough for the whole street to hear and Nellie shuffled to the edge of the couch. 'Let me go, they'll not be botherin' yer again, Mrs C.'

'No, I'll go,' Molly said, noting the apprehension on the old lady's face. 'It's no good startin' anythin' 'cos Mrs Corkhill's got to live here. I'll make some excuse, then when Corker comes home he can deal with them.'

Molly opened the door to the eldest of the two girls she'd seen playing ball. 'Yes?'

'I wanna see the old lady.'

The brazen look on such a young face took Molly's breath away, but she stayed calm. 'The old lady? I suppose yer mean Mrs Corkhill?'

'Is tha' 'er name? Well, I wanna see 'er.'

'You can't see 'er now, she's busy.'

The crafty look in the youngster's eyes warned Molly, and she was just in time to grab a thin arm as the girl made to dash past her. 'Ay, ay, where d'yer think you're goin'?'

'I'm goin' to see Mrs Whats-her-name, an' you can't stop me, yer don't live 'ere.'

Molly tightened her grip, amazed that a young girl would answer a grown-up back in such a defiant way. She'd belt hers if they did that. 'I've told yer, she's busy! Now get back home, where yer belong.'

'I won't! Me mam wants to borrer some tea, she hasn't got none in the 'ouse an' we want a drink.' The girl's leg came up and she aimed a kick at Molly, but missed when Molly stepped back just in time.

'You little faggot!' Molly's nostrils flared in anger. 'If yer were mine I'd have yer over me knee and give yer a damn good hidin'.'

'Let go of me arm or I'll call me mam.' The girl tried to wriggle free but Molly's grip was

45

tight. 'Me mam'll kill yer.'

'Oh, aye!' Nellie had been standing by the living room door, listening to everything that was said. Now she came up behind Molly. 'Did yer say yer mam was goin' to kill someone? Well, you go an' bring yer mam over an' we'll see about that.'

The girl weighed up the size of Nellie and her face lost some of its defiance. But still she brazened it out. 'My mam can fight anyone, so there!'

'This I've got to see.' Nellie touched Molly's arm. 'Let her go. I can't wait to see this female Joe Louis.'

As soon as Molly's grip relaxed, the girl fled, stopping halfway across the street to turn and stick her tongue out before running through the open door of the house opposite.

'Well, have yer ever seen such a hard-faced kid in all yer life?' Molly leaned back against the door. 'No wonder Mrs Corkhill gives them what they ask for, she's probably terrified of them.'

'Let's step outside, see if the mother comes out.' Nellie held on to the door frame as she lowered herself down into the street. 'D'yer know, girl, I hope she does! It's a long time since we had any excitement.'

Molly was thinking she could do without this kind of excitement when a picture of Corker flashed through her mind. He was six feet five, was Corker, and built like a battleship. He was well known in the area and well liked. Especially by the children. When he walked up the street with his sailor's bag slung over his back, word

46

would spread like wildfire and children would leave their ollies and footballs to run to meet him, drawn like a magnet to the gentle giant they called Sinbad.

He was gentle, too, until he saw anyone being badly treated, then, roaring like a lion, he would move into action to help the underdog. And if it was the mother he adored who was being put on, then heaven help the perpetrator.

As her imagination conjured up pictures, Molly let out a giggle.

Nellie raised her eyebrows. 'What's ticklin' yer fancy now?'

Molly's giggle turned into a full-blown laugh. 'I'd love to see their faces when they get a load of Corker! If they've heard Mrs C's got a son, they'll expect 'im to be small an' thin, like her, not a flamin' giant!'

Nellie began to see the funny side and her whole body shook with laughter. 'Ay, wouldn't it be funny if they sent over for a cup of sugar an' Corker opened the door? They'd do it in their kecks.'

'Oh, yez think it's funny, do yez?'

They looked across to the pavement opposite where a woman was shaking a fist at them. She was about the same height as the two friends, and her size was somewhere between Molly's eleven stone and Nellie's eighteen. Her red hair looked as though it hadn't been combed for months, the pinny she was wearing was filthy and the stained navy-blue cardigan had big holes in the elbows. 'Yez'll be laughin' the other side of yer faces if I get me hands on yez.'

Nellie ran the back of her hand across her nose. Wait till she told George about this! It was like a scene from one of Old Mother Riley's films. She tried to wipe the smile from her face, knowing it would only inflame the woman more, but her efforts were in vain. Walking to the edge of the kerb, she put her hands on her ample hips and stared the woman out. 'Me an' me friend don't need to ask your permission to 'ave a private conversation, do we? Anyway, are yer comin' over or not?'

Rolling her sleeves up, the woman took stock of the situation. The one with the fair hair was no threat, she could easily deal with her. But the big woman was a different kettle of fish, she looked as though she could handle herself. And some of the neighbours were standing at their doors now, attracted by the shouting. If she got stuck in and came off worse, she'd be a laughing stock.

'Go on, Mam, belt 'er one.' The daughter who'd got her into this mess was pulling on her skirt. 'Go on, yer said yer would.'

'Get back in the 'ouse, yer little flamer!' The woman bent and delivered a stinging slap to the girl's bare leg. 'Get in an' do as yer told.'

Rubbing her leg, the girl stumbled back into the house. What was the matter with her mam? She'd never dodged a fight before. She could lick anyone, her mam could. Why, she'd even knocked a man out in the street where they used to live.

'Are yer comin' over or not?' Nellie goaded, thinking of Mrs Corkhill being taken for a ride by this woman and her family. 'We've got other things to do, even if you haven't.'

Quickly deciding that the odds were stacked against her, the woman blustered, 'If I didn't 'ave a pan boilin' on the stove, I'd be over there like a shot an' sort yez out.' The rolled-up sleeves were rolled up even further. 'But I'm warnin' yez, I'll be on the lookout for yez in future.'

'I can't wait for the pleasure,' Nellie shouted back. 'Next time, pick a better excuse than a boilin' pan.'

Molly pulled on Nellie's arm. 'Come on, that's enough. Don't be eggin' her on.'

Nellie allowed herself to be propelled back into the house where Mrs Corkhill was standing twisting the corner of her pinny. 'Oh, dear, I'm sorry you got involved. It would 'ave been easier to 'ave given them what they wanted.'

'Not on yer life!' Molly exploded. 'Don't let them borrow anythin' off yer again, d'yer hear? If yer refuse them a few times, they'll soon get fed up an' leave yer alone. Let's see if they can find anyone else as daft as you.'

'It's over now, Mrs C, so why don't yer put the kettle on an' we'll have a nice cuppa?' Nellie's face was beaming. She'd enjoyed that little exchange and it had given her something to talk about to George.

While they were having their tea Corker's mam told of the trouble the new people had caused. 'All the neighbours are up in, arms over them. The children are allowed to do as they like, fightin' with the other kids in the street an'

49

pinchin' their toys. And they're still playing out at eleven o'clock at night.'

'Why aren't they at school?' Molly asked. 'It's a wonder the schoolboard hasn't been after them.'

'They haven't been to school since they moved in.' Mrs Corkhill passed a plate of biscuits around. 'There's a boy as well. He looks old enough to 'ave left school, but I don't think he's working because he doesn't leave the house until after nine in the mornings. The father must 'ave a job, though, 'cos he's out early.'

'What's their name?' Molly asked.

'Bradley. The girl yer've just seen, she said her name's Joyce. The boy has been over on the cadge as well, but I don't know his name. Real shifty-eyed he is, never looks yer straight in the face. I just wish they'd leave me alone.'

'They're a queer lot, if yer ask me,' Nellie said. Then her brow creased as she asked, 'They don't borrow money off yer, do they?'

Mrs Corkhill looked sheepish. 'Only the once, a tanner it was.'

Molly blew out in exasperation. 'I know it's a daft question, but did yer get it back?'

When the old lady shook her head, Nellie banged her fist on the arm of the couch. 'The bloody cheek of them! Yer'll never get rid of them, Mrs C, unless yer put yer foot down. Next time they come, tell them to sod off.'

'Never mind,' Molly said, as the worry lines deepened. 'Corker's due home this week, he'll sort them out.'

50

'That's what I'm worried about.' Mrs Corkhill sighed. 'I don't want any trouble.'

'Yer've already got it!' Molly huffed. 'But yer won't 'ave it for long, not when Corker's home. He'll soon send them packin' with a flea in their ear.' She leaned forward to put her cup on the table. 'We'd better be makin' tracks, Nellie, I want to call an' see old Miss Clegg before I go to the shops, in case she needs anythin'. You an' Mary 'ave been doin' me good deeds for me, but I'm back in the fold now, ready to do me share.'

'Give us a leg-up, will yer?' Nellie held her hands out and pushed herself forward when Molly pulled. 'Thanks, girl, I don't know what I'd do without yer.'

'I do!' Molly told her, laughing. 'Yer'd be sat on that couch until George came lookin' for yer tonight.'

'Ho, ho, very funny!' Nellie's gentle push was enough to send Molly tottering backwards. 'Yer that sharp yer'll be cuttin' yerself one of these days.'

Mrs Corkhill smiled, wishing these two were her neighbours. She'd never tell Corker, 'cos he worried too much, but she did get very lonely sometimes. But she wouldn't if Molly and Nellie were around, 'cos there'd never be a dull moment.

'Don't forget what we've told yer,' Molly said as they stood on the doorstep. 'If they come over again, don't give them anythin', not even the time of day.'

'Don't worry, I won't.' But Mrs Corkhill

51

didn't feel as confident as she sounded. She knew she wouldn't refuse to give a cup of sugar or a few rounds of bread, not if it meant a peaceful life. She was too old to be fighting with neighbours, and that lot opposite were a right tough bunch.

'We'll nip up in the mornin',' Molly said. 'Just for a few minutes to make sure everything's all right.'

'Yeah, we'll do that.' Nellie linked her arm through Molly's. 'Ta-ra, Mrs C, don't do anythin' I wouldn't do.'

'That gives 'er a wide scope, doesn't it?' Molly said as they waved goodbye. 'There's practically nothin' you wouldn't do.' She could feel Nellie's tummy shaking against her arm. 'What's tickling yer now?'

'Yer right, there's not much I wouldn't do. But if yer were to ask George, he'd tell yer there's some things I can't do because me tummy gets in the way. Right frustrating it can be, I tell yer.'

'Nellie McDonough, yer've got a filthy mind.'

'Yeah, I know! Loverly, isn't it?'

Jack turned the key in the lock and pushed the door open. Then he turned to Tommy, who was standing behind him. 'Not a word, d'yer hear? I'll tell them when we're havin' our dinner. I'm dying to see the look on their faces.'

Jill and Doreen were sitting at the table when their father and brother breezed in, and Molly was just coming through from the kitchen with a plate in each hand. She smiled a greeting.

'I'll dish yours up now. No overtime tonight then, love?'

'No.' Jack slipped his coat off and walked out to hang it on the hall stand. He felt so happy and excited he could hardly contain himself. But he wanted to wait for just the right moment. And that moment came halfway through dinner when he couldn't keep it to himself any longer or he'd burst. 'I've got a bit of good news for yez.'

'Oh, aye,' Molly said, picking at a piece of meat stuck between her teeth. 'Been made a foreman, have yer?'

Jack banged his knife on the table. 'Are you all listening?'

There was complete silence, except for the hissing of the coals on the fire, as all eyes turned expectantly to the head of the house. Even Tommy had a look of anticipation on his face, though he knew what his dad was going to say.

'I told yez we'd come up on the pools, but I didn't know how much we'd get. Well, according to this morning's paper, an' me mates in work, we'll each get twenty-seven pounds, ten shillings and sixpence.'

Molly's knife and fork clattered to her plate as her mouth gaped in surprise. 'Go 'way! Jack Bennett, if yer havin' me on I'll break yer flamin' neck, an' I'm not jokin'.'

'Molly, it's you who's got the warped sense of humour, not me!' Jack was relishing every second. For the first time since the children had come on the scene, he was going to be able to give his wife more money than she'd ever had in one go. 'We had five lines up, an' altogether it comes to a hundred and ninety-odd pounds. Split between the seven of us, it works out at twenty-seven pounds, ten shillings and sixpence.'

Molly didn't speak, she just sat white-faced and wide-eyed, staring at Jack. My God, all that money! It was a small fortune! She couldn't think straight, but it must be nearly eight weeks' wages!

She was brought out of her daze by the high, excited voices of the children. All she could hear was, 'Can I have this?' 'Can I have that?' 'When will yer get it, Dad?' and Ruthie's plea, 'Can I have a new doll, Dad?'

'Ay, yez can just cut it out,' Molly shouted. 'Don't be so flamin' greedy! Yer dad's gone without other things so he could 'ave a bet every week, so the money is all his, he can do what he likes with it.'

'No, love, the money's for you,' Jack said softly. 'I've never been on a good wage, never been able to give yer enough to buy something just for yerself. Yer've always 'ad to scrimp and save, makin' sure me an' the children came first, and never once 'ave yer complained that yer needed a new coat or that the shoes were fallin' off yer feet.'

'Don't you be runnin' yerself down, Jack Bennett.' Molly's voice was thick with unshed tears. 'Yer the best husband in the world, bar none, an' I love the bones of yer.'

The children sat with their eyes down, their

54

father's words filling them with shame. He was right, they were greedy thinking only of themselves. In their minds they were remembering how it had been when they were all young, with only their dad's wages coming in. Their mam must have had a terrible struggle to make ends meet, but there'd always been a smile on her face and they could never remember her complaining.

'Me dad's right, Mam, you should have the money to do what you like with.' Jill was the first to speak. 'Get yourself some new clothes, or something for the house.'

'Yeah.' Doreen touched her mother's arm. 'How about a nice new couch so yer can sit in comfort?'

'Nah,' Tommy growled. 'A couch would be for all of us, not just me mam. Let 'er buy somethin' for herself.'

'Spend all that money on meself?' Molly laughed nervously. 'Not on yer life I won't!' Her eyes roamed the room, taking in the worn, scratched sideboard, the rickety chairs and the couch with the broken springs. 'I bet I could buy all new stuff for this room with that much money.'

'Think about it, love,' Jack said. 'I probably won't get the cash in me hand until next Monday, so there's plenty of time to decide what yer want to do with it.'

Her dinner forgotten, Molly clapped her hands in excitement, her face aglow. 'D'yez know, I've never 'ad that much money in me life! When me an' yer dad got married, we had ten pounds and thought we were millionaires! An' we were in those days, 'cos with that ten pounds we were able to buy everythin' for this house. It was all second-hand stuff, mind you, but we didn't care.'

Tommy chuckled, waving his hand in the air. 'This is still the same furniture, isn't it?'

'Yeah, it's lasted well.' Molly was so happy she couldn't stop laughing. 'Except for the poor couch, that's on its last legs. I've got permanent marks on me backside with the flamin' springs stickin' out.' She pushed her plate away. 'I'm too excited to eat. Just wait till I tell me ma and da, they'll be thrilled to bits. In fact,' she scraped her chair back, 'I'm goin' to leave yez to wash up while I go round there. If I don't tell someone soon, I'll burst.'

Molly patted Ruthie on the head as she moved to where Jack was sitting. Putting her arms around his neck she hugged him tight. 'Yer a cracker, Jack Bennett, that's what yer are. I'm the luckiest woman in the world, with the best husband an' the best children. I love all of yer, an' I thank God every day for me blessings.'

'Will yer go out, woman, before yer've got us all blubbering.' Jack turned his head to kiss her cheek. 'Go an' tell yer ma yer news.'

'Yeah, you go, Mam,' Tommy said. 'We'll see to the dishes.'

Molly thumped Jack on the shoulder. 'Ay, if money does this to them, yer'd better win the pools every week.' She reached the door and turned. 'I'll probably only be an hour, but just

56

in case, put Ruthie to bed for us, will yer?'

'You looked pleased with yerself' Bob Jackson closed the door and followed his daughter down the hall. 'Had a good day, 'ave yer?'

'Da, yer don't know the half of it.' Molly had run nearly all the way and was out of breath. 'Just wait till yer hear.'

'Oh, it's yourself, is it?' Bridie lowered the pillowslip she was embroidering. 'I wasn't expecting to see you tonight.'

Molly blinked in the brightness of the electric light. What a difference from their dark, gas-lit room. Still, she'd be swanking soon, 'cos the men were due to start laying the electric cables in their street any time. She sat on the couch and waved her father to a chair. 'Sit down, Da, till I tell yer me news.'

Bridie and Bob listened in silence, only the expressions on their faces showing their surprise. When Molly had finished, Bridie fell back in her chair. 'Well, did yer hear that now, Bob? All that money, sure, it's a small fortune, so it is.'

'I'm happy for yer, lass,' Bob said. 'You an' Jack deserve all the luck in the world.'

'D'yer know, I don't know whether I'm on me head or me heels,' Molly laughed. 'Or, put it another way, I don't know whether I'm comin' or goin'!'

'Well 'tis glad I am for yer.' Bridie laid her embroidery on the floor at the side of her chair. 'An' I hope yer spend it wisely, not be givin' it away to every Tom, Dick

57

an' Harry. I know what yer like, wanting to share yer good fortune with everyone, but you'd do well to think hard before frittering Jack's winnings away. It'll be a long time before so much money comes your way again, so think on.'

'Ma, I've no intention of frittering it away, as you put it. Every penny will be accounted for, don't you worry. It wouldn't be fair on Jack to just let it slip through me fingers with nothin' to show for it. I haven't been able to think straight since he told me, but I'm goin' to sit down and think hard on what to buy with it. I'll make a list out an' see how far it'll go.'

Bob covered his mouth to hide a smile. 'If I can make a suggestion, a new couch wouldn't go amiss. The springs on that old thing play a tune every time yer sit on it. It's served yer well, but it's time to put it out to pasture.'

'Yeah, nearly twenty years we've had it, an' it was second hand then! It certainly doesn't owe us anythin'.' Molly grinned. 'I'd miss it, though, or at least me backside would.'

Bridie stood up. 'I'll put the kettle on. I'm afraid we've nothing stronger, so we'll have to celebrate with tea.'

A cold chill ran through Molly's body as she remembered the night, just a few months ago, when her mother had gone out to make a pot of tea, leaving her and Bob talking. Her father had looked fine, just as he did now, but within minutes he was doubled up with chest pains.

And an hour later he was in hospital having suffered a severe heart attack.

Molly shivered. For six weeks her da had been in intensive care, on the critical list, and it had been the worst time of her life. She hoped none of them would ever have to go through that trauma again.

'Yer look well, Da! Gettin' used to bein' home again, are yer?'

'I feel fine, lass. Get tired quickly, but that's all.' Bob smiled. 'Heaven knows why I get tired, 'cos yer ma won't let me lift a finger. But it's good to be home. Yer never realise what yer've got until it's taken away from yer.'

Bridie came through with a tray. 'Jill an' Steve were round the other night an' it did me heart good to see them together again. They make a fine-lookin' couple, so they do.'

'I'm over the moon they're back together.' Molly took the china cup and saucer from her mother. 'I didn't take to that Miles bloke one little bit. Too stuck-up for my liking.' She sipped her tea. 'Did I tell yer he's leavin' his job? Got one with the Ministry of Defence so he won't get called up if there's a war.'

'I think it's more a case of when there's a war, not if,' Bob said, a serious look on his still-handsome face. 'Hitler and his strutting sidekick, Mussolini, are playing games with us. Making promises while he builds up his forces. If this Government can't see that, then they're fools.'

'Ah, ray, Da, don't be puttin' a damper

on things! Here's me, all bright an' happy, an' yer have to go an' spoil it! There's not goin' to be a flamin' war, so let's talk about somethin' else.' Molly put her cup down. She couldn't talk without waving her hands about and her mother's best china was safer out of the way. 'I know it's only superstition, but yer know they say good and bad things happen in threes? Well, in my case it's come true.'

'I'll not be listening to superstitions.' Bridie blessed herself. 'I'm surprised at yer, so I am.'

'Oh, Ma, it's only in fun! Forget I used the word an' listen to the three good things that 'ave happened to me over the last week or so.' Molly rolled her eyes at Bob and he winked back. 'First, me da gets better. Second, our Jill makes it up with Steve, and third, Jack wins all this money! Now, superstition or not, yer can't fall out with that, can yer?'

In spite of herself, Bridie smiled. This daughter of hers, with a heart as big as a week, could talk herself out of anything. You could argue with her till you were blue in the face, but you'd always end up laughing. Bridie didn't know how she did it, but Molly had a knack of lighting up the most miserable of faces. What Bridie did know, though, was that her daughter and her family meant the world to her and Bob. They brought love and laughter into their lives, giving them a reason to look forward to each day that dawned.

Chapter Four

Molly was daydreaming as she watched the suds bursting into little bubbles over her hands. Any other day she'd have had Ruthie's gymslip and blouse washed and hanging on the line by now. But today wasn't just another day, it was very special, so she allowed herself the luxury of dawdling while she contemplated what she'd do with the unexpected windfall. She'd been agonising over it all through the long night, hadn't got one wink of sleep. Jack had dropped off as soon as his head hit the pillow and listening to his even breathing she'd been jealous. Her nerves were so wound up she just couldn't fall asleep.

First she decided she'd rig the family out with all new clothes, and what was left she'd spend on the house. Then she discarded that idea, telling herself she could buy clothes with a Sturla's cheque. Jack didn't object to the few bob a week she forked out to the club woman who called, but he'd never allow her to buy anything big on the never-never. He said that once you got into that kind of debt you'd never get out of it.

Molly was so deep in thought she didn't hear the latch on the entry door click, and when Nellie's face peered at her through the kitchen window she started with fright. 'Yer silly beggar,

I nearly jumped out of me flamin' skin!'

Nellie banged the door behind her. 'I came up the yard to save yer openin' the front door.' She swayed over to the draining board, rubbing her hands together as she smiled into Molly's face. 'Our Steve told us the good news last night. I was that excited for yer, I couldn't sleep.'

Molly pulled the plug out and shook the surplus water from her hands before reaching for the towel hanging on a nail behind the door. 'How d'yer think I feel? I've tossed and turned all night while Jack slept like a baby, not a care in the world.'

'He's like my George, never gets excited about anythin'. I bet if my feller won a hundred pounds he wouldn't turn a hair.' Nellie loosened the knot in the floral scarf she'd put over her head to hide the dinky curlers. She'd tied the knot too tight and it was digging into her throat. 'I'm that pleased, Molly, anyone would think it was me that 'ad won the blinkin' pools.'

'I've been walkin' round in a dream all mornin', wondering what to spend it on. Me ma knows what I'm like with money, it goes through me hands like water, an' she gave me a good talkin' to last night.' Molly grinned. 'She still treats me like a little girl, forgets I've got a grown-up family of me own. But what she said was right. I've got to be sensible and spend it on things we really need, 'cos I'll never 'ave the chance again.'

'That's the idea, girl.' Nellie nodded. 'Yer ma's got her head screwed on the right way.'

'With all the excitement, and goin' round

to me ma's, I forgot to tell Jack about Mrs Corkhill. Did you tell George?'

'I certainly did! Of course, I got a lecture about actin' like a fishwife, havin' a slanging match in the middle of the street and ready to do battle with the Bradley woman. That's the trouble with George, he's got no sense of humour.'

'Yer know what George is like, yer should have left that part out,' Molly said. 'But what did he think about that crowd scrounging off her?'

'He was disgusted.' Nellie's scarf had slowly been slipping backwards, now she gave it such a tug it ended up covering her eyes. Tutting loudly, she undid the knot and pulled the scarf free. 'Blasted nuisance! I only put it on in case I met someone.'

'Clark Gable doesn't come down our jigger, Nellie,' Molly laughed.

'Clark Gable doesn't worry me.' Nellie held her tummy as her laugh ricocheted around the four walls of the tiny kitchen. 'But what if I bumped into James Cagney?'

'Oh, go on with yer!' Molly put the plug in the sink and turned the tap on. 'If yer goin' to stand there, yer'll have to watch me work, 'cos our Ruthie needs these clothes for school tomorrow.'

'There's not much dry out, girl.'

'If I get the wet out, I can put them round the fire tonight an' iron them in the mornin' before she gets up. She's only got the one change an' it's a blinkin' nuisance.'

'I know, she'll have to get some new ones out of the money.'

'Uh, uh!' Molly sounded determined. 'If the others don't get new clothes, neither does Ruthie. A Sturla's cheque will do.'

'Are we goin' up to Mrs Corkhill's?' Nellie asked. 'We said we would.'

'If you don't buzz off an' let me get me work done, I won't 'ave time to go anywhere!' Molly plunged the clothes into the sink, a grimace on her face as her hands touched the cold water. 'Go on, poppy off an' I'll call for yer in an hour.'

'Okay, I'll see yer later.' Nellie reached the door, then turned. 'Wait till I tell George me best mate told me to bugger off!'

Molly lifted her hand out of the sink and shook it in Nellie's face, splashing her with the ice-cold water. 'On yer way!'

Her lips set in a straight line, Nellie marched from the kitchen, banging the door behind her. Molly saw her pass the window and waited, knowing her friend would be determined to have the last word. Sure enough, Nellie's face was soon pressed so hard against the pane of glass her button nose and chubby cheeks were distorted. And when she spoke her lips appeared to be made of rubber. 'That's goin' down in me book as well, missus! Me best mate not only tells me to bugger off, she throws a bucketful of cold water over me.'

Molly leaned on the edge of the sink, doubled up with laughter. When she looked up again, Nellie was standing with a huge grin on her face. 'See yer later, girl!'

Molly nodded. 'Ta-ra!' And as she shook the clothes out ready to hang on the line, she thought how lucky she was to have a friend who was as crazy as a coot.

As soon as Molly set eyes on Mrs Corkhill she knew there was something wrong. The old lady's face had a grey tinge to it, her eyes were blinking rapidly, and when she wasn't wringing her hands she was twisting the corner of her pinny. 'I'll put the kettle on.'

When Corker's mam left them alone, Nellie gave Molly a dig in the ribs. 'There's summat up.'

'Yeah, it's stickin' out a mile,' Molly said, keeping her voice low. 'But don't let's rush her, she'll tell us in her own time.'

But as Mrs Corkhill poured their tea into china cups that her son had brought from Japan, she kept firing questions at them so quickly she didn't give them the opportunity of asking her how she was. She wanted to know about Jack, George, and then every member of their families. Molly began to get worried as the shrill voice carried on. There was definitely something wrong. This agitated, restless woman wasn't the Mrs Corkhill they were used to. But did they have the right to interfere? If they did, would the old lady thank them for it?

Then Molly remembered her promise to Corker, that she'd keep an eye on his mother. 'That was a nice cup of tea, Mrs Corkhill.' She placed the cup and saucer carefully on the table. 'Now yer've asked about everyone that God ever made, are yer goin' to tell us what's botherin' yer?'

Mrs Corkhill's hand fluttered to her throat. 'Why, I don't know what yer mean. There's nothin' bothering me.'

Nellie couldn't lean forward, so she passed her cup to Molly. 'Come off it, Mrs C! Yer a nervous wreck, there's got to be a reason for it.'

The old lady dropped her head. What was the use of pretending when she was worried to death? And if she couldn't tell these two, who could she tell? 'It's that family over the road again. They're makin' my life hell.'

Molly sighed. 'What 'ave they been up to now?'

'Just the usual...borrowing...borrowing...borrowing. It never ends.'

'I think there's more to it than that,' Nellie said, her eyes screwed up. 'They were doin' that yesterday, but you weren't as upset as yer are today.'

'Nellie's right!' Molly took a frail hand in hers. 'Come on, sunshine, yer can tell us. Anythin' yer say won't go any further than these four walls, I promise.'

Taking a deep breath, Mrs Corkhill said, 'You'd only been gone five minutes yesterday when that Joyce came over to borrow some tea. I know I told yez I wouldn't lend them any more, but with bein' on me own I don't want no trouble from them. So I gave in, but I made her wait on the step while I fetched it from the kitchen.'

Molly could feel her temper rising, but she kept quiet because she had a feeling there was more to come. And there was.

Her voice shaking, Mrs Corkhill continued, 'An hour later she was back to ask for some marg. Like a fool I gave in again. But this time, when I came out of the kitchen, the cheeky thing was standing in here, by the sideboard. I shouted at her, told her she had no right to come into my house, but she just laughed, grabbed the marge from my hand and ran.'

'Ooh, I'd like to get me hands on that little faggot for five minutes.' Nellie's face was red with anger. 'I'd belt the daylights out of her.'

'It's her mother I blame.' Molly said. 'What sort of a mother is she to send her kids out scrounging off people? Fine example she is.'

'They're not only scroungers, Molly, they're thieves.'

Molly closed her eyes briefly, afraid to ask what she knew had to be asked. 'They've stolen somethin' off yer?'

Mrs Corkhill nodded. 'I'd left me purse on the sideboard, like I always do, and when I went to get the money out to buy the *Echo* there was half a crown missing. The girl must have taken it while I was in the kitchen.'

'Oh, dear God, are yer sure?' Nellie's face, like Molly's, had drained of colour. 'Could yer be mistaken?'

'No, I know exactly how much I had in the purse. Yer see, I only had a ten-bob note to me name yesterday, and I changed it when I went to the corner shop for a few things. I

67

got two half-crowns in the change, a two-bob piece, a shilling, a sixpence, threepenny bit an' some coppers. An' the only time I opened me purse after that was when the insurance man came an' I gave him twopence.'

'Have yer had a good look on the floor?' Molly asked, not wanting to believe that a young girl would steal from an old woman. Being cheeky was one thing, but stealing, that was serious. 'It might have rolled under the table, or the sideboard.'

'I've looked, Molly, but I knew I was wasting me time. The money was all there when I took the twopence out for the insurance man, and I never had cause to open the purse after that.' Corker's mother clenched her fist and banged it on the table. 'I know that cheeky bitch took it! Me purse was on the end of the sideboard and she was standing right by it when I came in.'

'Are yer sure Maisie gave the right change?' Molly asked. 'Could yer 'ave been mistaken?'

'Molly, I'm not in me dotage, not yet anyway. I counted the change out on me knee, sittin' in this very chair, so I know to the penny what I had. I might not 'ave noticed it so soon, 'cos I don't usually count me money, but it was with the insurance man coming. I had eight shillings and elevenpence. Takin' off me insurance money and the *Echo*, I should 'ave eight and sevenpence ha'penny. Instead, I've got six shillings and three ha'pence.'

'Oh, dear, I don't know what to say,' Molly said. 'There's not much yer can do about it.'

'Of course there is!' Nellie shouted. 'I'll go

over an' have it out with them! We can't just
let them get away with it, they'll be laughin'
their ruddy socks off!'

'Calm down, Nellie!' Molly warned. 'Yer
can't just go over an' accuse someone of
stealing, not when yer've no proof.' She gazed
at the worried face of Mrs Corkhill. 'When's
Corker due home?'

'His ship's supposed to dock today, so he
should be home in the morning, all being
well.'

'Then see what he's got to say, that's the best
thing,' Molly advised.

'In the meantime don't open the door to
them, not even if they threaten to break it
down.'

'What about yer neighbours, Mrs C?' Nellie
asked. 'Do they know about this borrowin'
lark?'

'A few of them 'ave stopped me in the street
an' told me not to be so daft. Apparently those
kids tried it on a few people and got chased. But
me, soft girl, haven't got the guts to chase them.
Mrs Chambers from next door but one, she said
they're as common as muck an' real hard cases.
Told me to have no truck with them, shut the
door in their faces, she said. But when yer get
to my age, an' yer livin' on yer own, it's not
that easy.'

'I've got an idea that might put a halt to
their gallop.' Nellie smacked her lips together.
'Nothin' for you to worry about, Mrs C, I won't
do anythin' that'll make trouble for yer.'

'What are yer cooking up now?' Molly asked,

knowing some of the tricks her friend could get up to. 'Whatever it is, yer can leave me out of it.'

'I'll tell yer when we're outside.' Nellie made three attempts to push her enormous body up, but to no avail. In disgust, she turned to Molly. 'Give us a hand.'

'Give yer two, yer mean.' Molly held her hands out. 'If I tried pulling yer up with one hand, I'd end up on top of yer.'

Mrs Corkhill put a hand on Molly's arm. 'Don't let her do anything to cause trouble, will yer?'

'Oh, don't be worryin' about Nellie, her bark's worse than her ruddy bite.' Molly kissed the wrinkled face. 'I'll be up tomorrow if Corker doesn't call to ours first.'

They said goodbye in the living room, telling Mrs Corkhill they'd close the door behind them. Outside, Molly went to walk down the street but Nellie pulled her back. 'I'm goin' over the road and I want yer there as a witness.'

'Oh no you don't!' Molly shook her head vigorously. 'Yer not gettin' me involved in a fightin' match.'

'There'll be no fightin', I promise. I've got a gem of an idea an' I think it might just pay off.' Nellie pulled Molly off the kerb. 'Come on, all yer've got to do is stand there an' look intelligent.'

Molly's tummy started to flutter with nerves, but she knew if she didn't go with her friend, Nellie would go on her own. So even though she was afraid, she wouldn't let her mate down.

The young girl, Joyce, answered their knock. 'What d'yer want?'

'I'd like to see yer mother,' Nellie said, bracing herself. 'Ask 'er to come to the door a minute.'

The girl folded her arms and leaned against the door jamb. 'Mam, there's someone wants to see yer. It's that fat woman from yisterdey.'

Oh, that did it! If Nellie had had qualms about what she was doing, the girl's description of her dispelled them and got her dander up. So it was an angry face that confronted the girl's mother when she came down the hall wearing the same dirty pinny and cardigan. 'What the 'ell d'you want?'

'I believe you borrowed some margarine off the old lady across the street? Not the first time you've borrowed from her, either, apparently. But yesterday she gave you all the margarine she had in the house and had to eat dry bread because she didn't have a penny to her name.'

'That's a lie!' young Joyce said hotly. 'She did 'ave money, I saw it in 'er purse.'

'Oh, did you?' Nellie raised her eyebrows until they were nearly touching her hairline. 'Now I wonder how that came about?'

After giving Nellie a look to kill, the woman turned on the girl and gave her such a belt across the ears it sent her reeling and crying out in pain. 'Get in before I give yer another one, yer soddin' little bleeder.'

'Charming language, I must say.' Nellie drew herself up to her full height, shoulders back and huge bosom thrust forward. 'I've said all I want to say, heard all I want to hear, so my friend and I will bid you goodbye.'

The woman shook her fist in Nellie's face. 'Don't think yer gettin' away with callin' my daughter a thief, yer bleedin' fat cow! Just yer wait till my feller gets 'ome, he'll soddin' pulverise yer.'

'I didn't call your daughter a thief, so I wonder why you think I did? Guilty conscience, perhaps?' Nellie spoke calmly but her tummy was churning with anger. For two pins she'd have put her fist in the woman's face, and it was only the thought of Molly that stopped her. 'By the way, I live in number twenty-six if your husband is interested.'

'Yer big fat bleedin' cow! Once round you, twice round the bloody gasworks.' The woman searched her mind for insults. 'Yer've got a bigger bleedin' arse than Fatty Arbuckle.'

Molly stepped forward. She wasn't going to stand there and listen to her friend being insulted. 'You're a fine one to talk, I must say! Have yer tried lookin' in the mirror lately? I'd say it was a toss-up which is the biggest...your mouth or the entrance to the Mersey Tunnel!'

Nellie had been hurt by the insults, but she had no intention of letting the woman know. 'Don't waste yer breath on her, Molly, she's not worth it.' She slipped her hand through her friend's arm and turned her to face down the street. They'd taken two steps when Nellie turned. Sounding a lot calmer than she felt, she called, 'Oh, by the way, Mrs Whats-yer-name, next time you send your children scrounging, make sure they don't go to Mrs Corkhill's. And if you must borrow anything, make it something you really need...like a block of carbolic to scrub your filthy mouth out with.'

The friends didn't speak until they were crossing the road that cut through their street, then Molly found her voice. 'Honest to God, Nellie, yer were a bloody hero! Yer didn't half put her in her place. An' the posh voice on yer, as well!'

'I can put the talk on when I want to.' Nellie's hurt was soothed by her friend's praise. After all, a few insults weren't going to kill her. And all in all she felt she'd got the better of the woman. 'Mind you, I couldn't keep talkin' as though I 'ad a plum on me mouth for long, I was beginnin' to get on me own nerves.'

'An' that girl did pinch the money, didn't she?' Molly said. 'But fancy you catchin' her out like that, yer crafty beggar.'

'I took a chance an' it paid off. But now we know, what do we do about it?'

'Nothing!' Molly sounded very definite. 'From now on it's up to Corker, he'll know 'ow to deal with them.'

They'd reached Nellie's front door by this time. 'Are yer goin' to the shops?'

Molly shook her head. 'No, I only want bread an' I can get that at Maisie's. Why, d'you need messages?'

Nellie's tongue darted out to lick her lips. 'D'yer know where I could buy a pair of boxing gloves? If that Bradley feller comes down, George will need them.'

'Nellie McDonough, I don't think it's funny, an' I'm damn sure George won't, either!'

The gurgle started deep in Nellie's tummy and built up to a roar of laughter. 'Molly, yer should see yer face! Honest to God, yer'd fall for the flamin' cat, you would! Of course what's happened isn't funny, neither is me gettin' called a fat-arsed cow! But the thought of George with a pair of boxing gloves on his mitts, well, I think that's bloody hilarious! My feller couldn't fight 'is way out of a paper bag, an' you know it!'

Molly wanted to say she couldn't see anything remotely funny in getting a gentle man like George involved in fisticuffs. She'd never known him raise his voice, never mind his fists! But her imagination was as vivid as Nellie's, and when a vision flashed through her mind of George wearing a pair of boxing gloves and wading in, she had to admit Nellie was right, it was hilarious. 'What happens, then, if the bloke comes down determined to knock the stuffin' out of someone for callin' his daughter a thief? I suppose you'll be the one to take 'im on?'

'Nah! George will lick 'im, have no fear.' Nellie grabbed Molly's arm and held on tight as she gasped for air. 'My feller can't fight, but by God, he can run. By the time the feller caught up he'd be at the Pier Head and the poor bloke would be so out of breath he wouldn't be able to fight 'is own flamin' shadow.'

Mary Watson across the street came out of her door and saw the two women clinging to each other, their laughter filling the air. 'Well, it's nice to be some people, I must say! Have you two got nothin' better to do?'

Nellie wiped her hand across her eyes before calling back, 'Haven't yer heard, Mary, Molly's come into money? She's hired a maid now, an', bein' her best mate, like, she's kindly offered to let 'er clean my 'ouse as well.'

'Oh,' Mary laughed, 'one of the idle rich now, eh?'

'Take no notice of 'er, Mary, she's in one of 'er funny moods.' Molly gave Nellie a push. 'I'm goin' to get some work done. And for heaven's sake stay out of trouble, will yer?'

'I ain't promisin' anythin', girl, but I'll try. Anyway, I'll be down later for me afternoon cup of tea.' Nellie waited until Molly was putting her key in the lock before shouting, 'Don't bother bakin' a cake, girl, I wouldn't want yer puttin' yerself out.'

'Will yer go 'ome, Nellie McDonough?' Molly waved. 'Ta-ra!'

'Now we're all together, shall I read yez the list I've made? It's what I think we should do with the money, an' I want to know what yez think.' Molly gazed around the table. 'I know we're not all here, our Ruthie's in bed, but she's too young to understand anyway.'

'Go ahead, love.' Jack said, 'but I've already told yer to spend it as yer see fit.'

'I know yer have, sunshine, an' I'm goin' to. But I'd like us all to talk about it first, as a family.' Molly took a slip of paper from the pocket of her pinny. 'I think we should spend most of it on furniture, brighten this place up a bit. That way we'll all get some enjoyment out of it. So what I thought was, I'd spend the odd ten and six on a new school gymslip and blouse for Ruthie, give these three a pound each to buy whatever they want, and two pound for you, Jack. I'll get meself a new pair of shoes, and that will leave me twenty-one pound to spend on the house.' She folded the paper and put it back in her pocket. 'How does that sound?'

'Don't bother about me, love.' Jack smiled across the table. 'My clothes 'ave still got plenty of wear in them, they'll last me a while.'

'And I don't need anything, Mam,' Jill said. 'So you can put my pound towards the house.'

Molly caught the looks exchanged between Doreen and Tommy and knew they were thinking that if they didn't offer to go without, they'd look greedy. But they were different from Jill, they didn't get half the pocket money she did. Doreen worked in Johnson's dye works, and although she loved her job and the firm were good to their employees, the wages were very low. And Tommy only earned buttons as an apprentice. 'No, fair's fair,' Molly said, 'yez all get the same.'

When Jill saw the smiles on the faces of her sister and brother, she guessed what was on her mother's mind and didn't object. She'd find a way around it, perhaps buy something for the room when it was refurnished.

'Now that's settled, I've got somethin' else to tell yez that isn't so pleasant. But if any of yez repeat one word outside this 'ouse, I'll have yer guts for garters, so remember.' Molly went on to tell them in detail about the previous day's visit to Mrs Corkhill's. Then, when she saw they were going to give vent to their disgust, she held a hand up. 'Hang on, there's worse to come.'

Molly related every word and every action from the time they knocked on the old lady's door this morning until they closed it on their way out.

'That is despicable,' Jack snorted in contempt. 'Only the lowest of the low would do that to an old lady.'

The three children were loud in their anger and revulsion. Tommy said, 'If it 'ad been a feller did it, I'd go up there an' knock 'is block off.'

'If I find out who she is, I'll belt 'er.' The look on Doreen's face told them she meant it.

'Poor Mrs Corkhill.' Jill's face was sad. 'She's a lovely little thing, always bright and cheerful. They must be a horrible lot.'

'I still haven't finished,' Molly told them. 'I don't think I can do justice to what happened next, but I'll do me best.' She rose from her chair. 'I'll 'ave to stand up for this. Now, pretend I'm Nellie, an' I swear that every word I'm going to say is the truth.' Stretching her arms first, Molly then folded them across her tummy, a pose everyone recognised as Nellie's. Her head tilted back to look as though she was talking to someone standing on the top step, she began to act out her version of her friend's encounter with the red-haired woman. Apart from the insults hurled at Nellie, she told the lot, ending up with the laugh they'd had over the boxing gloves.

'So the girl really did steal the money?' Jack shook his head sadly. 'What a state of affairs when a young girl will rob anyone, let alone an old lady.'

'Auntie Nellie didn't say all those things, did she, Mam?' Doreen was biting on her nails. 'Ooh, I'd 'ave loved to 'ave seen her.'

'She was absolutely brilliant,' Molly said. 'I felt proud of 'er.'

Jill was grinning. It sounded just the sort of thing Steve's mother would do. She was fond of all his family. His dad was lovely, and she got on like a house on fire with his sister, Lily, who was the same age as herself, and his brother, Peter, who was fifteen. But it was his mother she loved. Always a smile on her face, a joke on her lips, and a heart full of warmth and compassion. 'Wait till I see her tonight, I'll pull her leg soft.'

'Don't do that, sunshine,' Molly warned. 'Mr McDonough won't think it's very funny, especially if that bloke comes down an' offers him out.'

'D'yer think that's likely?' Jack asked, a frown on his face.

'I don't know, love! I don't know what sort of a man he is, do I? If he's anythin' like the wife, then he'll be down with fists flyin'.'

'Nah!' Tommy said. 'If he knows the girl stole the money he'll stay well away. Stands to sense, doesn't it?'

'Yeah, I think yer've got a point there, son.' Jack pulled on the lobe of his ear, a habit he had when he was thinking. 'Just to be on the safe side, though, Jill, tell Auntie Nellie to send someone down here if he comes. An extra pair of hands might come in useful.'

'I'll keep an eye out,' Tommy said, sounding all grown-up. 'Ginger lives a bit higher up the street, so we'll hang around. If I see anythin' I'll run down and tell yer.'

'I hope it blows over until Corker's home,' Molly said. 'I'd love to see them tangle with him.'

A slow smile spread across Jack's face. 'Now, that is somethin' I'd give anythin' to see. They'd throw the towel in before the fight began.'

Chapter Five

Nellie pulled a face when another sharp pain seared her chest. 'Keep goin', yer nearly there,' she muttered through clenched teeth, hurrying up the street as fast as her cumbersome body would allow. She could feel the sweat running freely down her face and neck, meeting in the valley between her breasts to form a pool within the confines of her brassiere. Finally she reached Molly's door and just had enough breath left to bang with the knocker before falling back against the side wall. 'If I'd kept that up much longer, I'd 'ave killed meself.' She wiped the sleeve of her coat across her brow. 'I'll 'ave to get rid of some of this fat, it's no good.'

'Who yer talkin' to, soft girl?' Molly asked, carefully stepping over the step she'd donkey-stoned not half an hour since. 'They'll be cartin' yer away in a straitjacket one of these days, talkin' to yerself.'

A hand to her chest, Nellie panted, 'I was just tellin' meself I'll 'ave to stop eatin', try an' get me weight down. It's either that or take a Bob Martin's conditionin' powder.'

Molly eyed the red face and heaving chest. 'The sweat's pourin' off yer! Why have yer been runnin'?'

'Yer can hardly call it runnin', girl, more like a hop, skip an' a jump.' Nellie drew away from the wall. 'I saw Corker go into the greengrocer's an' I thought I'd let yer know in case yer want to nab 'im before he goes home. He'll be turnin' the corner any minute, probably only went to get his mam a bunch of flowers, like he always does.'

'What d'yer think, Nellie? Perhaps we should leave it an' let his mam tell him herself.'

'I'll lay yer ten to one she won't breathe a word! Yer know she never says anythin' to worry him.' A huge beam spread across Nellie's face as she waved her hand high in the air. 'Here he comes, yer better make up yer mind quick.'

Molly spun round, her smile of welcome matching that of the giant of a man walking towards them, his seaman's bag slung over his shoulder, a bunch of white marguerites dangling from his hand. He'd stand out in any crowd, would Corker, and not just because of his size. Everything about him was colourful, from his

80

ruddy complexion to his mop of sandy hair and matching thick moustache and beard.

'Molly, me darlin', yer a sight for sore eyes.' Jimmy Corkhill swung his bag from his shoulder, put it on the ground with the bunch of flowers on top, then encircled Molly's waist and lifted her off her feet. 'I swear, the older yer get, the prettier yer get.'

Molly laughed down into the twinkling blue eyes of the man she thought was one of the finest God ever made, and one of the most handsome. He towered above all the other men in the street—even her Jack, and he was six foot. 'Let me down, yer big soft thing.' Molly kicked her legs backwards. 'Yer'll 'ave the neighbours talkin'.'

Corker was enjoying her embarrassment. 'While yer up there, tell me how yer father is.'

'He's out of 'ospital an' he looks fine. When yer've got a minute, he'd love to see yer.' Molly beat her fists on his shoulder. 'Now, will yer let go of me?'

'Give us a kiss first.'

Molly planted a kiss on his cheek, her nose twitching as his beard tickled her skin. 'Now put me down, yer've got me dress pulled up an' I'm showin' everythin' I've got.'

'Got yer frilly ones on, have yer?' Corker roared as he lowered Molly to the ground, bringing a smile to the face of Nellie who was watching with amusement. But when Corker turned towards her, his arms outstretched, she backed away. 'Oh no yer don't, Corker! I know yer a big feller, like, but yer'd need the 'elp of King Kong to lift me.'

''Tis a kiss I'm after, Nellie me darlin', not a broken back.' Corker cupped her chubby face between his enormous hands and kissed her full on the lips. 'That's me welcome home present.'

'Oh, aye,' Nellie laughed, nodding to the flowers. 'An' I suppose they're a welcome 'ome present for yer fancy woman?'

'I've got the best fancy woman in the world, Nellie, an' I've had her since the day I was born.' Corker smiled as he picked up the marguerites. 'Me ma loves fresh flowers in the house.'

Molly bit her lip when Corker lifted his bag by the drawstrings, her mind torn between telling him about the trouble his mother had had with the new neighbours and leaving it to see if she told him herself.

When Corker swung the bag over his shoulder, Molly quickly made up her mind. 'Corker, 'ave yer got a minute? There's somethin' I want to talk to yer about.'

'I'll call in later, Molly, I think I'd better get home first. Me ma's probably lookin' out for me.'

'It's yer ma I want to talk to you about.' Molly nodded to the open door. 'I think yer should come in, it'll not take but a few minutes.'

The smile dropped from Corker's face. 'She's not ill, is she?'

'No, she's in fine health,' Molly assured him.

'But she 'as got a problem, an' me an' Nellie think she might be too frightened to tell yer herself.'

'Lead the way.' Corker followed them into the house, dropping his bag at the bottom of the stairs before ducking his head to get through the living room door. 'Now, what's all the mystery?'

Molly indicated that he should sit down, but for once she didn't offer to make him a drink. He wanted to get home and she knew his mother would be back and forward to the front door watching for sight of him. So she didn't waste any time as she hurriedly told the story, with just a few interruptions from Nellie when she remembered something her friend had left out.

Corker listened in silence, his head bowed, staring at his clasped hands. And when Molly had finished speaking, he stayed in that position for several minutes, causing Molly and Nellie to exchange looks of surprise. This wasn't the reaction they'd expected, not from Corker. They thought he'd blow his top and rant and rave. But when he raised his head, the cold steel of his blue eyes told them of his inner anger. 'Yer say this family moved into the Culshaws' old house?'

Molly nodded. 'Nobody knew Mr Henry had let it, he never said a dickie bird! They just turned up one day with a cartload of furniture.'

'So nobody knows who they are, where they came from?' When Molly shook her head,

Corker stood up and shook the creases from his trousers. 'Right! I'll be off home an' see how the land lies.'

'Corker, yer ma doesn't know about Nellie's little confrontation with the Bradley woman. She probably knows we went over, 'cos I've a feeling she was watching from behind her curtains, but she doesn't know Nellie caught the girl out.'

'I'll sort it out, Molly, they won't bother Ma again, yer can be sure of that! But I'd like to thank the pair of yez for keepin' an eye on her, I appreciate it.'

Nellie squinted up at the big man. Anyone who didn't know him would think he was taking it very calmly, because he didn't seem a bit perturbed. But they'd be very wrong. This was the calm before the storm, and Nellie thought she wouldn't be in the Bradleys' shoes for a big clock. 'What'll yer do, Corker?'

'What I'd like to do an' what I will do, Nellie, are two different things.' Corker's laugh was hollow. 'They deserve to be punished for pickin' on an old lady, and I'll find a way of doing it. But there's more than one way of skinning a cat. In all the years we've lived in that house me ma hasn't had a cross word with any of her neighbours, so I'll not be doin' anything that would shame her.' His face was thoughtful as he stroked his bristly beard. 'But they'll not get away with it, yer can bet yer life on that! I've got a week's leave, plenty of time to do what's got to be done. And by the time I'm due back on board, the Bradleys will wonder what's hit them.'

'Well, yer know where we are, Corker, if yer need us,' Molly said. 'Just yell out.'

'I'll not be doin' anything in a hurry, Molly. Just askin' a few questions here an' there, get the lay of the land.' Corker nodded to both women before bending his head to walk through the door 'Thanks again.'

'I'll let you out.' Molly followed on his heels. 'We'll see yer when we see yer, eh?'

'I'll be comin' down to see Ellen and the kids tonight, so if yer see 'er will yer let her know?' Corker raised his bushy eyebrows. 'If I think me ma's all right to leave for a few hours, I might give yer a knock to ask Jack out for a pint.'

'Okay.' Corker had walked a few steps when Molly called after him. 'Would yer like me to ask Jill and Steve to sit with Ellen's children while yer take her out for an hour?'

Corker raised his thumb, a hint of a smile on his face. 'Molly, me darlin', yer a little cracker.'

'Flatterer! I bet yer say that to all the girls.' Molly laughed. 'Anyway, get home to yer ma, now, she'll be worryin'. See yer later.'

Corker crossed the road dividing the two ends of the street, then paused briefly before turning left. If he went up the entry and in the back door, no one would know he was home. So anyone coming on the cadge would be in for a surprise.

Lizzie Corkhill heard the latch on the entry door click and dashed to the back window. Her face lit up when she saw her son striding up the

85

yard. It never ceased to amaze her that she, not the size of sixpennorth of copper, had produced this mountain of a man. She'd had a hard time giving birth because he was a big baby, eleven pounds, but never in her wildest dreams had she, or her husband Ted, imagined he'd grow to be the man he was. Oh, how happy her life had been then, with a husband she adored and a son they both idolised.

When her husband had come home from work one day complaining of a heavy cold, little did she realise it was the beginning of the end of her happiness. The cold had quickly developed into pneumonia and within a week her forty-year-old husband was dead. She was heartbroken and would have lost her sanity but for Corker. He was only fourteen at the time, but he had enough sense to know he had to make his mother carry on from one day to the next, otherwise she'd die of grief. So Corker suffered his own pain in silence. He took over the mantle of the man of the house and he'd cared for his mother ever since.

'What's the big idea?' Lizzie Corkhill opened her arms wide as Corker reached for her. 'Yer've never come in the back way before.'

Corker lifted her up and spun her around. 'I was checkin' on yer to make sure the yard's kept clean.' He held her tight, tears of love glistening in his eyes. 'How's my sweetheart?'

'Just fine!' She tugged playfully on his beard. 'I don't need to ask how you are, you look the picture of health.'

'I'm glad to be home, Ma.' Corker set her

down gently. 'Just think, I've got a whole week of you spoiling me with yer apple pies and pans of scouse. The cook on the ship is hopeless, wouldn't know a pan of scouse from a rice puddin'.'

'I've got a rice puddin' in the oven right now, doin' nice and slow, just the way you like it. Plenty of sugar in and nutmeg on the top.' Lizzie touched her snow-white hair, making sure the waves she'd set with sugar and water were still in place. 'I'll make us a nice cup of tea and put those flowers in water.'

Corker threw his bag down in the hall and hung his navy-blue reefer jacket and peaked cap on the small hall stand which boasted a round mirror with a bevelled edge. He stared at his reflection for a few seconds, wondering how he should react if his mother did confide in him. Deciding the best plan would be to play it by ear, he made for the chair already drawn up to the fire for him and took his packet of Capstan Full Strength from his pocket. After lighting up, he stretched his long legs out and surveyed the room. Spick and span as usual. She was real house-proud, his mother. And for her age she did very well, keeping the place like a new pin all the time, inside and out. The back yard was swilled down every day, and once a week, come hail, rain or shine, she'd be out scrubbing the red-raddled windowsill and donkey-stoning the front step.

Corker drew on his cigarette. He worried sometimes about what would happen when she could no longer look after herself. If he had a trade he wouldn't go to sea, he'd stay home and look after her. But he wasn't skilled, and a labourer's job didn't pay much, certainly not the sort of money he got in the merchant navy.

'Move yer legs out of the way, son, an' make room for this.' Lizzie set a small table down by the side of him. 'I'll bring the tray in.'

Corker studied his mother's face as she poured the tea. She was chattering away and had a smile on her face, but he sensed a tension in her voice and manner that just didn't sit right with her. 'Have yer been managing all right, Ma?' He took the cup and saucer and steadied it on his knee. 'Plenty of coal an' everythin'?'

'Yes, Tucker always makes sure I've got enough coal in.' Lizzie smiled. 'He throws me two bags in every week when the weather's bad, doesn't even ask.'

Corker was watching his mother's face when the knock came and saw the flicker of nervous apprehension as she stood up. 'I'll just see who it is.'

'Stay where you are,' Corker said softly. 'I'll go.'

'There's no need to disturb yerself, it'll only be a hawker.'

'Ma, I said I'll go.' Corker's voice was quiet but firm. 'If it is someone sellin' things, I'll soon get rid of them.'

Corker opened the door wide. 'Yes?'

Joyce Bradley put a hand to her mouth and stared. She'd never seen anyone as big, he was like a giant out of the story books. She swallowed hard, so surprised she was rooted to the spot, unable to move or utter a sound.

'What is it?' Corker asked. 'Have yer come to the wrong house?' The girl shook her head. If she went back home without the bread she'd been told to borrow, she knew she'd get a thick ear. She hadn't wanted to come, not after what happened yesterday, but her mam had kicked her out of the door cursing and swearing, telling her the old lady was a soft touch.

Corker took stock of the dirty, lank hair, the tidemark around the girl's neck, her grubby, torn dress and scuffed shoes. He could have found pity in his heart for her, because children were what their parents made them, but there was an insolence in the eyes that told him that what he'd heard from Molly was true. So he hardened his heart. 'I'm waiting.'

The girl considered her options. She knew what to expect from her mother, but this man was an unknown quantity. Still, she couldn't lose anything by trying. 'Me...er...me...me mam wants to know...er...if she can borrow a few slices of bread.'

'I was right,' Corker said, 'you have come to the wrong house. We don't borrow in this house, and we don't lend. So away yer go and pass the message on to your mother.' He didn't like what was happening, he felt like a big bully shouting at a little girl. But the face staring back at him wasn't the face of an innocent child. This one was tough, with no respect or compassion for an old lady. She was also a thief. 'Would yer like me to come over with you and tell her meself?'

The girl took to her heels and fled, leaving Corker to close the door with a look of sadness on his face.

'Are yer going to tell me about it, Ma?' Corker caught his mother's eye as he eased himself down in the chair.

'Tell yer what, son?' Lizzie looked away, running a hand down the front of her dress to smooth out the creases. 'What is it yer want me to tell yer?'

'Ma, don't try an' pull the wool over me eyes, it won't do yer no good. I met Molly and Nellie on the way up.'

'Oh dear!' Lizzie's hands fluttered nervously. 'I was goin' to tell yer, honest! But I wanted to give yer time to settle in first, not be moaning at yer as soon as yer walked in the door.'

'Okay, Ma, don't be gettin' yerself all upset.' Corker twisted the end of his moustache. 'I'll get it sorted out, they'll not bother you again. And I promise there'll be no fighting, so there's no need for yer to fret.'

'I'm not the only one had trouble with them,' Lizzie said, defending her stupidity. 'None of the neighbours like them, but it's all right for them 'cos they've got big families, they're not on their own like me.'

'I'm surprised at Mr Henry, lettin' the house to the likes of them,' Corker said. 'Does he know what's goin' on?'

'He didn't come himself last week, it was another collector. He said Mr Henry wasn't well.' Lizzie was beginning to feel better now it was all out in the open. It was just as well because she couldn't have put up with it much longer. Especially since that half-crown was stolen, she'd been sick with worry. It had got to the stage where she dreaded getting out of bed in the morning, dreaded every knock on the door. 'The rent's due tomorrow, so if Mr Henry comes himself I'll have a word with him.'

'Uh, uh!' Corker grunted. '*I'll* have a word with Mr Henry. In fact, I'll have more than a word with 'im. If he doesn't come himself tomorrow, I'll go down to their office. Do they still 'ave that place in Spellow Lane, just past Burton's tailors?'

Lizzie nodded. 'As far as I know. But he'll be here tomorrow, I've never known Mr Henry miss two weeks.'

'Then let's forget all about it for today.' Corker stretched his arms before clasping his hands behind his head. 'Now, what's for dinner?'

'I've got mutton chops braising on the top shelf of the oven. They've been in as long as the rice puddin', so they should be nice an' tender. The potatoes are peeled, so I can have the dinner ready in half an hour, is that okay?'

'That'll suit me fine, Ma, 'cos I've got a bit of business to see to this afternoon. And if yer don't mind being left on yer own, I thought I'd go for a pint tonight, with Jack Bennett.'

'Of course I'm all right,' Lizzie huffed. 'Why shouldn't I be?' She left her chair to pull on his beard, smiling into his face. 'I suppose yer takin' Ellen for a drink as well?'

'Don't miss much, do yer, Ma?' Corker returned her smile. 'If she'll come, yes, I am!' Their eyes locked. 'Yer don't mind me bein' friends with Ellen, do yer, Ma?'

Lizzie straightened up. 'I like Ellen well enough, she's a nice woman. But I worry about yer, son, 'cos nothing can come of it, not with her being a married woman.'

'She's married in name only, Ma! Nobby will never come out of that place, he's there for as long as he lives. And she had a lousy life with 'im, you know that! He was a right bastard to her an' the kids.'

Lizzie lifted her hand. 'I'm not sitting in judgement, son, it's just that I don't want you to get hurt. There's nothin' I'd like better than to see you married and settled down, with a family of your own. I'd go to my grave in peace then, knowing you weren't alone in the world.'

'You're not goin' to yer grave or anywhere else, Ma, not for a long time.' Corker threw back his head, a deep chuckle rumbling in his throat. 'I forbid it, d'yer hear? I mean, who's going to make sure I have a clean hankie in me pocket and clean underpants on? And what about the apple pies? There's no one in the whole world who can make an apple pie like you.'

'One thing yer are good at, son, is changing the subject,' Lizzie said drily. 'One minute we're talkin' about Ellen, the next it's apple pies!'

'Ma, I'm forty years of age, old enough to know what I'm doing. I like Ellen, have done since we were youngsters together. If I'd have had any sense I'd 'ave married her then, but the sea was in me blood an' I was away too often. Now, well, we'll have to wait an' see. Ellen will never let me be any more than a friend to her, not while Nobby's still alive, but that satisfies me. What the future has in store, well, only God knows that.'

'Hi-ya, Ellen!' Molly was draining the water from the potatoes when Ellen walked through to the kitchen for her nightly five-minute chat. 'I'll be with yer in a minute.' She put the pan back on the stove, waving her hand through the steam which swirled like clouds in the tiny kitchen. 'I wish these kitchens were bigger, yer can't even swing the flamin' cat around in here.'

Ellen grinned. 'Yer haven't got a cat.'

'See what I mean?' Molly giggled. 'What's the use of havin' a cat if yer can't swing it round?' She took Ellen's arm and pulled her through to the living room. 'Corker's 'ome, an' he said to tell yer he'd be down later to see you an' the kids.'

Ellen coloured. 'I'd better get home an' tidy up then.'

'Hang on a minute, missus! I said I'd ask Jill to sit with the kids so yer could go for a drink with him. Is that all right with you?'

'I should say I'm not goin' for a drink with him, but I won't!' Ellen raised her head defiantly. 'To hell with what the neighbours think! I was left on me own in the shop all mornin' 'cos Tony had to go to the abattoir, and I was run off me feet. So I deserve a nice quiet sit-down an' a glass of sherry.'

'Go an' get yerself dolled up then.' Molly pushed her towards the door. 'By the time yer've given the kids their tea and put the young ones to bed, he'll be here.'

Ellen was in the hall when she remembered the parcel under her arm. 'Oh, I nearly forgot.' She marched back into the living room and placed the parcel on the table. As she unwrapped the newspaper, she explained, 'Tony gave me a big piece of dripping. I've cut it in three, a piece each for you an' Nellie an' meself.'

'God bless yer!' Molly dashed out for a plate, then picked out two pieces of the dripping. 'Thanks, Ellen, yer a pal.' She wrapped the remaining piece up and handed it over. 'Now scarper, an' get yerself titivated up.'

'Will yer let me know what Jill says?' Ellen asked over her shoulder as she was being pushed along the hall. 'She might 'ave made other arrangements.'

'She'll be there, don't worry! Her an' Steve will be glad of a place to be on their own. They can sit an' hold hands all night, all gooey-eyed.'

'They won't be on their own, our Phoebe and Dorothy don't go to bed till about ten.'

Then they can sit an' watch.' Molly waved, 'Goodbye, Ellen! If yer've any more questions, write me a flamin' note!'

Ellen and Corker were ready to leave when Jill arrived with Steve. 'We won't be late,'

Corker promised as he cupped Ellen's elbow. 'I'm callin' in to say hello to yer dad and the rest of the family, then we'll be in the pub on the corner if yer need us.'

Phoebe and Dorothy had happy smiles on their faces when Jill walked in with Steve. The couple had sat with them before when their mam went out with Sinbad, but they hadn't seen them since Christmas, and when they'd asked their mam why, she'd told them that Jill and Steve had fallen out. The girls had been saddened by the news because they had grown fond of the couple. The Bennett family were the first real friends they'd ever had. When their dad was home nobody ever came to the house. They thought Jill looked like a fairy princess with her long blonde hair, slim figure and pretty face, and Steve was handsome enough to be a Prince Charming.

'Hi, girls.' There was a look of pride on Steve's face as he pulled a chair out for Jill before sitting down himself. 'What is it tonight, a game of cards, or snakes and ladders?'

But Phoebe wasn't interested in games, she had other things on her mind. And she wasn't backward in coming forward. 'Are youse two courtin' again?'

Jill blushed. 'It looks like it, doesn't it?'

It was Dorothy's turn to satisfy her curiosity. 'Will yez be gettin' married then?'

Steve tapped his nose. 'Nosy, aren't yer?' But seeing he was never happier than talking of the day he and Jill would be married, he was more than pleased to answer the question. 'Yeah, we'll

95

be gettin' married, won't we, Jill?'

'When we're a bit older.'

'Can we still be bridesmaids, like yez promised?' Phoebe's face was eager. 'Remember, before yez fell out, yer did promise us.'

When Steve smiled, the dimples in his cheeks became deep hollows. 'We won't break our promise, will we, Jill?'

Jill gazed at the faces of the two girls who were willing her to say what they wanted to hear. Poor kids, they hadn't had much to be happy about. Up till nine months ago they, and their two younger brothers, had suffered the most miserable lives imaginable, with a father who was always drunk and thought nothing of lashing out with his hands and feet. They'd come out a lot since he'd left, laughing when they felt like it or playing in the street with the other kids, things they couldn't do when he was around. But the mental scars must still be there, Jill thought now, and they had to learn there were people they could trust. 'No, of course we won't break our promise.'

'Ooh, our Phoebe, isn't that the gear?' Dorothy clapped her hands in delight. She'd never even been to a wedding, never mind been a bridesmaid, and the prospect filled her with joy.

But Phoebe wanted to know more. Never in her life had there been anything she could brag about to the girls in school, and she wanted more details so they'd believe her. 'When will yez be gettin' married, then?'

'It'll be a long time yet,' Jill told her. 'I'm only sixteen.'

'You'll be seventeen in a few months,' Steve was quick to remind her, 'and I'll be eighteen.' He hung his head in embarrassment. 'I was goin' to ask yer to get engaged on yer birthday.'

'You were?' Jill faced him, her eyes shining. 'Oh, yes, please!' Then, disappointment in her voice, she added, 'But we've no money for a ring.'

'I've been savin' a few coppers each week,' Steve said, taking her hands in his. 'I'd have enough if we didn't go to the pictures every week.'

'Ooh, I don't mind missing the pictures,' Jill said, her thumb stroking his hand. 'I'd much rather get engaged.'

Forgotten by the two sweethearts, Phoebe and Dorothy looked on, enthralled. With their elbows on the table and their thin faces cupped in their hands, they listened as their fairy princess and Prince Charming discussed how much a ring would cost. They sat up straight when Steve raised his voice to say it was up to him to buy the engagement ring, and he wasn't having Jill pay towards it. For a few horrible seconds they thought the two were going to fall out again, putting an end to their dreams of being bridesmaids. But they soon relaxed when Jill gave in. Yes, it was the right and proper thing for the man to buy the engagement ring. But you could get engagement rings for men as well, so she'd save up because she wanted to give him a ring on the day they got engaged.

When Phoebe and Dorothy were snuggled up to each other in bed that night, they were too excited to sleep. 'Wasn't it dead romantic?' Phoebe whispered. 'Just like yer see on the pictures.'

'Yeah.' Dorothy's sigh was one of bliss. 'An' they're goin' to let us choose the colour of the bridesmaids' dresses.' Again she sighed. 'Five bridesmaids, it's goin' to be a proper posh weddin'.'

'Ooh, I can't wait, I wish it was temorrer.' Phoebe snuggled closer. 'An' don't forget it's a secret, our Dorothy, yer've not to tell a soul.'

'Scout's honour, I won't open me mouth.' Dorothy pulled the sheet up to her chin. 'Good night and God bless, our Phoebe.'

'Good night, sis! Sleep tight an' mind the fleas don't bite.'

Chapter Six

The table was set for dinner, the room was neat and tidy and a fire burned cheerfully in the grate. Molly gave one more glance around to make sure there were no shoes left lying around or newspapers peeping out from under the cushions, then she nodded in satisfaction and pulled out a chair, relishing the rare opportunity of having half an hour's peace and quiet to herself. Jack and Tommy usually got home about half one on a Saturday but today they were going straight from work to Norris Green, where the man who did the coupon for the syndicate lived. He was reluctant to carry so much money into work with him, said it was too much of a responsibility. So all the winners were going to his home to pick up their share, and Tommy was tagging along.

Molly laid her palms flat on the table and stared at the flames licking the bars of the grate. If they were getting new furniture for this room they'd have to decorate first. No good spoiling the ship for the sake of a ha'porth of tar. Light wallpaper, something like her mother's with little sprigs of flowers on, that would brighten the place up. And they'd have white paintwork instead of the miserable brown they had now. The trouble was, anything too light would show every mark and Ruthie wasn't fussy where she put her dirty hands.

Molly's eyes went to the ceiling when she heard her daughter running down the hall, shouting, 'Mam, can I 'ave a jam buttie?'

'I might 'ave known it was too good to be true.' Molly swivelled in her chair and groaned at the sight of her daughter. Hair dishevelled, nose running, streaks of dirt on her face and the socks that had been white a couple of hours ago filthy dirty and wrinkled around her ankles. 'In the name of God will yer look at the state of yer? Honest, people will wonder what sort of a home yer come from!'

'I'm only playin' with Bella!' Ruthie looked disgusted. How could yer play ollies without getting dirty? She ran the sleeve of her coat across her nose. 'Can I 'ave a jam buttie?'

Molly tutted. 'That's a dirty habit, that is,

wipin' yer nose on yer sleeve.' White paintwork indeed, she thought, I must be out of my mind! I'd spend my life washing dirty, sticky finger-marks off it. 'Go out an' play, there's a good girl. Yer can't 'ave a buttie 'cos it'll put yer off yer dinner.'

'Ah, ray, Mam!'

'Don't give me any lip, Ruthie, or I'll keep you in.' That was the worst of having a baby when the rest of your family were grown-up, you didn't have the same patience. Still, she admitted to herself, it wasn't the child's fault, she hadn't asked to be born. And she was no worse than the others had been at her age. Jill wasn't so bad, she always managed to keep herself clean, but Doreen and Tommy had been little terrors, always filthy and always in trouble. 'Be a good girl, sunshine, an' go out an' play. It won't be long before yer dad and Tommy are home, an' we'll be havin' a big dinner.' The look of disappointment on the child's face and the down-turned mouth brought forth a wave of sympathy. 'I'll give yer a penny after dinner to buy some sweets, how about that?'

The mouth turned upwards and a smile hovered on the pixie-like face. 'Okay, Mam, give us a shout when me dinner's ready.'

She's easily pleased, Molly thought, listening as her daughter skipped down the hall. Mind you, what kid wouldn't be after being bribed with the promise of a penny? When I was her age I was dead chuffed to get a farthing!

'Mam!'

'What is it now?'

'The rent man's 'ere.'

Molly jumped up, frowning. She'd paid her rent, what was the matter with the man? She pulled the sideboard drawer open, muttering to herself as she searched for the brown book. 'I bet he's never marked it in 'is book, the silly beggar. But that's 'is lookout, 'cos if he thinks I'm payin' again, he's got another think comin'.'

'Ah, here it is.' Flicking through the book for the last page, Molly hurried down the hall. 'Look, it's...' Her words petered out and her mouth gaped. 'Mr Henry! What on earth 'ave yer done to yerself?'

The landlord's right hand, cradled in a sling, was covered in a plaster cast which was partly hidden by the sleeve of his coat. Looking past him, Molly could see his car and a woman sitting behind the steering wheel. 'I tripped over some books on the office floor and fell awkwardly.' Mr Henry pulled a face. 'Broke my wrist.'

'The other bloke didn't say what was wrong with yer, just told us yer were ill,' Molly said. 'I thought it was funny you bein' off two weeks, I've never known yer be sick all the years yer've been comin'.'

'I can't drive, and it'll be several weeks before the cast comes off. But the collector said there'd been complaints about the new people at the top of the street, so I asked the wife to drive me down to find out what it's all about.'

'Are yer comin' in?'

'If you don't mind, just for a few minutes.' Mr Henry leaned towards the car window, lifted up five fingers then followed Molly into the house. 'I thought you'd be the best one to ask. There's no point in me going up there without knowing what the Bradleys are doing, and who they're doing it to.'

'Yer shouldn't 'ave bothered, not the way yer are,' Molly told him, pointing to his hand. 'Yer must be in agony.'

'No, it's not too bad if I don't move it. Actually, it's more itchy than painful and I can't get at it to have a good scratch.' He laughed. 'I got one of the wife's knitting needles down the cast this morning, and I was really enjoying myself having a good scratch when she came in and caught me. Boxed my ears, she did.'

'No more than yer deserve.' Molly indicated a chair. 'Sit yerself down and I'll spill the beans.'

When she'd finished, the landlord shook his head. 'Oh, dear, they sound like troublemakers.' He looked puzzled. 'I'm surprised really, because the woman who recommended them is one of my best tenants. She said they were good friends of hers.'

'If they're her friends, I'd hate to see 'er enemies! God bless us, Mr Henry, the woman's as tough as old boots! I don't know about the 'usband, I've never seen 'im, but I wouldn't touch her with a flamin' bargepole! An' wait till yer see the mess the house is in, yer'll 'ave a fit! The Culshaws mightn't 'ave had any money, but at least they were clean an' they weren't rowdy. That lot are as common as muck.'

'There's not much I can do about it right now, not until I'm back collecting and can

102

see for myself. But I'm surprised at Mrs Black recommending them, she's such a nice person.'

'Does she live around 'ere, this Mrs Black?' Molly asked.

'No, in Tetlow Street, off Rice Lane. We've got six houses in that street and we've never had trouble with any of them.'

'Well, if a house comes empty next to this Mrs Black, stick the Bradleys in it an' see how she likes it.' Molly saw the concern on Mr Henry's face and felt sorry for him. He'd always been a good landlord, always understood if you were skint one week and couldn't afford the rent. And he'd let you pay the arrears off at a couple of bob a week. 'Look, don't be worryin' about anythin' till yer feel up to it. Corker sent them packin' when they tried to borrow off his ma, an' they haven't been back since, so perhaps they're got the message. You just go 'ome and forget about it until yer better.'

'If anything untoward does happen, will you send word up to the office, Molly?'

''Course I will! An' I'm seein' Corker tonight, so I'll tell 'im. We're all goin' out for a drink.' She told him about Jack's good fortune and was delighted when it brought a smile to his face. 'So yer see, Mr Henry, life's not all bad. An' when we're all tanked up, singin' our heads off, I'll think of yer. Unless I 'ave one over the eight, then I won't be capable of thinkin' straight, I'll be legless.' Molly stood up. 'I'm goin' to chase yer now, otherwise the dinner will be burned to a cinder.'

Jack threw the brown paper bag on to the table in front of Molly. 'There you are, love.' His face was wreathed in smiles. 'There's sixpence short because the bank charged for changing the cheque.'

Molly was all of a dither as she opened the bag and took out the notes. 'What's this?' She fingered a large white piece of paper. 'Where's the money?'

Jack laughed. 'That *is* money! There's five five-pound notes, two one pound, and a ten-bob one.'

'In the name of God, I've never seen one of these in me life!' Molly held one of the notes nearer to her eyes and read the wording on it. 'Well, I'll be blowed! It doesn't look like money, does it?'

'I wouldn't mind a fistful of them, Mam.' Tommy fingered one of the notes, a look of wonder on his face. 'Just think, five pound an' it just looks like a scrap of paper.'

'Put them back in the bag while I see to the dinner,' Molly said. 'I expected yez in before now.'

'It was further than I thought.' Jack came back from hanging his coat up. 'We got a tram to the East Lancs Road, then had to get a bus the rest of the way.'

'I've been keeping yer dinner warm, I hope it's not dried up.' Molly made her way to the kitchen. 'Give Ruthie a shout, will yer, Tommy?'

Jack stood by the kitchen door. 'Where are the girls?'

'Jill went out with Steve about half ten.' With a towel to protect her hands, Molly lifted a plate from the top of a pan of hot water. 'Move out of the way, love, this is red hot.' She put the plate on the table before saying, 'They've gone into town, window-shopping. Right now I bet they've got their noses pressed against a jeweller's window, seein' how much the engagement rings are.'

'They're not gettin' engaged, are they?' Jack stepped back a pace to let her pass. 'Nobody's said anythin' to me about gettin' engaged.'

'They've not said anythin' to me, either, but I've a feeling it's in the wind.' Molly gave him a peck as she made the return journey to the kitchen. 'It's bound to happen sometime, love, 'cos they're crazy about each other.'

'Aye, I keep forgettin' they're growing up.' Jack sat down and picked up his knife and fork. 'What's this? Lamb chops!'

'I thought I'd give yez a treat, seein' as it's a special day.' Molly put a hot plate down in front of Tommy. 'Watch yer hands on that, son, it's red hot.'

'Did I hear yer say our Jill's gettin' engaged?' Tommy looked surprised. 'I've not heard anythin'.'

Ruthie stood by the door, her nose still running, a bag of ollies in one hand and a piece of chalk in the other. 'Ooh, er, is our Jill gettin' engaged?'

'Oh, dear God, now it'll be all over the street!' Molly screwed her eyes up. All this had developed from one innocent remark. 'No, she's not gettin' engaged! And from this minute we're goin' to be like those three monkeys...we see nowt, hear nowt, an' say nowt, d'yez hear? If I hear one word repeated outside this room, so help me I'll batter the lot of yez.'

'It's my fault, I misunderstood.' Jack picked the chop up with his fingers and bit into it. 'Mmm, this is lovely.'

'Holy sufferin' ducks, I forgot the mint sauce!' Molly dashed out to return with a small glass jug. 'First time we've 'ad lamb for donkey's years an' I almost forgot the best part.'

'Where's our Doreen, Mam?' Tommy asked. 'She's usually home by now.'

'She's gone to Blackler's with Maureen to buy some material.' Molly poured the sauce liberally over her dinner before passing the jug to Jack. 'She's stayin' in tonight while me an' yer dad go for a drink, so Maureen's comin' back with her an' they're goin' to spend the night cutting a dress pattern out.'

Doreen worked in the sewing room at Johnson's dye works and she made up for the low wages by making her own clothes. She was good at it, too, there was nothing she couldn't turn her hand to. She made all Molly's and Ruthie's clothes as well, and earned herself a couple of bob sewing for the neighbours.

'Jill and Steve going in next door tonight?' Jack asked, gravy running down his chin. He was turning the chop in his fingers to see if he'd missed any of the succulent meat.

Molly nodded. 'They don't mind, in fact I think they enjoy it. And Ellen said Phoebe and

106

Dorothy are over the moon, they love it when their mam goes out and Jill and Steve sit with them.'

Tommy patted his full tummy and heaved a sigh of pleasure as he pushed his plate away. 'That was lovely, Mam, I really enjoyed it.'

'Can't beat a lamb chop,' Molly agreed. 'Even the bones are sweet.'

'Can I get washed in the kitchen before yer start on the dishes?' Tommy coaxed. 'I told Ginger I'd call for 'im at three o'clock an' I'm late now.'

'Okay, but don't make a mess 'cos I've scrubbed that place from top to bottom.' Molly leaned her elbows on the table and watched Ruthie lift her plate to her mouth to lick the remains of the gravy. 'It's bad manners to do that, sunshine, but I'll let yer off this once, seeing as it's a special day.'

Ruthie lowered the plate to the table, her small tongue running over her lips. 'Can I go out an' play, Mam?'

'Rinse yer mouth first, yer look a sight.' Molly smiled across at Jack when she heard her daughter shouting at Tommy because he wouldn't let her get to the sink. 'Brotherly love.'

Ruthie was back in a flash to stand beside her mother, her hand held out palm upwards. 'Yer promised me a penny, Mam.'

'So I did, sunshine.' Molly delved into the pocket of her pinny. 'Here yer are, but don't be mean, share it with Bella.' She grabbed her

107

daughter's arm as the girl turned away. 'Let's see yer face.'

'I couldn't wash it proper 'cos our Tommy wouldn't let me in the sink.' Ruthie scowled. 'I wiped it on the towel.'

'Oh, go on with yer.' Molly patted her bottom. 'Yer'll be as black as the hobs of hell in five minutes, anyway.'

When they were alone, Molly reached for the paper bag. 'I'll 'ave to ask Maisie if she'll change one of these five-pound notes for me, so as I can give the kids the money I promised them.' She handed the two one-pound notes to Jack. 'You take these, love, 'cos yer'll have to buy a few rounds tonight, mug them all.'

'I won't need that much, love, one will do.'

'Not on yer life!' Molly was determined. 'There'll be eight of us, an' I'm not havin' yer sittin' there countin' yer coppers, not after winning all this money.'

Jack put the notes behind the clock on the mantelpiece. 'You'll have none left, the way you're goin' on.'

'I might be cabbage-lookin', Jack, but I'm not green.' Molly left one of the white notes on the arm of the couch then carefully folded the bag and pushed it under one of the cushions. 'I've got it all worked out to the penny. After I've seen to the kids, I'll have twenty-two pound left. The odd two will buy wallpaper and paint, the rest is for furniture.'

'I don't care what yer do with it, love, as long as it makes yer happy.' Jack knew that the money he and the children turned over every week was enough to pay the weekly bills and keep them, but there was never any over for luxuries. Now Molly could go out and buy what she wanted without worrying about having to go short on something else 'That's all I want from life, love, to see you happy.'

'Jack, I'm over the moon with the money. Delighted, delirious, ecstatic, even! But if yer asked me what made me the happiest, the money or me family, then me family would come first any time.' Molly rose to cup his face in her hands. 'I love every hair on yer heads.'

Jack raised his brows, a grin on his face. 'We've got the house to ourselves, how about goin' upstairs for half an hour?'

'Yer can sod off, Jack Bennett!' Molly's laugh filled the room. 'Right now I'm off to Maisie's to swank, an' change the first five-pound note I've ever 'ad in me life. Then I'm nipping over to Miss Clegg's for five minutes, see 'ow she is. I've neglected her for the last few months with me da being ill, left it to Nellie an' Mary to look after her, but I'll make it up to her.'

Molly picked up the note and folded it as she walked to the door. Then she turned, a twinkle in her eyes. 'Yer know what I'm like after a few drinks, love, so try yer hand tonight, I think yer might just be lucky.'

Chapter Seven

'There's two tables over there, in the corner. Pull them together an' we'll all get around them.' With her hand in the small of Jack's back, Molly pushed him forward. 'Quick, before someone else beats us to it.'

'Da, you sit here in the corner with Ma, save you getting yer head knocked off every time someone passes.' Jack helped Bob and Bridie to their seats. 'In half an hour's time yer won't be able to breathe in here.'

'I'll sit next to me da.' Molly plonked herself down. It was the first time Bob had been out at night since he'd come home from hospital and Molly intended to keep an eye on him. 'The rest of yez can fend for yerselves.'

'I'll bag one of the stools so me backside can hang over the sides.' Nellie patted an empty chair at the side of her. 'Come on, George, sit by yer ever-loving wife.'

After making sure Ellen was comfortable, Corker stood beside Jack. 'Now, what'll it be?'

'This is my round, Corker, but yer can give me a hand with the drinks,' Jack said, feeling very rich with two pounds in his pockets. 'Is it sherry for the ladies and pints of bitter for the men?'

'Just a glass for me, son,' Bob said. 'I don't want to overdo it.'

The pub got busier and noisier as the night wore on. A group of regulars who'd been drinking heavily started singing, and a few of the other customers joined in. But they were all waiting for the star turn, who was standing by the bar slowly sipping pints. He was an insignificant little man, as thin as a rake, with a sickly complexion, a receding hairline and most of his front teeth long gone. But Joe Pinnington had been blessed with a rare gift, a voice that was so rich and powerful people came from miles around to hear him. He brought so much custom to the pub that the landlord kept him supplied with free beer. He had a routine, did Joe, and no amount of coaxing would shift him from it. Two pints before he started, then one always at hand to wet his whistle. He lived a dull, monotonous life for six days of the week, but on a Saturday night he was a star.

Joe downed the last of his pint and moved away from the bar, leaving the counter free for those wishing to buy drinks. As he took up his regular position a silence descended, and the lounge was suddenly filled to overflowing as customers from the snug brought their drinks through. After clearing his throat, Joe began to sing, and even those who heard him every week were thrilled by the richness of his voice. '"She's my lady love, she is my love, my turtle dove."'

Molly saw her father take his wife's hand, and she smiled when she heard him say, 'One of our favourites, sweetheart.'

Soon the rafters were ringing to the tune

of 'Lily of Laguna', followed by 'My Wild Irish Rose' and other well-known favourites. Joe would sing the songs first, before inviting everyone to join in. Not that anyone needed any encouragement: this was what they'd all come for.

Molly kept a close watch on her father, worried that the noise and excitement might be too much for him. He'd been firm in his refusal to have more than two half-pints of bitter, saying he didn't need drink to enjoy himself. And his pleasure was evident on his face as he sang along with Bridie, her hand held fast in his. Like two lovebirds, Molly thought before transferring her gaze to Corker, whose arm was draped casually around Ellen's shoulders as he sang at the top of his voice.

Then came a ten-minute interval, time for Joe to oil his parched throat and for the customers to get their drinks in.

'He should be on the stage, that feller,' Nellie said, her chins moving in different directions. 'He's as good as any I've heard.'

'Bob, I think yer've had enough for one night.' Bridie squeezed her husband's hand. 'Let's away now while we've got the chance. I'd not like to walk out when the man's singing, it wouldn't be polite.'

Molly butted in when she saw her father was about to protest. The ma's right, Da, I think yer should call it a day.'

Reluctantly, Bob nodded. 'I suppose you're right.'

'I'll walk you home,' Jack said. 'It'll only take

me a quarter of an hour to get there and back.'
After giving them time to say their farewells,
he pushed a way through the crowd, Bob and
Bridie following in his wake.

They'd not been gone long when a voice
from the other end of the room shouted,
'Come on, Joe, on yer feet! Give us one of
Al Jolson's.'

Joe took a swig of beer, wiped a hand across
his lips, then started. '"Mammy, Mammy, the
sun shines east, the sun shines west."'

'Oh, God, I don't 'alf love this one.' Nellie,
with four glasses of sherry inside her, put her
hands on the table and pushed herself up.
Ignoring George's pleas, and pushing his hand
away, she opened her mouth and let rip. It
wouldn't be fair to say Nellie was tone deaf,
but her singing caused Joe to change key several
times to try and keep in tune with her. It was an
impossible task, but Nellie was so well known
and liked in the area he did his best, while
the customers clapped their hands and egged
her on.

'That's right, girl, you let 'em have it,' Corker
roared, singing along with them. Even Ellen,
usually so quiet, was laughing as Nellie's face
performed contortions and her hands followed
Joe's actions.

George looked at his wife, her mouth wide
open, her hands waving, and dropped his head
in his hands. 'Don't let on she's with me.'

'Oh, come on, George,' Molly laughed. 'She's
enjoyin' herself an' makin' everyone happy. As
me ma would say, sure, wouldn't the world be

a better place if everyone was as cheerful as Nellie?'

'I'm only jokin', Molly.' George winked before looking through his fingers at his wife. The song was coming to an end now and Nellie was punching her fist in the air as she belted out, '"I'd walk a million miles, for one of yer smiles, my Mam-mam-ammeee!"'

'More!' shouted the crowd, clapping wildly. 'Encore!'

With a wide sweep of her hand, Nellie gave an exaggerated bow. 'Ladies and gentlemen...' She was stopped in mid-sentence when George, to hoots of laughter from the crowd, reached over and pulled her unceremoniously back to her stool. 'What the...!'

'You're cramping Joe's style,' George growled, handing over her glass of sherry. 'Drink that an' stay put.'

The look of amazement on Nellie's chubby face had Molly, Corker and Ellen doubled up. Then the big woman's humour surfaced and she played along, pretending she was the worse for drink. 'What, hic, did yer, hic, say, love?' She downed her drink in one go and, swaying slightly, held the glass out to George. 'Yes, hic, I will 'ave another, hic, drink. It's hic, kind of yer, hic, to ask.'

Molly was wiping her eyes when she saw Jack pushing his way through the crowd. 'You've been quick, love! Oh, yer should 'ave been here five minutes ago, yer'd have died laughin'.'

'I left Ma an Da at their door.' Jack's face looked troubled. 'There's fightin' going on at the top of our street and I thought, with yer mother bein' on her own, Corker, perhaps yer should go home.'

Corker leaned forward. 'Who's fightin'?'

The whole flamin' street is out, but I didn't stay to find out what was goin' on 'cos I thought it best to get back here quick and let you know. I could hear shoutin' and screamin', and there's dozens of people out, but it was too dark to see clearly who they were.'

'I better get home.' Corker nearly knocked the table over in his haste. 'If anyone's frightened me ma, I'll strangle them.'

'You run on, Corker.' Molly slipped her arms into her coat. 'We'll be right behind you.'

'I bet it's that Bradley family,' Nellie said, scowling. 'We've had the odd row in the street before now, but never fightin'.'

Jack and George chased after Corker, leaving Ellen and Molly to each take one of Nellie's arms to help her move faster. They could hear the shouting and screaming from the bottom of the street and it increased in volume as they drew nearer. 'In the name of God, it sounds as though they're killing each other.' Molly remembered that Tommy's friend, Ginger, lived at the top and she felt a stab of fear as she prayed her son wasn't involved.

'Look, Corker's got hold of someone.' Ellen let go of Nellie's arm. From the dim light given out by the street gas lamps, she could see Corker trying to restrain a man who was shouting and waving his arms about.

'We've had nowt but trouble since you lot

115

moved in,' the man screamed, 'but yer'll not get away with stealin' my son's bike. I want that bike back or I'll break yer bloody neck for yer.'

'That's Barney Coleman.' Molly's voice was high with surprise. 'I've never seen 'im like this before.'

'Look, there's the Bradley woman,' Nellie said, 'an' that must be her husband, the one shoutin' and swearin'.'

The neighbours not in the crowd that had gathered were standing at their doors, shaking their fists at the Bradleys and shouting their support for Barney. Most of them had lived in the street nearly all their lives and never had they witnessed a scene like this.

The three women edged closer, in time to hear Corker say, 'Calm down, Barney, and tell me what it's all about.'

'I'll tell yer what it's about, Corker, it's about that crowd of thieving swines.' Barney was beside himself with rage. 'There's all sorts of things gone missing since they moved in, but no one could prove anythin'. But this time they were seen takin' our Malcolm's bike.'

'Yer a liar!' Mr Bradley was average in height, but it was hard to see his features in the darkness, except that his black hair was long and straggly and he was dressed like a tramp. 'None of mine touched yer bleedin' bike!'

Mrs Bradley joined her husband. 'Call any o' mine a thief an' I'll scratch yer bleedin' eyes out.' She started towards Barney but Jack stood in front of her, blocking her path. 'Get out

116

of me way, yer bastard, let me get me hands on 'im.'

'Your son did take me bike.' Barney's twelve-year-old son, Malcolm, was nearly in tears. 'I was at the top of the entry an' I saw him take it out of our back yard an' put it in yours.'

'Yer lyin' bastard!' Mrs Bradley darted around Jack before he knew what was happening and went for Malcolm. 'Little bugger!' Her hands were around the terrified boy's throat and she was shaking him like a rag doll when Jack came up behind her and lifted her off her feet. 'That's enough of that, Mrs Whatever-yer-name-is!' He carried her, kicking and screaming, to deposit her on her front step. 'If yer know what's good for yer, yer'll stay there.'

As Jack turned away the woman lunged at him. She jumped on his back, wrapped her arms around his neck and began to head-butt him, her feet kicking wildly into the backs of his knees. He tried to shake her off but she hung on like a leech, her arms threatening to cut off his air supply.

'I'll kill her!' Molly darted forward, followed quickly by Nellie and George. 'So help me, if she hurts 'im, I'll swing for her.'

'Don't do that, girl, yer'll only make it worse,' Nellie said as Molly tried to pull the woman off Jack's back. She was so angry she didn't realise her attempts were only making the woman hang on tighter. 'Step aside, Molly.'

Nellie did no more than grab the woman's feet and lift them up backwards, higher and higher until they were on a level with her

117

head. She got such a shock she relaxed her grip on Jack as she tried to free her feet. 'Keep these up,' Nellie said, jerking her head at George to indicate he should take one foot and Molly the other. When she was sure they had a firm grip, she moved away. 'Don't let go until I tell yez.' The shouting stopped as everyone watched Nellie's actions. Even Mr Bradley seemed too mesmerised to go to his wife's aid. They saw Nellie stoop until she was under Mrs Bradley's chest, then she stood up and shouted, 'When I say "go", drop them an' move out of the way.'

Jack felt the weight being taken off his back and, rubbing his throat, he turned to witness the most amazing sight he'd ever seen. The woman who'd been clinging to him seconds before was now horizontal in mid-air, supported under her chest by Nellie's head and with her feet held up by Molly and George.

'Okay, yez can let go now!' As soon as Nellie felt the woman's body slipping backwards, she moved away and Mrs Bradley fell to the ground.

But although the woman was down, she certainly wasn't out. She could hear the sniggers of the crowd and the sound fuelled her anger. 'I'll get yer for this, yer big fat cow!'

Nellie stood over her, shaking a fist. 'Yer'll get this in yer face if yer touch one of me friends again! Mind you, if yer 'ad yer face bashed in it'd be an improvement.'

Corker didn't have time now to appreciate what he'd seen, but he knew when he got to bed he'd relive that scene over and over again.

He led Barney over to stand by the wall. 'Are yer sure about this, Barney?'

'As sure as God is my judge, Corker. The bike was there one minute and gone the next. I'd sent Malcolm to the corner shop for two ounces of baccy, and he wasn't away more than five minutes. He came runnin' in to say he'd seen one of the Bradley lads wheeling the bike out of our yard and taking it into theirs. He ran after him an' banged on the yard door, but no one answered an' when he tried the door it was bolted.'

'Hey, Dad!' A young lad of about sixteen came out of the Bradleys' house to lean against the wall. He had a smug smile on his face, as he said, 'If they're so sure we took the bleedin' bike, why don't yer let them search the 'ouse, see if they can find it?'

Corker didn't miss the look exchanged between father and son. They must think we were born yesterday, he thought. Still, I'm wised up to them now. He whispered to Barney, 'They've shifted it somewhere else. Proper cocky young feller that one, too clever for his own good. Go along with me, Barney, don't let them rile yer. Tell young Malcolm I'll get 'is bike back for him, one way or t'other. If I don't, I'll fix him up with another one.'

'Okay, Corker, thanks. But they shouldn't be allowed to get away with it.'

'They won't, Barney, just trust me.' Corker walked over to Mr Bradley and looked down at him. 'We won't come in, it'd be a waste of time. But tell that cocky son of yours not to

119

try an' move the bike from where he's stashed it, 'cos every eye in the street will be watching him, and the rest of yer family. Yer won't be able to blink without us knowing about it.'

'We didn't take it, mister,' Mr Bradley whined, his head back as he gazed up at Corker. Getting on the wrong side of this big bloke could land them in real trouble. 'Honest!'

'That's a funny word comin' out of your mouth.' Corker threw him a look of scorn before turning to the crowd. 'A kid's bike 'as been stolen an' we've got a good idea who took it. Yez all know the saying that thieves never prosper, well these won't. I can promise yez that! But we can't do anythin' tonight, it's too late and tempers are frayed. So away home to yer beds an' we'll see what tomorrow brings.'

Miss Victoria Clegg had been in bed for an hour when she was awakened by the sound of raised voices. At first she thought it was a crowd passing on their way home from the pub, but when the sound didn't go away she got up to peep out of the bedroom window. There wasn't a soul in sight. 'I must be hearing things,' she muttered, climbing back into bed and pulling the clothes up to her chin. 'They say you lose the run of your senses when you get older.'

Victoria was eighty-six years of age, and a spinster. She'd been born in this house, an only child. And when her parents had died over forty years ago, she'd been left alone in the world, without kith or kin. She hadn't minded living on her own, even after she'd retired from Crawford's biscuit factory when she was sixty. There was plenty to keep her occupied, what with the housework, washing and shopping. She'd looked after herself, too, never going a day without making a hot dinner even though there wasn't much fun in sitting down to eat on her own. But lately she worried about growing old and not being able to do the things she was used to doing. Like pulling the furniture out to clean behind, or changing the curtains. Last year she'd fallen off a chair while cleaning the windows, and if the neighbours hadn't broken into the house when they became worried because they hadn't seen her for three days, she'd probably have died.

Victoria turned on to her side, sighing. She was lucky with her neighbours, particularly Molly and Nellie from across the street, and Mary next door. They'd been marvellous since her accident, taking it in turns to do her shopping, helping with the cleaning and making sure she got a hot dinner every single day.

Victoria sat up in bed. She definitely wasn't imagining things, there was shouting going on somewhere. Once more she felt her way around the dressing table to the window and pulled the curtain back. The street was completely deserted, not a sign of a living soul. 'I wonder if it's coming from the entry?' Victoria asked herself. 'Might be a couple of drunks having a fight.' With her arms outstretched feeling her way, she made for the back bedroom. No one ever slept in there so the curtains were never drawn. It had been her bedroom from when she was a baby until her parents died. Her mother had passed away just two years after her father, and Victoria had moved into the larger, brighter bedroom overlooking the street.

It took several seconds for Victoria's eyes to adjust to the darkness outside. There was a gas lamp at the end of the entry but its glow didn't reach as far as her house, which was in the middle of the terrace. 'Oh my God!' Victoria's hand went to her mouth. 'There's someone sitting on the yard wall!' It was too dark to make out who it was, but it had to be a man, a girl couldn't have scaled the high wall. As she watched, the shape dropped down into her yard, then she heard the bolt on the entry door being drawn back.

Rigid with fear, Victoria was rooted to the spot, her hand covering her mouth to stop herself from screaming. She thought of running downstairs and out the front door, but she was afraid. What if there was someone already in the house? Oh, dear God, don't let them come into the house, please! The shape was moving silently, first into the entry, then back inside the yard. He seemed to be pushing something but before Victoria could make out what it was he had disappeared from view into the space beside the coal shed. There came a faint scraping sound, then the back yard door was closed and the bolt shot back into place. Before she had time to wonder why the man had locked himself in, Victoria saw his shape on top of the wall again for a fraction of a second before hearing the soft thud of his feet landing in the entry.

Victoria's heart was thumping like mad. Why should someone want to come into her yard? There was nothing there for them to steal, and why go to all the trouble of unbolting the door, then bolting it again after them? It just didn't make sense! Slowly she made her way back to her bed, but not to sleep. All night she lay awake trying to make sense of what she'd seen. 'It was probably a big dog!' she said aloud. 'I've let my imagination run away with me.' She was comforted by the thought until a voice in her head told her it would have to be a clever dog to open and close the door, and slip the bolt.

Victoria pulled the sides of her hairnet over her ears. 'Oh, dear, I'm all mixed up. It all happened so quickly. I'm not really sure now whether I saw anything or not!'

One thing she was sure of, though, was that the kitchen door would stay firmly bolted tomorrow until Molly came over. Thank goodness Nellie had filled the two coal scuttles, because she wasn't going down that yard on her own, not for all the tea in China.

The next morning in the Bennett house, breakfast was a noisy affair. The children were firing questions across the table, first at Jack then at Molly, wanting to know every little detail of the exciting events of the night before. Jill and Doreen had been told briefly that there'd been trouble, but Molly had been so tired by the time they got home, all she wanted to do was go

123

to bed. Tommy had been to the second house pictures with Ginger and had missed the lot. By the time he got in everyone was in bed.

'That's enough for now.' Molly's head was beginning to ache. 'It's time yer got yerselves ready for Mass.'

'Mam, tell us again about what Auntie Nellie did.' There was porridge running down Ruthie's chin. 'Just once more, Mam, please?'

'Not now, sunshine. I've got a splitting headache. Ask yer dad.'

'No, I want you to tell me,' Ruthie banged the handle of her spoon on the table, sending splashes of porridge all over the place. 'You tell it better than me dad.'

'Yeah, go on, Mam,' Tommy coaxed. 'I think it's dead funny.'

'Yer wouldn't 'ave thought it funny if yer'd been there! That flamin' woman nearly strangled yer dad!' The memory of Mrs Bradley hanging on to Jack's back was enough to send Molly's pulses racing. 'Anyway, Corker's comin' this afternoon, so yer'll hear it all over again.'

Jack shook Ruthie's arm. 'Eat up, love, or you'll be late for Mass. And you three put a move on.'

'Do I 'ave to go to Mass today?' Tommy knew he was fighting a losing battle, as he did every Sunday, but nevertheless he tried. 'Can't I skip it, just this once?'

Molly glared. 'Get goin' before me patience runs out.' She stood up and began to clear the table. 'I want to get the dinner over early an' this place tidied up before Corker comes, so

124

come straight 'ome from church to give us a hand.'

Jack stood by the kitchen door watching Molly dish the dinner out. 'What time is Corker coming, did he say?'

Molly shook her head. 'As soon as he's 'ad his dinner, I suppose.'

Jack was eyeing the plates. 'Yer've got one too many, love.'

'No, it's my turn for Miss Clegg.' Molly spooned gravy over the dinners then put the pan back on the stove. 'Start takin' them in, love, while I see to Miss Clegg's.'

Jack picked up a plate in each hand. 'Which is which?'

'They're all the same, except Ruthie's.' Molly picked up a plate she had put on one side. 'I'll nip over with this.' She covered the plate with another one, then wrapped a towel around to keep it warm. 'I won't be long.'

Miss Clegg answered the door so quickly Molly guessed she'd been watching from the window. 'Here yer are, sunshine, a nice bit of shin beef, carrots and turnip and roast tatties.'

A small card table stood in front of the fire, covered with a white cloth with embroidery at the corners, and beside a knife and fork stood a glass of water. 'I see yer all ready!' Molly removed the towel and top plate. 'Now eat every bit, d'yer hear? Got to keep yer strength up.'

'You're very kind, I don't know what I'd do without you and Nellie and Mary.'

'Kind me backside!' Molly grinned. 'We only

do it so we can swank about our cookin'. Now sit down an' get stuck in while it's hot.'

But Miss Clegg made no move towards her chair. Wringing her hands, she asked, 'Have you got a minute, Molly?'

Molly thought of her own dinner going cold, but didn't let it show on her face. 'For you, sunshine, I've got all the time in the world! Why, is there somethin' on yer mind?'

The old lady had been asking herself all morning whether she should tell Molly or not. She'd half convinced herself that she'd been dreaming, but there was that niggle of doubt at the back of her mind that wouldn't go away. What if it hadn't been a dream and the person came back? There was no one else she could tell, because once Molly closed the door behind her she wouldn't see another soul until tomorrow, and it might be too late then. 'A funny thing happened last night, Molly, and it's got me worried.'

'Oh, there's no need to worry, Miss Clegg! There was a fight at the top of the street an' yer probably heard them shoutin' and screaming.'

Victoria nodded. 'Yes, it was the noise woke me up. But that's not what I wanted to talk to you about.'

Molly gazed at the dinner which wasn't going to be fit to eat if it was left much longer. 'Let's put this on the hob, keep it warm for yer.' She put the extra plate on top and set the dinner down on the hob, near the fire. 'Now, sit yerself down and tell Auntie Molly all about it.' Molly's mind was on her own

126

dinner as Victoria started to speak. It was to be hoped Jack had the sense to put it back in the oven. But as the old woman's words began to sink in, Molly forgot everything else, her gaze riveted on the lined face. 'Have yer been in the yard this mornin', to look?'

'No fear! The door's been barred and bolted all morning.'

'There's only one way to find out.' Molly jumped to her feet and hurried from the room. Victoria heard the two bolts being drawn back, then saw Molly passing the window. The seconds ticking away slowly on the big Westminster chiming clock on the sideboard was the only sound breaking the silence. Then Molly came running up the yard, her face agog.

'Well, was there anything?' Victoria asked. 'Or am I just a crazy old woman?'

'Yer far from crazy, sunshine!' Molly sank to her knees and put her arms around the frail shoulders. 'Yer brilliant, that's what yer are.' She kissed the fine white hair before struggling to her feet. 'Just listen to what I've got to tell yer.'

Victoria wore her hair parted right down the middle from forehead to the nape of her neck. Each side was plaited and wound into a bun at either side of her head, like large earphones. And as Molly explained the reason for the fighting the night before, Victoria kept fingering the buns nervously.

'An' the bike that caused all the fightin' is now propped up against your coal shed!' Molly ended on a high note. 'It's unbelievable, bloody unbelievable! Wait till Malcolm Coleman knows he's got his bike back, he'll be over the moon!'

But Victoria didn't share Molly's excitement. 'What if the boy comes back for it? And what made him choose my yard? I don't even know the family, so why pick on me?'

Molly frowned. She hadn't thought of that. Why *had* they picked on Miss Clegg's house? She answered her own question. Because they probably know she's old and lives on her own. The type they are, they've more than likely got the whole street sussed out by now. But she couldn't tell the old lady that, she'd never sleep in her bed again.

'What time did yer go to bed, sunshine?'

'I went early because there was nothing worth listening to on the wireless. I'm not sure, but it must have been before ten.'

'That's why, then! Your house would be the only one with no lights on!' Molly tried to keep her tone light, but inside she was filled with mixed emotions. Pleasure for Malcolm getting his bike back, anger at the Bradleys for being thieves, and sadness that they'd upset this dear old lady. 'They were in a hurry to get rid of the evidence, an' with your place bein' in darkness they must 'ave thought the family was out for the night.'

'But they must intend coming back for it, mustn't they?'

'I'm not a detective, Miss Clegg, but I think they intended comin' back for it last night, when they thought everyone would be in bed.

But Corker put a spoke in their wheel an' they were probably too frightened to come for it. He told everyone in the street to watch their house, back an' front, an' he said it loud enough for the Bradleys to hear.'

'Oh dear,' Victoria cried. 'I'm not used to this, it's a terrible way to live.'

'There's no need to get yerself upset about it, they don't know you from Adam, wouldn't know yer if they fell over yer. It was just pure chance that they picked on your place. An' there'll be no need for them to come back, I can put yer mind at rest on that score. Malcolm will get his bike back this afternoon an' Corker will take great delight in telling the Bradleys.' Molly rose to her feet. 'I'll 'ave to get back, but I'll be over later with Jack or Corker, an' we'll take the bike.' Using the towel, Molly carried the plate from the hob and set it in front of Victoria. 'Yer've put a halt to the gallop of those thieves an' they'll think twice about tryin' to pull a stunt like that again. Yer'll be a hero in the street after this, you mark my words.'

Victoria's lashes fluttered coyly. 'I haven't done anything.'

'Oh, but yes yer have! If you hadn't been brave enough to go to the window to see what was goin' on, heaven only knows whether we'd ever 'ave seen the bike again.' Molly picked up the knife and fork and held them out. 'Get on with yer dinner now an' I'll see yer later.'

At the door, Molly turned. The old lady was cutting into a roast potato and she looked more contented than she had done earlier. But Molly

129

didn't feel contented, she felt angry. Those Bradleys certainly knew who to target. First Corker's mother, now Miss Clegg. Something had to be done to stop them, but what?

'Victoria!'

Miss Clegg looked up in surprise. 'Yes?'

'It is Sunday, so I can call yer by yer Sunday name.' There was tenderness in Molly's smile. 'D'yer want to know somethin'?'

'Only if it's something nice.' The wrinkles deepened as Victoria returned Molly's smile. 'I've had enough unpleasant things happen to last me a lifetime.'

'Oh, it's nice all right. I just wanted to say that not only are yer a hero in my eyes, but a little love into the bargain.'

Chapter Eight

On Sunday afternoon Molly's living room resembled a board meeting. The surroundings may have been less opulent, but to the neighbours sitting around her table the subject under discussion was as important to them as the fluctuating price of cotton would be to directors of an importing company.

Two wooden chairs had been brought down from the bedrooms so all the grown-ups were able to sit around the table, while the children perched on any surface they could find. Only Ruthie was missing. For the first time in her life she had to be sent out to play under protest. She knew something was afoot and didn't want to miss it. But she was a very talkative child and anything she heard would be all over the street in no time.

Corker had called for Ellen on his way down, Nellie and George were there, and Barney Coleman and Malcolm had been sent for. The house hadn't been built to accommodate such a crowd and Molly's table wasn't big enough for eight pairs of elbows to rest on in comfort. But no one cared about the crush or discomfort as they voiced their suggestions on how to deal with the return of Malcolm's bike so it would have the maximum impact on the Bradleys.

The bike was now propped up against the wall in Molly's yard, brought there by Corker who had made a detour through all the back alleys so he wouldn't be seen.

'Why don't we just walk up there, bold as brass, an' tell them we know all about their little game?' Nellie didn't believe in messing around. Go straight for the jugular, that was her motto.

'No! I don't want to get Miss Clegg involved!' Molly gave a determined shake of her head. 'She's frightened as it is, an' I promised we wouldn't let on where we got the bike from.'

'They'll flamin' well know where we got it from!' Nellie snorted. 'They put the ruddy thing there!'

'That doesn't mean they know about Miss Clegg.' Corker tapped his fingers on the table. 'Like Molly said, her house was the only one

131

without a light on, an' I'll bet a pound to a pinch of snuff that the young cocky feller had every intention of goin' back for it when everyone was in bed. The only reason he didn't was because he knew every eye in the street was on him.'

Corker passed his cigarette packet to Jack, then after he'd lit both cigarettes, he turned to Molly. 'When I was in the entry I noticed none of the yard doors 'ave numbers on them, an' I wondered how he'd recognise the door again. I'd just come to the conclusion that he must have counted the number of doors as he went back up the entry, when something caught me eye.' Corker drew hard on his cigarette as he gazed around the table. 'It was a little chalk mark, in the shape of a cross, near the latch.' He heard gasps from his audience and grinned. 'He's a cunning little bugger, that Bradley lad. Had it all worked out, or so he thought.'

'Oh dear, that means he'll go back to Miss Clegg's.' Molly bit on her bottom lip. 'D'yer know, I'll break 'is neck if I find he's been near her.'

'Not to worry, Molly me darlin', he'll 'ave a helluva job to find her house again.' A deep throaty chuckle came from between Corker's moustache and beard. 'Young Bella was playin' hopscotch outside her house, so I borrowed her piece of chalk. Now every door in that entry has a cross on it, in exactly the same place, under the latches.'

When Nellie started to laugh, her enormous tummy lifted the table, and the legs hovered

132

inches from the floor until the weight of her heavy bosom anchored it again. 'Corker, yer a flamin' genius! Yer deserve a bloody medal for thinkin' of that!'

The room was ringing with laughter and it was a while before order was restored. 'Come on.' Corker banged his huge fist on the table. 'This isn't goin' to get the baby a new coat, so let's get down to business. Anybody got any suggestions to make? If so, spit them out an' we'll see which one we think is the best. How about you, Barney?'

'Anythin' you decide will be all right with me, Corker. I think the Bradleys should be taught a lesson, and if it was up to me I'd belt the father, 'cos he's the one should take the blame. Yer can't tell me he didn't know the bike was in his yard.'

Malcolm was silent as he listened to the grown-ups. He'd spent most of the night crying, because the bike had been the first one he'd ever owned, and he loved it. It was second hand when his mother bought it him for Christmas, and it had been in a sorry state, all rusty and peeling paintwork. But he'd worked on it every spare minute he had, rubbing and polishing until his hands were sore. And just when he had it shining like new, it had been stolen from him. He never thought he'd see it again, so when he heard it was in the Bennetts' yard it felt like Christmas all over again.

Ideas were being aired and chewed over. Going to the police had been George's suggestion, but that was turned down because if the police were called Miss Clegg would be involved. And confronting the Bradleys was dismissed for the same reason. They couldn't make accusations without mentioning what the old lady had seen.

'What about you, Jack?' Corker asked. 'Any ideas?'

'I can't see how we can do much about it, certainly as far as punishing them goes. I know what I'd do if it was up to me, but I don't think any of yer would agree with me.'

'We've not come up with anythin' so far that we're all in agreement with, Jack, so let's hear what you think.'

Jack lowered his head and laid his palms flat on the table. 'I'd give Malcolm his bike back and let 'im ride it in the street.'

'What?' every voice cried in unison, registering varying degrees of surprise and shock. Even the children seemed stunned as they scrambled from their seats to stand by the table.

'Let them get away with it, Jack?' Corker asked, his voice quiet. 'Just like that?'

'No, Corker, not just like that. Listen...'

'As soon as we've gone, will yer take these chairs upstairs an' call our Ruthie in?' Molly struggled into her coat. 'An' don't let her out no matter how much she creates.'

'Don't worry, Mam, I'll see to her.' Jill smiled. 'I wish you luck.'

'And I'll help tidy up.' Doreen's eyes were shining. Fancy her dad being so clever! 'Hurry back an' let's know what happens.'

Jack tied the woollen muffler around his neck. 'Are we ready then?'

Corker nodded before glancing at Malcolm. 'Are yer sure yer know what to say, son?'

'Yeah, Sinbad! I think it's a great idea.'

'Not frightened of them, are yer?'

'Nah!' Knowing that this giant would be watching every move gave Malcolm the courage of a lion. 'They don't scare me.'

Barney took his son's arm. 'We'll go down your entry to the main road, up the next street, then down the top of our entry so we won't have to pass their house. Give us a quarter of an hour, then Malcolm will wheel his bike out and ride it up and down.'

'I'll come with yez and call at Ginger's.' Tommy found all this cloak-and-dagger stuff very exciting. 'I'll stand by the window an' the first sign of trouble I'll be out like a shot.'

'Ay, you!' Molly shook a warning finger. 'Don't you dare start anythin' or yer'll have me to answer to.'

'Come on, get a move on.' Jack sounded impatient. 'It'll be dark before we know it.'

The look of happiness on Malcolm's face as he gripped the handlebars was a joy to behold. And as he preceded his father into the entry he appeared to grow six inches in stature. He'd learned his lesson the hard way. Never again would anyone get a chance to steal his beloved bike. He'd save all his pocket money and buy a lock and chain.

'This is where we part company.' Molly closed the entry door behind her. 'We'll see yez later.'

'Okay and thanks, Molly.' Barney nodded to where his son was walking ahead with Tommy. 'Yer've put the smile back on his face.'

'Away with yer! It's Miss Clegg yer should be thankin', not me.'

'And I'll be doing that too! Get today over, an' I'll give her a call.' Barney set off after his son. 'See yer later.'

Nellie linked her arm through her husband's as they set off in the opposite direction. 'Ay, this is like one of them Edward G. Robinson films.'

'You an' yer flamin' film stars!' Molly, walking behind with Jack, chuckled. 'Ay, George, yer wife likes tough guys, like James Cagney an' Edward G. Robinson. Yer want to try knockin' her around, she'll think more of yer.'

'I wouldn't try if I were you, George.' Corker was bringing up the rear with Ellen. 'One swipe off Nellie an' yer'd be out for the count.'

George turned his head, a wide smile creasing his face. 'I only ever hit her once, an' she belted me back.' He touched his thinning hair. 'I've still got the scar to prove it. I know when I'm beat, so I never tried it again.'

The look of astonishment on Lizzie Corkhill's face when they all trooped in turned to one of dismay. Oh dear, she wasn't expecting visitors and didn't have enough cakes to go around this lot. Then she remembered the nice boiled ham she had on a plate in the larder, and cheered up. At least she could offer them a sandwich and a chocolate wafer biscuit. 'Sit yerselves down,' Lizzie fussed, shaking cushions and

136

pulling chairs forward. 'To what do I owe this pleasure?'

Ellen felt most uncomfortable. This was the first time she'd been in Corker's house and her nerves were gone. She knew his mother, of course, hadn't they lived in the same street for years? But they'd been neighbours, nothing more. And although Corker said his mother had no objection to him being friends with her, Ellen had her doubts. What mother would want her son to be knocking around with a married woman? 'I hope you don't mind us barging in on yer like this, Mrs Corkhill?' Ellen sounded as nervous as she felt. 'We won't stay long.'

'You'll stay an' have a cup of tea.' Lizzie Corkhill couldn't help feeling sorry for Ellen. She was a nice little thing, but if only she weren't married! 'I'm glad to see you, and you're all more than welcome. But I don't need a crystal ball to tell me there's more to this than meets the eye.'

'You're right, Ma, as usual.' From his position by the window, Corker began explaining the plot they'd hatched. He was halfway through when he turned and grinned at them. 'First part of the operation gone according to plan. I can see your Tommy standing by the window of 'is mate's house.'

Lizzie tutted. 'You've seen too many detective pictures.'

'There y'are!' Nellie wriggled her button of a nose. 'I told yez it was like a gangster film.'

'I'd be glad to see the back of that family,' Lizzie said. 'They're a bad lot.'

'They won't bother you no more, Mrs C.' Jack winked at her. 'Not now they've seen the size of yer son.'

'Makes no matter,' Lizzie huffed. 'The street would be a better place without the likes of them.'

'I agree, sunshine!' Molly stood up. 'Lets you an' me make a nice cup of tea, eh?'

'Come here, quick!' Corker jerked his head. 'Malcolm's just bringin' his bike out.'

The first one to reach the window was Lizzie. The last one was Nellie. She'd been daft enough to sit in a low chair and couldn't get up. It took a hefty jerk from George to dislodge her.

Joyce Bradley and her younger sister, Clare, were playing with a rubber ball, bouncing it from one to the other. Joyce was facing up the street and was the first to see Malcolm wheeling his bike out. She gaped in surprise, missing the ball Clare had bounced her way.

'Why didn't yer catch it, yer daft thing?' Clare watched the ball speeding up the street, then stuck her tongue out at her sister. 'Yer needn't think I'm runnin' after it, 'cos I'm not, so there!'

'Oh, shut yer gob!' Joyce said, before flying into the house as though the devil was on her heels.

Malcolm pedalled down the street, turned and rode back. He was passing the Bradley house when the son, Brian, came out with his sister. They watched in amazement as Malcolm rode towards the top of the street then the boy bent his head to whisper something to Joyce, who turned and ran back into the house.

Tommy's friend Ginger had spread the word to all the neighbours, so behind every curtain eyes were watching the proceedings. Unaware that he had an audience, Brian lolled against the wall until Malcolm was on his way back down the street. Then, timing it nicely, he stepped into the road just as Malcolm came abreast of him and grabbed the handlebars. Anticipating what was going to happen, Malcolm tightened his hold on the handlebars and leaned to one side to gain a foothold on the ground.

'Got yer bike back, eh?'

The sneering expression on Brian's face would have scared the younger boy if he hadn't known Sinbad was watching and could be by his side in seconds. The knowledge gave him the courage to stay calm and remember exactly what he'd been told. 'Not blind, are yer?'

Enraged, the Bradley boy began to shake the bike violently. 'Who told yer where it was, eh?'

'What's it got to do with you?' Malcolm asked, struggling to keep his foot on the ground. 'It's none of your business.'

'I asked yer who told yer, an' if yer've got any sense in that thick 'ead of yours, yer'll answer me question, or else.'

'An' I told yer it's none of yer business.'

'I'm makin' it me bleedin' business.' Once more the bike was pushed and pulled. 'If yer know what's good for yer, yer'll tell me what I want to know. Now, where did yer get the bike from?'

Before Malcolm had time to answer, Mr Bradley appeared by his son's side. 'What's goin' on?'

Brian turned his head. 'He won't tell me where'e got it from. Had the bleedin' cheek to tell me it was none of me business.'

'Oh, clever bugger, are yer?' Mr Bradley's tone was menacing as he put his hand on the crossbar. 'Now, where did yer get it an' who told yer?'

Malcolm could feel his skin tingling with fear but he didn't let it show. He did wish someone would put in an appearance, though, 'cos by the look on the man's face he was in for a hiding. 'It's got nothin' to do with you, so mind yer own business.'

'Yer little bleeder!' The man's hand left the crossbar to grip Malcolm's arm. 'I've a good mind to...' His words were cut off when his son elbowed him.

'Watch out, Dad,' Brian said under his breath, 'we've got company.'

Mr Bradley took his eyes off Malcolm and his jaw dropped when he saw Corker and Jack coming towards them, followed by Molly and Nellie. But it was the sight of the big man that brought about a rapid change in his attitude. The anger on his face was replaced by a smile that revealed yellow, rotting teeth. 'I was just tellin' the lad how glad we are he's got 'is bike back.'

'Yes, I know.' Corker looked down from his great height. 'I've been watching from the window an' I could see how pleased yer were.'

Feeling brave again, Malcolm glared at the boy, who was still holding on to the handlebars. 'Take yer hands off me bike.'

Brian removed his hands so fast you'd have thought the bike was on fire. 'I was tellin' 'im how lucky he was, like.' Apart from the bad teeth, Brian was the spitting image of his father. Long greasy hair reaching down to his shoulders, a sickly complexion and shifty eyes. They looked as though they were used to living rough, like gypsies or tramps. 'I was askin' 'im who told...er...I mean, 'ow he managed to get it back.'

'The police got it back for him.' Corker was rewarded by the startled looks exchanged between father and son. He derived great pleasure out of seeing these two squirm. And he hadn't finished with them yet. 'The police will be around later, asking questions, trying to find out who the thieves are. Yer'll probably get a call from them.'

'We don't want no coppers comin' to our 'ouse.' The fear in the man's eyes didn't go unnoticed by Corker. 'There's no cause for them to come to us, we've done nothin' wrong.'

'Me dad's right,' Brian said, looking decidedly nervous. 'We ain't done nothin'.'

'In that case yer've nothin' to worry about, have yez?' Corker's heavy brows drew together. 'Only someone with a guilty conscience has cause to fear the police.'

'I've got no guilty conscience.' Mr Bradley's act of bravado didn't quite come off. He was scared and it showed in the dirty look he threw at his son. 'I just don't want no bleedin' coppers knockin' on my door.'

'Oh, it won't be an ordinary copper,' Corker told him, 'it'll be a detective in plain clothes.'

'They can go to soddin' hell.' Mr Bradley jerked his head at his son. 'Come on.'

Corker waited until they were inside their house, then smiled at Malcolm. 'You did well, son, I'm proud of yer.'

'I wasn't a bit frightened, Sinbad, honest!'

'I know yer weren't, son.' Corker patted the boy's head. 'Now yer can ride yer bike to yer heart's content.'

'Nah, I'll have to take it in now, Sinbad, 'cos me mam doesn't let me play out on a Sunday.'

Lizzie Corkhill was watching through the window, and when she saw Corker pat Malcolm's head, tears came to her eyes. Her son loved children and was so good with them. It was a cause of sadness to Lizzie that he'd never married and had a family of his own. He'd make a wonderful father. She ran a hand across her eye to wipe away the sign of tears, before saying to Ellen and George, 'They're coming now. Will you help with the tea, Ellen?'

Molly was the first in. 'I still think they're gettin' off light,' she sniffed. 'Thieving swines, that's what they are.'

'I agree with yer, girl!' Nellie looked at the chair she'd occupied before and shook her head: she wasn't going to go through that again. So she chose one of the straight dining chairs and plonked herself down. 'I wish there *was* a detective goin' to see them.'

'Will you all sit down.' Lizzie and Ellen had been busy while they were out. The table was set with plates of sandwiches and biscuits, and the teapot, with its knitted cosy keeping it warm, was standing on the hob. 'It's not much but I wasn't expectin' visitors.'

'It's just the job, Mrs C,' Molly said. 'I'm gasping for a drink.' She took a sandwich from the plate Ellen was holding out and put it to her lips. But before she took a bite, she said angrily, 'After all the things they've done, they're gettin' off scot-free! Ooh, me blood's boiling!'

Corker was leaning forward, his elbows on his knees. He waved away the plate of sandwiches Ellen held out. 'No thanks, love.' The dainty triangles wouldn't even fill the gap in his teeth. He'd make his own later, like the ones he was used to on board, as thick as doorsteps. 'There's somethin' fishy about that family,' he said. 'I think the father's spent some time inside.'

'Yer mean in prison?' Jack showed no surprise. 'The thought had crossed my mind, as well.'

'Oh lord, that's all we need!' Molly rolled her eyes. 'Flamin' convicts in our street!'

'Now we're only guessing, Molly, so be careful,' Jack warned. 'Yer could land yerself in trouble.'

Ellen sat down as far away from Corker as she could get. She'd gone the colour of beetroot when he'd called her 'love', and although no one seemed to have noticed, she'd busied herself pouring tea out until the colour she could feel burning her face had subsided. 'Mrs Bradley's

143

got a terrible tongue in her head. She came in the shop yesterday, and being Saturday we were packed out. The language she came out with was somethin' shockin', and all the customers were disgusted. In the end Tony told her to watch her mouth and she got real snotty with him. I won't repeat what she said, but it amounted to takin' her custom elsewhere.'

'What happened then, love?' Corker asked.

Oh, please don't let me blush, Ellen prayed silently. Doesn't he realise I'm embarrassed enough being in his house? 'Tony told her it would be good riddance to bad rubbish. She got on her high horse when the customers voiced their agreement with Tony, and flounced out, cursing and swearin' as loud as yer like.'

'I'm goin' to make some enquiries about them.' Corker sat up straight, his huge body eclipsing the chair he was sitting on. 'One of the policemen down at the dock is a good mate of mine, I'll ask him to find out.'

'Good idea, Corker.' George, always the quiet one, nodded. 'Even if we can't do anythin' about it, it's best if we know what we're dealing with.'

Nellie beamed proudly. 'See, my feller doesn't say much, but when he does, it's worth listening to.'

'I only seem quiet because I can never get a word in with you around.' George ducked to escape the blow Nellie aimed at him. 'It's a mystery to me how yer can go on so long without stoppin' to take a breath.'

'Here's her mate.' Jack jerked his thumb at

Molly. 'It's a toss-up who talks the most.'

Molly and Nellie gazed at each other for several seconds, then burst out laughing. What was the good of denying something they knew was the truth? They did talk too much. It was their favourite pastime! 'There's worse things than being gas-bags, yer know.' Molly giggled. 'We could be off down to Lime Street every day, flogging our bodies.'

'Oh, that's where the action is, is it?' Corker's roar of laughter filled the room. 'Thanks for the tip, Molly.'

'Wouldn't do me much good.' Nellie put on a sad face. 'I'd never make any money. In fact, I'd probably end up havin' to pay the feller.'

'Aah, yer poor thing.' Molly tutted sympathetically. 'Tell yer what, seein' as how yer me best mate, I'll let you count me takings.'

'Gee, kid, thanks!' Nellie clapped her hands. 'Yer kindness is crushing, like yer big feet.'

Lizzie was relaxed now and enjoying the fun. She was fed up worrying about that Bradley family, they were beginning to come between her and her sleep. 'More tea, anyone?'

'No, ta, Mrs C.' Molly leaned over to put her cup on the table. 'We'll have to get back to the family or they'll think we've left home.'

'Or gone down to Lime Street.' Nellie couldn't resist, even though George was giving her daggers. 'Earning a few bob towards doin' yer room out.'

'Ooh, yeah!' Molly hugged herself, a look of anticipated pleasure on her face. 'I'm off to buy the wallpaper tomorrow.' She looked towards Jack. 'Yer'll have to tell me how many rolls of paper we need, an' how much border.'

'Your room's the same as this, so yer need six rolls.' Corker narrowed his eyes, mentally measuring the walls. 'And about twenty yards of border.'

'I won't be doin' the papering until I've painted the ceiling and frieze, so make sure yer get the paint for that first.' Jack looked pained. 'Proper slave-driver, this one, Corker. If she had her way I wouldn't see me bed until the whole room was finished. An' I'm a fool to meself, 'cos once it's done and she's got her new furniture in, life won't be worth living. It'll be "don't sit there", an' "keep yer fingers off"!'

'I could do the ceiling for yer,' Corker offered. 'I could 'ave it done in a day, while yer were at work.'

A gleam of hope shone briefly in Jack's eyes, then he shook his head. 'I couldn't let yer do that, Corker, it wouldn't be fair. Yer only home for a few days.'

'Nonsense! I don't go away until Thursday, so if Molly gets the stuff tomorrow I can spend Tuesday on it.'

'Take him up on it, Jack,' Nellie said. 'Corker doesn't need a ladder to do the ceiling, he can reach that high without one.'

Corker burst out laughing. 'Not quite, Nellie! I don't need a ladder, but I will need a chair or stool.'

'That's the gear, Corker, yer a real pal.' Molly

closed her eyes, thinking of the treasure hidden under the cushion on the couch. She was really going to enjoy spending that money. And who better to share her pleasure than her best mate. 'Are yer comin' with me tomorrow, Nellie, help me choose the paper?'

'Yer didn't think for one moment I'd let yer go on yer own, did yer?' Nellie blew out huffily. 'You need me, mate! Without my guiding hand, my impeccable good taste, yer'd end up buying paper in sky-blue pink with a finny-haddy border.'

'D'yer know, Nellie, I'm glad yer reminded me of that!' Molly, like her friend, kept her face straight. 'I'd forgotten about my taste bein' in me backside.'

'That's what friends are for, girl! To be there in times of trouble, to hold yer hand, wipe yer tears away, wipe yer flamin' backside if need be, and stick like bloody glue to yer mate when she's in the money.' Her arms folded and resting on the ledge made by her tummy, Nellie asked, 'So I'll call for yer at ten in the mornin', shall I?'

Corker stroked his beard, laughter shining in his eyes. 'Are these two always like this?'

George nodded his head. 'Always.'

'Never known them any different.' Jack winked. 'D'yer still want to do our ceiling? Just think, a full day with someone who can talk the hind leg off a donkey.'

'I'll go along,' Nellie grinned, 'just to make sure there's no hanky-panky. All this talk about Lime Street might have put ideas into Corker's head. But don't worry, Jack, I'll keep me eye on them.'

'Oh God!' Corker groaned. 'That's two women talking the hind legs off two donkeys!'

Chapter Nine

'How d'yer like this one, Molly?' Nellie picked up a roll of wallpaper and opened it up for her friend's inspection. 'He's sellin' it off cheap, fourpence a roll.'

'No, it's too dark.' Molly dismissed it with a wave of her hand. 'I want somethin' light to brighten the room up.' She gazed about the walls of the shop where pieces of wallpaper were on display, her eyes lingering longer on some patterns than on others. Then she smiled and pointed a finger. 'There, that's more like it.'

Nellie's eyes became slits as they followed the line of her friend's finger. 'That one's ninepence ha'penny, more than twice the price of this.'

'That's only goin' cheap because they can't sell it! Even if they were givin' it away I wouldn't want it, it's too dark and miserable. I've got to live with it every day, so I might as well 'ave somethin' that'll cheer me up.'

'Suit yerself, girl.' Nellie rolled the offending wallpaper up and placed it on the counter. 'You get what yer want, otherwise I'll never hear the end of it.'

Molly beckoned the assistant over. 'Could you

let me see a roll of that one, please? And some border yer think will match it.'

They watched the man climb a ladder to reach one of the top shelves, and Molly moved forward to take the roll he handed down. She opened it and grinned with pleasure. 'D'yer know, Nellie, this is exactly what I 'ad in mind.'

Nellie gazed at the light beige paper with its pattern of small flowers and leaves. 'Yeah, it is nice, girl, definitely oh-la-la-posh.'

The assistant came over with five rolls of border. 'Try them against the paper, see if there's one you like. If not, I'll get some more down.'

'That's it!' Molly cried with delight as the man held the third sample of border against the wallpaper. 'It sets it off beautiful.'

'How much is it?' Nellie asked.

'Threepence a roll.' The assistant was being crafty. Monday was a slack day for decorating materials, so a sale would stand him in good stead with the boss. And the best way to make a sale was to let the customer think they were getting a bargain. 'Mind you, if you're buying the wallpaper, I can let you have the border cheaper, say twopence a roll.'

I wonder who he thinks he's kidding? Nellie asked herself. Still, two can play at that game. She gave Molly a gentle tap with her foot, a warning to keep quiet. 'Me friend is lookin' for paint as well. For the ceilin' and the paintwork. We were goin' to T. J. Hughes' 'cos we heard it's cheaper there, but it's no joke carryin' paint

149

all that way on the tram. How about knockin'
another ha'penny off the price of the border an'
she can get everythin' she wants here.'

The man did a quick calculation in his head.
If he refused, it was possible he'd lose the order
altogether, and his boss would go mad if he
let a couple of pounds' worth of business slip
through his fingers for the sake of, at the most,
tenpence. 'I'll probably get me block knocked
off, but okay, you can have the border for three
ha'pence a roll.'

Twenty minutes later the friends walked from
the shop laden down with paper and paint.
'You're a case, you are, Nellie McDonough.'
Molly made a grab for a roll of paper that
was threatening to slip from the wrapping. 'But
thank God yer are, yer saved me tenpence.'

'Yer've got to be up to them, girl, otherwise
they'd do yer all roads.' Nellie stopped in her
tracks. 'Hang on a minute till I change hands,
this paint's not 'alf heavy.'

'I'll start trimmin' the paper this afternoon
while I've got an hour to meself.' Molly was
so elated she felt she was walking on air. 'I
can't wait to see it all done and me new
furniture in.'

'Where yer goin' for the dining room suite?'

'I don't know yet, I'll 'ave a good look around
before I decide on anythin'. It'll have to last me
a helluva long time so it's got to be solid as well
as nice to look at.'

'Why don't yer try that little shop in Stanley
Road? I believe he 'as some nice stuff an' he's
reasonable.'

'Which shop is that?' Molly asked as they turned the corner of their street. 'There's a few furniture shops in Stanley Road.'

'It's at the far end, near Scottie Road. Yer must 'ave seen it, he has furniture outside on the pavement, but that's mostly second hand.'

Molly shook her head. 'Can't say I've ever noticed.'

'I think it's called Greenberg's, he's Jewish. I've heard he sells good stuff and is very reasonable.' They'd reached Molly's door and Nellie let out a long sigh. 'Get that key out quick, me flippin' arms are droppin' off.'

Molly laid her parcels on the table and took the paint from Nellie. 'Sit down, sunshine, an' I'll make yer a nice cup of tea.'

Nellie listened to the kettle being filled. 'I'll come with yer to Greenberg's one day, if yer like. Wouldn't mind havin' a gander meself in case I come into money.'

Molly popped her head around the door. 'That's an idea! No harm in having a look before I try the shops in town.'

'How about goin' now, after we've 'ad a drink?'

'I couldn't go today, I haven't even thought about what we're 'aving for dinner yet.'

'Oh, to hell with dinner!' Nellie snorted. 'Give them bacon and eggs, somethin' easy.' She saw the doubt on her friend's face and snorted again. 'An' don't make the excuse yer've got to trim the paper, 'cos I'll give yer a hand with it tomorrow, while Corker's paintin' the ceiling.'

Molly didn't need much persuading. For years

151

everything she'd seen that she liked had been behind shop windows, out of her reach. Now, with money in her pocket, she could go into the shops knowing she was in a position to buy. Not that she intended to buy just for the sake of it, it had to be something they really needed, and good value, 'cos once the money had gone, it would never be replaced. Unless Jack came up on the pools again, but that was a chance in a million. 'I'll make us a buttie, then we'll nip down and have a look around, okay?'

'It doesn't look very big.' Molly was disappointed at the sight of the small corner shop, which had chairs and tables arranged on the pavement outside. 'They can't 'ave much of a selection.'

'For God's sake, don't start moanin' before yer even get inside.' Nellie withdrew her hand from Molly's arm and pushed her friend towards the open door. 'If there's nothin' there to suit yer, all we've lost is the tuppence tram fare, an' that's not goin' to skint us.'

Molly stood inside the shop and her disappointment mounted. It was so packed with furniture it looked a mess. Chairs were piled on top of couches and sideboards, and from what Molly could see, most of the stuff was in a worse condition than her own furniture. 'There's nothin' here for me.' She bumped into Nellie as she turned to walk out. 'It's all second-hand stuff.'

Nellie blocked her path. 'He sells new furniture as well, so there must be another room at the back.'

'Can I help you, ladies?'

Molly spun round and stared at the man standing before them. Where on earth had he come from? She couldn't see a door, but there must be one somewhere, probably behind the big wardrobe at the back. He was a small, chubby man wearing a grey three-piece suit. The bottom button on his waistcoat was undone, not through neglect but because it obviously wouldn't fasten across his enormous tummy. He had a round, friendly face with rosy cheeks and eyes that smiled at them through steel-rimmed glasses.

Molly returned his smile. 'I was looking for a dinin' room suite, but I see yer only sell second-hand furniture.'

'In here, yes, but there's a showroom at the rear. If you'd like to follow me I'll show you what we have in stock.'

As Molly followed the man, Nellie gave her a dig in the back. 'See! I told yer, didn't I?'

Walking into the showroom was like walking into another world and Molly gasped with pleasure. There were three dining room suites on display, but the one that caught Molly's eye was a beauty. 'Ooh, look at that, Nellie, isn't it gorgeous?'

The suite was in mahogany, with a square table and four chairs. The chairs were the nicest Molly had ever seen. The seats were sprung and covered in a maroon plush material, and the high backs were curved at the top and decorated with carvings. Molly ran her hands lovingly over the top of the gleaming table and sighed. It was beautiful, but way out of her reach.

'It's no good yer lookin' all dreamy over that one, girl,' Nellie whispered softly. 'Unless yer meant what yer said about goin' down Lime Street. An' yer'd need to flog yer body a few hundred times to be able to afford that!'

Mr Greenberg came to stand beside them. 'That one isn't new.'

'What?' Molly looked at him as though he was stark staring mad. 'It's brand new!'

'No.' There was amusement in the man's eyes. 'It's been restored.'

'Well I never!' Nellie was flabbergasted. 'I'd never 'ave guessed, not in a million years.'

'It's a beautiful suite,' Mr Greenberg said. 'Must have cost the earth when it was new. Came from one of the big houses in Mossley Hill'

'And who did this...this restoring, or whatever yer call it?'

'I did, it's my trade.'

'Well, I'll tell yer what,' Nellie said, 'yer've made a bloody good job of it. I'd never 'ave guessed it wasn't new.'

Molly gazed at the suite, imagining it in their room. Go on, an inner voice urged, ask him how much. If you never ask, you'll never get. But Molly didn't dare. Just looking at it was enough to know it was beyond her means.

Nellie was watching her friend's face. Then she turned to Mr Greenberg and enquired, casually, 'How much yer askin' for it?'

'Twenty pounds.'

Molly's heart sank. Even though she'd

resigned herself to the fact that the suite would never be hers, she still felt sad.

'Anythin' off for cash?' Nellie asked. 'All the money in one go, in yer 'and.'

A smile crossed Sol Greenberg's face. He only had to look at Nellie to know she was a kindred spirit. Someone who, like himself, couldn't resist the temptations of food. He knew by the look in her eyes that it wasn't the only thing they had in common, either! They both liked to barter, to get the best bargain they could. He was going to enjoy this. 'I could probably come down a pound or two.'

Nellie pursed her lips and glanced at Molly. She saw the disappointment in her friend's eyes and turned back to Mr Greenberg to try again. 'It's not me, yer understand, it's me mate. She's only got so much money, an' she's got certain things to buy with it. She hasn't got a big mouth like me, so I'm goin' to stand in for her. Is that all right, Molly?'

Molly nodded. It was probably a waste of time, but if Nellie could perform a miracle then she'd be in debt to her for the rest of her life.

'Right, I'll put the cards on the table.' Nellie drew herself up to her full height. 'An' put meself in your hands.'

The sound that came from Mr Greenberg's mouth took them both by surprise. It was more of a wheeze than a laugh, so funny it brought smiles to the faces of the two women. 'Please, don't put yourself in my hands.' He gulped in air. 'I don't think I could stand the weight.'

Nellie joined in his laughter. Thank God the

man had a sense of humour, it was half the battle. She waited until the wheezing ceased, then said, 'I don't know what I was laughin' at, Mr Greenberg, that was a flamin' insult!'

'Call me Sol, everyone round here does.' He took his glasses off and fished a handkerchief out of his pocket. 'It wasn't meant as an insult, I can assure you. It would be a case of the pot calling the kettle black, 'cos I doubt if there's a pound difference between us.'

'Don't worry, Sol, I don't take the huff easy.' Nellie grinned. 'Now, down to business. Me mate's got twenty pound between her an' the workhouse, an' with that she's got to get a dining room suite an' a couch. So, what can yer do for 'er?'

'That's a tall order!' Sol wiped his eyes before replacing his glasses. 'We could probably work something out if she'd consider one of the other suites. They're brand new, but of course not in the same league as this one.'

'This is definitely the one she wants.' Nellie smiled sweetly. 'Can't yer come up with anythin'?'

A podgy hand scratched the thinning brown hair. 'What about the furniture she's got? Perhaps I could take that in part exchange.'

'No!' Molly felt she had to butt in before Nellie got her into trouble. Her friend meant well, but no one in their right mind would buy the furniture she had, it was falling to pieces! 'My stuff is only fit for the...'

'Oh my Gawd!' Nellie interrupted with a growl. 'D'yer know what, Sol, Molly's me

156

best mate and we get on like a house on fire. But she's got one fault, she's too bloody honest! She was just about to tell yer that her furniture is only fit for the rag and bone man! It is in a bad state, I'll grant yer that. The sideboard's got marks all over it, same as the table top, and the legs on the chairs are wobbly. But if yer clever enough to do them up, like yer 'ave this one,' she waved her hand at the restored dining room suite, 'then someone will be glad of them. To hear me mate talk, yer'd think they were sittin' on flamin' orange boxes.'

Sol Greenberg thought of all the desperately poor people who lived around the shop who were, literally, sitting on orange boxes. A chair to them would be a luxury. 'Are you still using the furniture, Mrs...er?'

'Bennett. Molly Bennett.' Molly pushed a strand of hair from her eyes. 'Yes, of course we're still using it! In fact, if my husband hadn't won on the pools we'd have had to make do with it for another few years.'

'In that case I'll be able to sell it for a few pounds. Now we've got the question of a couch.' He held his chin in his hands as he mentally went through all his stock. 'Ah, I think I might have something! Will you come with me.'

With Nellie poking her in the ribs, Molly followed. They walked into a small side room, more like a passage, really, in which the only thing was a couch. It looked really comfortable, and very attractive, in a fawn uncut moquette,

157

with just a sprinkling of small squares in a deep maroon colour. Molly could imagine Jack sitting in it, a cigarette in his mouth and the *Echo* open on his knee. Then she came down to earth. I'll never get that with the few pounds I'm going to have over after paying for the suite.

'This came from the same house in Mossley Hill.' Sol was pulling the couch away from the wall as he spoke. 'It's got a tear in the back, and I put it out here until I can get it repaired.' He beckoned the two women over. 'Look, near the bottom.'

'Yer can't hardly see it!' Nellie bent closer. 'If it was against the wall it would never be noticed.'

Sol pushed the couch, puffing from the exertion. 'Apart from that it's in very good condition.'

Molly put her hands behind her back and crossed her fingers. 'How much d'yer want for it?'

'With the dining room suite, you can have it for twenty pound and your furniture. And you've got yourself a very good bargain.'

Molly's shoulders sagged in relief while Nellie beamed all over her face. 'Thank you, Mr Greenberg.' Molly felt so happy she wanted to throw her arms around his neck. 'I'm very grateful.'

'Yer a real gent, that's what yer are.' Nellie's pat on the back would have sent a lesser man reeling. 'When my feller wins the pools I'll be right down 'ere like a shot.'

'I'll bring the money in tomorrow, shall I?' Molly asked, terrified that someone else might come in and snap up her bargain. Then she reminded herself that not everyone had a mate like Nellie.

'No need for that.' Sol was feeling in a good mood. The dining room suite was worth more than he was getting, but it had been a pleasure doing business with these two. They'd brightened up a miserable Monday. 'You can pay cash on delivery. The van that comes will drop your new furniture off and pick up your old. Pay the driver but make sure he gives you a receipt.'

While he was writing down Molly's address and the day she wanted the delivery made, he said, 'You've picked a good time to buy new furniture, because when the war starts they'll be making armaments and not tables and chairs.'

'Oh, don't say that, Mr Greenberg!' Molly's happiness started to ebb. 'Yer don't really think there's going to be a war, do yer?'

Sol bent over the paper he was writing on to hide the anguish he knew they would see in his eyes. The news filtering through to the Jewish community in the city about the atrocities taking place in Germany was enough to send a person insane. Jews being tortured and sent to concentration camps to be slaughtered in their thousands, men, women and even children. It didn't bear thinking about. Unless someone took a gun to Hitler and stopped his brutality and butchery, war was inevitable. 'The writing on

159

the wall is very clear. I'll be surprised if we aren't at war with Germany within the next few months.'

Molly had steadfastly refused to listen to any talk of war. She didn't read the papers and would turn the wireless off if it was mentioned. But she couldn't help overhearing what people were saying in the shops, or on the newsreel when she went to the pictures. And although she wouldn't allow her mind to dwell on it, she knew something of Hitler's treatment of Jews. Now she wondered why he hated them so much. This man was Jewish, but he was no different from her or anyone else. In fact, in the half-hour they'd been in the shop he'd been more courteous than many men she knew, more helpful, and certainly more generous.

Molly sighed. Why was it that men like Hitler were so greedy for power they didn't care who they killed or hurt to get it? But he'd get paid back, God would see to that.

Sol Greenberg was holding his hand out. 'It's been a pleasure doing business with you, Mrs Bennett.'

'Thank you.' Molly shook his hand warmly. 'You're a good man.'

He turned to Nellie. 'I'll see you when your husband wins the pools, then, Mrs...er?'

Nellie pumped his hand up and down. 'McDonough. Helen Theresa McDonough.'

Molly hurried from the shop before she burst out laughing. Helen Theresa McDonough indeed! Oh, Nellie would never hear the last of that! But as Molly watched her friend edging her huge body through the shop door, a wave of tenderness swept over her. She was a friend and a half was Nellie, and if she wanted to call herself the Angel Gabriel it was all right with Molly.

Nellie tucked her arm through Molly's as they crossed the wide road. 'Not a bad day's work, eh, girl?'

'Thanks to you it's been a wonderful day!' Molly glanced sideways. 'I'd never 'ave done it without you, sunshine! I've got everythin' I wanted, more than I thought the money would stretch to, an' it's all thanks to you.'

'I need me head testin', girl,' Nellie said with a cheeky grin. 'I've helped yer get all posh stuff for your 'ouse and I'm lumbered with me old sticks of furniture! Show me up, that's what yer'll do. Still, I'm not too proud to sit on yer new couch.'

A tram came trundling to a halt and Molly let Nellie board first, pushing her bottom to give her a lift up.

'You sit by the window, girl, I'm better on the outside, let me backside hang over.'

When the conductor came along the aisle clicking his ticket machine, Molly had the money ready in her hand. 'Two tuppenny, please.'

'Eh, I knew there was somethin' I had to tell yer, an' I've just remembered what it was.' Nellie was gripping the seat in front as the tram swayed on its way. 'I ran out of sugar for breakfast this mornin' an' I 'ad

161

to run up to Maisie's. D'yer know what she told me?' Without pausing, she went on, 'Our street's next to 'ave the electric put in.'

'Go 'way! How does she know?'

'Someone from the electricity came to tell 'er. Supposed to be startin' a week on Monday.' Nellie realised her dress was riding up, pulled it down over her knees and kept her hand on it. 'I'm showin' all I've got, knickers, garters, the lot!'

'That's good news, that is!' Molly smiled happily. 'No more tryin' to read or sew by flamin' gaslight! An' it'll show me new decoratin' and furniture up a treat.' Then the smile slipped from her face. 'Oh God, I've just thought on! Jack's doin' the papering this week, then they'll be round to make a mess of it! Me ma's paper all got torn when they were puttin' the switches in, they ruined it!'

'Ooh, I never thought of that, girl! Well, yer know what to do, get another roll of wallpaper an' Jack can patch it up after they've finished.'

'Yeah, I better had. The shop's right by the tram stop so I'll call in an' get one.'

'Have yer got enough money on yer? I've got a couple of bob yer can have if yer skint.'

'No, I'll manage. I can always borrow a few bob off our Jill if I run short.' Molly put an arm across her friend's shoulders and squeezed. 'Yer've done enough for me for one day, Helen Theresa McDonough.'

162

Chapter Ten

'I'll say this much for Corker, he's a damn good worker.' Running his fingers through the thick mop of hair flattened by his working cap, Jack surveyed Corker's handiwork. 'The ceiling looks a treat and it hasn't half brightened the room up.'

'He had it done in a couple of hours,' said Molly with a smile. 'Brought 'is own stool an' got cracking right away. I covered the furniture with old sheets so it wouldn't get any splashes on, and while he was doing the paintin', me an' Nellie trimmed four rolls of paper.'

Jack slipped his coat off and went to hang it in the hall. 'It's a big help that! It would've taken me two nights to do it.'

'He's comin' back in the mornin' to make sure there's no patches.' Molly pointed to the carved rosette in the middle of the ceiling. 'He thinks that'll need another coat, it was black with smoke from the gaslight.'

'When I've had me dinner I'll start scrapin' the walls.' Jack turned to raise his brows at Tommy. 'If you're not goin' anywhere special, yer can give me a hand.'

'Yeah, okay, Dad.' Tommy pulled a chair out from the table and winked at Molly. 'Does he know it's double pay for overtime?'

'Some hopes you've got.' She ruffled his hair

on the way to the kitchen. 'If I got paid for workin' after six o'clock there wouldn't be enough money comin' in to the house to pay me.'

'Ah, but yours is a labour of love.' Jack followed, intending to wash his hands at the kitchen sink. But Jill was there, up to her elbows in soapy water washing pans, while Doreen stood by, a tea towel ready to dry the pots as they were passed to her. 'I see it's all hands on deck tonight.'

'It certainly is.' Molly bent to take two plates from the warm oven. 'Everyone is goin' to benefit, so they can all get stuck in an' do their bit.'

'Steve's coming down to help.' Jill tossed her head, shaking the hair from her face. 'It won't take long if we all pull our weight.'

'And Mike's promised to come.' Doreen rubbed the tea towel around the inside of a pan then stood on tiptoe to place it upside-down on the top shelf. Mike was a mechanic at Johnson's and, with his friend Sammy and Doreen's friend Maureen, he made up a foursome to go dancing with. 'We'll 'ave the walls stripped in no time.'

'If I'd known that, I'd have asked yer mam to get some sandpaper to rub the paintwork down. It won't take all of us to strip the walls.'

Molly, two hot plates in her hand, pushed him out of the way. 'Corker beat yer to it, sunshine! He said yer'd need it and went down to the shop for a few sheets.' She quickly dropped the plates

164

on the table and blew on her fingers. 'Blinkin' hot, they are.'

'I can't get to the sink so I'll leave me hands.' Jack pulled a chair out. 'They're not that bad, an' what's a bit of dirt between friends, anyway?'

'As soon as yer've finished yer dinner we'll stack everythin' in the middle of the room, then I'll wet the walls with the sweeping brush. The paper comes off easier when it's wet.'

'Ah, ray, Mam!' Tommy's face wore a pained expression. 'We need a cup of tea before we start.'

'And a cigarette.' Jack smiled. 'I'll work twice as fast after a fag.'

Molly clicked her tongue against the roof of her mouth. 'You an' yer flamin' ciggies! I think yer'd rather have a fag than a hot dinner.' She lowered herself on to a chair. 'I may as well rest me legs while I'm waitin' for yez. I've been on the go all day, an' our Ruthie had to pick tonight to be contrary. Kicked up a proper stink when I tried to get 'er to bed. She can be a right little so-and-so when she's in one of her moods.'

'Did yer manage to get all the paper trimmed, love?'

'No, I told yer, we only did four rolls. Still, I can do the rest tomorrow.' Molly leaned forward on the table, a twinkle in her eyes. 'We didn't 'alf have a good laugh today. I'd stacked everythin' on the table to give Corker room to move around, an' me an' Nellie were sittin' on these chairs cuttin' the paper. It was awkward, I'll grant yer that, but I was managing all right. Poor Nellie, though, when I looked at her I nearly wet meself laughing. Her face was all screwed up, her tongue hanging out of the side of her mouth, her turban had slipped to one side and she was cutting that slow we'd have been at it until Pancake Tuesday. She really was havin' a helluva time...her tummy's so big there was no room on her lap for the paper and she couldn't see what she was doing. In the end I had to clear the table for her to sit at, otherwise the border would 'ave been all skewwhiff.'

Jack let out a deep chuckle. 'I can just picture it!'

'Corker enjoyed himself...she had 'im in stitches tellin' him about me posh new furniture. When he said he'd 'ave to wipe his feet before he came in, she told 'im he'd 'ave to wipe his backside as well, before I'd let him sit on me new chairs.' Molly giggled at the memory. 'An' she told 'im I wouldn't take his word for it, there'd be an inspection at the front door.'

Jill and Doreen appeared in the doorway. Any tale involving Nellie was bound to be worth listening to.

Tommy wiped a hand across his mouth. 'I bet Sinbad had an answer to that!'

'Well, it started 'im off on his school days. Said no one had seen his bare backside since his teacher, a Mr Braithwaite, used to give him the cane. Apparently this teacher was a real puny little feller, looked as though a puff of wind would blow 'im over. But Corker said after three strokes of the cane off him, yer couldn't

166

sit down for hours. Not that the fear of it put Corker off, 'cos from the sound of things he was a real scallywag. Always givin' old buck to the teacher, smoking at the back of the school...you name it and Corker did it, even though he knew it meant gettin' the cane.'

'You do surprise me,' Jack said, a potato halfway to his mouth. 'I never would 'ave thought that of Corker.'

'Oh, you ain't heard nothin' yet, kid! Wait till I tell yez about me mate Nellie! Not to be outdone by Corker, she told us about some of the tricks she used to get up to at school. Now I know I shouldn't laugh at this 'cos what she did was a sin, but yer know what Nellie's like, she turns everythin' into a joke an' yer can't help but laugh. Anyway, she used to get the cane for not knowing her Catechism off by heart. She said she knew most of it, but sure as eggs the priest would ask her a question she didn't know an' then she'd 'ave to go to the headmistress for two strokes of the cane. Now Nellie didn't like gettin' the cane, did she, so what did the crafty beggar do? She bribed the girl who sat next to her, that's what! When Father Mooney asked her a question she couldn't answer, Nellie would give the girl a nudge and she'd whisper the answer! Then, at playtime, her friend would be rewarded with a sweet.'

'Well, I'll be blowed!' Jack broke the silence, then laughter erupted around the table.

'I told her she was still a heathen to this day.' Molly chuckled. 'I've added her to the list of people I pray for in bed every night. If the list gets much longer I'll 'ave to start goin' to bed at eight o'clock to fit them all in.'

The chairs had been stacked on the table, the couch and sideboard moved away from the walls and Jack's chair carried out to the hallway. Molly heaved a sigh, wiping the sweat from her face with the corner of her pinny. 'I'll be glad when it's over. All this just to be posh!'

'It'll be worth it in the end, love.' Jack gave her a hug. 'Just a few days an' yer won't know the place'

'If I last out that long.' Molly pulled a face. 'I'll get a bucket of water an' the brush...start wetting the walls. If I stand in the one spot too long I'll fall asleep.'

'I'll go and tell Steve to put a move on.' Jill gave a quick glance in the mirror before making for the door. 'We'll be right back.'

Jack watched Molly take the brush from the bucket of water and opened his mouth to warn her...but it was too late. Instead of letting the excess water drip from it, she raised the brush over her head to reach the top of the wall and ended up being drenched by the torrent that descended on her head and shoulders. 'Oh my God,' she screamed, 'I'm drowned!'

'Here, let me do it.' Jack was grinning as he took the brush. 'It's the way yer hold yer mouth, love.'

'Well, seein' as you're so clever, I'll let yer get on with it.'

'What d'yer want me to do, Dad?' Tommy asked. 'Shall I start scrapin' the part yer've wet?'

Jack shook his head, 'No, let it soak for a while. Yer can start rubbing the skirting board down with the sandpaper. Make a start on the far wall, under the window.'

'I'll go an' meet Mike off the tram.' Doreen slipped her arms into the sleeves of her coat. 'I won't be long, Mam.'

'I'll 'ave yer life if yer are, madam! We've got two days to get this room ready, so just bear that in mind.'

Tommy was laying newspapers on the floor to kneel on when Jack rested his hands on the brush handle. 'Do us a favour, son. Nip to the corner shop for a packet of fags.'

'Oh dear, oh dear.' Molly reached for her purse off the mantelpiece. 'I'll give him the money, you carry on with the job.'

When Tommy had gone, she tapped Jack on the back. 'Have yer noticed, we're on our lonesome?'

'They haven't deserted us, they'll be back in a minute.' He cocked his head, and hearing footsteps, nodded. 'See...what did I tell yer?'

Jill and Steve skipped through the door hand in hand, happiness written on their faces. 'Hiya, Mr and Mrs B.'

'Hello, son.' They made a handsome couple, and as nice inside as out. Then Molly took a closer look. They were always happy in each other's company, but tonight they seemed radiant, brimming over with excitement. 'You two are lookin' pleased with yerselves.'

Steve glanced towards the kitchen. 'On yer own, are yez?'

169

'Only for a minute... Tommy's nipped to the shop an' Doreen's gone to meet Mike. Why?'

Molly glimpsed Steve squeezing Jill's hand, and when she looked up his face was crimson with embarrassment. 'Can I ask yez something while there's no one here?'

With his back to them, Jack was oblivious to Steve's discomfort. 'Of course yer can, son. What is it?'

Steve swallowed hard before blurting out, 'Will yez let me an' Jill get engaged on her birthday?'

Before Jack had time to digest the news, Molly had rushed forward to fling her arms around the couple. In between planting noisy kisses on each of their faces, she said, 'Oh, I'm so happy for yez I could cry! I've waited for this day for as long as I can remember.'

'Excuse me, missus!' Jack disentangled her arms. 'Can I get a look in, please?' He held Jill close, tears threatening. His firstborn, now old enough to get engaged. 'Congratulations, sweetheart, and all the luck in the world. You'll not go far wrong with Steve... I couldn't wish for a better son-in-law.' He gripped Steve's hand. 'Congratulations, son, an' welcome to the family.'

Molly sniffed and wiped away a tear. 'I'm abso-bloody-lutely delighted. I really am. An' I bet yer mam is too, Steve.'

'I haven't told her yet,' he said sheepishly, his eyes on the lino. 'I thought I'd better ask you first.'

'D'yez want to run back an' tell her? She'll

go mad if she thinks I know somethin' she doesn't.'

'No, we'll get cracking here first, otherwise it'll never get done.' Jill gazed into Steve's handsome face. 'That's all right with you, isn't it, Steve?'

Steve was so happy he felt like shouting his news from the rooftops. But he managed to keep his excitement in check. After all, knowing his mam and Molly, it would be all over the street tomorrow anyway. 'Yeah, let's get stuck in.'

Work came to a halt when Tommy came in, followed closely by Doreen and Mike. The room was filled with laughter and excitement as kisses and congratulations were exchanged. For a while Jack was content to lean on the brush, enjoying the happy scene. Then worry took over. He had three nights to get this room papered and painted...a daunting prospect. 'I hate to be a wet blanket, but if this room's to be ready for Thursday night we need to roll our sleeves up and get stuck in.'

The room became a hive of activity after that. As Jack finished damping a wall, Doreen and Mike would move in to scrape the paper off while Steve and Tommy got busy rubbing the paintwork down. Molly and Jill moved into the hall out of the way, taking with them the rolls of paper to be trimmed and the border.

'D'you think it'll be finished in time, Mam?' Jill rested the scissors on her lap. She was sitting in Jack's chair with Molly perched on the second stair. 'There's only two nights after tonight.'

'Hang on a minute, sunshine.' The scissors

moved quickly and surely along the border line to the end of the roll. 'There...that's one more off me mind.' Molly heaved a sigh of relief as she stood the roll against the wall. 'Yer dad's a quick worker so we're in with a chance.'

She leaned forward to peep into the living room. 'They're all hard at it, so it won't be for want of tryin' if it's not finished.' She spied Mike pulling playfully at Doreen's hair and smiled when her daughter thumped him in the chest. He was a nice lad, was Mike. A bit on the shy side, but better that than being rowdy.

Molly rested her elbows on her knees as she studied Mike's face. He was teasing Doreen, draping bits of wallpaper over her head, and the look in his eyes gave Molly pause for thought. She'd seen that look before, many times. 'Is our Doreen keen on Mike, d'yer think, sunshine?'

Jill laughed. 'Oh, go 'way, Mam! You know what our Doreen's like...she only sees Mike when it suits her! They're friends, that's all!'

Molly passed over the last roll of paper to be trimmed. 'You finish that one, sunshine, while I start on the border.' Taking one last look at Mike, she muttered under her breath, 'If his intentions towards our Doreen are strictly platonic I'll eat me flamin' hat...at least I would if I 'ad one, like!'

By half past ten the walls had all been stripped, the paintwork rubbed down and the rubbish shovelled into a cardboard box and placed in the yard ready for the binman to take away.

With a smile of satisfaction on his face, Jack carried his chair through from the hall and flopped into it. 'Yer know that expression yer ma uses, love, about being deliciously tired? I've always thought it was a daft expression, but I've changed me mind. That's just the way I feel now. Every bone in me body is aching but I'm as happy as Larry.'

'We've done well, haven't we?' Tommy sat on the arm of his father's chair. 'Better than yer thought, eh, Dad?'

'Never in me wildest dreams did I think we'd get so much done in one night.' Jack struck a match and drew hard on the first cigarette he'd been allowed since they'd started work. He winked at Molly. 'We'd never 'ave managed it on our own, would we, love?'

'They've all been bricks,' agreed Molly, 'an' they deserve a nice cup of tea.' On her way to the kitchen she glanced at Mike. 'Have you got time for a drink, Mike?'

He glanced at the clock on the mantelpiece. 'It'll have to be a quick one, Mrs Bennett, I don't want to miss the last tram.'

'Mam, would you mind if me and Steve went to see his mam and dad?' Jill was holding on tight to Steve's hand. 'It's only fair we tell them together.'

'Of course it is!' Molly waved her hand towards the door. 'Go on, off yez pop.' They were halfway down the hall when she called after them, 'Tell Nellie I'll 'ave her for the biggest hat.'

The footsteps stopped. 'What's this about big

173

hats?' Jill appeared in the doorway. 'I don't understand.'

'She'll know what I'm on about.' Picturing Nellie in her mind's eye, Molly tittered, 'Just tell 'er what I said.'

Mike drank his tea with one eye on the clock. This was one night he couldn't face that long walk home, so he emptied his cup, said a hasty farewell and fled. After seeing him out, Doreen stretched her arms over her head and yawned. 'I can't keep me eyes open any longer, I'm off to bed.' She kissed Molly's cheek. 'I'll see yez in the morning if I can drag meself out of bed. Good night and God bless, Mam, an' you, Dad.'

'I'm off, too!' Tommy planted a quick kiss on Molly's forehead. 'Good night and God bless.' After a salute to his dad, he followed Doreen up the dark, narrow stairs. They were tired, but it was a nice, satisfying tiredness. The last time the room had been decorated they'd been very young and could only remember being sent to bed early out of the way. But tonight they'd been involved in grown-up work...treated like adults, and they were proud of themselves.

'Our Jill's a long time, she'll never get up for work in the morning.' Molly held a piece of newspaper in front of the fire, hoping to coax a flame out of the few coals that were still smouldering. 'It's not worth puttin' any more coal on, is it?'

'Not for me, I'll be off meself soon.' Jack squinted through a haze of cigarette smoke.

174

'What's the mystery about big hats?'

Molly took the newspaper away and grunted in disgust. 'Not even a flicker.' She grinned at Jack as she folded the paper and threw it on the hearth. 'Me an' Nellie 'ave always hoped our Jill and Steve would get married...even when they were only kids we used to talk about it. Anyway, when they fell out a few months ago, we were havin' a natter, an' I said they'd soon be back together, 'cos if ever a couple were made for each other, it's them.'

She moved to sit on Jack's knee. 'Yer know what me an' Nellie are like when we start gassing, we get carried away. I said the day our Jill married her son, I'd be wearin' the biggest hat I could find...one as big as a cartwheel.'

Jack pulled her close. 'An' what did Nellie have to say?'

'She was stumped. Said she couldn't think of anythin' bigger than a cartwheel so she'd stand under mine.'

Jack's head fell back and he let out a hearty chuckle. 'Honest to God, the things you two find to talk about! I often wonder what yer'd do if yer didn't have Nellie.'

'Be bloody miserable, that's what!' Molly jumped up. 'There's our Jill now, I'll open the door.'

To Molly's surprise, Jill wasn't alone. Nellie and Corker stood behind her, their faces wreathed in smiles. 'I've come to ask a question,' said Nellie, her hand on Jill's shoulder. 'If she's goin' to be me daughter-in-law, what does that make you?'

'Tuppence short of a shilling, that's what it makes me.' Molly kept her face straight. 'If I was in me' right mind I'd forbid my daughter to marry into your family.' She appealed to Corker. 'Don't yer think I want me bumps feelin', Corker?'

'Don't bring me into it!' His booming laugh echoed in the dark, deserted street. 'I've seen Nellie in action, there's no way I'm gettin' on the wrong side of her.'

Nellie squared her shoulders, pushing her enormous bust forward. 'At least I've got manners, Mrs Bennett! I invite people into me house...I don't leave them standing on the step.'

'If yer had any manners, Mrs McDonough, yer wouldn't be visitin' at this time of night.' Feigning indignation, Molly opened the door wide and stepped aside. 'Still, seeing as yer practically family now, I suppose I'll 'ave to let yer in.'

Jill touched Nellie's arm. 'After you, Mrs Mac.'

Nellie was squeezing past Molly when she turned her head. 'Seein' as yer'll soon be me daughter-in-law, yer can call me Mummy.'

'Mummy!' Molly spluttered. 'Honest, Helen Theresa McDonough, there's times when yer get too big for yer flamin' boots.'

She watched Nellie waddle down the hall and a surge of affection swept over her. God had certainly been looking after her when he brought Nellie into her life. The best friend in the world she was, and Molly loved every last ounce of her.

'Hiya, Jack!' Nellie's chubby face beamed. 'Never know the minute, do yer, kid?'

'Never know what to expect with you around, Nellie.' Jack returned her smile before turning his gaze to the giant standing behind her. 'I'm surprised to see you, Corker!'

'I was on me way home when I bumped into these two. I wouldn't have dared to come this time of night, but Nellie said yer wouldn't mind.'

'That's right, put the blame on me! I don't care...me shoulders are wide enough.' Nellie eyed the wooden chairs suspiciously. Better not try, she thought...I might just break one and then Molly will have me life. So she plumped for the couch, telling herself she'd worry about getting out of it when the time came. 'Well, what d'yez think of the good news?'

'Delighted, Nellie, delighted.' Jack's eyes were tender as he gazed at Jill. She was beautiful, kind, generous and caring, and he was so proud of her. 'I'll be the happiest man in Liverpool when I walk down the aisle with her on me arm.'

'Oh, Dad, it'll be years yet!' Jill could feel all eyes on her and she blushed. 'Steve won't be out of his time for three years.'

'Something to look forward to, though, isn't it, sweetheart?' In a show of affection, Corker laid an arm across her shoulders. 'I'll make sure I'm home when it happens... I wouldn't miss your wedding for all the tea in China.'

'We'll help yer start yer bottom drawer, won't we, Molly?' Nellie was so excited she knew she'd never get a wink of sleep that night. 'A little bit each week an' by the time yer get married yer'll 'ave everythin' yer need.'

'What she needs right now is her beauty sleep,' Molly said firmly. 'It's work tomorrow.'

'Yes, I am tired.' Jill's smile covered everyone. 'Good night and God bless.'

They waited until she was out of earshot, then Corker said, 'She's one little princess, is Jill. Your Steve's a lucky feller, Nellie.'

Molly was quick to defend the boy she looked on as a second son. 'Jill's the lucky one... Steve's a smashing lad.'

Satisfied that her son wasn't being left out of the compliments, Nellie patted the space beside her on the couch. 'Sit 'ere, Molly, an' I don't have to twist me neck to see yer.'

When Molly was seated, Nellie said, 'We'll 'ave to 'ave a do for their engagement, kid! Jars out, knees up...the lot!'

Jack jerked his head at Corker. 'They're in their element now. It'll be all over the neighbourhood by dinnertime tomorrow.'

'It'll keep them out of mischief.' Corker was gazing around the room. 'I see yer've been busy.'

'Many hands make light work.' Jack took two cigarettes from his packet and passed one over. 'But if it hadn't been for you, I'd still be doin' the ceiling. I can't thank yer enough, Corker.'

'Think nothin' of it, it was a pleasure.' Stroking his beard, the big man leaned forward.

'I've got a few hours spare in the morning, I could start on the undercoating. Every little helps.'

'I couldn't impose on yer like that! Yer go away again on Thursday.'

Corker brushed his protests aside. 'It won't kill me. I'm meeting someone at one o'clock so I'll 'ave to be away by twelve. But if I come about nine I can get a couple of hours in.'

'I'm not one to look a gift horse in the mouth, so I'll take yer up on it. Thanks, Corker.' Jack drew on his cigarette. 'Been for a pint tonight, have yer?'

'Yeah, I took Ellen out for an hour. I was just comin' out of next door when Nellie an' Jill passed.' Corker leaned further forward and lowered his voice. 'I spent a few hours this afternoon checking up on the Bradley family.'

'Oh, aye! Find out anythin', did yer?'

'Well, the Bradleys are well known to the police. In fact, the father's done a stretch inside!'

'Go 'way!' Molly had been listening to Nellie and keeping track of the men's conversation at the same time. 'I knew there was somethin' fishy about that family.'

'Now, Molly,' Corker lifted a warning finger, 'what yer've just heard isn't to go any further than this room. It's true the man's been in prison, but as yet I don't know what for. Until I know for sure, I want you an' Nellie to promise not to tell a living soul. I've heard a lot of rumours about the family, but I want to be sure of me facts before doing anything.'

'Yer can rely on us, can't he, Nellie?'

'Cross my heart an' hope to die.' Nellie's podgy finger made a cross where she imagined her heart was. 'Wild horses wouldn't drag it out of me.'

'I've got a few friends snooping around, so when I get home on leave again I'll know everythin' there is to know about them.' Corker raised his bushy brows. 'Did yer know they 'ad two sons, Molly?'

'No, I didn't.'

'From what I've heard, the other lad's a different kettle of fish from the rest of the family.' Corker wafted the smoke from his eyes. 'He works in Chadburn's, and me friend says he's a decent, hardworking lad.'

'I feel sorry for him then, stuck with that lot.' Molly glanced at the clock and gasped when she saw the time. 'Ay, come on, missus.' She gave Nellie a dig. 'It's nearly midnight! Jack's got to be up at half six.'

Nellie shuffled to the edge of the couch. 'Give us a hand up, then, moanin' Minnie.'

'Nellie, I haven't got the energy to get meself up, never mind you!'

'Blimey!' Nellie huffed. 'That's friendship for yer.'

'Here, grab hold of me hand.' Corker held out his massive paw and pulled Nellie up as though she was a feather. 'There yer go, girl!'

'Oh, for a real he-man!' Nellie beamed. 'Are yer comin', Corker?'

'Let him and Jack finish their ciggies.' Molly linked arms with her friend and steered her towards the door. 'I'll see yer get home safe.'

'You would, spoilsport!' Nellie's rosy cheeks moved upwards as she winked at the men. 'She's jealous of me, yer know. Green-eyed with envy 'cos the men can't keep their 'ands off me.'

'Out yer get, missus.' Molly put both hands in the small of her friend's back and pushed her through the door and along the hall, Nellie protesting with every step.

'I was dead tired before, now I'm wide awake.' Jack grinned. 'Nellie has that effect on me.' He brushed the dust off his trousers and crossed his legs, the smile slipping from his face. 'Things don't look so good with Germany, do they, Corker?'

'Jack, I'll bet me bottom dollar that calling-up papers will be dropping through letter boxes before the summer. Every country in Europe is expecting war...preparing for it! We've left it too late, given Hitler too much time to build his forces up. I can tell by the cargoes we carry. It used to be light stuff...toys, clothes and household goods. Now it's parts for making war machines, spares for tanks, that sort of thing. But it's like putting a cat down to face a lion! Germany is so strong those little countries won't stand an earthly! And what gets my goat is Hitler knows we're not prepared...he's got spies everywhere. Even in his own country.'

Corker's face was red with anger. 'Not everyone in Germany agrees with him, but they daren't speak out. If they do they end up in the concentration camps with the poor Jews.'

Jack let out a long sigh. 'It doesn't bear thinking about, Steve is eighteen in a few months, he'll be one of the first to be called up. He's only a kid, for God's sake! I was watching him an' our Jill tonight...they're crazy about each other and can't wait to get married. All they want out of life is to be together, raise a family and be happy. Not much to ask, is it? So why should a madman be allowed to spoil their lives just because he craves power?'

'Two crazy men, Jack...don't forget Hitler's sidekick, Mussolini. He's not as clever as Hitler, but just as dangerous. And it's always the young men get called up first...they make the best cannon fodder.'

Molly came bustling in, rubbing her arms. 'It's cold out there.' She noted the serious faces and groaned. 'You two aren't talkin' about war again, are yez?'

Jack and Corker exchanged glances. Then the big man stood up, setting his cap on his head at a jaunty angle. 'As a matter of fact, Molly me darlin', me an' Jack have been thinkin' of ways to stop Hitler. And we've come up with the perfect solution.'

'Oh, aye? A ruddy big dose of arsenic?'

'Better than that, Molly! We're going to send Nellie over to him. She'd talk the man to death.'

182

Chapter Eleven

'I thought they'd 'ave been here by now. If they don't come soon I'll be a nervous wreck,' said Molly, a frown on her face as she paced back and forth in the confined space of the kitchen. 'Just look.' She shoved her open hand under Nellie's nose. 'I've bitten me nails right down to the quick.'

Nellie, leaning against the sink, huffed. 'An' I feel like one of Lewis's standin' here! I don't know why we can't sit down...rest our legs while we're waitin'.'

Molly shook her head vigorously. 'I've polished that furniture so much it's a wonder it hasn't fallen to pieces, an' I don't want fingermarks all over it when the men come.'

'For cryin' out loud, they won't even notice what it's like!' Nellie sounded exasperated. 'It'll get thrown in the back of the van an' be as bad as ever by the time it gets to the shop. Yer worryin' yerself to death for nothin'.'

Molly stopped her pacing and held a finger up. 'There's the van now.' She flew down the hall and threw the door open.

The older of the two men touched the peak of his cap. 'Mrs Bennett? We've got a delivery an' a pick-up.'

Neither of the men uttered another word as they carried the old furniture out to stand on the pavement. Watching through the net curtains, Molly felt a pang of regret as she saw her old table and chairs being dumped outside the window. They were old and tatty, and heaven only knew she'd had more than her money's worth out of them, but she'd had them since the day she and Jack moved into the house as newly-weds. Swallowing hard, she sniffed. 'It's like losing one of the family.'

'Yer'll get over it.' Nellie rolled her eyes. 'Honest to God, there's no pleasin' yer.'

'I know I'm daft, but I can't help it.' Molly quickly moved aside as the men carried her new sideboard in. She indicated the wall it was to stand against and watched as they set it down carefully and manoeuvred it into position. And when they returned to the van Molly's sadness went out of the door with them. She hadn't paid much attention to the sideboard when she was in the shop, she was so taken up with the table and chairs. But seeing it now, set against the newly decorated wall, she was overcome with emotion. It was in solid mahogany, with two long drawers, three cupboards and metal handles twisted into an ornate design. 'It's beautiful, isn't it, Nellie?'

'You ain't kiddin'! Sol's put some work into polishin' that...yer can see yer face in it!'

'Let's go in the kitchen, out of the way.' Molly pulled Nellie after her. 'I've got the money ready for them.' She opened a drawer and took out an envelope. 'D'yer think sixpence tip is enough?'

'I should say it is! They'll think it's their birthday!'

Molly leaned against the sink, tapping the envelope on her chin. 'I can't wait to see me room all poshed up.'

'Won't be long now, kid.' From her vantage point by the door Nellie was able to see what was going on. 'Unless I'm very much mistaken, the last chair's just comin' in.' Her folded arms resting on her tummy, she winked broadly. 'Not very talkative, are they? It's like watchin' one of the old silent movies.'

Before Molly could reply, a voice called, 'We've finished, missus.'

Handing the envelope to the older of the two men, Molly said, 'It's just right, but yer'd better count it to make sure.'

The man licked his finger before counting the notes, then reached into the inside pocket of his coat. 'Here's yer receipt.'

'Thank you.' Molly slipped a sixpence into his hand. 'Buy yerselves a packet of fags.'

The man smiled for the first time. Doffing his cap, he said, 'Ta very much, missus.'

Molly followed them along the hall, thanked them again, then closed the door and flew back to the living room. She stood just inside the door and clapped her hands in excitement. 'Nellie, for the first time in me life I can't find words to explain how I feel.'

'I'll do the talkin' for yer, then.' With a wide grin covering her chubby face, Nellie waved a hand. 'I've never been in a posh 'ouse, but this is what I imagine one would look like. The table an' sideboard are that shiny they're makin' me eyes water. An' look how the maroon seats of

185

the chairs match the couch...yer'd think they were made for each other.'

Molly flung her arms around her friend's neck and cried into her shoulder. 'Ooh, Nellie.'

'Go on with yer, yer silly sod!' Nellie struggled free. 'What the 'ell yer cryin' for?'

'I'm crying with happiness.' Molly rubbed a hand across her eyes and took a deep breath before turning to survey the room. 'Those men must be mind-readers...they've put everythin' just where I wanted it.' She ran her fingers lovingly over the table. 'It's as smooth as silk.'

'Don't be goin' all poetic on me, for God's sake,' grunted Nellie, feeling quite emotional herself. 'There's a thin layer of dust on the spindles of the chairs...get me a nice clean cloth an' I'll dust them for yer.'

'Yeah!' Molly sprang into action. 'While you're doin' that, I'll get me ornaments out. They're not much cop, but they'll have to do.' She opened the cupboard in the recess at the side of the fireplace and took out an old pillowslip. 'Here yer are, kid, use this.'

She walked through to the kitchen, leaving Nellie eyeing one of the chairs, a speculative expression on her face. She daren't up-end it, Molly would have her guts for garters. And if she got down on her knees she'd never get up again. Her chin in her hand, her brow furrowed, she sought a solution. Then out of the blue she had a brainwave. Lifting the coal tongs from the companion set on the hearth, she wrapped the duster around them and found she could reach the spindles merely by bending down. Feeling

186

pleased with herself, she was humming a tune when Molly came through carrying the only two ornaments she possessed. The plaster donkey had had its tail knocked off years ago, and the green and yellow dog had an ear missing. 'Don't tell me yer puttin' those things on that beautiful sideboard? They'd look ridiculous!'

'I know,' sighed Molly, eyeing the battered ornaments. 'But it looks so bare with nothin' on.'

'Better bare than 'aving those mangy things standin' on it.' Nellie felt quite indignant. 'Where's yer taste, kid? In yer ruddy backside?'

'Don't you get cocky with me, Nellie McDonough, or...' A knock on the front door brought Molly's hand to cover her mouth. 'I bet this is me ma and da.' She thrust the offending ornaments at her friend. 'Put these in the kitchen for us, will yer? Oh, and straighten that chair, please.'

'Who was yer servant before I came along?' Nellie shouted after Molly's retreating back. 'Yer've only 'ad the furniture half an hour an' yer a flamin' snob already!'

When she opened the door to her mother and father there was a grin covering Molly's face. 'Did yer hear me mate callin' me a snob?'

'I did an' all.' Handing over a bunch of flowers, Bridie stepped into the hall. She held her cheek out for a kiss, saying, 'Sure, I hope you two won't come to blows.'

'She's hit me twice already.' Molly put the carnations to her nose and closed her eyes as she breathed in their perfume. 'They're lovely, Ma.'

'And this is to put them in, lass.' Bob handed over a brown paper parcel. 'It's a glass vase, so be careful with it.'

'Yer an angel, Da.' A noisy kiss was planted on his cheek. 'Just what I needed to set me new sideboard off.'

Bridie had brought two small, round mats she'd crocheted, and while Molly put the flowers in her new vase, Bridie set one mat on the sideboard and the other in the centre of the table. Then all four stood back in admiration. The whole room had been transformed. Set against the bright walls, the gleaming furniture looked beautiful.

''Tis a sight for sore eyes, lass,' Bridie said softly. 'Sure, I haven't seen anything so grand since I worked in the big house.' Her mind travelled back in time to when she'd left her home in County Wicklow. Her family were poor and there was no work for a young girl in the village where she was born. So at the tender age of sixteen she'd come to Liverpool hoping to find work so she could send money back to her family. After a week living with an Irish family who were distant relatives, she got herself a job in service at the home of a rich shipping merchant in Princes Avenue, down Toxteth way. The work was very hard...being the youngest member of staff, Bridie was no more than a skivvy. Up at six every morning and on the go until ten at night, at everyone's beck and call. Her only time off was an evening a week and a full day once a month. And for that she was paid four shillings a month and her keep.

188

But even though the work was hard, she wasn't unhappy. She had never known such wealth and opulence...and she derived much pleasure out of polishing the beautiful furniture and arranging the rich, heavy drapes at the windows. Those few years at the big house had taught her to appreciate fine things, but she was never envious of the people who owned them. And when Bob came along she had no regrets about exchanging life at the big house for a two-up two-down terrace and the love of a good man.

Bob was watching his wife's face and knew she was in a world of her own. It grieved him that he'd never been able to afford to take her back to the lush green fields of her beloved Ireland. Even when her parents had died, many years ago, they couldn't rake enough money together to pay the fare so she could attend the funerals. He had promised himself that one day he would take her back to see her only living relative, her sister Eileen, who had been fourteen when Bridie left home. Now she was married with a family of her own.

Bob sighed softly as he reached for his wife's hand. He wasn't able to work now, so he'd never be able to fulfil that promise. 'The room looks a treat, doesn't it, sweetheart?'

Bridie shook her head to clear her mind before turning to meet the eyes of the man she adored. 'It does that, me darlin', it's a credit to her, so it is.'

'Ay, you two!' Molly feigned indignation. 'Don't worry about me, I only live 'ere!'

'Then shouldn't yerself be inviting us to sit

189

down? Have I brought me daughter up to have no manners?'

'Sit down!' Molly lifted her hands in mock horror. 'Yer don't think I'm goin' to let yez sit on me new furniture, do yez?'

Bob chuckled. 'If we get a cup of tea, will we be sent out to the yard to drink it?'

'Oh, sod that for a lark!' Nellie pulled a chair out and plonked herself down. 'Like it or not, I'm christening this one.' Her face wore a pained expression as she gazed at Bridie. 'I've been 'ere since ten o'clock an' this is the first time I've sat down. Bloody slave-driver, that daughter of yours.'

'Oh, stop yer moanin'.' Molly smiled at her father as she pointed to the couch. 'D'yer want to christen that, Da?'

'I wouldn't mind resting me legs, lass.' Bob laid his arm across Bridie's shoulders. 'Sit next to me, sweetheart.'

Molly waited for their reaction and was rewarded when they smiled in appreciation after sinking into the well-sprung couch. 'It's very comfortable, lass.'

'It's got to be an improvement on the old thing she had.' Nellie went to lean on the table, then thought better of it. 'The springs on that used to leave marks on me backside.'

'How would you know?' Molly asked with a smile. 'Yer can't see yer own backside.'

Nellie's shaking tummy gave warning of the roar that was to come. 'Yer can if yer bend down in front of the mirror in the wardrobe.' She rocked back and forth with laughter. 'Mind

190

you, it's not a sight for the faint-hearted.'

'I'm goin' to put the kettle on before she starts tellin' dirty jokes.' Molly made for the kitchen, saying over her shoulder, 'I'm not goin' to cover the table until Jack an' the kids come in. It would spoil the effect an' I want to see their faces.'

'They'll be delighted, me darlin', so they will.' Bridie's eyes travelled the room. 'Everythin' looks beautiful...the nicest room I've seen in many a long day.'

'That does it!' Nellie forgot herself and banged her fist on the table. 'What me mate's got, I want. I'm not havin' her looking down her nose at me, thank you very much. So my feller 'ad better come up on the pools soon, or I'll break 'is ruddy neck for him.'

Molly poked her head around the door. 'George doesn't do the pools, does he?'

'No, clever clogs, he doesn't! But he can start next week, can't he? That means we should get our winnings the week after an' I can shoot down to see Sol Greenberg. I'll haunt his flamin' shop until he gets me some furniture that'll knock yours into a cocked hat.'

'Nellie, my Jack's been doin' the pools for years an' this is the first decent win he's had.'

'Molly,' Nellie looked the picture of innocence, 'if I told yer it was rainin', would yer dash outside an' bring yer washing in?'

Molly's face was blank. 'I haven't got any washin' out.'

Nellie winked at Bridie and Bob. 'How Laurel and Hardy ever get a laugh out of your daughter

I'll never know. She doesn't appreciate my humour one little bit. It's like floggin' a dead horse.' She smiled sweetly at Molly. 'But I love yer for all yer faults.'

The dinner was ready when the girls came in from work but Molly made them wait in the kitchen until Jack and Tommy came home. She wanted them to see the room in all its glory before covering the polished table with the square of thick baize she had ready to put under the tablecloth.

Ruthie had been allowed to stay up and she clung to Molly's skirt as the whole family gazed with wonder at the transformation. 'If I didn't know better, I'd think I was in the wrong house.' There was a look of surprise and pleasure on Jack's face. Molly had been going on about the furniture all week, but he was so used to her exaggerating he took all she said with a pinch of salt. He certainly hadn't expected anything as good as this. 'You did well, love, I'm proud of yer.'

'The room looks brilliant, Mam.' Tommy gave her a cuddle. 'Dead posh.'

'Look at this, Dad.' Doreen opened one of the sideboard drawers. 'See, it's all lined with green felt and these sections are for the cutlery.'

Molly poked Jack in the ribs. 'Talk about a fur coat an' no knickers, our six knives, forks an' spoons are goin' to look a bit daft in there.'

'Now, yer never know yer luck in a big city,' Jack told her, grinning. 'I might come up on the pools again an' yer can buy a full canteen of cutlery.'

Ruthie had begun to lose interest. 'What about me dinner, Mam?' She pulled on Molly's skirt. 'I'm hungry.'

Jack bent down to ruffle her hair. 'Haven't you had anythin' to eat, sweetheart?'

'Only a sugar buttie.' Ruthie was feeling sorry for herself. 'Me tummy's rumbling.'

'I'll see to the dinner.' Molly bustled towards the kitchen. 'Set the table for us, Jill, but don't forget to put the underfelt on...I don't want any marks on me new table, 'cos it's got to last me a lifetime.'

Molly raised her head from the sock she was darning and closed her eyes. It was a strain trying to sew by gaslight and she'd be glad when they had electric. The men had started digging at the top of the street yesterday, so all being well they should be sitting pretty by the time the summer came. It would be nice if it was all finished before Jill's birthday in May.

She glanced round the room and sighed with pleasure. It did look nice...but how much nicer it would be when the room was lit up by electric light. Show her furniture off a treat, it would.

Molly bent her head and returned to the job in hand, savouring the peace and quiet. She loved her children dearly, but it was nice to have a break from them for a couple of hours. To wind down, relax and let her thoughts wander without fear of interruption. The only sounds in the room were so familiar to her she didn't even hear them...the hissing of the coals, the ticking of the clock and the rustle of paper when Jack turned a page of the newspaper he was reading.

It had been quite a day, no two ways about that! But remembering the surprise and pleasure on each face when they'd walked through the door and set eyes on the new furniture, a warm glow spread through Molly's body. And she smiled when she recalled the pride on Jill's face when Steve called for her. All the cupboards and drawers had to be opened for his inspection and approval, then the tablecloth had been whipped off so he could appreciate the beauty of the shining mahogany top. And Jill had been so happy with his reaction. Down on his knees admiring the carving on the table legs, his handsome face beaming, he'd looked up and said, 'When we're married, I'll buy yer something as nice as this.'

Thinking of Steve took Molly's mind forward to the next exciting event on her calendar...the engagement of her daughter to the boy who was already almost like a son to her. She'd have to start saving with a vengeance to give them the best engagement party anyone ever had. It was only what they deserved because they were a smashing couple. With Nellie's help she'd give them a do they'd remember all their lives.

Molly was so deep in thought she didn't hear the knock and she jumped when Jack prodded her leg with his foot. 'In the name of God, Jack, yer frightened the livin' daylights out of me!'

'There's someone at the door, love.'

'Oh, no!' Molly rested the sock on her knee. 'Talk about no peace for the wicked...we never get any time on our own!'

'Shall I go?'

Molly nodded. 'Don't invite anyone in, though... I've 'ad enough visitors for one day.'

With her ear cocked, Molly heard the door open, then the sound of raised voices. She recognised Jack's, but couldn't place the other one. 'Whoever it is, I hope they go away,' she muttered. 'I feel more like flying than entertaining.'

But when Barney Coleman followed Jack into the room, Molly didn't let her disappointment show. 'This is a surprise, Barney!'

'Aye, well, there's trouble up the street again.' A brief flicker of interest crossed Barney's face when he noticed the difference in the room from the last time he was there, but he was in no mood to be sidetracked from the reason for his call. 'It's that Bradley family again...a right lot of crooks, they are!'

Sighing, Molly stuck her needle in the sock and put it to one side. 'What 'ave they been up to now?'

'It would be quicker to tell yez what they haven't been up to!' In a gesture of frustration, Barney ran a hand through his hair. 'I wouldn't bother yer, Molly, but I wondered if Corker had found out anythin' about the family? I didn't see him before he went away, otherwise I'd have asked him meself.'

Molly exchanged glances with Jack before answering. 'Corker did ask around, but he

195

wouldn't tell us anythin'.' She looked to her husband for help. 'Would he, Jack?'

'Sit down, Barney.' Jack pointed to the couch and waited until the man was seated. 'Corker's got a few friends making enquiries...he said he'll know more next time he's home.' He offered his packet of Woodbines and lit the two cigarettes before continuing. 'As he said, yer can't go accusing anyone unless yer've got yer facts right.'

Barney looked at the smoke floating upwards from his cigarette. 'Never a ha'porth of trouble in this street until that family moved in. Now, not a day goes by without somethin' getting nicked. The neighbours are up in arms...they'll take the law into their own hands if things carry on as they are.'

'I would have thought those Bradleys would have learned their lesson over your Malcolm's bike.' Molly pulled her skirt down when she realised she was showing more knee than was respectable. 'What 'ave they been stealin'?'

'Anythin' and everythin', Molly! If it's movable, they'll move it. Nothing is safe from them.' Barney beat a fist on his knee. 'I can't believe the things they get up to...don't know how they've got the nerve! Little Dolly Lawton's tricycle went missing out of their yard while they were in bed...and the poor kid's cried every night since. Mrs Lawrence went to the shops yesterday, and when she got back all the washing had disappeared from her line and her larder had been cleaned out of food.'

Molly gasped. 'Go 'way! Yer mean they went in her house?'

'As bold as brass, an' in broad daylight! Mrs Lawrence had locked the entry door but she hadn't bothered lockin' the kitchen door because there's never been any need to. We've never 'ad thieves for neighbours before.'

'Are yer sure it's them?' Jack asked. 'It couldn't be anyone else, could it?'

'Oh, come off it, Jack! For twenty years my wife 'as left the milk money on the step every mornin' an' it's never been pinched. She leaves the insurance money on the hall table an' the door on the latch if she's got to go out when the collector's due, an' that's never been pinched, either! Yer can't tell me it's just coincidence that these things start happenin' when the Bradleys move in.'

'Of course it's them!' Molly was surprised her husband had any doubts. 'Yer've only got to look at them to know what they are...common as muck an' hard as nails.'

'If we weren't sure before, we are after what happened today.' Barney gazed at Molly. 'D'yer know that old lady in the next street...Mrs Tewson or something?'

'Mrs Townson.' Molly nodded knowingly. 'Little, thin as a rake, an' she's got a twitch at the side of her mouth.'

'That's the one.' Barney leaned forward. 'She was in the corner shop today, gettin' a few things, an' she put her purse in the basket on top of the groceries. But when she got home the purse had gone. An' guess who was standin' next to her in the shop? The Bradley girl... I think her name's Joyce.' He turned to Jack. 'Ask Maisie if yer think I'm being bad-minded. She'll tell yer she saw the old lady put the purse in her basket, and she'll also tell yer who opened the shop door to let her out.'

'I don't know how they can do it!' Molly looked and sounded angry. 'That old lady never has two ha'pennies to rub together! She looks as though she never sees a decent meal.'

'She went back to the shop to see if she'd left the purse there, an' Maisie said she thought she was goin' to faint when she found she hadn't. Every penny she possessed was in it, including her rent money.'

'Ay, Barney,' Molly narrowed her eyes. 'How come those two Bradley girls never go to school? If it was one of mine, the school board would be knockin' on me door an' I'd be in trouble.'

'The neighbours 'ave been wonderin' the same thing. All I can think is that they live like gypsies, always on the move, an' the education people never know where they are.'

'We could always inform them.' Jack threw his cigarette end into the fire. 'That would put a stop to some of the thieving.'

'It would put a stop to a lot of it! Those two girls play in the street all day, watching the comings and goings. They know everyone's habits, an' I think they're the lookouts. When they know a house is empty, that brazen brother of theirs moves in.' There was no warmth in Barney's smile. 'They'd leave you an' me standing, Jack, an' that's a fact. Crafty as a

198

cartload of monkeys, and just as devious.'

'Corker said somethin' about there bein' another son.' Molly chose her words carefully: she'd promised Corker not to say too much. 'Have you seen another lad, Barney?'

'Aye, an' that's another mystery! He's not like the others to look at, he's got blond hair and he's tall an' broad...not like the other upstart. He mightn't be one of the family, but he certainly lives there. The queer thing about it is he comes an' goes the back way. No one's ever seen him in the street. The only reason I've seen him is that he goes out the same time as me in the mornings. I use the entry because it's handy to nip down the back jiggers to the tram stop, an' I see him most days. But he never lets on...doesn't look right nor left. With a pair of navy-blue overalls rolled up under his arm, he legs it down the entry like he's got wings on his heels.'

Molly could feel Jack's eyes on her, but she didn't need his warning. She had more sense than to repeat what Corker had told them. 'Has anyone said anythin' to the Bradleys?'

Barney nodded, half smiling at the memory. 'The whole street was out last night, shouting and accusing...I thought there was goin' to be a riot! But all it achieved was an invitation to search their house if we thought they were the thieves, and a whole lot of abuse. Their language was choice, I can tell yer. I hear plenty of swearin' down at the docks, an' I can do me fair share, but even the dockers would draw the line at some of the things they came out with.'

199

Jack's chest heaved, then he let out a long-drawn-out sigh. 'As yer said, Barney, it's a mystery. An' there's not much yer can do about it, unless yer catch them in the act. The police can't do anythin' unless yer've got proof.'

Barney nodded in agreement. 'I know that, Jack, an' they know it too! That's the maddening thing about it! They're laughin' their flamin' heads off at us and there's nowt we can do about it. I don't know where they stash their ill-gotten gains, but I do know if we'd taken up their offer of searching their house we wouldn't 'ave found Dolly's tricycle or Mrs Lawrence's clothes.'

A spark from the fire landed on the rug in front of the hearth and Molly rushed to stamp it out. It was a tatty old rug—spoiled the look of the room really—but it would have to do until she could save up enough to buy a new one. Standing with her hands on her hips, Molly gazed at Barney, sympathy in her eyes. 'Look, I know Corker's away for two weeks, but don't do anythin' till he gets home. If yer take the law into your own hands it's you that'll end up in trouble, not the Bradleys.'

'Molly's right.' Jack took the cigarette Barney offered and reached in his pocket for matches. 'I know how yer feel...how any red-blooded man would feel in your place...but hold yer hand till Corker gets back. If anyone can sort it out, it's him.'

Barney drew hard on the cigarette. He knew Jack was right, but it went against the grain to give in to a nasty little sod like the Bradley man.

If he had his way, he'd strangle the bastard. 'It's all we can do, I suppose. We've already agreed to keep our eyes open...to be more careful about lockin' doors and not leaving anythin' in the yards at night.' He ground his teeth together. 'What a bloody way to live, though, eh?'

'It won't be for long, just till Corker gets home. He'll put them in their place, don't you worry.' Molly pinched at the fat around her elbow. 'I'm thinkin' about poor Mrs Townson. She's a proud little thing, always pays her dues. She'll be mortified havin' to tell the rent man she's got no money.'

She rested her chin on a curled fist, her mind ticking over. 'I could ask the neighbours to 'ave a whip-round. It wouldn't be much, mind, 'cos most people are strugglin' themselves. But I'm sure they could spare a few coppers, an' every little helps. At least the old lady could pay somethin' off her rent.'

'Come up to our end, they'll all give somethin'.' Barney stood up and leaning towards Molly whispered, 'Yer could even try the Bradleys, they're probably better off than any of us.'

'I might just do that, Barney! At least I'll stand behind Nellie when she asks. She'll be holdin' the collecting tin.'

Barney made for the door, feeling a damn sight better than when he'd arrived. His hand on the knob, he turned. 'Men don't usually notice things...not like you women. But I've got to say, Molly, yer room looks a treat.'

Chapter Twelve

'Ay, Mo,' Doreen clutched her friend's arm, 'don't look now, but there's a feller just come in an' he's gorgeous. Talk about tall, blond an' handsome isn't in it, he's like someone yer see in the films but never in real life.'

They were standing at the bottom of the room, by the stage, and Maureen turned her head casually to scan the group standing inside the door of Barlows Lane dance hall. And when she saw a boy fitting the description she whistled through her teeth. 'You ain't kiddin', he's a smasher! I wonder if he's with a girl?'

'Doesn't seem to be, he's standin' on his own.'

'She's probably puttin' her coat in the cloakroom.' Maureen pulled a face. 'With his looks he's bound to have a girlfriend.'

The band leader announced the next dance as an excuse-me quickstep and the two friends were quickly snapped up. As soon as Doreen's partner took her hand and stretched their arms sideways to their full extent, she knew she'd got a raw beginner. Holding her a yard away from him he started off on the wrong foot and trod heavily on her toes. 'I'm sorry,' he muttered, and plodded on, his body as stiff as a board and his steps completely out of time with the beat of the music. Doreen did her best to follow him but after a few steps she gave it up as a bad job and concentrated on keeping out of the way of his feet.

When they'd walked the length of the room —you certainly couldn't call it dancing—the boy was in trouble. He had no idea how to negotiate the turn and came to a full stop. His face the colour of beetroot, he said, 'I'm not very good...it's me first time.'

'Yer'll soon get the hang of it.' Doreen tried to sound sympathetic as she manoeuvred him into the right position, but told herself if she saw him coming towards her again she'd make a beeline for the cloakroom.

The boy's heel came down heavily on her toes and she cried out in pain. 'I...I...I'm sorry,' he stuttered. 'Have I hurt yer?'

Wincing with the pain, Doreen growled through clenched teeth, 'Yer only nearly took me flamin' foot off, that's all!' She happened to glance over his shoulder and found herself looking into the eyes of the blond boy. He was half smiling and she was so filled with embarrassment she pulled her partner forward so roughly he almost lost his balance. 'I'm all right now, keep movin'.'

They'd only gone a few steps when Doreen felt a hand on her elbow. 'Can I cut in, please?' After gazing briefly into the bluest eyes she'd ever seen, she withdrew her hand from her partner, saying, 'Thank you.'

Doreen's new partner held her close and twirled her around before gliding down the room with the ease of an accomplished dancer.

His stride long, his body rising and falling with each movement and his hand on her back guiding her, he chuckled, 'How are yer feet?'

Doreen felt as though she was floating on air. He was doing all the steps she'd learned at Connie Millington's and their bodies were moving as one. He was definitely the best partner she'd ever had. 'Pardon? What did yer say?'

'I asked how yer feet are,' he whispered in her ear. 'He seemed to be givin' yer a hard time.'

Doreen waited until they'd completed a sequence of intricate steps before answering. 'Oh, I didn't mind. He's got to practise on someone.'

'You're a good dancer.'

'Thank you.' Doreen grinned into his face. 'Yer not bad yerself.'

'I've never seen yer here before.'

'That's because I've never been before. Me an' me mate usually go to the Grafton or Blair Hall. An' now and again we go to Connie Millington's.'

'So that's where yer learned to dance! I thought I recognised the style.'

'Why?' Doreen's surprise showed on her face. 'Don't tell me you've been there?'

'I used to go, but it's over a year now. Before I went there I was even worse than the bloke yer've just danced with.'

Doreen sighed inwardly when the dance came to an end...she could have gone on for ever. 'Thank you.' She turned to walk away but a hand on her arm held her back. 'What's yer name?'

'Doreen.'

'Well, Doreen, will yer save the next slow foxtrot for me?'

Thrilled to pieces, Doreen nodded. Oh, boy, wait till she told Maureen!

'Yeah, okay. But aren't yer goin' to tell me your name?'

'Philip...but me mates call me Phil.'

Doreen blushed when she realised they were the only two left on the dance floor. 'I'll see yer later, then, Phil.'

Maureen's face was eager as she hopped from one foot to the other. 'Yer lucky blighter! D'yer know, if you fell down a lavatory yer'd come up smellin' of roses.'

'Mo, he's absolutely gorgeous! He's got the bluest eyes in the whole world and lovely white teeth. I felt like swooning every time he looked at me.'

Maureen rolled her eyes. 'Been reading *True Confessions*, have yer? Swooning, indeed! I thought that word went out with the ark.'

For once there was no quick retort to Maureen's friendly sarcasm. Doreen had other things on her mind. 'He can't half dance, Mo. An' he's asked me to save the next slow foxtrot for him.'

'Then yer better start swooning,' Maureen said drily, ''cos he's halfway across the floor an' the band haven't even started up yet.'

Doreen could feel her nails digging into the palms of her hands as she waited. Her tummy was churning with excitement but she wasn't going to let him see she was that eager, so she stubbornly stood with her back to the dance floor until she felt a tap on her arm. 'Would yer like to dance?'

Doreen glanced at her friend for a second. 'See you later, Mo.' Then she walked into Phil's outstretched arms and was soon gliding down the floor with a boy she'd just met, but who was making her heart beat like mad. The slow foxtrot was her favourite dance, but never had she enjoyed it as she was now. Their body movements and steps matched so perfectly it was hard to believe they'd never laid eyes on each other until tonight. Phil slowed down and held her away from him. 'Will yer be here on Saturday?'

Taken aback by the question, Doreen floundered. 'I, er, I don't think so...I always go out with Maureen on a Saturday.'

'Well, she's with yer tonight, so why can't she come with yer on Saturday?'

Doreen's mind ticked over quickly. There was no point in telling him a lie because he might mention it to Maureen and her friend would unwittingly let the cat out of the bag. 'We usually go out as a foursome on a Saturday, with two of the boys from work.'

Disappointment showed on Phil's face. 'Yer've got a boyfriend, then?'

'No! We're all just good mates!' That wasn't a lie because although she liked Mike, it was only as a friend. 'It only started because me mam said I was too young to walk home from a dance on me own. She knows Mike and Sammy and trusts them to get me home safe.'

'They're not with yer tonight.'

'No...that's why I'll have to leave early.'

'Yer look capable enough to be let out on yer own.' Phil's brow furrowed. 'How old are yer?'

'Sixteen.' Then Doreen shook her head, grinning. 'Actually, I'm not sixteen for another ten weeks.'

Phil waited for the right beat, then danced away from the corner where they'd been marking time. 'In that case I'd better make the most of it.' He squeezed her hand. 'Will yer have every dance with me?' Doreen felt so happy she thought her heart would burst, but her mind was clear enough to know she mustn't appear too eager. So, as casually as she could, she answered, 'If yer like.'

'I do like.' A smile lit up his handsome face. 'Will yer be here next Tuesday?'

'Perhaps.' Doreen lifted her hand from his shoulder to wave at Maureen, who was dancing with a tall, skinny, sandy-haired boy whose face was covered in pimples. He was trying to waltz to the tempo of the slow foxtrot and looked confused because Maureen's steps weren't matching his own. And the look of disgust on her face was a picture no artist could paint. 'Me mate's having a bad time of it.' Doreen stretched her neck to smile into Phil's face. The feller she's dancing with doesn't know his left foot from his right.'

But Phil wasn't interested in anyone but the girl he'd been attracted to from the moment he'd set eyes on her. He had to see her again. 'Promise yer'll come next Tuesday?'

Doreen didn't answer right away. She wanted more than anything to see him again but she couldn't afford to go dancing twice in one week. The only way she'd been able to come tonight was by borrowing off Jill, and by the time she paid her sister back she'd be lucky if she had enough pocket money left for the Grafton on Saturday. 'I'll try, but I can't promise.'

'Ah, go on, say yer'll come,' Phil coaxed. 'I want to see you again.'

'It's not that I don't want to come.' Doreen decided to tell the truth and shame the devil. 'I just can't afford to. I get lousy wages and they don't run to two nights out a week.'

'If that's all that's stoppin' yer, I'll pay for yer.' He gazed down into her eyes. 'I can meet yer outside.'

Doreen shook her head, sending her long blonde hair swinging across her face. 'I wouldn't come without Mo, we go everywhere together.'

They danced in silence for a while, both deep in concentration. Phil was only an apprentice and didn't earn much himself, certainly not enough to pay for Doreen and her friend. He let out a deep sigh. 'It looks as though I'll never see yer again.'

'Yes yer will... I'll be here next Tuesday.' There was a mischievous smile playing around the corners of Doreen's mouth. 'Come hell or high water, I'll meet yer here at eight o'clock.'

The look of surprise on Phil's face turned to

one of suspicion. 'D'yer mean it, or are yer just fobbing me off?'

'I wouldn't say it if I didn't mean it. I promise yer I'll be here next Tuesday.'

'Smashing!' Phil spun her around and around, ignoring the glares of the couples they brushed against. 'The week won't go quick enough for me.'

The music came to an end, and as Doreen clapped in appreciation of the band, she was thinking that the week better hadn't go too quickly or she wouldn't be able to keep her promise.

'You're late.' Molly closed the door behind Doreen. 'What's yer excuse this time, young lady? And don't give me the one about not bein' able to find yer coat in the cloakroom...that one's got bells on.'

'Ah, ray, Mam, I'm only ten minutes late! We just missed the tram by the skin of our teeth an' had to wait ten minutes for the next one.'

'Then yer should have left the dance five minutes earlier.' Jack was sprawled in his chair, his legs stretched out in front of the hearth. 'When yer Mam tells yer to be in by half ten, she means half ten, not a quarter to eleven.'

Doreen put her dance shoes down at the side of the couch before undoing the buttons on her coat. She was so happy she didn't mind getting told off. And she wasn't going to answer back tonight either, 'cos she needed to get her mother in a good mood.

'Did yer go window-shoppin', Jill?' Doreen came back after hanging her coat on the hall stand. 'Seen the ring yer want yet?'

Jill nodded, her eyes sparkling. 'We went down to that little jeweller's shop in London Road...I think it's called Brown's...and there it was, right in the middle of a tray in the front of the window. As soon as I saw it I fell in love with it. It's a cluster, with a diamond in the centre surrounded by red stones. It mightn't fit me, of course, but Steve said they can alter it. He's taking me on Saturday to try it on and leave a deposit.'

'I thought you wanted a solitaire?' Doreen sat beside her mother on the couch. 'That's what yer've always said.'

'I know.' Jill sighed dreamily. 'But as soon as I saw this one I knew it was the one I wanted.' She tapped the small notebook resting on her lap. 'I've just been adding up what we've got saved and how many more weeks we've got left.'

'How much is the ring?' Doreen grimaced when her mother delivered a sharp dig to her ribs. 'What was that for?'

'For bein' so flamin' nosy!' Molly huffed. 'Honest, that mouth of yours will get yer hung one of these days.'

'It's all right, Mam, I don't mind.' Jill smiled at her sister. 'Four pounds, ten shillings and sixpence.'

'Phew!' Doreen whistled through her teeth. 'Yer don't come cheap, do yer, sis?'

'Well, getting engaged is a once-in-a-lifetime

thing, so Steve said I should only settle for a ring I really like.'

'He's right, too!' Doreen flicked her hair back over her shoulders and crossed her long, slim legs. 'Life's short, so get what yer can out of it.'

Molly leaned forward and tapped Jack's leg with her toes. 'D'yer hear that, love? Sweet fifteen an' talkin' about life being short. Not much down for us, is there? We must be ready for the knacker's yard.'

'I didn't mean it like that,' Doreen said quickly. 'I just meant that we should try an' get the best out of life.'

Molly leaned an elbow on the arm of the couch and rested her chin on her clenched fist while she gazed at her daughter. She noted the sparkling eyes and sensed the tension in the slim body. She's all on edge, this one, she thought. I bet a pound to a pinch of snuff she's after something. 'How did the dance go? Did yer meet any tall, dark, handsome fellers?'

Doreen moved closer and whispered in her ear, 'Actually, he was a tall, blond, handsome feller, Mam, an' he couldn't half dance.'

'Dancing's not the be-all and end-all, yer know, sunshine! It's a person's character yer should be interested in, not his flamin' footwork.'

'Mam, I only met the bloke tonight...had a few dances with him. I could hardly ask him for his family history, now could I? All I know is his name's Philip, he's a smashin' dancer an' he goes to Barlows Lane every Tuesday.'

211

I wasn't far wrong, Molly told herself. I can always tell with her, she gives herself away. 'So yer'll be goin' to Barlows Lane again, eh?'

Doreen tossed her head. This wasn't turning out as she'd hoped, but now she'd started there was no going back. 'It all depends.'

Jack was looking on with interest. 'Depends upon what, love?'

'Whether me mam will let me get me sewing machine out.'

'Not on your nellie!' Molly said indignantly, sitting up straight. 'I'm not havin' that heavy thing on me new table.'

'I'll put a cloth over it, Mam, it won't do no harm!'

Jack lifted his hand for silence. 'Just hang on a minute, yer've completely lost me! What on earth has the sewing machine got to do with going to a dance at Barlows Lane?'

'Well I was makin' a dress for Mary, from over the road, but me mam put a stop to it,' Doreen got in quickly, hoping to gain sympathy before her mother had her say. 'It'll only take a couple of hours to finish it off, but I've nowhere to put the machine.' She gazed at him with eyes begging for understanding. 'Mary always gives me a shilling for making her a dress and if I got that I'd be able to pay our Jill back and have enough left to go to the dance.'

'Yer can soft-soap yer dad as much as yer like,' said Molly with a determined shake of her head. 'In fact, yer can talk till the cows come home, but it won't make any difference. Yer not puttin' that heavy machine on me new table.'

Jack was torn between the two of them. He didn't like disagreeing with Molly in front of the children but he could see Doreen's point of view. The few bob she earned by making clothes made all the difference to her. And he admired her initiative in trying to earn extra money instead of moaning about being skint. He stroked his chin while seeking a solution. It was no good trying to get around Molly, she wouldn't even let him put his packet of cigarettes on the table, never mind a heavy sewing machine. The novelty would wear off eventually, but right now she guarded that furniture as though her life depended on it.

Jack's eyes lit on the aspidistra plant standing on the little table under the back window. 'What about that table, wouldn't it serve the purpose?'

'No, it's too small.' Close to tears, Doreen hung her head. It didn't look as though she'd see Phil again after all her promises. 'The machine will fit on it, but there's no room to spread the material out. It hangs down, pulls at the needle, breaks the cotton and the stitches go all wonky.'

'I could sit at the side and hold the material,' Jill offered. 'I wouldn't mind.'

Molly shifted her gaze from Jill to Jack, and when she saw the look in his eyes she groaned inwardly. They're on her side...they think I'm being mean. A feeling of guilt grew quickly, and with it the thought that they were right...she was being mean and childish. After all, what did she want for her children, a nice posh house where they were afraid of touching anything, or a proper home where they were comfortable and happy?

'Okay, I give in! Yer can use the ruddy table.'

A wide smile spread across Doreen's face. 'Oh, thanks, Mam!' She threw her arms around Molly's neck and hugged her. 'I promise I'll be careful.'

'I'll make sure yer careful, sunshine! There'll be a thick blanket on the table an' I'll be watchin' yer like a hawk.'

Jack grinned as he struck a match to light his cigarette. He knew that if his wife hadn't given in tonight she would have done so in the morning, after a sleepless night. She tried to make out she was strict, but deep down she was as soft as a brush, especially where the children were concerned: she'd run to the ends of the earth to make them happy.

He lifted his cigarette and sent a ring of smoke rising to the ceiling. As he watched its progress, he sighed happily. Ah, well, we'll all sleep soundly tonight.

The loud rap on the door sounded urgent, and Molly hurried down the hall wiping her hands on the corner of her pinny. One look at Mary Watson's face told her this wasn't a social call. 'What is it?'

'I'm not sure, but I think there's something wrong with Miss Clegg.' Mary's face was drained of colour. 'I heard a funny noise on our wall, like a cup or something being thrown at it and

214

smashing. I waited for a while, then it came again, the same kind of sound. I've banged and banged on her front door but there's no answer. I've even been around the back to try and get in but the entry door's bolted.'

'Hang on a minute while I get me coat an' me keys.' Molly ran through to the kitchen, turned the gas low under the pan, grabbed her keys off the mantelpiece and collected her coat as she passed the hall stand. 'Nellie's got the front-door key...it's her turn to see to Miss Clegg's dinner today.'

Nellie's beaming smile faded when she heard the reason for the unexpected visit from her two neighbours. 'I've got 'er keys in here.' She tapped the bulging pocket of her pinny as she led the way across the street. 'I hope to God she's all right.'

'Better knock first in case we frighten her.' Molly rapped on the knocker then pressed her ear to a panel on the door. 'Not a dickiebird, Nellie, yer better open up.'

Nellie hesitated in the dark, narrow, silent hallway. 'Coo-ee, Miss Clegg, are yer there?'

When there was no answer, her eyes swivelled to Molly. 'Shall we just go in?'

'Of course we go in, yer silly nit!' Molly hissed. 'Isn't that what we're here for?'

Nellie pressed herself back against the wall to let Molly pass. 'You better go first, girl, I'm all of a dither.'

Molly shot her friend a withering look before moving quickly down the hall. When she reached the living room door she stopped dead in her

215

tracks and an icy chill ran through her body. Miss Clegg was sitting in her rocking chair by the side of the hearth, and at first glance it looked as though she had just fallen asleep. But the unnatural position of her body told Molly this was no ordinary sleep. The old lady was slumped to one side and an arm hung limply over the chair arm. Molly glanced back along the hall and beckoned. 'Nellie, Mary, come quick.'

Mary, stood just inside the door, nervously biting her nails while Molly and Nellie gently sat the old lady up straight.

'There now, that's better.' The faded grey eyes that looked into Molly's were filled with terror, and it took all her self-control to keep her voice light. 'First off, we'll make yer a drink. Then we'll see what yer've been an' gone an' done to yerself.'

Dragging Nellie with her, Molly headed for the kitchen. 'We'll 'ave to send for the doctor. Poor soul's had a stroke.'

'Are yer sure?'

'Nellie, it's as plain as the nose on yer face.' Molly put the kettle under the tap and turned the water on. 'There's no life in her right arm an' her mouth is all lopsided.'

Mary appeared in the doorway. 'What's wrong with her?'

Molly put a finger to her lips and whispered, 'Poor old thing's had a stroke.'

Tears welled up in Mary's eyes. Miss Clegg had been her neighbour for years and she loved the old lady. 'Oh, dear God!' she cried. 'What's goin' to happen to her?'

'I don't know until the doctor's been.' Molly struck a match under the kettle. 'But I know what'll happen to you if yer go in there weepin' and wailing...I'll flatten yer! So buck yer ideas up, Mary, an' when yer go in there an' tell her yer going to send for the doctor, put a flamin' smile on yer face. The poor old dear is frightened enough without you lookin' like death warmed up.'

Mary sniffed and straightened her shoulders. 'Shall I go to the corner shop an' ask Maisie to ring for the doctor?'

'Yes please.' Molly put her hand on Mary's arm. 'I'm sorry, Mary, I didn't mean to flare up. But I'm worried to death about Miss Clegg an' if I don't pick on someone to shout at, I'll end up bawlin' me eyes out.'

When Mary had left, Molly went back into the living room, followed closely by Nellie. 'While we're waitin' for the kettle to boil, let's have a look at yer, sunshine.' With a smile on her face, Molly put a hand under the old lady's chin. 'Not in pain, are yer?'

When Miss Clegg shook her head Molly could feel the saliva, running unchecked from the distorted mouth, falling on to her hand. The doctor won't be long an' he'll soon have yer sorted out.' She turned her head. 'Nellie, see if there's a flannel in the kitchen, will yer? If not, wet the end of a towel so I can clean her face up.' With a cheerfulness she was far from feeling, she grinned into the stricken face. 'Got to make yer look glamorous for the doctor comin', haven't we?'

Dr Whiteside put the stethoscope to Miss Clegg's chest and listened for a few seconds. 'Heartbeat's a bit fast, but that's only to be expected.' He put the instrument in his bag before turning kindly eyes on the old lady. 'You've had a slight stroke, my dear, and it's affected your right arm and one side of your face.' When he saw the flicker of fear in the faded grey eyes, he patted her arm. 'Don't start worrying yet, it might not be permanent.' He glanced at Molly, who was hovering by the kitchen door, and held out his hands. 'Is there anywhere I can wash my hands?'

'Yes, of course.' Molly walked ahead of him into the kitchen and made a sign with her eyes for Nellie and Mary to move away from the sink. 'It's a bit crowded in here, Doctor.'

'It's nice to know the old lady has neighbours who care for her, Molly.' John Whiteside had pure white hair, striking blue eyes and a healthy pink complexion. He was well past retiring age, but had no intention of putting himself out to pasture. He preferred tending the sick to tending his garden.

'It's only a mild stroke, but at her age it's difficult to say whether she'll recover fully.' John shook the excess, water from his hands before reaching for the towel Molly was holding out to him. 'In any case, she'll have to go into hospital, she can't do anything for herself the way she is.'

'Oh dear.' Molly was remembering when the old lady had fallen off a chair a while back and had had to go into hospital. She could still see the fear in her eyes, and her tearful admission that she was terrified of hospitals. 'Couldn't she stay home for a few days...see how it goes? As yer said, Doctor, she could get better. An' we'd take turns lookin' after her, wouldn't we, girls?'

'Yes!' Nellie said, while Mary nodded. 'We do that now anyway. One of us comes every day with a hot dinner for her.'

'It's not that simple.' John handed the towel back. 'She needs twenty-four-hour care at the moment. She won't be able to wash or dress herself, go to the toilet without help, or climb the stairs to bed.'

Molly had figured that out. 'We can bring a bed downstairs. She's got a single one in the back bedroom...if we move the furniture around we'd easy get it in the livin' room.'

'You'd have your work cut out, Molly, what with your own families to see to. Far better let her go into hospital where she'd get round-the-clock care.'

Molly's heart was thumping. She had this terrible feeling that if Miss Clegg went into hospital she'd never come out again. The old lady was shy and didn't mix easily, and if she was stuck in a ward with strangers she'd give up on life and just fade away. 'We could try it for a week, see how it goes. If she doesn't seem to be improving, or if we find we can't manage, then we'll have another think about it.' She looked

219

to Nellie for support. 'What d'yer say, Nellie?'

'I agree with yer, girl! We could get a couple of the other women to help out, they'd jump at the chance.' Nellie sent her chins swaying in all directions when she nodded her head at the doctor. 'She's very popular in this street, yer know.'

John Whiteside lifted his hands in mock surrender. 'Okay, I give in. I'll call tomorrow to see how she's progressing, and if you've had a change of heart it won't be too late to send her to hospital.'

'We won't 'ave a change of heart,' Molly said, her chin jutting out in a gesture of determination. 'An' yer've no need to worry, Doctor, she'll be well looked after.'

John grinned as he scratched his head. 'Still as stubborn as a mule, eh, Molly?'

'She can bloody well kick like one, too!' Nellie's remark was said under her breath, but John heard it as he made his way back to the living room. And when he put his hands either side of Miss Clegg's chair and gazed down into her face, he was grinning. 'I was going to suggest a few days in hospital, dear, but your friends have talked me out of it. They're going to look after you.' The relief on the lined face told him he'd been wise to listen to Molly. Gently he stroked the wispy white hair. 'They say that laughter is the best medicine in the world...if it's true, you should be up and about in no time, because that's one thing you won't be short of.'

220

Chapter Thirteen

Molly was on her knees in front of the fire, brushing up flakes of soot that had fallen from the chimney to blacken the hearth. Her face red with temper and chest heaving, she sat back on her heels to gaze first at Bridie then at Bob. 'Yer wouldn't credit it, would yer? It's me own fault for not gettin' the chimney swept before we started decoratin', but I never gave it a thought.' She set the shovel down carefully before waving her arms around the room. 'Now everything is going to be ruined...the fire's belching smoke an' the soot's comin' down in bucketfuls. If it keeps on like this, the walls and ceiling will be filthy in no time. Honest, Ma, I feel like kickin' meself.'

'Get the chimney-sweep in as soon as yer can.' Bridie, sitting next to her husband on the couch, clucked her tongue against the roof of her mouth in sympathy. 'Sure, it would be a shame if all Jack's work was ruined, so it would.'

'Get that Jimmy Smith to do it.' Bob leaned forward. 'He's the best chimney-sweep around. He puts a box inside the grate and covers the front up with a piece of wood so all the soot falls into the box, an' he's got one of those newfangled things that sucks up any dirt left in the grate and the hearth. He's very quick...in and out before yer know it.'

'I'll nip around an' see him when Jack comes in from work. He's usually home before one o'clock on a Saturday.' Molly struggled to her feet, holding the shovel steady in her hand. 'How much does he charge?'

'It was a shilling last time he did ours, wasn't it, sweetheart?'

Bridie nodded. 'An' worth every penny, so it was. Not a speck of dust anywhere when he'd finished.'

'I'll just empty this in the bin.' Molly made for the kitchen, saying over her shoulder, 'With a bit of luck he might be able to come on Monday.' When she reappeared, Bridie reminded her, 'Don't forget to clean the grate out the night before, lass.'

They heard the key in the door, then Doreen's laugh rang out, followed by a loud guffaw from Maureen. Molly smiled. 'What it is to be young, eh, Da? Not a ruddy care in the world.'

'Sure, isn't that the way it should be?' Bridie's eyes were on the door, eager as always for the sight of one of her beloved grandchildren. 'An' weren't you the same at their age?'

'Hello, Nan, Granda.' Doreen was about to put her handbag on the sideboard when she felt her mother's eyes on her and remembered it wasn't allowed any more. Winking broadly, she bent to put it on the floor at the side of the couch. 'Yer nearly had me there, Mam.'

'Yes, by the flamin' throat!'

'Hello, Mrs B.'

Molly returned Maureen's smile. 'You two seem happy.'

'No good havin' a miserable gob on yer, Mrs B, it turns the milk sour.'

Maureen was completely the opposite to Doreen in looks and colouring, but was just as attractive. Her jet-black hair, cut in a short bob with a thick fringe reaching down to her well-arched eyebrows, framed a round face with rosy cheeks, dark brown eyes, full lips with a generous cupid's bow, and a set of perfect white teeth. She had a sunny disposition and had been a hit with Molly from the time she'd set eyes on her.

'I see yer've brought yer dancin' shoes with yer.' Molly nodded to the parcel tucked under Maureen's arm. 'Goin' out straight from here, are yer?'

'Yeah, no point in goin' all that way home.' Maureen undid the buttons on her coat and opened it wide before doing a twirl. 'See, I went to work in me glad rags.'

'Going somewhere special, are yez?' Bridie asked. 'Heavy dates?'

'They're goin' to the Grafton tonight,' Molly explained, 'but this afternoon they're going to sit with Miss Clegg for a few hours to give us a break.'

'That's what we came round for, really,' Bob said, 'to ask after the old lady. Is she improving at all?'

'Yer know, Da, if they were givin' out medals for guts, the old dear would be first in line. I wouldn't have given tuppence for her chances a few days ago, but she's surprised us all...even the doctor. Her mouth has improved a lot...it's still a bit lopsided, but Dr Whiteside said if she goes on as she is, it should be back to normal in a week or so. Her right arm is useless, though, that hasn't improved at all.' Molly sat down and leaning forward, rested her elbows on her knees. 'Her speech is slurred, but it certainly doesn't stop her from making herself understood. Honest, she's as stubborn as a flamin' mule. We walk her down the yard, but under no circumstances will she let us go in the lavvy with her. How she manages her knickers an' things with one arm I'll never know, but she won't let us help.' Molly began to giggle. 'I was waitin' in the yard for her yesterday, an' when she came out of the lavvy her dress was tucked into her knickers at the back. I offered her my arm but she wasn't having any...said she wasn't a baby. And as I followed her up the yard all I could see were these blue fleecy-lined bloomers, miles too big for her, reaching down to her garters.' Molly glanced at her mother. 'I know yer goin' to say I shouldn't be laughin' at her, Ma, but honest to God, I wasn't laughin' at her, I was laughin' at the situation. There she was, her head held high, too proud to let me help her, and showing her bloomers to the whole wide world.'

Bridie could see the scene in her mind's eye, and she had to admit it must have been funny. Especially to someone with as keen a sense of humour as her daughter. Nevertheless, a woman of eighty-six deserved more respect. 'Sure, I hope yer didn't belittle the old lady. Pride and independence are important when yer get to her age, so they are. Take them away from her and you leave her with nothing to live for.'

'Thanks for the lecture, Ma, but I really don't need it. I love that old lady, an' I wouldn't hurt her for the world. In fact, I'd strangle anyone who looked sideways at her.'

'How did yer get around it, Mrs B?' Maureen's eyes were bright with interest as she cupped her face in her hands. 'About the bloomers, I mean.'

'I gave her a big cuddle, an' while me arms were around her waist I pulled her dress free.' Molly, her brows raised, looked at Bridie. 'Does that satisfy yer, Ma?'

'I knew yer wouldn't do anythin' to hurt her, so I did.' Bridie smiled that gentle smile that Molly loved so much. 'Sure, 'tis a big mouth yer have on yer all right, but didn't the good Lord bless yer with a big heart to go with it?'

'Now you two have sorted that out,' said Bob, smiling, 'why don't me and yer ma sit with Miss Clegg for a few hours?'

'No!' Doreen said quickly, glancing sideways to see Maureen nodding in agreement. 'We like sitting with her, an' we promised. We tell her all the things that happen in work, what dances we go to and what dresses we wear. An' she's really interested.'

Molly leaned back in the chair, a mischievous glint in her eyes. 'Talkin' about dances, Mo, I believe our Doreen clicked with a feller at Barlows Lane on Tuesday.'

'Ah, ray, Mam!' Doreen blushed. 'I didn't

say I clicked...I only had a few dances with the bloke.'

But Maureen was more forthcoming. 'Ooh, ay, Mrs B, yer should 'ave seen him! A great big hunk of a feller...looks like a film star. He didn't half fancy your Doreen...danced every dance with 'er.'

'An' are you going to Barlows Lane on Tuesday as well?'

Maureen pulled a face. 'I don't fancy playin' gooseberry, but me mate said she'd never speak to me again if I don't go.'

'I've told yer, I won't leave yer on yer own.' Doreen looked daggers at her friend. 'Anyway, he mightn't turn up.'

Bridie wore a puzzled expression. 'Now I don't want yez thinking I'm a nosy old biddy, but I thought Mike was your boyfriend an' Sammy was Maureen's.'

Doreen had had enough. She stood up quickly, almost sending the chair crashing. 'Mike is not me boyfriend! We're just mates, aren't we, Mo?'

Maureen was torn between loyalty to her friend and her liking for Mike. He worked with Sammy in the same part of the factory as the girls and they were both really nice blokes. 'I don't think Mike sees it that way.'

'Then that's his lookout, isn't it?' Doreen's face spoke volumes. Wait till she got her friend on her own...fancy sticking up for Mike! 'Come on, let's go over the road.'

Molly covered her mouth with her hand until she heard the front door slam, then she burst out laughing. 'I wouldn't be in Mo's shoes for a big clock! She'll be gettin' a right earful off our Doreen.'

'I think Maureen's quite capable of stickin' up for herself.' There was a smile on Bob's face. 'She's a girl after me own heart...open and straightforward.'

'Yeah, she's a nice kid. I never worry about Doreen when she's out with Mo, 'cos I think she's a good influence on her.'

'An' I like Mike!' Bridie intended getting her twopennyworth in. 'Fine and upstanding...a real broth of a boy, so he is.'

'Oh, don't be worryin', Ma! Doreen's not sixteen yet, she'll have dozens of boyfriends before she's finished.'

'An' who should know that better than anyone?' Bridie asked drily. 'Sure isn't it yourself she takes after?'

'I don't know how yer do it, Ma, but somehow I always end up getting the blame.' Molly adopted the Irish accent she'd been hearing all her life. 'But sure an' begorrah, me shoulders are broad enough to take it, so they are.'

'Oh, yer've done it!' Molly looked at the jeweller's receipt which stated that a two pounds and ten shilling deposit had been paid on a garnet and diamond cluster ring. 'Half paid for, eh?' She felt Jack's arm fall across her shoulder. 'They've done well, haven't they, love?'

Jack glanced briefly at the slip of paper before looking into Jill's smiling face. 'Yer

227

mam's right...yer've done very well an' I take me hat off to you both. Yer've done without a lot of things to save up that money.'

Steve's face was one big dimple. 'Won't be long now, Mr B, only three months or so.'

'When is the big day, son?'

Feeling important, Steve squared his shoulders. 'It's my birthday on the sixth of May, and Jill's on the twelfth. So we're getting engaged on the Saturday in between our birthdays.' His face creased in a smile, he glanced from his future father-in-law to Molly. 'That's if it's okay with you.'

'Of course it is!' As he looked from Steve's proud, handsome face to the gentle beauty of his daughter's, Jack felt a veil of sadness envelop him. They were so happy, so much in love, it would devastate them if anything came along to part them.

Jack let his arm fall from Molly's shoulder. 'I'm goin' down for the *Echo*,' he said gruffly. 'They should be in the shops now.'

Molly looked surprised. 'Let one of the kids go for it.'

Jack shook his head. 'No, I feel like a breath of fresh air.'

Molly knew her husband's moods inside out and was quick to recognise that there was something bothering him. Still, she told herself as she heard the front door close after him, it can't be anything to worry about or he'd have told me as soon as he came in from work.

But if she'd been able to read Jack's mind as he walked down the street she would have known that his was a worry he wouldn't burden her with. Not now, anyway, not when she was so happy.

Jack waved to one of the neighbours, pulled the collar of his coat up against the cold wind, and plunged his hands deep into his pockets. If the news bulletins in the papers and on the wireless were anything to go by, war was inevitable. In spite of his words to the contrary, Hitler was continuing to build up his forces...just last week Germany had launched a new battleship, the *Bismarck*. And if anybody doubted the evil the man was capable of, they only had to look at the way Jews were being treated in Germany. They'd been ordered to hand over all their precious possessions, been uprooted from their jobs and made to work for the Reich, and Gentiles were forbidden even to speak to them! Those who dared to disobey, or spoke out against what was happening, were dragged off to one of the dreaded concentration camps. Jack sighed as he turned the corner of the street. Only a miracle could stop a war, and miracles were in short supply. Britain had been caught with its trousers down, totally unprepared for a war against the massive armies Hitler had built up while the world looked on and did nothing. Now, too late, the Government was spending five hundred and eighty million pounds on defence. If that wasn't a sign of things to come, then nothing was.

Jack pushed open the door of the newsagent's and was hit by the warmth inside the busy shop. 'The *Echo*, please, Joe.'

'Don't usually see you on a Saturday, Jack.' Joe Quinn folded the paper and passed it over. 'Had a fight with the missus, 'ave yer?'

'Yeah.' Jack put a sixpence into the outstretched hand. 'The rolling pin missed me by inches.' His eyes lit on the glass cabinet filled with a selection of sweets. 'Give us a tuppenny slab of Cadbury's an' a quarter of Dolly Mixtures.'

Joe Quinn chuckled as he stretched to reach the glass bottle on the shelf behind him. 'That should put the rolling pin back in the drawer.' He kept his eye on the scales as he measured the coloured sweets. 'Why God invented women I'll never understand...they're nowt but a load of trouble.'

Mrs Quinn finished serving her customer then walked down the length of the counter. 'What did you say, Joe Quinn?'

'Who, me?' Joe feigned surprise. 'Why, I was just sayin' what a blessing women are. Don't know what we'd do without them.' He tipped the sweets into a small paper bag and handed them across the counter, a smile on his face. 'That's right, isn't it, Jack? An' didn't I say you an' I had two of the best?'

'Something like that.' Jack grinned as he dropped the sweets into his pocket. 'They weren't the exact words, but they were near enough.'

'Will yer do us a favour when yer get home, Jack?' Olive Quinn leaned on the counter and turned her head from her husband so he couldn't see her wink. 'Send one of the kids

230

down with Molly's rolling pin, will yer? See if it'll have the same effect on my feller as it's had on you.'

Jack was laughing as he left the shop. He rolled the *Echo* up, put it under his arm and strode purposefully up the street. He'd take a leaf out of Molly's book, that was what he'd do. If she could fill her mind with the happy things in life, like Jill and Steve getting engaged, then he'd do the same. After all, worrying wasn't going to help...it wouldn't alter the course of events.

Jack closed the door behind him and shouted down the hall, 'Get off yer backside, missus, an' put the kettle on. It's freezing out.'

Molly was standing stiffly to attention when he entered the room, her open hand at the side of her forehead in a salute. 'Aye, aye, sir! Would yer like anything else, sir?'

Jack glanced at Ruthie before meeting his wife's eyes. 'Yes, I would! But I'll wait until we're,' he pointed a finger to the ceiling, 'you know where.'

'Jack Bennett, yer've got a one-track mind.'

'Does that mean I'm not on?'

'Er, let me see now.' Molly closed her eyes and pinched the bridge of her nose as though considering. Then she smiled. 'I think yer in with a chance.'

Jack bent to give Ruthie her bag of sweets, then wafted the slab of Cadbury's under Molly's nose. 'Shall I give yer this now, or keep it until later to bribe yer with?'

'Give us it now.' Molly snatched the chocolate

231

and tore at the silver paper. 'There's two things I can't resist...you and chocolate.' She broke off a square and handed it to him. 'It's a good job the others aren't here to hear yer talking like that.'

'Where've they all vanished to?'

'God alone knows where Tommy is, I haven't seen him since dinnertime.' Molly sucked on the chocolate, a look of bliss on her face. 'Jill and Steve have gone up to Nellie's, and Doreen and Mo are upstairs gettin' dolled up.'

Jack put his arms around her waist and held her tight. 'Give us a kiss.'

His lips lingering on hers, Molly could feel her body responding and sighed as she pushed him away. 'Patience, my love, patience.'

Jack kept his voice to a whisper. 'Let's have an early night in bed, eh?'

'I'll think about it.' Molly closed her eyes briefly before whispering, 'After due consideration, will eight o'clock suit yer?'

Ruthie looked up with a frown on her face. She couldn't understand grown-ups, they could be awful daft sometimes. Just look at the way her mam and dad were giggling now. Nothing funny had happened, no one had told a joke, so what was there to laugh at?

Ruthie sighed and went back to her picture book. No, she'd never understand grown-ups.

Molly and Jack broke apart when they heard the two girls clattering down the stairs. Flushed with embarrassment, Molly moved to stand behind Ruthie's chair, patting her hair back into place with one hand while smoothing the front of her dress with the other. 'You two make enough noise to wake the dead.'

'Mam, d'yer like me hair?' Doreen's hair had been parted down the middle and braided tightly into two plaits which hung each side of her face, tied at the ends with bows of blue ribbon. 'D'yer think it suits me?'

'No, I don't!' Molly was quick to give her opinion. 'It makes yer face look too thin.'

Doreen rolled her eyes before seeking support from her father. 'What about you, Dad?'

'I agree with yer mam, love, I think the style is too severe for yer.' Jack noticed the disappointment in the blue eyes and, forever the appeaser, added softly, 'Yer've got beautiful hair, love, why tie it up? Many a girl would give her eye-teeth for a head of hair like yours.'

'I told yer that, didn't I?' Maureen pursed her lips. 'But no, yer wouldn't have it.'

Mollified by her father's praise, Doreen grinned at her friend. 'I thought yer were only sayin' it 'cos yer didn't want me to look nice and attract all the fellers.'

'If that was the case, I'd have said nothin' and let yer go out looking like somethin' the cat had dragged in.' Maureen jerked her head at Molly. 'I wouldn't say yer daughter was big-headed, Mrs B, but have yer ever noticed she has trouble getting through the door?'

Molly chuckled. Her da was right, Maureen was quite capable of sticking up for herself. 'Come here, Doreen, an' let me undo those flamin' plaits. Yer look like a country bumpkin... all yer need is a piece of straw stickin' out of yer

233

ears.' She was halfway through unwinding one of the plaits when there was a loud rap on the door. 'Oh, dear, who can this be?'

'I'll go, Mrs B.' Maureen skipped along the hall, singing, '"I don't want to set the world on fire."'

'I should bloody well hope not!' Nellie grinned into Maureen's face as she brushed past. 'I know it's cold, but settin' the whole ruddy world on fire is goin' a bit too far.' She waddled down the hall singing at the top of her voice, '"It's only me from over the sea, said Barnacle Bill the sailor."'

Nellie's bosom entered the room seconds before the rest of her. 'Good evening, playmates!'

Keeping her face straight, Molly glanced at Jack. 'Is that Arthur Askey, or that nosy neighbour of ours?'

'Oh, that's charming, that is.' Nellie stood inside the door, her hands on her hips. 'An' from someone who's supposed to be me best mate.' She dropped her head and began to sob. 'I'd best be off, then. I don't need the house to fall on me to know when I'm not wanted.'

Ruthie was off her chair like a shot. 'Don't cry, Auntie Nellie.' She put her arms around her favourite auntie's waist and pressed her face into the soft, cushiony tummy. 'Me mam didn't mean it, did yer, Mam?'

Oh God, she's taken me seriously! Molly rushed to sweep the child into her arms. 'Of course I didn't mean it, silly! Isn't Nellie me best friend in the whole wide world?'

'Then yer shouldn't 'ave said it.' Ruthie

glared, her brow furrowed. 'Look what yer've done, yer've made her cry.'

'She's only pretending.' Molly spun around so her daughter could see over her shoulder, 'See, she's laughing her head off.'

Ruthie wriggled free and slid to the floor. Wagging a tiny finger, she said, 'Yer were teasin', Auntie Nellie, an' that's naughty.'

'I know, I'm very naughty.' Nellie bent down and pushed a finger into one of her chubby cheeks. 'Here yer are, sweetheart, give Auntie Nellie a smack...right there.'

Ruthie clasped her hands behind her back, giggling. 'Oh, you are funny, Auntie Nellie.'

Doreen glanced at the clock for the umpteenth time, her patience,wearing thin. 'Mam, will yer stop actin' the goat an' finish me hair? It'll be time to come home before we get there!'

'Sit yerself down, Nellie, while I sort this one out.' Molly went to work on the plaits and soon Doreen's hair was once again hanging loose about her shoulders. 'Just run a comb through an' yer can titivate yerself up properly when yer get there.'

Doreen dashed from the room, and as she took the stairs two at a time she shouted down, 'Get yer coat on, Mo, I'll only be two shakes of a lamb's tail.'

Molly shook her head as she sat down. 'Yer'd think it was a matter of life and death, wouldn't yer?'

'Oh, it is, Mrs B.' Maureen slipped her arms into her coat. 'Just think how awful it would be if we missed the Spot Waltz.'

When Doreen came down she had her coat on and her dance shoes tucked under her arm. 'See yez later, folks.'

'Don't you be late, mind!' Molly lifted a warning finger. 'Half ten an' no later.'

Doreen waited until she had the front door open before answering, 'Mam, every time I go out yer say the same thing! Yer like a flippin' gramophone record that got stuck.'

Molly opened her mouth to reply, but closed it when she heard the door slam. 'She's a cheeky little faggot, that one.'

'Mine are just the same,' Nellie said, 'they think they know it all.'

'They probably do, too! Girls are much more advanced than we were at their age.' Molly pulled Ruthie towards her. 'Come on, sunshine, let's get you ready for bed.'

'Ah, Mam, let me stay up for another ten minutes, please?'

'No, it's way past your bedtime.' Molly's grip tightened on the struggling child. 'Behave yerself or I'll box yer ears for yer.'

'It's not fair.' Ruthie stamped her feet in temper. 'I don't 'ave to go to school tomorrer.'

'Yer can argue till yer blue in the face, sunshine, but yer still going to bed.' Molly pulled her daughter's dress over her head and threw it on the floor ready for the wash tub. 'Jack, pass that nightie off the maiden, will yer?'

Ruthie calmed down when she felt the warmth of the nightie on her body. She had the sense to know that when her mam used that tone of voice she meant business. 'Can I take the rest of me sweeties to bed with me?'

'I suppose so.' Molly cupped the pixie-like face between her hands. 'Yer can be a little demon at times, but I love the bones of yer.'

'I'll take her up,' Jack said, reaching for his daughter's hand. 'I'll light a candle and read her a story so you an' Nellie can natter in peace.'

'I didn't come for a natter.' Nellie wiped a hand across her forehead which was glistening with perspiration. Pushing her chair back from the fire, she said, 'I came to ask Molly if she felt like comin' to the Gainsborough with us. I heard it was a good picture... Spencer Tracy an' Pat O'Brien are in it.'

Jack stopped by the door and turned to Molly. 'It's up to you, love,' he said gruffly, 'if yer want to go.'

'No, I couldn't be bothered makin' the effort.' Molly's eyes sent him a message. 'Go on, take Ruthie up.'

'Ah, come on, girl,' Nellie coaxed. 'Yer don't 'ave to get dolled up, no one will see yer. Just put yer coat on an' come as yer are.'

Molly waited for Jack's footsteps to fade before answering. 'We'd promised ourselves an early night, Nellie. Every night this week Jack's worked overtime and he's worn out.'

'There's nothin' to stop Jack goin' to bed on his own, is there?' Nellie looked hard at her friend, then slowly her cheeks moved upwards into a grin. Her eyes almost lost in the folds of flesh, she leaned forward and gave Molly a dig

237

in the ribs. 'Oh, I get it...he's on a promise, is he?'

'Nellie McDonough, yer've got a mind like a muck midden.' But try as she might, Molly couldn't stop the colour rising from her neck to cover her face. 'It's a good job Jack's not here...yer'd make a saint blush, you would.'

'An' you ain't no saint.' Nellie rocked with laughter. 'Yer should see yer face...guilt written all over it.'

'Honest to God, Nellie, I don't know what I'm goin' to do with you.' Molly could never hold out against her friend's humour, and her slow smile soon developed into a roar of laughter. 'What the hell am I feeling guilty for? All right, clever clogs, so Jack's on a promise! But we are married, yer know...there's no law against it.'

'Did I say there was?' Nellie's face was a picture of innocence. 'No, girl, my motto is get all the pleasure out of life that yer can.'

Molly knew her friend too well to be fooled by the angelic look on her face. 'One word out of you when Jack comes down, and so help me I'll strangle yer. D'yer hear me, Helen Theresa McDonough?'

'Oh, I'm not waitin' for Jack to come down.' Nellie shuffled to the edge of the chair. 'I'm goin' home to see if I can get my feller in the mood.' She stood up and began to button her coat. 'When yer come to think of it, it's as good as goin' to the pictures. Yer can have a laugh, get yerself all het up, and yer not kept in suspense 'cos yer know there'll be a happy ending. Besides all that, it doesn't cost yer anythin'...only energy.' She was chuckling as she made her way to the door. At the bottom of the stairs she stopped and looked up. 'Will Ruthie be asleep by now?'

Molly shook her head. 'Probably halfway through "The Three Bears" or "Little Red Riding Hood".'

The temptation was too much for Nellie. 'Molly tells me yez are havin' an early night, Jack,' she bawled. 'Enjoy yerselves.'

Molly gave her a none-too-gentle push. 'On yer way, Nellie McDonough, before I die of shame.'

'There's no shame in cuddlin' up to yer own husband in bed.' Nellie opened the door and stepped into the street. 'Besides, what a lovely way to die...with a smile on yer face.'

Mike was holding Doreen's hand as they walked from the dance floor. 'It's packed here tonight, yer can hardly move.'

'I know.' Doreen pulled a face. 'Yer frightened to let yerself go in case yer bump into someone.' She pulled her hand free as they reached the corner where Maureen and Sammy were standing. 'You two soon got fed up.'

'There's no pleasure in shuffling around,' Maureen said, 'an' that's all yer can do. I know what a sardine feels like now.'

Sammy pushed a wayward lock of sandy hair from his eyes. 'I was just sayin' to Mo, why don't me an' Mike come to Barlows Lane with yez on Tuesday?'

Doreen's jaw dropped. 'Oh, no, yer can't!' She saw the surprised expressions on the boys' faces and floundered. For the life of her she couldn't think of an excuse to put them off. But if Mike came along, and tagged on to her all night, Phil would steer clear. 'We, er, we don't even know whether we're goin' ourselves yet, do we, Mo?'

Maureen glanced at Mike before answering. He was a nice bloke and she was very fond of him. He wasn't what you'd call handsome, he was too tall and thin for that, but he was kind and considerate. Anyway, looks weren't everything... as her mam always said, 'handsome is as handsome does'. 'No, we haven't made our minds up yet,' she said finally, glaring at Doreen. What a cheek she's got, expecting me to tell lies for her! Just wait until we're on our own, she won't half get a piece of my mind. I'll tell her straight it wasn't her I was thinking about, but Mike. I don't want to see him hurt or made a fool of, he's too nice. 'It all depends upon whether we've got any money...we might be skint an' happy by Tuesday.'

Mike took Doreen's hand. 'We'll pay for yez.'

'No!' Doreen said quickly. 'When we started goin' out as a foursome we all agreed we'd go Dutch. You don't earn enough to be forkin' out for me, so if I haven't got the money to go to Barlows Lane then it's just too bad.'

'You will tell us if yer goin', though, won't yer?'

'Yes, of course we will.' Doreen was so

240

relieved she smiled up into his face. 'Shall we dance?'

Sammy had been taking it all in, and although he said nothing, he thought plenty. He watched them walk to the dance floor, then turned to Maureen. 'Unless I'm very much mistaken, she's lying through her teeth.' He quirked an eyebrow, 'Am I right or wrong?'

Maureen shrugged her shoulders. 'Leave me out of it, Sammy. If yer want to know, ask her yerself.'

'I might do better than that,' Sammy said, mysteriously. Then he grinned and held out his arms. 'Come on, kid, let's show 'em how it's done.'

Chapter Fourteen

'Oh my gawd!' Molly jumped from her chair when she saw the visitors Jack had just let in. Ellen was standing in the doorway, with Corker towering behind her. Throwing her neighbour a dirty look, she quickly gathered up Ruthie's cast-off clothing from the couch. 'Yer might have told me when yer called in from work that Corker was home.'

'I didn't know meself until half an hour ago.' Ellen felt a hand in her back propelling her into the room. 'He caught me on the hop, too!'

'I didn't expect to see you until next week, Corker.' Molly saw the big man cast an

241

appreciative eye around the room and groaned when she remembered that he hadn't seen it since the transformation. 'Yer might have warned me.'

Leaving the visitors standing, Molly made a dash for the kitchen and threw the clothes into the dolly tub to steep overnight. She was back in a flash, and as one hand whipped the chenille cloth from the table, the other hand was reaching for the old sheet used to protect the couch from grubby hands. 'There yer are, that's better.' Holding the bundle to her chest, Molly grinned. 'What d'yer think, Corker?'

'Molly me darlin', it looks a treat. Yer've really done yerself proud.' Corker tilted his head as he stroked his beard. 'Especially the ceiling...now that's what I call a real professional job.'

'Did yer hear that, Jack? Talk about blowin' yer own trumpet isn't in it.'

'If yer don't blow yer own trumpet, love, no one's goin' to blow it for yer.' Jack's smile was warm and welcoming. 'It's good to see yer, Corker, sit yerselves down.' He saw the big man eyeing the couch. 'It's all right, she allows visitors to sit.'

Corker waited until Ellen was settled before lowering his huge frame to sit beside her. 'I didn't expect to be home meself until next week, but they had us working around the clock at Rotterdam, unloading the cargo.' He bent to put his cap on the floor between his feet. 'We're only staying in port long enough to load up, then we're off again. And from

242

the looks of it it's a sign of things to come. France, Holland, all those little countries are crying out for armaments...we can't deliver them fast enough.'

Molly bent until her face was on a level with his. 'Corker, how many times do I 'ave to tell yer...there's not going to be a ruddy war! I know they say Hitler's a madman, but even he's not crazy enough to take all those countries on. And don't forget Canada, Australia and New Zealand...they'd all join in if he started any shenanigans.'

'He's crazy all right, Molly, crazy for power. You mark my words he's only biding his time, laughing up his sleeve at the lot of us. When he's ready, he'll strike...then it'll be God help us.'

Jack watched his wife walk to the kitchen to put the cloths on the draining board and decided a change in the conversation was called for. 'How long are yer home for, then, Corker?'

'Two days...three at the most. Still,' Corker patted Ellen's knee, 'it's better than a kick in the teeth, isn't it, love?'

Blushing to the roots of her hair, Ellen nodded before moving on to safer ground. 'I bet yer mam was glad to see you.'

Corker's roar of laughter filled the tiny room. 'Yer know, the older I get the more she treats me like a little boy. I go through a kit inspection every time I come home. She checks everything...me shirt, socks, hankies, and woe betide me if she can't see her face in the shine of me shoes. I'm sure if she could reach she'd

243

check to see me ears were clean an' I didn't have a tidemark.'

Molly came in wiping her hands on a piece of towelling. 'I'll 'ave a word with her tomorrow, tell her to stand on a chair.' Turning, she threw the towel in the direction of the wash tub and smiled when it hit its target. 'Did she tell yer there's been more trouble with the Bradleys?'

'No, she never mentioned them.'

'With yer just gettin' home, she probably didn't want to upset yer.' Molly pulled a chair from the table and sat down. 'Barney called one night last week and told us there'd been blue murder up that end.' She quickly told him about Dolly Lawton's tricycle going missing from their yard, how Mrs Lawrence had come back from the shops to find her washing gone from the line and her larder emptied of all the food. Finally she told him about old Mrs Townson's purse being stolen. 'The old dear didn't 'ave a penny to her name, so we had a whip-round in the street and collected nearly ten bob for her.'

Corker listened in silence, twirling his moustache. When Molly had finished, the anger he felt could be heard in the word he spat out, 'Bastards.'

'Corker!' Ellen, usually as quiet and frightened as a mouse, gave him a dig. 'Watch your language.'

'I'm sorry, love, I forgot there were ladies present.' Corker looked like a child who'd been reprimanded. 'Sorry, Molly.'

Well, Molly was thinking, there's a turn-up for the books. Ellen Clarke, who wouldn't say boo to a goose, putting her foot down and getting away with it! 'That's all right, Corker.' Molly grinned. 'It takes a lot to upset me. Besides, I can't think of a better word to describe the Bradley family.'

'I'll get out bright an' early in the morning to see if me mates have come up with anything.' Corker took two Capstan Full Strength from a packet and passed one to Jack. 'If they've been in trouble, or are up to anythin', me mates will have found out.' He leaned forward to light his cigarette from the match Jack was holding towards him. 'All I need is proof that they're no good, then I'll go and see Mr Henry and ask him to throw them out.'

'Mr Henry's still not back at work yet. I've been waitin' to see him meself.'

After glancing at the clock, Ellen nudged Corker's arm. 'If yer want to go for a pint we'd better be makin' a move. Don't forget, I've left Phoebe lookin' after the children.'

'Right, we'll be on our way.' Corker reached for his cap before standing up. 'I'll be on the high seas by Saturday, so how about goin' out tomorrow night for a pint?'

Molly did a quick calculation in her head. She only had about seven bob in her purse and she knew Jack wouldn't have enough for a night out. It would mean being skint and happy until pay day, but what the hell! And anyway, they wouldn't starve. There was always the corner shop to fall back on... Maisie wouldn't mind giving her some things on tick. 'Yeah, we'd like that, wouldn't we, Jack?'

'If we can afford it.' Jack was looking doubtful. 'I've only got enough for me fares to work and me ciggies.'

'We'll be all right.' Molly sent him a knowing look before grinning at Corker. 'Shall I ask Nellie and George?'

'Of course! It wouldn't be a show without Punch, would it? We're always sure of a laugh with Nellie. An' I'd like to see yer ma and da, if they'll come.'

'I'll sort it out,' Molly said with confidence. 'An' I'll ask Jill and Steve to sit with the children, Ellen.'

'Thanks, Molly.' Ellen's mind was racing ahead. It was Wednesday tomorrow, half-day closing. She'd borrow Molly's curling tongs and do something with her hair to make herself presentable.

Corker glanced once more around the room, then gazed down at Ellen. 'One of these days we'll have your place looking like this.'

Oh, why does he have to embarrass me? Ellen asked herself as she felt the colour rise in her cheeks. It's bad enough going out for a drink with him, me being a married woman, without him acting as though we're a courting couple. For a brief second she allowed her mind to dwell on how marvellous life would be if they *were* a courting couple. He was so good and kind...life with him would be far better than any she'd ever known.

Molly sensed Ellen's discomfort and came to her aid. 'No good doin' your place up while the kids are so young, is it, Ellen?'

Ellen shook her head to rid her mind of something that was just an impossible dream. While her husband was alive, she was tied to him. 'You're right, Molly. Perhaps in a few years.'

Corker took her arm. 'Come on, love, let's go for that drink. I'm spittin' feathers.'

As she followed them down the hall, Molly once again wondered where this relationship would end. It was sad really, because Corker would be so good for Ellen and the children. If only Nobby would oblige and die peacefully in his sleep. But knowing Nobby, if he was capable of rational thought he'd live to be a hundred just for spite.

'I know we'll be seein' yez tomorrow night, but yer will call in before if yer've any news, won't yer, Corker?'

'You'll be the first to know, I promise.' Corker cupped Ellen's elbow. 'Good night, Molly.'

'Ta-ra, Corker, ta-ra, Ellen.' Molly was closing the door as Doreen skipped lightly down the stairs. 'All dolled up for the new man in yer life, are yer?'

'I've only got me blue dress on, nothin' special.' Doreen tried to sound casual but her tummy was doing somersaults. She'd die if Phil didn't turn up after she'd thought of nothing else all week. Not to mention Maureen having the last laugh. 'Mam, can I stay out until eleven tonight, please?'

'Can yer heck! Half past ten is late enough at your age.'

'Ah, ray, Mam! Just this once, please? An'
I'm sixteen in nine weeks, remember, I'm not
a baby.'

'Ay, less cheek from you, young lady, or yer'll
get a thick lip.'

Molly could feel Jack watching and turned to
him. 'Well, what 'ave you got to say?'

'I was just thinking...why don't yez compro-
mise? Meet each other halfway an' make it a
quarter to eleven.'

Doreen waited with bated breath while her
mother stood with her chin in her hand,
considering her husband's suggestion. A quarter
of an hour was better than nothing...it meant an
extra dance.

'Oh, all right, I give in.' Molly waved her
away. 'Vamoose, before I change me mind.'

Doreen let her breath out. 'Thanks, Mam. In
case yer in bed when I get home, I'll say good
night and God bless.'

Running down the street as though she had
wings on her heels, Doreen was planning ahead.
Only nine more weeks and she'd ask if she could
stay out until eleven o'clock on a Tuesday. After
all, at sixteen you weren't a girl any more, you
were a young lady.

'Here, you may as well pay for both of us.'
They were nearing the entrance to Barlows
Lane dance hall and Doreen could feel her
hand shaking as she passed the sixpence to
Maureen. 'I'll put our coats in the cloakroom.'
She'd been praying silently all the way on the
tram that Phil wouldn't let her down. She'd

thought of nothing else all week, and the idea that he mightn't turn up was too horrible to contemplate.

'You haven't half got it bad,' Maureen said, amusement in her dark eyes, 'yer as white as a sheet.'

'Oh, don't be so daft.' Doreen walked ahead of her friend and pushed the door open. 'I couldn't care...' She pulled up so suddenly Maureen couldn't prevent a collision.

'You stupid nit!' Maureen bent to pick up one of the dance shoes that had slipped out of the bag under her arm. 'I only nearly broke one of me flamin' toes.'

It was only when Maureen straightened up that she realised there was something odd going on. Doreen was standing so still it was as though she'd been turned to stone. Her unblinking eyes were wide and staring, as if she was seeing a ghost. 'What's up with you?' Maureen followed her friend's gaze and when she saw the cause of the trouble she didn't know whether to laugh or cry. For there, leaning casually against the wall facing them, was Sammy. He was wearing his best suit, his hair was sleeked back with brilliantine and the cheeky grin on his face seemed to be mocking them.

'Hiya, Sammy!' Maureen gave Doreen a sharp dig in the ribs as she moved forward. 'Fancy seeing you here!'

'Well, yez raved about it so much I thought I'd come an' see for meself.' Sammy lowered his voice before adding. 'Take a gander at her face, she doesn't know what's hit her.'

249

'Don't you dare let on I told yer we were coming,' Maureen hissed. 'If yer do, I'll never speak to yer again.'

'Scout's honour.' Sammy looked down at his shoes. 'She shouldn't have lied to Mike, though, that was a lousy trick.'

'It was only a half-lie...she said we weren't sure.' Maureen felt she had to be loyal to her friend, even though she agreed with Sammy that it was a dirty trick. 'Anyway, we'll see yer later.' She turned and took Doreen's arm. 'Come on, let's pay an' put our coats in the cloakroom.'

Doreen leaned against a wall in the ladies' toilet. 'Mike's not with him, is he?'

As Maureen shook her head she blurted out, 'It would serve yer right if he was! Why couldn't yer tell the lad the truth?'

'Because I didn't want him to come! He'd only have tagged along an' spoilt the night for me.'

'Yer know, Doreen, yer can be awful selfish sometimes.'

Doreen had the grace to blush. 'I know, an' I'm not proud of meself. I felt terrible lying to him, 'cos he's a nice bloke and I do like him. But I've been lookin' forward to seeing Phil an' I didn't want Mike spoiling me chances.'

'In other words, yer want yer cake and eat it! All I can say is, I hope this Phil comes up to your expectations, kid, 'cos if Mike finds out yer've double-crossed him, he'll give yer the elbow.'

Doreen's face was unhappy as she ran a comb through her long hair. 'Sammy is bound to tell him.' She picked the stray hairs from the comb before returning it to her handbag, then looked Maureen straight in the eyes. 'You told Sammy we were comin', didn't yer?'

'Yes, I did!' Maureen was unrepentant. 'You can lie through yer teeth if yer want to, but don't expect me to do the same.' With a toss of her head, she opened the door. 'I'm goin' in before they start playing the last waltz.'

Doreen followed closely on her heels. 'Be a pal an' ask Sammy not to say anythin' to Mike, will yer?'

Maureen turned to face her. 'I'll tell him yer don't want Mike to know, an' that's all. The rest is up to him.'

Doreen grabbed her arm. 'Don't let's fall out, Mo, please! I'm sorry I've got yer involved in this, honest I am.' She took a deep breath. 'I'll come clean with Mike tomorrow, I promise.'

'Oh, aye, an' I don't think!'

'I bet yer a tanner I do!' Doreen put an arm across her friend's shoulders as they walked towards the door of the dance hall. 'You're me best mate, Mo, an' I'd rather tell Phil and Mike to go and jump in the lake than be out of friends with you.'

The corners of Maureen's mouth twitched as her humour was restored. 'Two dances with the blond hunk an' it's me yer'll be telling to jump in a lake.' The strains of a slow foxtrot met them as they entered the hall, and there was Sammy, his arms outstretched to claim Maureen. 'Here yer are.' She passed her handbag to Doreen.

251

'Put it behind one of the chairs down by the stage.'

Although she was dying to look around for sight of a blond head, Doreen decided it would be the wrong tactic to let him think she was so interested, and she gazed straight ahead as she weaved her way between the people gathered at the edge of the dance hall. Girls hoping for a partner, boys eyeing the girls up to see which one they fancied. Most of the chairs had handbags or coats on to reserve them, but Doreen found two at the very bottom of the hall that looked as though they hadn't already been claimed. She was stooping to put the two handbags down when she heard a voice behind her. 'I was beginnin' to think yer weren't goin' to show up.'

Her heart thumping fit to burst, Doreen took her time pushing the bags out of sight before facing him. 'Oh, hiya, Phil!' He was even more handsome than she remembered. 'Me mam had visitors an' I was late getting out.' Not for the world would she admit she'd stood on the landing waiting for Corker and Ellen to leave so she could ask permission to stay out late.

'I'll forgive yer where thousands wouldn't.' Phil's teeth gleamed as he held out his hand. 'Come on, let's dance.'

Doreen was in a trance as they circled the floor, her happiness knowing no bounds. She was so absorbed she didn't notice Sammy waving, but Phil did. 'D'yer know that bloke dancin' with yer mate?'

Doreen turned her head. 'Yes, he works with

us.' She hesitated before adding, 'He's one of the blokes we go to the Grafton with on a Saturday.'

'Is he yer mate's boyfriend?'

'No, they're just friends.'

'Where's the other bloke...why isn't he here?'

'I dunno, he probably didn't want to come. Doreen bit her lip...she was getting too good at telling lies. 'That's not true. He's not here because I didn't tell him I was comin'.'

'Why didn't yer tell him?' Phil moved back to look into her face. 'Was it because of me?'

'Yeah, he's not as good a dancer as you.' Flushed with embarrassment, Doreen didn't know what to say. No boy had ever spoken to her like this...as though he was jealous. She lowered her eyes. 'No, that's not fair, Mike's a good dancer.' She added mentally that Mike wasn't in the same street as Phil when it came to dancing, but she wasn't prepared to be disloyal to Mike by saying so.

When the music came to an end Phil seemed reluctant to let her go. 'Stay with me for the next dance.'

Doreen would have liked nothing better, but the thought of what Sammy would make of it made her refuse. He had enough tales to tell without adding to them. 'I can't do that, Mo would kill me.'

'Well if anyone else asks yer, tell them yer spoken for.'

Doreen grinned. 'Okay, I'll tell 'em I'm took.'

Sammy was standing with Maureen and it

was obvious he had every intention of staying put. 'That guy yer were dancing with is a bit of all right. Good-lookin' an' a good dancer.' There was no smile on Sammy's face. He was angry with Doreen, and with himself. Doreen for what he saw as belittling his friend, and himself because he knew he wouldn't tell Mike even though he thought he should be told. But he knew his friend was crazy about Doreen and he wasn't going to be the one to upset him. 'Know him, do yer?'

'Not really,' Doreen said, shrugging her shapely shoulders. 'I had a few dances with him last week, that's all.'

'It's nice here.' Sammy's words were slow and deliberate. 'Mike would enjoy it.'

'Yeah, it's not as crowded as the Grafton. The band's not as good, but at least yer can get around without gettin' bumped into.'

As the band leader announced a quickstep, Maureen saw Phil leave the group of men standing by the door and walk quickly in their direction. She held her arms out. 'Are yer dancin' with me, Sammy?'

'No, I'll dance this one with Doreen.' He put his hand on Doreen's back and moved her forward. 'Can't leave her on her own all night, so yer'll have to share me...seein' as Mike's not here.'

Phil reached them just as Sammy was leading Doreen on to the dance floor, and his face fell. He hesitated for a second before smiling at Maureen. 'Would yer like to dance?'

Oh, boy, can this boy move! Maureen felt

herself floating effortlessly across the floor. Even if he was as ugly as sin he'd still be worth dancing with. She bit on the inside of her cheek to keep the laughter back as she thought how yer could always put a paper bag over his head if he was as ugly as sin, then yer wouldn't know the difference. It's no wonder Doreen's fallen for him, he is def-in-itely the best. She looked for her friend and nearly burst out laughing when she saw the dark, threatening glare being directed at her over Sammy's shoulder. She's terrified of me telling tales out of school! Well, serves her right...let her be jealous for a change.

'I can tell yer another of Connie Millington's pupils.' Phil smiled down at her. 'She must be the best teacher in Liverpool.'

'Yeah, she's great. I used to go there with Doreen.'

'And yer boyfriend?' Phil raised his blond eyebrows. 'That is yer boyfriend, isn't it?'

'Not really.' That was true, Maureen consoled herself, me and Sammy are not courting as such. 'I'm too young to 'ave a proper boyfriend.'

'Sixteen in a few weeks like Doreen, are yer?'

Maureen looked at him hard to see if he was making fun of her, but no, he looked really interested. 'There's only a week between our birthdays. I'm seven days older than her, so I get to be the boss.'

Phil chuckled as he led her into a quick spin. 'I can't see anyone bossing Doreen around.'

'Blimey, you catch on quick.' Maureen found

255

herself liking this lad who seemed to have everything going for him. Good looks, a smashing dancer and nice into the bargain. 'Yer could say me mate's high-spirited.'

'The boy who isn't yer boyfriend, on account of yer being too young to be courtin', doesn't seem to approve of me…if looks could kill, I'd be a dead duck.'

'Oh, Sammy's all right,' Maureen said, 'he's just got a cob on 'cos Doreen didn't tell Mike she was comin' here tonight.'

'She doesn't have to, does she. Not unless they're going serious.'

'Nah, they're not serious. I think Mike would like to be, but Doreen doesn't feel the same way.' Maureen was sorry when the music stopped. Sammy wasn't a bad dancer but he wasn't in the same league as Phil. She smiled and started to walk away. 'Thank you, I enjoyed that.'

'Yeah, me too.' Phil touched her arm lightly. 'Will yer ask Doreen to save me the next dance?'

'I told yer I'm the boss…I won't ask her, I'll tell her!' With that, Maureen turned in search of her friend and Sammy.

'I'm goin' to the toilet.' Doreen bent to retrieve her bag from under the chair. 'Are yer comin', Mo?'

Maureen pulled a face. 'Do I have a choice?'

Doreen linked her arm. 'Come with me, save me walking through that lot on me own.'

'Be back soon, Sammy,' Maureen called over her shoulder as she was marched away. 'Just goin' to comb me hair.'

Doreen didn't speak until they were safely inside the toilet. Then she couldn't get the words out quick enough. 'What did he say? Did he mention me? What were yez talkin' about?'

'Oh dear, oh dear, oh dear!' Maureen leaned back against the white-tiled wall. 'The third degree, is it?'

'Ah, come on, Mo...what did he say? Did he mention me?'

'No, he asked me if he could take me to the pictures tomorrow night.' Maureen saw the dismay on her friend's face and moved away from the wall. 'God, Doreen, yer'd fall for the flamin' cat, you would! He said to tell yer to save the next dance for him, an' if we'don't get back quick, he'll think yer not interested.'

Doreen nodded, her face eager as she opened the door and let her friend walk through first. 'He's nice, isn't he, Mo?'

'That's putting it mild,' Maureen said. 'He's gorgeous.' She grinned impishly. 'If yer not careful, I'll make a play for him meself...give yer a run for yer money.'

'Don't you dare!' Doreen started when she saw Phil standing outside the door to the dance hall. 'Yer not goin' home, are yer?'

'I'm making sure I get yer before the boy who isn't Maureen's boyfriend claims yer.' Phil held the door open. 'It's a nice dreamy waltz.'

'Mo, take me bag for me, will yer?' Doreen's face was creased in a smile that said she was blissfully happy. 'I'll see yer later.'

'Yer better had!' Maureen called as she

watched the pair join the dancers on the floor. She could understand her friend falling for Phil; she could fall for him herself.

'She's nice, yer friend.' Phil slowed down to a walk as he gazed into Doreen's eyes. 'I bet she's full of fun.'

'Yeah, she's a good scout, is Mo.' Doreen's heart was thumping so hard she thought he must surely hear it. Those vivid blue eyes of his were flirting with her and she was loving every second of it.

'I may as well come an' stand with yez, save me having to dash across the floor all the time.'

Doreen came down to earth. 'No, don't do that! Not tonight, anyway. Sammy won't be here next week, then yer can stand with us.'

'Can I walk yer home, then?'

Doreen felt so light-headed she thought she would faint. This must be what falling in love was like. She wanted so much for Phil to walk her home and was sorely tempted to say to hell with what anyone thought. But even in her euphoric state she could hear warning bells. It wasn't only what her friends thought that mattered...there was her mam to worry about. She'd have a duck egg if she knew her daughter had let a strange lad walk her home. She'd never trust Doreen again, and that would queer her pitch for any favours she might want...like staying out late again next Tuesday. 'No, I came with Mo, so I'll have to leave with her. Yer see, me mam's very strict, she likes to know who I'm mixing with.'

'I can hardly ask yer mam if I can walk yer home when I don't even know her.' Phil began to chuckle. 'Yer know, it's a novelty to me, havin' to get permission from a girl's mother before I can walk her home.'

Doreen thought he was making fun of her and took the huff. 'In that case, why don't yer walk one of yer other girlfriends home? I'm sure yer've got plenty of them.'

'Because it's you I want to take home, that's why.' Phil found his interest growing. He was used to girls throwing themselves at him and found Doreen's attitude a refreshing change. He knew by the innocence in her eyes that she was telling the truth and not just playing hard to get. 'So when do I get to meet yer mam?'

'When I've known yer a bit longer.' Doreen was surprised at her own self-assurance. If she was truthful she'd have to admit she'd like nothing better than to see Phil every day of her life. He was everything in a boy she'd ever dreamed of. But she knew nothing about him...he might have half a dozen girlfriends for all she knew. 'Me mam won't let me bring a boy home yet, she says I'm too young. An' we don't know each other, not really. After all, we've only seen each other twice.'

'So it's a case of a few dances every Tuesday, eh?' Phil sounded disappointed. 'We'll never get to know each other at that rate.'

'When I'm sixteen I'll take yer home to see if me parents approve.' Doreen tilted her head, her eyes twinkling. 'That's if you're still around an' I'm still interested.'

'Oh, I'll still be around...will you still be interested?'

'Yes, I think so.' Doreen lowered her lashes. Like every young person does at some time, she was wishing her life away. The next nine weeks wouldn't go quick enough for, her. 'So yer'll be here next Tuesday, then?'

'Wild horses wouldn't keep me away.' Phil pulled her close. 'I won't pretend I'm not disappointed, 'cos I am. But I agree with yer mam, she's right to keep an eye on yer. Shows she's a good mother and cares for yer.'

Chapter Fifteen

Corker pulled a crumpled ten-bob note from his pocket and smoothed it out before placing it on the counter. 'It's quiet in here tonight, Les.'

'Wednesday night, Corker, there's no money around.' The barman glanced around the snug as he pulled a pint. There were two workmen standing at the other end of the bar with pint glasses in their hands. They were wearing their working caps and overalls and their hands still bore the grime of a hard day's toil. They came in every night, straight off the tram, for one pint of bitter before going home. He could set his clock by them...they arrived dead on the dot every night. Apart from them, the only other customers were three elderly men sitting on the benches along the wall. They came in regular every night too, just for some male company. Retired from work, they were glad to get away from their wives for a couple of hours. All they ever bought was a half-glass of beer, and that would last them all night. What they spent wouldn't pay his wages, but Les didn't mind, it was better than having an empty pub, lent a bit of atmosphere.

'Was it four glasses of sherry, Corker?' Les had been delighted when the big man walked in, followed by what looked like a small army. His takings would be well up on a usual Wednesday night, 'cos Corker always spent a few bob.

'I'll take these and come back for the sherry.' Corker picked the four pint glasses up in his two huge hands and carried them to a table in the corner. 'I got yer a pint, Bob, is that all right?'

'Is it drunk yer'll have him?' Bridie asked, before Bob could open his mouth. She eyed the large glass with misgiving. 'Sure he's a man of moderation, so he is, an' that's altogether too much for him.'

Bob winked at Corker before taking his wife's hand in his. 'Don't worry, sweetheart, this will last me till closing time.'

'Truer words yer never spoke, Bob Jackson.' Bridie slapped his hand. ''Cos won't I be having me eye on yer all night?'

When all the drinks were on the table, Corker raised his glass. 'Here's to us and ours.'

Molly waited until they'd wished each other well, then leaned forward on her stool. 'Go on, Corker, tell them what yer've found out.'

'Molly!' Jack tutted. 'For heaven's sake let the man have a drink in peace.'

'Eh, you!' Nellie's dig in the ribs knocked Jack sideways. 'Never mind leave the man in peace! I'm dyin' to go to the lavvy, but I'm not movin' until I hear what Molly's bein' so mysterious about. Sure as eggs, if I move I'll miss something.'

Corker roared with laughter as he licked the froth from his moustache. 'Go to the lavvy, Nellie, I'd hate yer to have an accident. I promise me lips will be sealed until yer get back.'

'Uh, uh!' Nellie shook her head emphatically. 'It's not that I don't trust yer, Corker, it's me mate I don't trust. She's on pins, an' I bet a pound to a penny that by the time my backside hit the lavatory seat she'd have it out of yer.'

'Well, thanks very much!' Molly's attempt to keep her face straight failed miserably. 'Oh, all right,' she tittered, 'but don't blame us if yer wet yer knickers.'

'An' what sort of talk is that from a lady?' Bridie asked. 'Sure, haven't I asked meself a thousand times who it is yer take after?'

'And how many times 'ave I asked what the milkman an' the coalman looked like?' Molly stood up and leaned across the table to kiss her mother's cheek. 'Don't look so shocked, Ma, I'm only acting daft.' She tilted her head to one side and in an accent that would fool even an Irishman said, 'Sure, now, isn't it yer dear sweet self I take after?'

'D'yer know, I could 'ave spent a penny by

now.' Nellie clucked in disgust. 'Will yer sit down, missus, an' stop hoggin' the limelight? Corker can't get a word in edgeways.'

'Wait till I wet me whistle.' Corker lifted his glass and to everyone's amazement emptied it in one go. 'Mmmm, that was good.' He wiped the back of his hand across his mouth and turned to Ellen, who was seated next to him. 'All right, love?'

'Yes, I'm fine.' She lowered her eyes and plucked at a loose strand of cotton hanging from the sleeve of her coat. Even the curls she'd coaxed with the help of Molly's curling tongs and the make-up she'd taken ages to apply didn't give her the confidence to feel at ease. 'Go on, tell them what yer found out.'

'Not much, really! Nothing to get excited about. Only that the Bradleys have got a scrapyard down Westminster Road. The father and that weed of a son run it between them. One goes out with a handcart, like a rag an' bone man, while the other stays at the yard and buys second-hand stuff that people bring in.' The three old men in the corner looked over when Corker's loud guffaw filled the room. 'Me mate said they'd buy anythin' from a jam jar to a tram car.'

Jack looked thoughtful. 'Good way of getting rid of any stuff they knock off, though, isn't it?'

'Aye, the thought had crossed my mind, too,' Corker said. 'But how do we find out if any of the things he's got in the yard 'ave been nicked? We need proof before we can do anythin',

263

an' none of us could just go in and mooch around...he knows us too well for that.'

'Ooh, isn't it maddening?' Nellie was perched on her stool with her legs wide open, showing the tops of her stockings which were held up by a piece of elastic tied in a knot just above her knees. 'Mind you, little Dolly Lawton's bike will be well gone by now. He probably flogged it for a few bob to get rid of it quick.'

'There's another little bit of tittle-tattle. Me mate said Mrs Bradley had a bun in the oven when they got married.' Corker picked up his empty glass, a twinkle in his eye. 'The talk in the neighbourhood at that time was that they had to get hitched because of her being in the family way. But when the baby arrived it didn't look a bit like either of them. It had blond hair, an' as yer know, she's red-headed and he's jet black. The wagging tongues had a field day, so I'm told. They reckoned the baby wasn't his.'

'Well, I'll go to the foot of our stairs.' Nellie's face was doing contortions. 'She must 'ave pulled a fast one on him.'

'How d'yer know all this, Corker?' Jack asked.

'She used to live in Bullens Terrace, near the railway station in Marsh Lane, an' one of me mates lived a few doors from her. They stopped with her family for two years until they got a place of their own. The neighbours weren't sorry when they moved...they weren't very popular.'

'I bet she was the talk of the wash-house.' Nellie's chubby cheeks moved upward and her eyes disappeared in the flesh. 'I was goin' to say she was lucky anyone would marry 'er in that condition, but he's no cop, is he?'

'Now, love, don't you go around spreadin' tales,' George cautioned, knowing his wife's penchant for gossip. 'After all, it mightn't be true.'

'Oh, trust you to put a damper on things.' Nellie gazed around the group, looking for sympathy. 'He's a proper spoilsport is my feller...hates to see me enjoying meself.'

'He's right though, Nellie.' Corker said, nodding to Jack and George to finish their drinks so he could get another round in. 'Least said, soonest mended.' He grinned at Bob as he reached for the three empty glasses. 'Sorry, mate, but I'm not goin' to ask yer to drink up, 'cos yer wife will kill me.'

'I'll come with yer, Corker. 'Jack squeezed past Molly's legs, careful not to rock the table. 'This round's on me.'

'I've got a better idea.' George fished in his pocket and brought out half a crown. 'We'll have a kitty...that's the best way—'

Corker opened his mouth to protest, then changed his mind. He knew they didn't have much money, would probably have to scrimp and save for the rest of the week, but they had their pride. 'Okay, we'll do it your way. Four sherrys and three pints coming up.'

Setting a glass down in front of each of the ladies, Corker told them, 'I've got to report back to the ship at four tomorrow, we're sailing at six.'

'Ye gods, it wasn't worth yer comin' home!'

265

Molly was disappointed. So far they didn't have enough on the Bradleys to go to Mr Henry, and with Corker away they wouldn't be getting any more. 'How long will yer be away this time?'

'Only God knows that, Molly, an' He won't tell. I didn't expect to be sailing so soon, but the way things are, yer can never tell. I knew this was goin' to be a quick turnaround, but not this quick. The dockers must be working around the clock...non-stop.' Corker turned to Ellen and patted her knee. 'With a bit of luck it'll be a short run, eh, love?'

With all eyes on her, Ellen coloured. 'Yer can never tell with you.' She played with a strand of hair that had lost its curl and was hanging limply down the side of her cheek. Remembering how he'd caught her out yesterday, she cringed inside. She hadn't been in long when he called and was still wearing her working overall which was covered in bloodstains where she'd wiped her hands down the front after serving customers. 'It's a case of here today an' gone tomorrow.'

Molly picked up her glass and sipped slowly at the sherry as she wondered about the couple facing her. With Ellen you could never tell. When Corker was there she never looked you straight in the eye, never dropped her guard. When he wasn't there she wouldn't talk about him...always steered the conversation on to safer ground. But the big man was a different kettle of fish. He showed his feelings openly and didn't give a damn what people thought.

Molly set her glass on the table. He was one

266

of the best, was Corker, they didn't come any better.

Ellen was surprised when she walked in to see her two daughters sitting at the table playing ludo with Jill and Steve. 'Eh, what are you two doin' up? Yer should 'ave been in bed ages ago.'

'We did try, Mrs Clarke,' Jill said apologetically, 'but they wouldn't budge until they'd seen Uncle Corker.'

'What's all this then?' There was a wide grin on Corker's face as he threw his cap on to the couch. 'Old Nick will be after you.'

The two girls rushed to stand in front of him. 'Yer goin' away tomorrow, Sinbad, an' we wanted to see yer before yer went.' Phoebe said, hanging on to his arm. 'D'yer 'ave to go?'

Dorothy didn't give him a chance to answer. Grabbing his other arm, she gazed up at the giant who was idolised by the four Clarke children. He'd made such a difference to their lives, shown them a warmth and kindness they'd never known before. Always patient, he would sit and talk to them, make them laugh and have them wide-eyed at his feet as he told them of his adventures on the high seas. And although they were too young to realise it, he had taught them that not all men were violent bullies like the father they'd been terrified of.

'It's not fair,' Dorothy cried. 'We haven't seen nothin' of yer.'

'Well now.' Corker put a hand on each of their heads and ruffled their hair. 'When I go

267

aboard, I'll tell the Captain that yer said he's got to let me stay home longer next time. How about that, eh?'

'Ooh, er, will yer really tell the Captain that?' Phoebe was impressed.

'I most certainly will! An' I won't pull me punches, either.' Looking down from his great height, Corker smiled. 'Now, how about givin' me a big kiss before yer go to bed?'

'Yer'll have to bend down,' Dorothy giggled, 'we can't reach.'

Ellen's heart was heavy as she watched. This was the sort of affection the children had lacked all their young lives. And it was all her fault. She'd been swept off her feet by Nobby Clarke, thought she was in for a lifetime of happiness. And when she'd found out, too late, what he was really like, she hadn't had the courage to stand up to him.

'Come on now, girls, yer'll never get up for school in the morning.' She steered them to the narrow staircase. 'Say good night and thank you to Jill an' Steve.'

When they'd left the room, Corker turned his attention to the young couple. 'The big day won't be long now, eh?'

'Just a couple of months,' Steve said proudly, his arm across Jill's shoulders. 'It'll soon pass.'

'I suppose yer know how lucky yer are?' Corker lowered his huge frame into a chair. 'She's the prettiest girl in the neighbourhood, is my princess, an' if I'd been twenty years younger I'd have given yer a run for yer money.'

Jill, blushing at the compliment, turned her

268

bright eyes to Steve. 'I think I'm getting the best of the bargain.'

'You were made for each other, an' I hope I'm home for the engagement party to join in the toast.' Corker's head swivelled as Ellen entered the room. 'Are they settled?'

'They're nattering away to each other, but they'll probably drop off soon.' Ellen rubbed her arms briskly. 'It's cold up there. I'll put the kettle on.'

'Not for us, thanks, Mrs Clarke.' Steve pushed his chair back. He hadn't been alone with Jill all night and was longing to hold her in his arms and kiss her. 'We'll be on our way.'

'Are yer sure?'

'Yes, it's getting late.' Jill lifted her coat from the back of a chair. 'I hope you're back soon, Uncle Corker.'

'So do I, princess, so do I.' Corker raised his brows at Steve. 'Am I allowed a kiss?'

'You don't have to ask him.' Jill grinned as she leaned towards him. 'You're my uncle, aren't you?'

'I'll see you to the door,' Ellen said.

'No, I'll do it.' Corker stood up. 'You put the kettle on, love.'

Ellen was in the kitchen when she heard Corker come back. 'I won't be a minute, the kettle's just on the boil.'

'They make a smashing couple, don't they?' Corker's frame filled the doorway. 'Their marriage shouldn't have any problems.'

Ellen poured the boiling water into the pot. 'They've got everythin' going for them. Good

269

looks and nice natures.' She smiled. 'They won't have any problems...Molly an' Nellie will see to that.'

While Ellen poured the tea, Corker placed a couple of pieces of coal on the fire. 'Warm you up before yer go to bed.'

They sat in silence for a while, both thoughtful. Then Corker asked, 'I don't suppose yer've been in to see Nobby?'

Ellen felt a shiver run through her body at the mention of her husband's name. 'No, I can't bring meself to go.' She curled her hands around her cup for warmth. 'It costs a couple of bob to get there, which I can ill afford...and for what? He doesn't even know who I am. An' he frightens the life out of me the way he just sits and stares, never saying one word. I keep expectin' him to jump up and belt me one.'

'I'll come with yer next time I'm home.' Corker pulled his chair nearer. 'It's best to keep in touch to see if there's any change.'

'He won't change.' Ellen stared at the flames that were licking around the coals Corker had put on the fire. 'They told me last time I was there that there was no chance of him improving. He's mentally insane and will stay that way until he dies.'

'You could get a divorce, yer know.'

'What?' Ellen lowered the cup so quickly the tea spilled over into her lap. 'I couldn't get a divorce!'

'Why not? You've got grounds enough.'

'Oh, I couldn't do that, Corker. I couldn't divorce him.'

Corker combed his fingers through his bushy beard. 'D'yer want to stay married to him?'

Again Ellen felt a cold shiver run through her body. Even though her husband was miles away, locked up behind bars, he still had the power to fill her with fear. 'Of course I don't want to stay married to 'im. But yer know I'm a Catholic, and the Church doesn't believe in divorce.'

Corker snorted. 'Not even the Church would expect yer to stay married to a madman.' He put his cup on the table and leaned forward. 'What about us, Ellen?'

'What d'yer mean, what about us?'

Corker put a hand under her chin and turned her face towards him. 'Come off it, love. We're not kids any more, we don't have to pretend. Yer must know how I feel about you.'

Nervous and agitated, Ellen jerked her head free. 'We shouldn't be talkin' like this, Corker, it's not proper.'

'We've got to talk about it, love. We can't go on as we are, an' you know it.' He took the cup from her hand and put it on the table. 'Look at me, Ellen.'

When he saw the tears glistening in her eyes, Corker slid from the chair and knelt in front of her. Taking her hand, he said softly, 'Don't cry, love, please. It's got to come to a head sometime, so it might as well be now. Let's be sensible and bring it all out in the open. When we've had our say, if yer don't want me in yer life, then I'll just walk away with no hard feelings.'

Ellen felt her heart miss a beat. What would

271

she do without Corker? Not only her, but the children? He'd come into their lives when they most needed someone and now she couldn't imagine a life without him. He'd given her back her self-respect, made her feel like a woman again. She missed him when he was away and was always excited when his ship was due in. But divorce... She'd been brought up to believe that when you got married, you stayed married. Otherwise you were committing a sin in the eyes of God.

She heard Corker groan as he lifted one of his knees to rub. 'Get up, Corker, yer'll have sore knees.'

'It is bloody uncomfortable.' Corker struggled to his feet and held out his hand. 'Come an' sit next to me on the couch.'

Still holding hands, they sat close on the old horsehair couch. 'Now, I'll have my say first, eh?' Corker could feel her hand shaking and squeezed it gently. 'There's no need to get upset, love, it's not the end of the world. As I said, if yer want to, yer can show me the door. But not until I get what I've got to say off me chest. Okay?' He waited for Ellen's nod, then continued. 'I've always had a soft spot for yer, even when we were young and lived in the same neighbourhood. I thought yer were my girl, 'cos I used to take yer to the flicks an' the local hops. But we know what happened...I started goin' away to sea an' before I got down to askin' yer to marry me, yer'd upped and wed Nobby Clarke. We won't go into the years you were married to him, or the life he led yer, that's all in the past. But we've been given another chance, an' I for one would like to grab it with both hands. My feelings for yer are very strong, and for the kids. But I don't just want yer friendship, Ellen, I want more than that.'

The tears were now flowing freely down Ellen's face. For the first time she allowed the truth to enter her mind and stay. She loved this gentle giant and wasn't going to pretend otherwise. He'd been honest with her, he deserved no less in return. Her voice shaking, she asked, 'What can we do about it, Corker?'

'We can start by you telling me if yer feel the same about me as I do about you.'

Ellen wasn't going to let her shyness stop her this time. There was too much at stake. 'You must know that I do. Otherwise I wouldn't be seen out with yer...giving the wagging tongues a field day.'

Corker pulled her to him. 'That's all I want to know. To hell with the waggin' tongues...they don't pay the rent for yer.'

'I'm being unkind about the neighbours, they've all been marvellous to me since...er... since Nobby's accident. Especially Molly, Nellie and a few others.' Daring to do something she'd long desired, Ellen put a hand to his cheek. 'What are we goin' to do, Corker?'

'Right now yer goin' to give me me first kiss.' Corker's massive arms held her tight as he pressed his lips to hers. It was a long kiss, but gentle. And with that, Corker was satisfied. He'd waited a long time, a little longer wouldn't hurt. For her peace of mind he wanted to do things right. 'When I come home again we'll go to Winwick to see Nobby, and I'll have a word with one of the doctors. But I don't want yer worrying while I'm away. Whatever happens, I promise that one day we'll be together. You, me and the children.'

In the shelter of his arms, Ellen had never felt so safe and contented. If he was right, and they could find a way of being together, life would be heaven. Not only for her, but for the children as well. He'd make a marvellous husband and a loving, caring father.

Ellen sighed with contentment. They'd be a close, happy family, like the Bennetts and the McDonoughs. Like their neighbours, their home would be warm and filled with laughter.

A cloud of doubt threatened to spoil Ellen's happiness, but she brushed it aside. She'd put her hopes and trust in Corker...he wouldn't let her down.

Chapter Sixteen

'I'm not sittin' down until I've got the washing out.' Molly jerked her head at Nellie. 'Come an' give us a hand...yer can hold the pegs.'

'I suppose yer'd liked me to hold them in me mouth to keep me quiet.' Nellie held her apron out while Molly threw the pegs in. 'It's a good drying day, isn't it, kid? Nice and mild, with a little breeze.'

'That's why I want to get it out now, before the weather changes.' Molly shook a nightdress out without thinking and sent a spray of water over Nellie. 'Sorry about that, sunshine, but it'll save yer washing yer ugly mug.'

'We can't all be glamorous,' Nellie said, handing over two pegs. 'Everyone is gifted in different ways. I might 'ave been behind the door when looks were given out, but as yer ma would say, sure, didn't the good Lord bless me with a voice like an angel?'

'Nellie, yer've got a voice like a hooter on one of the tug boats on the Mersey! Yer want to listen to yerself sometime.'

'Jealousy gets yer nowhere, girl.' Undaunted, Nellie threw her head back and began to sing, '"Wait till the sun shines, Nellie, and the clouds go drifting by."'

Molly clapped a hand over her friend's mouth. 'In the name of God, Nellie, yer'll have the neighbours out! Yer sound like someone in agony.'

As Nellie doubled up with laughter pegs fell from the side of her apron and scattered in all directions. 'Look what yer've made me do now.' Snorting noisily, she dropped the corners of her apron and the remaining pegs. 'It's your fault, so you can pick them up. I can't bend down, yer see, girl, not with my complaint.'

Molly rescued two pegs and hung a shirt of Jack's on the line before facing her friend. 'And what, pray, is this complaint that stops yer from bending down?'

Her face creased in a smile. Nellie patted her

275

enormous tummy. 'This is what stops me from bending down.' She moved back to lean against the yard wall. 'D'yer want to know somethin', girl? I haven't seen me feet for nearly twenty years. Wouldn't know I had any, except for the corns on me little toes givin' me gyp.'

'Nellie McDonough, yer past the post, you really are.' But there was affection in Molly's eyes as she gazed at her friend. She was nearly as wide as she was tall, but Molly loved every ounce of her. 'Anyway, what are yer doin' down here this time of the mornin'? Why aren't yer gettin' yer washing on the line, like me?'

'I don't hang about, girl, me clothes were on the line hours ago.' Nellie waddled after Molly into the kitchen. 'I woke about five o'clock an' was frightened to drop off again in case we overslept, so I decided to get up an' start on me washin'. And while me hands were busy, so was me brain.' She folded her arms and hitched up her mountainous bosom. 'How about you an' me gettin' the tram down to Westminster Road an' see if we can find this scrapyard of the Bradleys'?'

Molly looked puzzled. 'What good would that do us?'

'How the hell do I know? But it's worth a try, isn't it?'

'Uh, uh, Nellie...you can get me into enough trouble without goin' looking for it. And anyway, they've been keepin' their noses clean lately.'

'That's what you think.' Nellie's expression was as effective as sticking her tongue out. 'I went down for the paper early on, an' I met that

276

woman who lives next door but two to Corker. The milk's been pinched off her doorstep for three mornings on the trot. Her husband's 'ad to have conny-onny in his tea, an' he's none too pleased. An' she said she's not the only one it's happened to.'

'Go 'way!' Molly was really interested now. 'Well I never! The thieving buggers!'

'So they're still at it, yer see, girl! And they'll keep at it unless someone stops them.'

'Aye, yer right there,' Molly agreed, 'once a thief, always a thief.'

'So, are yer comin' with me to spy out the lay of the land?' Nellie asked, her eyes narrowed to slits. 'Yer never know, girl, we might just come up with somethin'.'

'But we don't even know where it is!'

'Oh, for cryin' out loud, girl, have yer got any more excuses? We've got tongues in our flamin' heads, haven't we?' Nellie was getting impatient. 'If I sit on one side of the tram, an' you on the other, we can't miss it, can we?'

Molly was thoughtful for a while. 'Yer wouldn't do anythin' to get us into trouble, would yer?'

'Now would I do that to you?'

'Yes, yer ruddy well would! I've lost count of the times yer've landed me in it.'

Knowing this to be true, Nellie wisely didn't argue. 'Look, if I promise not to open me mouth, or take a step without askin' yer first, will yer come?'

'Oh, all right.' Molly gave in. 'But I want to peel the spuds before I go out, 'cos it's my turn to pick Ruthie an' Bella up from school. So give me half an hour.'

Careful not to smile in case her friend thought she was gloating, Nellie swayed towards the door. 'Yer on, girl. Ta-ra.'

Nellie had the seat on the tram to herself. There were people standing in the aisles, but no one was prepared to perch on the mere six inches not covered by her backside. When the tram trundled past the scrapyard, she shuffled to the edge of the seat, calling to Molly, 'Come on, girl, this is where we get off.'

They stood on the pavement until the tram moved on, then Molly asked, 'Where is it?'

'On the corner, about two streets back. It looks a right dump from what I could see of it.' Nellie raised her arm and pointed. 'Look, yer can see it from here.'

'For God's sake, Nellie, stop pointing!' Molly raised her eyes to the sky. 'I don't know why I let yer talk me into this, it's crazy. What do we do now...stand her like two flamin' lemons?'

'I don't think it would be wise, girl, not under the circumstances. Don't turn around, but the queer feller is comin' towards us, pushing a handcart.'

'Oh, dear God in heaven.' Molly grabbed her friend's arm and dragged her into the doorway of the nearest shop. 'You'll get me hung one of these days, Nellie McDonough.'

Totally unconcerned, Nellie popped her head out of the doorway. 'He's nearly on top of us, we'd better get in the shop.'

Before being unceremoniously pushed through the doorway, Molly had time to note that it was a sweet shop. She thanked her lucky stars it wasn't a butcher's...she could just about afford a penny for sweets for Ruthie, but anything dearer would have been out of the question.

'I won't keep you a minute.' A middle-aged woman was bending down in front of a little girl who was sobbing her heart out. 'Don't cry, love, there's a good girl. Your mam will come for you soon.'

'Is she lost?' Molly asked, her own fears forgotten as she gazed on the tear-stained face.

The woman straightened up. 'Her older brother brought her in for some sweets, but he ran off and left her.' She lowered her voice. 'Taking the sweets with him, of course. He's a cute little blighter and I'm surprised Mrs Birchall trusts her with him she's only two.'

'Ah, bless her little cotton socks.' Nellie bent towards the child, who had curls like Shirley Temple, but unlike the child film star her hair was a rich auburn. 'Yer mam will come for yer, you'll see. She wouldn't want to lose a pretty little girl like you.'

'I'd take her home meself,' the woman said, 'but I'm on me own in the shop and I can't leave it.'

'Does she live far?' Molly asked.

'No, only the next street. Third door down on the left, number six.'

'We'll walk her home,' Molly offered. 'That's if yer'll trust us with her.'

The woman's face brightened. 'Of course I

will. It's very kind of you...and a load off my mind. I'd be grateful if you would explain to Mrs Birchall what happened, and that I'm sorry I couldn't bring Susan myself.'

Molly nodded as she held her hand out. 'Come on, sunshine, yer mam will be worried stiff about yer.'

'She won't have missed her yet. Robert, her brother, won't go home until all the sweets are eaten, you can be sure of that. He's a proper little imp if ever there was one.'

'He sounds it.' Nellie brought a scruffy purse from her pocket. 'Give Little Dolly Daydreams a pennyworth of sweets...mix them for 'er.'

Happy with the bag of sweets in her hand and a smiling lady each side of her, Susan went willingly. 'I dunno, there's never a dull moment when I'm out with you,' Molly muttered as they turned into the side street. 'This morning I 'ad all me day planned...the bedrooms were going to get a thorough clean-out.' Shaking her head, she glared at Nellie. 'I must want me bumps feeling, letting yer talk me into anything. I could have had me bedrooms done by now, all nice and clean. But no, I listen to Helen Theresa McDonough, an' what happens? I find meself walking down a strange street with a child I've never seen in me life before!'

'Oh, stop yer flamin' moaning! The child did us a good turn, didn't she? If it hadn't been for her, we might 'ave been run over by the queer feller's handcart.'

'Here's number six.' Molly gazed at the neatly kept terraced house. The windows were

280

gleaming and the net curtains as white as snow. Susan's mother was obviously very house-proud. 'Shall I knock?'

Nellie put a hand to her mouth to hide the smile. 'Well, yer could try booting the door in.'

Molly tutted as she reached for the shining brass knocker. 'You want yer head seein' to, you do.'

The door was opened by an attractive young woman who looked to be in her late twenties. Her auburn hair was naturally curly like her daughter's, and her appearance was as neat and tidy as the outside of the house. She looked at the two women with surprise, and as Molly was explaining their presence, she swept the tiny tot into her arms and held her tight. 'Thank you, I'm very grateful. just wait until that little tinker comes in, I'll tan 'is backside so hard he won't be able to sit down for a week.' Her eyes were curious as she gazed from one to the other. 'You're not from around here, are you?'

It was Nellie who answered, an idea forming in her mind. 'No, we were on the tram into town when we noticed a scrapyard, the one around the corner, and we decided to have a look-see. Me an' me mate here, we love rummaging through old junk.'

'I'd keep away from that place if I were you. They're nothing but bloomin' robbers.' Millicent Birchall decided she liked the look of the pair and asked, 'Would you like to come in for a cuppa? It's the least I can offer after yer've been so good.'

'D'yer know, I could murder a cuppa.' Nellie avoided Molly's eyes. What she didn't see she needn't worry about. 'That's if it's no trouble?'

'Not at all...I'll be glad of a bit of company.' Millicent led the way down the narrow hall. 'Leave the front door ajar, please, in case Robert comes in.'

'Yer've got yer house nice.' Molly said, scanning the spotlessly clean well-furnished living room. She gave Nellie a dig and pointed to the modern tiled fire surround. 'Ay, doesn't that make a difference?'

'We had the old black grate taken out last year.' Millicent was very house-proud and the compliment brought a smile of pleasure to her pretty face as she lowered Susan to the floor. 'It used to give me the willies...great big iron monster. It took up half the room an' was murder to keep clean. That one's a doddle...only needs a wipe over with a wet cloth.'

'Yeah, it doesn't half make a difference.' Molly nodded in agreement. 'If we hadn't just decorated I'd be havin' a word with my Jack.'

'Won't yer sit down, er...' Millicent grinned. 'I don't even know yer names.'

'I'm Nellie, an' this is me mate, Molly.' Nellie was eyeing the couch with apprehension. If she sat on that she'd never get up. 'D'yer mind if I sit on one of the wooden chairs? As yer can see, I'm a big girl an' yer'd need a block an' tackle to get me off the couch.'

'Be my guest.' Millicent made her way to the kitchen, saying over her shoulder. 'Make yerselves at home while I put the kettle on.'

While the tap water was running, Nellie said softly, 'Nice 'ouse, isn't it?'

'It is,' Molly hissed, 'but what the 'ell are we doing in it?'

'Oh, stop yer moanin', will yer? Sit back, relax an' enjoy yerself.'

Susan's eyes were moving from one to the other as she sucked on a bull's-eye. 'Where's me bruvver?'

'He'll be home any minute, sunshine.' Molly stroked her thick, glossy hair. 'You'll see.'

'He took my sweeties.'

'Yes, that was very naughty of him. But Auntie Nellie bought you some sweeties, didn't she? An' I bet you've got more than him.'

Millicent came through carrying a wooden tray covered with a pretty embroidered cloth and set with dainty china cups and saucers. 'He's probably skulking in the entry, frightened to come in.' She poured milk into the cups before lifting the teapot. 'He's a handful, is Robert. A real boy, always into mischief.'

'You don't need to tell us, we've been through it.' Molly took the proferred cup and saucer gingerly. Tea always tasted nicer out of a china cup, but when it belonged to somebody else the fear of breaking it took the pleasure away. She'd have been much happier with an old chipped cup. 'We've both got boys, haven't we, Nellie?'

'Yeah...and right little horrors they were.' Nellie was perched on a small dining chair, her tongue peeping out of the side of her

283

mouth as she tried to get her plump finger through the handle of the delicate cup. In the end she gave up. 'Yer'll 'ave to forgive me manners, Millicent, but I'll 'ave to hold the cup in me hands.' After waiting for a nod of understanding, she said casually, 'Yer were tellin' us about the scrapyard. Waste of time us goin', is it?'

'I wouldn't go near it.' Millicent took a hankie from the sleeve of her navy-blue cardi and wiped Susan's red-stained, sticky mouth. 'A man an' his son have it, an' they're horrible. Mind you, the way the father carries on, he thinks he's God's gift to women. There's a broken-down old shed at the back of the yard and he's always got some woman in there, chattin' them up. All I can say is, their taste must be in their backsides because he's a slimy little toad...yellow teeth, greasy hair, smelly...ugh, he's horrible.'

'Yer don't say!' Nellie glanced at Molly and her eyes spoke volumes. 'He sounds a right little twerp.'

'It's not only that... I mean, after all, no one can help what they look like.' Millicent sat back and crossed her shapely legs. 'But they've got a terrible name around here for thieving. I think half the stuff they sell is knock-off. Loads of things 'ave gone missing from houses and yards, and although we know it's down to them, we can't prove anythin', 'cos the things are never in the scrapyard. My husband thinks they steal to order an' the goods are whipped away quick in the handcart.'

'This is all very interestin', isn't it Molly?'

Nellie gave a sigh of relief as she carefully placed her cup and saucer on the tray. They were very nice, but too delicate for her clumsy hands. 'Sounds like someone we know, eh, girl?'

'Yeah.' Molly chewed on her bottom lip for a few seconds, then nodded. 'Go on, tell her.'

That was all the encouragement Nellie needed. Without pausing for breath she told the startled Millicent the real reason for their visit to Westminster Road. 'We didn't know what good it would do, but we 'ad to do something. Yer can't just sit back and let sods like that get away with it. I mean, it's not as though he's Robin Hood...stealin' from the rich to give to the poor.'

'I can't believe it!' There was amazement on Millicent's face. 'Fancy you comin' all this way and ending up in my house! What a coincidence!'

'If you knew my friend,' Molly said drily, 'yer'd know nothing is a coincidence with her. There's a method in everythin' she does. Oh, I'm not sayin' she knew we'd end up in your house, but sure as eggs, and by hook or by crook, she'd 'ave found someone who knew the Bradleys.'

Millicent let out a high-pitched laugh. 'Yer know, you two are hilarious!' She studied Nellie's huge body before letting out another shriek of laughter. 'It's not as though yer'd go unnoticed!'

'Ay, we'll 'ave less of that.' Nellie pushed out her bosom. 'Don't yer know we're in disguise? I'm Charlie Chan an' this,' she jerked her thumb at Molly, 'is me sidekick.'

Millicent doubled up. 'Oh, you are funny. I'm really glad our Robert was naughty...so glad, I'll probably give him a hug when he comes in, instead of a clout. Just wait until I tell me husband, he'll have hysterics. He can't stand the Bradleys...had many a set-to with them...an' he'll be made up to know you're on the warpath.'

Molly knew what was coming when the chair Nellie was sitting on started to creak, but Millicent wasn't prepared for the loud guffaws that filled the room. And although she didn't know the cause of the big woman's mirth, it was so infectious it wasn't long before her high-pitched laugh joined the guffaws.

Wiping her eyes with the back of her hand, and gasping for breath, Nellie wheezed, 'Tell your feller he can hire us if he wants. We don't come cheap, mind, but we're good detectives. If he gets us, he's gettin' the best. For tuppence an hour, we'll trail the villains until we catch them red-handed. An' to set his mind at rest, yer can tell him we're so good the Bradleys won't even know they're being followed.'

'Oh, dear God, please help me.' Molly's sides were aching with laughter and she dug her curled fists into each side of her waist to numb the pain. 'Nellie, yer'd stick out like a sore thumb! Yer might as well say nobody would notice a ruddy big oak tree standing between the tram lines in Scotland Road.'

Millicent felt in her sleeve for the hankie to wipe away the tears running down her cheeks.

But when she opened it up and saw the sticky mess she shoved it back in her sleeve and used the backs of her hands. 'D'yer know, you two are as good as a tonic. It's ages since I laughed so much.'

'It's laughter makes the world go around, girl. Better than a bottle of milk stout any day.'

'It's a good job we've had a laugh, 'cos otherwise it would 'ave been a wasted journey,' Molly said, remembering why they were here. 'We know no more about the Bradleys than we already knew.'

'There is somethin' you don't seem to know. An' I'm not tellin' tales out of school, either, 'cos everyone round here knows about it.' Millicent paused long enough to make sure she had their undivided attention. 'A woman down the street had a baby to Mr Bradley about eighteen months ago.'

'Go 'way!' Nellie leaned forward so quickly she nearly overbalanced. Just in time she managed to grab the end of the table to stop herself falling head first into the fire. 'Is that gospel?'

Millicent nodded. 'Yeah, she makes no bones about it. The hard-faced so-and-so makes my blood boil. There's no shame in her, she walks around as though she owns the place.'

'Hasn't she got a husband?' Molly asked.

'She's got one, but where he is is a mystery. He did a disappearing act about three years ago an' I don't blame him. She was carryin' on with every Tom, Dick and Harry behind his back...man-mad she is, chases anything in a pair of trousers.'

'An' does she admit it's Bradley's baby?'

'Admit it...she told everyone! Not that anyone needed telling, mind you, because he slips down to her house every afternoon for a few hours. And beside that, the baby's the spittin' image of him.'

'Ooh, er!' Nellie's eyes were bright with excitement. 'I wonder if 'is wife knows?'

'I wouldn't know. Nobody has ever seen his wife.'

'Ay, Molly.' Nellie's brain was racing ahead. 'That would put the cat amongst the pigeons, wouldn't it?'

Molly grinned. 'Yer right there, sunshine.' Her grin widened when she looked at Millicent. 'If yer knew his wife yer'd understand what we're on about. She's a real firebrand, is Mrs Bradley. Common as muck an' as tough as old rope. I've got a feelin' she doesn't know about her husband's extramarital affair, an' if she were to find out there'd be skin an' hair flying.'

'Now, Molly, yer surely not wicked enough to snitch on him, are yer?' Nellie was in her element. It hadn't been a wasted journey after all. 'That would be a lousy, underhanded trick, that would.'

'I'm not goin' to snitch! But I know someone who would, an' she's not a million miles from me now.' Molly winked at Millicent. 'Meet the biggest stirrer-up in Liverpool... Helen Theresa McDonough.'

Millicent gazed at Nellie, her eyes wide. 'Are yer goin' to tell her?'

'Ooh, I'll have to put me thinkin' cap on for

this.' Nellie tapped the side of her head. 'Can't rush into an operation of this size without a lot of planning. Besides, my feller's got no sense of humour and if he found out I was up to somethin' he'd have me guts for garters.'

Susan, the now-empty sweet bag in her hand, pulled on her mother's skirt for attention. 'I want to wee-wee, Mummy.'

'All right, darling, I'll take you down the yard.' Millicent lifted a finger. 'Not a word till I get back.'

'She's a nice woman.' Molly watched Millicent pass the window carrying her daughter. 'I've enjoyed meself the last hour.'

'An' we've learned somethin' to our advantage.' Nellie's chins did a quickstep. 'I don't know what we can do about it, but it's a card up our sleeve.'

'We'll do nothin' till we see Corker,' Molly warned. 'I'm not gettin' meself mixed up with people like that.'

'What can Corker do? He's been away a month, an' according to Ellen he doesn't know when he'll be home.'

'I don't care, Nellie, I'm not gettin' involved. An' don't try an' talk me into anything, 'cos this time I mean it.'

They heard the latch on the back door click and Millicent's voice carried through to them. 'I'll pull yer knickers up properly, darling, just give me time. We can't leave our visitors sittin' on their own, 'cos it's bad manners.'

'Tell 'er the truth,' Nellie bawled, 'that yer frightened of missing anythin'.'

Millicent was grinning when she led her daughter into the room. 'She's never spent a penny so fast in all her life.'

'Yer could have let her take her time, there's been no great plot hatched while yer were away.'

Millicent lifted her daughter on to the couch. 'Yer mean you haven't come up with anything exciting?'

Nellie sat hunched forward, her elbows resting on her knees, her thumbs circling each other. 'I'm game, but me mate isn't. She's frightened of gettin' into trouble.'

'What she means is, I don't relish ending up in hospital or jail.' Molly nodded her head vigorously. 'An' she's right, I don't!'

Nellie suddenly sat up straight, the expression on her face resembling someone who had just found the right answer to a crossword clue. 'I've got it! The perfect plan! How about it if we send one of those enon...amon...oh, what's the word I'm lookin' for? Yer know, when someone sends a letter an' doesn't put their name on it?'

Millicent raised her brows. 'Yer mean anonymous?'

'That's it, girl, that's the word!' Nellie clapped her hands in glee. 'What it is to be educated, eh?'

'Hey, that's a great idea!' Millicent was suitably impressed. 'You'd get away with it, too! No one would dream it was you, with not livin' around here...I mean, it's just a sheer fluke you called at my house, isn't it? An' if you posted the letter in a postbox in this area, they'd think someone around here had sent it.'

'Just a minute, hang on!' Molly lifted her hand. 'I don't want to be a wet blanket, but I've got to say I don't think you two are thinkin' straight.' She appealed to Nellie, 'What good would it do us if Bradley's wife did find out about the baby? Seein' as one of her children is supposed to be illegitimate, she can hardly play the wronged wife, now can she? She'd probably raise ructions, batter him senseless, but at the end of the day they'd still be livin' in our street, still thieving from our neighbours.'

Looking deflated, Nellie pulled a face at Millicent. 'Yer know, for a while there, girl, I was really enjoying meself. Thought I was a proper clever-clogs...the bee's knees. But Molly's right, it wouldn't do us no good.'

'I'm not saying forget the idea,' Molly told her. 'I just think we should wait an' ask Corker.'

'Corker? Who's Corker?'

'You tell her,' Molly said, thinking it would cheer her friend up. She'd enjoy it too, 'cos no one could tell a tale better than Nellie. So she sat back to listen and smile as her friend's hands moved as quickly as her mouth. Helen Theresa McDonough, she thought, you don't half exaggerate! Corker was a big man, no doubt about that. But according to Nellie, he was about nine feet tall and had to bend double to get through doors. She had his beard down to his tummy, his hands the size of ham shanks, and he could fight half a dozen men at the same time.

291

'He sounds quite a character.' Millicent's face was alive with interest. 'I'd love to meet him.'

'Well, yer never know yer luck in a big city, girl! We might be able to arrange a meeting.'

Molly was getting fidgety. It was all right for Nellie, she could talk till the cows came home, but if they didn't make a move she'd be late getting to the school. 'Come on, missus, let's get goin'.'

'All right, girl, I'm on me way.' With both hands pressing on the table, Nellie levered herself up. 'It's been a very interesting couple of hours, Millicent, thanks to you.'

'Yes, you've been very kind.' Molly felt in her pocket for a loose penny and handed it to Susan. 'Here yer are, sunshine, that's for bein' a good girl.'

'I'm sorry you've got to go.' Millicent was clearly disappointed. She'd really enjoyed the company and her voice was hopeful as she asked, 'Will yer come again?'

'Oh, I don't think that would be wise, do you, Nellie?'

Nellie shook her head and her chins. 'Not under the circumstances. Yer see, we might decide to send that letter an' it wouldn't do if we were seen in the vicinity. They'd soon put two an' two together.'

'Well how will I know what's going on?' Millicent cried. 'Yer can't leave me in the dark, now can yer?'

'Write down yer name an' address an' we'll write an' tell yer what we're up to.'

Millicent pulled open a drawer of the

sideboard and rummaged until she found a piece of paper and a pencil. 'Don't yer let me down, now,' she said as she scribbled. 'I'll be watchin' for the postman.'

'Scout's honour.' Nellie folded the paper and pushed it in her pocket. Then she bent to kiss Susan. 'Yer've been as good as gold...a credit to yer mam.'

They were walking down the hall when Millicent grabbed Molly's arm. 'Oh, I've just remembered something! I heard that the Bradley man's been told they're taking his railings away from around the yard.'

'Who's takin' his railings?' Molly looked puzzled. 'An' why?'

'Haven't yer heard? They're taking all the railings from around the parks and everywhere. Anything made of iron is being confiscated to be used to make guns an' tanks...that's what my husband says.'

'They're not gettin' my poker,' Nellie said before Molly could argue about the certainty of there being a war. 'I use that for me own personal war...to keep my feller on his toes.' Laughing at her own joke, she waddled towards the front door.

Millicent stood on the step, sorry to see them go. Then she had a thought which brought a smile to her face. 'Without those high railings, the scrapyard'll be easy pickings, won't it? He'll come in one mornin' an' find everything's been nicked. That would be real justice, wouldn't it?'

'Yeah.' Nellie's imagination was fired. 'Couldn't

yer get a posse up, like they do in the cowboy pictures? Empty the whole bloody place out? Oh, what I'd give to see his face if yer did. Give him a taste of his own medicine an' see how he likes it.'

'If I had your address, I could write an' let yer know if I hear anythin' that might be of interest to yer.'

Molly pulled on Nellie's arm, worried that she had to go home first to put the dinner on, then out again to pick Ruthie up. 'I'll drop yer a line in the next day or two, an' me address will be on the letter. But right now we'll have to dash...ta-ra.'

Nellie, being dragged sideways down the street, waved. 'See yer, Milly! Don't take any wooden nickels...ta-ra!'

Chapter Seventeen

Maisie handed the customer her change. 'There yer are, Mrs Purley, a thrupenny joey...don't go mad an' spend it all in one shop.' She reached for the basket standing on the counter. 'I'll put yer shopping in for yer.' Glancing down to where Molly was waiting patiently, she winked. 'Won't be a tick, Molly.'

'Time's on our side, sunshine, I'm in no hurry.'

'There yer go, love.' Maisie lifted the handle of the basket. 'It's pretty heavy! If yer not waiting for the groceries I could have it delivered to your house, save yer lugging it. Young Peter Clarke would nip around with it when he comes home from school.'

Mrs Purley tested the weight. 'No, I can manage. I'll keep swapping hands. Thanks, Maisie, I'll be seein' yer.'

Molly ran to open the shop door for the slight elderly woman. 'Ta-ra, sunshine.'

'I was hoping yer'd come.' Maisie lifted her foot and grimaced. 'D'yer know, I've got a corn on me little toe an' it's giving me hell.'

'That's not why yer were hopin' I'd come, is it?' Molly grinned. 'So yer could have a good old moan?'

'No, but now yer come to mention it, I may as well make use of yer. Keep an eye on the shop for us while I put a corn plaster on.'

'Where's Alec?'

'We're running low on bread, so he's nipped to the bakery.' Maisie's voice grew fainter as she walked through to the back. 'He shouldn't be long.'

'If he's more than half an hour I'll be clockin' on for wages.' Molly leaned her elbows on the counter. 'What was it yer wanted to see me about?'

'Hang on a minute.' There was silence for a while, then Maisie reappeared, wincing each time she put her right foot to the floor. 'I'll have to put a hot poultice on it tonight, see if I can draw the blasted thing out.'

'Thank God I don't suffer with corns. Nellie

does though...she's got them on both of her little toes.'

'She has my sympathy.' Maisie pulled a small three-legged stool from under the counter and sat down. 'May as well rest it while there's no customers in the shop.'

'Gee, thanks, pal! Don't I count as a customer?'

'Oh, yer know what I mean,' Maisie said, reaching into the glass display cabinet and picking out a slab of chocolate. She broke it in two and slid one of the pieces along the counter to Molly. 'Get yer mouth around that while I give yer the message. I had a phone call from Corker an' he asked me to tell his mam, an' Ellen, that his ship's docked in Portsmouth. He's tryin' to get a few days' leave but he's not sure yet. Either way, he's goin' to let me know.'

Cadbury's chocolate was one of Molly's failings. She couldn't resist its creamy-smooth texture and would suck it slowly to make it last longer. 'It's been a long trip for Corker this time.' Her tongue flicked over her lips. 'An' he won't be very happy bein' stuck down in Portsmouth. Even if he does get a few days' leave, two of them will be spent travelling there and back. I wonder how come they docked there instead of Liverpool?'

'I dunno, Molly, but things are changin' so fast yer can't rely on anythin'. We notice it more, having a shop. There's a shortage of lots of things that up until lately we took for granted. For instance, our delivery from the wholesaler this week was way down on what we'd ordered. Alec rang them to see if they'd sent us the wrong order, but they told him their supplies had been cut an' they couldn't do anything about it. So take my advice, Molly, an' shop early on in the week before we run out of the likes of butter an' marg. An' yer can forget bananas, they're a thing of the past...can't get hold of them for love nor money.'

'Things are lookin' pretty grim, aren't they?' Even Molly could no longer delude herself about the possibility of war. Every night in the *Echo* there was talk of factories being taken over to make uniforms, gas masks and parachutes. Air-raid shelters were being built in different parts of the city, and shops were advertising material for making blackout curtains.

Molly let out a deep sigh. 'It's a great life if yer don't weaken, isn't it, Maisie? Yer just get the kids grown up, have a few bob in yer pocket when they start work, an' what happens? Some stupid, jumped-up bugger starts a flamin' war!'

'I lie awake in bed every night thinkin' about it.' Maisie rolled the silver paper from the chocolate bar into a ball and threw it on the floor. 'Our fellers won't be called up...not at the beginning, anyway. It's the young ones that'll go first.' She rubbed a finger over a crack in the counter. 'You remember the last war, don't yer, Molly?'

'Too true I remember it! I'd only just left school when it was over.' Molly's laugh was hollow. 'Wasn't it supposed to be the war that ended all wars? Some joke, eh?'

'It's the young lads I feel sorry for...the likes of Steve. Nobody asks them if they want to fight, they just get a letter tellin' them they're goin' in the army or the navy an' they have to like it or lump it.'

'Yeah, yer right there, sunshine. D'yer know what I think? I think that the people who decide there's going to be a war, well, they're the ones that should be in the firing line. Put a rifle in their hands and stick them in the front of the troops, see how they like it.'

'It isn't that easy, Molly.'

'No? Well, I think it is. The first sign of fightin' and they'd do it in their kecks as they were runnin' for cover. If they want a war, let them have a bloody war, but leave the rest of us out of it.' Molly banged her fist on the counter. 'The big nobs won't be anywhere near the fighting! Stuck behind a desk somewhere safe, they won't be in any danger. Like that Miles, in Jill's office! His father's in the know, so he's got himself a nice safe job in the Ministry of Defence. They say money talks, and by God it's true.'

'But it's not us that wants a war, Molly,' Maisie said, in an attempt to make her see reason, 'it's that Hitler. An' we can't just sit back and let him get away with what he's doin'.'

'I could...very easily.' Molly's chest was heaving and she could feel herself getting all het up. And for what? It wouldn't solve anything. 'Anyway, Maisie, it hasn't started yet, so let's just live in hope that either Hitler comes to his senses or some bugger shoots him. I'll pass Corker's message on to Ellen an' she can let his mam know.' She squared her shoulders and rose to her full height. 'Now, corn or no corn, yer can get off yer backside an' get me a quarter of brawn, a tin loaf an' half of marg.'

'Okay, boss!' Maisie held on to the counter and pulled herself up. 'I'd love to see you in a room with Hitler...yer'd flatten him.'

'Flatten him! I'd bloody crucify him... an' all his ruddy cronies. An' I wouldn't need any help, the way I feel now. I'd do it all on me own.'

'The love of your life 'as just come in.' Maureen nudged her friend. 'His eyes are everywhere, lookin' for yer.'

'Don't let him see you lookin',' Doreen hissed. 'I don't want 'im to think I'm runnin' after him.'

'If yer not running after him, what the hell are we doin' here?' After a quick glance across the room, Maureen smiled knowingly. 'Ay out, he's on his way over.'

'Don't you let on yer've seen him, Maureen Shepherd, or I'll never speak to yer again.' Doreen felt a light touch on her arm and in the short time it took her to spin around, the frown on her face had been replaced by a smile. 'Hello, Phil.'

'I'm a bit late tonight, I had to work overtime.' Phil took her elbow. 'Shall we dance?' He was leading her towards the dance floor when he turned his head and grinned at Maureen. 'Hiya, Mo.'

'Hiya.' God, but he's handsome, Maureen thought, her heart beating fifteen to the dozen. He stands out a mile from all the other blokes. If he wasn't so smitten with Doreen I'd make a play for him myself.

'I nearly didn't make it tonight.' Holding Doreen close, Phil slowed down to gaze into her face. 'We're mad busy an' the boss asked me to work until ten o'clock.'

'How did yer get out of it?'

'Told him I had a heavy date with a girl outside Reece's.' White teeth gleamed and blue eyes twinkled. 'I said if I didn't turn up she'd be left stranded in town on her own.'

'You fibber! Fancy tellin' lies like that!'

'Why? Didn't yer care whether I came or not?' The look in Phil's eyes was so tender it made Doreen go weak at the knees. 'If I hadn't turned up, wouldn't yer have been a teeny-weeny bit disappointed?'

It was six weeks since they'd met and Thursday nights were the high spots of Doreen's life. She was counting the days to her sixteenth birthday, when she thought her mother wouldn't object to her going out on a date with Phil. She'd take him home first, of course, to meet the family, so they'd know she was in safe hands. After all, no one could help but like him, he was nice in every way. 'Yes, I would 'ave been disappointed.' She smiled into his face. 'I'd have had no one to dance with.'

Content with her response, Phil lengthened

his strides to match the tempo of the slow foxtrot. 'Is this the night I get to walk yer home?'

'I've explained to yer about Mo... I can't leave her. An' I can't expect her to tag along with us, she'd be embarrassed. Apart from that, me mam would do her nut if she knew I was on me own with a feller she didn't know. But when I'm sixteen yer can walk me home an' I'll take yer in to meet me mam an' dad.'

'Where do yer live, by the way?'

Doreen was looking over his shoulder when she gave him her address and missed seeing his face drain of colour. But when he stumbled and trod on her toe, she cried, 'Hey, watch it! Yer nearly crippled me!'

'Sorry.' Phil Bradley felt as though he'd been punched in the stomach. The only girl he'd ever really fallen for, and she had to live in the same street as himself. She'd know all about his family. It wouldn't do any good telling her he wasn't like the rest of them, that he hated the life they led and was waiting for the day when he would earn enough money to get a place of his own, somewhere miles away. As long as he lived under the same roof he'd be tarred with the same brush.

'What's the matter?' Doreen asked. 'Yer've gone very quiet.'

'I'm tired, that's all.' His heart filled with despair and a sense of hopelessness, Phil tried to smile. 'I've been workin' too hard.' Not for the first time, Phil wondered why his mother had married Tom Bradley. He would rather have been branded illegitimate than be a member of that family. He'd known from an early age that the man he called 'Dad' wasn't his real father. Hadn't he had the word 'bastard' thrown at him every time he refused to go out stealing? To give his mother her due, she had tried to shield him, because in her own way she did love him. But she was under the thumb of the man she'd married, and over the years Phil had seen her grow harder and coarser. There were times when, hearing her cursing and shouting obscenities in the street, he came close to hating her for bringing him into the world.

'Yer do look tired.' Doreen searched his face. 'Have yer far to walk home?'

'Er, no! I only live five minutes' walk from here.' Even as he spoke, Phil was asking himself what was the use of lying. He couldn't hide who he was from someone who only lived down the other end of their street. The only reason they'd never bumped into each other before now was because he always used the back entries.

His head pounding, Phil went through the dance routine automatically. Why was life so unfair? He was ashamed of his family, but never had he done anything himself to be ashamed of...not that anyone would believe it, with the reputation the Bradleys had. So what could he do? Tell Doreen the truth and hope she'd understand, or disappear from her life? Neither of the options appealed to him. He couldn't bear her rejection, it would break his heart. And even if she herself didn't reject him, her family certainly wouldn't welcome him with open arms. And who could blame them?

No, it was best to make a clean break. Taking a deep breath, Phil said, 'If I'm not here next week, yer'll know I've had to work late.'

'Ah, no! We only see each other once a week as it is!'

The disappointment on Doreen's face caused hope to flare in Phil's heart. She's as taken with me as I am with her! Perhaps if I... No, you can put that out of your head, he told himself. She likes you right enough, but she doesn't know your name is Philip Bradley.

'Go on, don't be a meanie.' Doreen fluttered her lashes at him. The thought of going two weeks without seeing him was one she couldn't bear. 'Tell them yer not feelin' well or something.'

As he looked into her eyes his resolve melted, while the hatred he felt for his family built up. Because of them, he was going to lose the girl he had fallen in love with. But he had to see her again, just one more time. 'Okay, I'll do me best.'

'That's not good enough.' Doreen pouted. 'I want yer to promise yer'll definitely be here.'

Phil smiled, even though his heart was aching. 'I promise.'

'The way you're goin' on, yer'll be married before your Jill.' Maureen grinned as she rubbed the sleeve of her coat across the steamed-up window of the tram. 'Like two flamin' lovebirds, yez are.'

'He is lovely, though, isn't he, Mo?' Doreen's

eyes were dreamy. He definitely liked her, she could tell by the sad look on his face when she'd said good night to him...as though he didn't want her to leave. 'I think me mam will approve, don't you?'

'If she doesn't, my mam will.' Maureen peered through the cleared glass. 'This is your stop, kiddo. I'll see yer in the mornin'.'

'Yeah, okay. Ta-ra, Mo.'

Doreen jumped from the tram, waved to Maureen, then ran up the street, hugging herself. In a couple of weeks, when he's walking me home, I wonder if he'll kiss me? I hope so, because I've never been kissed before. Not a real kiss, like you see on the pictures. Mike's had been more brotherly pecks. He was a nice lad, was Mike, and she was fond of him. But he didn't thrill her as Phil did, didn't stir her emotions.

Doreen rummaged in her bag for her door key, and as she slipped it into the lock she was humming with happiness. She'd heard people talking about love at first sight and had thought it was a load of old tripe...but it was true! The minute she'd clapped eyes on Phil she'd fallen for him, hook, line and sinker.

'I thought yer'd be in bed by now.' Doreen was surprised to see her mother and father sitting quietly listening to the wireless. The serious expressions on their faces caused her to ask, 'What's up?'

'Bloody Hitler, that's what's up!' Molly lifted her hand. 'Sshh, let's listen.'

Doreen dropped her dance shoes and slipped

304

out of her coat. Standing by the door, she listened to the words coming from the set. From the tone of the man's voice, whatever had happened was serious. Hitler's name was mentioned, then soldiers, guns and tanks. 'What's happened, Dad?'

Jack took a deep breath and let it out slowly between clenched teeth. 'Germany's invaded Czechoslovakia.' He took another deep breath and there was anger in his voice when he continued. 'It's been stickin' out a mile what he was up to. They've had soldiers massed at the border for weeks, and anyone with half an ounce of intelligence could see what he was going to do. But apart from a few warnings from the likes of Chamberlain, no one did anythin' about it. Now he's lifted his two fingers up to the lot of us and marched into Czechoslovakia with whole armies, tanks and aeroplanes. And I'll bet a pound to a pinch of snuff he gets away with it, because no one is strong enough to bloody well stand up to him.' Jack only ever swore when he was worried or in a temper, and right now he was blazing. 'He's been gearing up for this for years and we should have seen it coming. But instead of building our forces up, we've sat on our bloody backsides and let it happen.'

'Perhaps the Czechoslovakian people will stop him,' Molly's face was drained of colour. 'They're bound to fight back—they won't just stand there and let Hitler take over their country.'

'Well I can't see them being able to stop him. He's got enough forces and armaments to take

305

on the whole of Europe. Yer'd have thought we'd have learned our lesson from the last war, but no, we've well and truly been caught with our trousers down.'

Doreen sat on the arm of the couch. 'Will we get dragged into a war, Dad?'

'I'm not very clever, love, but to me it's as plain as the nose on yer face. If Hitler takes Czechoslovakia—and I've no doubts he will—he won't be content. He'll go for another small country, and then another.' Jack lit a cigarette and drew deeply. 'He's got to be stopped.'

Doreen met her mother's eyes. 'Does that mean all the young fellers will be called up?'

'I dunno, sunshine, I don't know what to think.' Molly ran her fingers through her hair. 'It's beyond me why men want to fight each other.'

'Sshh!' Jack lifted a hand for silence. His ear cocked towards the wireless, he listened intently. Then he shook his head. 'That's the beginning... Chamberlain has denounced Hitler and recalled our ambassador.'

'Does that mean we're at war?' Molly asked, her hands tightly clasped on her lap.

'Not yet...not officially. But mark my words, it won't be long before we are.'

'They wouldn't call you up, would they, Dad?'

'No, not an old crock like me.' Jack noticed the frown on his daughter's pretty face and cursed himself for helping to put it there. Time enough to worry when and if his gut feeling was turned into reality. 'Anyway, as the saying goes, "don't worry, it may never happen".'

'Ooh, I hope not.'

They heard the key in the lock and three pairs of eyes were on the door when Jill came through. 'I'm sorry I'm a bit late, Mam, but I was listening to the news on the wireless at Steve's.' She put her handbag down on the floor. 'Sounds pretty grim, doesn't it?'

'Well, it's certainly nothin' to celebrate.' Molly put her hands on the sides of her chair and pushed herself up. 'It's a pity Hitler's mother didn't drown him at birth...she'd have been doin' us all a favour.'

'Now as yer come to mention it,' Jack's brow was furrowed, 'isn't it funny that all they've written in the papers about Hitler, there's never been one word said about his family?'

'They've probably disowned 'im,' Molly grunted. 'Who in their right mind would want him for a son, or a brother?'

'Funny that,' Jack mused, 'he must have some family.'

'I dunno, an' I don't ruddy well care.' As she untied the knots in her pinny, a sudden smile crossed Molly's face. 'Perhaps he's been made up of nuts and bolts...like that Frankenstein monster.'

'Don't be daft, Mam, that wasn't real! It was only a picture!' Too late, Doreen saw the twinkle in her mother's eye and blushed. 'Oh, you!'

'Me mam's right about one thing,' Jill said, 'Hitler is a monster.'

'Whatever he is, I'm not goin' to lose any

sleep over him.' Molly yawned and stretched her arms aloft. 'If I do dream, it'll be about Ray Milland or Cary Grant, not a little feller with a stupid moustache who struts around with his hand in the air shouting "Heil Hitler".'

'Ay, come off it!' Jack pointed a stiffened finger. 'If you do dream, it had better be about me or I'll want to know why.'

'Don't be gettin' yer knickers in a twist.' Molly bent towards him and rubbed her nose against his. 'Yer see, in me dreams I'm not me! I mean, with the best will in the world, yer can't see Clark Gable kissing me, now can yer? So I make believe I'm Jean Harlow, Myrna Loy or Constance Bennett. I wear glamorous chiffon or flowing silk dresses, an' I lay on a chaise-longue with a glass of champagne in one hand and a cigarette holder in the other. An' I have all these handsome men kneeling in front of me, paying homage, like.'

All thoughts of war forgotten, Jack's hearty chuckle filled the room. 'No wonder yer like going to bed early, yer have a fine time in this secret life of yours.'

Jill had pulled out a chair and sat down, her elbows resting on the table, her face cupped in her hands. 'Go on, Mam, it was just gettin' interesting.'

'Yeah, go 'ed, Mam.' Doreen sounded eager. 'Tell us what happens.'

'Oh, how soft you are!' Molly gave Jack a broad wink before straightening up. 'Yez can go and find yer own dreams, 'cos yer not being invited into mine.'

'Oh, all right, meanie.' Doreen stuck her tongue out cheekily. 'I won't tell yer about my dreams, so there!'

Jill turned to her sister, a smile on her face. 'Talking about dreams, was your dreamboat at the dance?'

Doreen blushed to the roots of her hair. 'He's not my dreamboat, just a bloke I dance with.' Then she realised she was being stupid. After all, she'd be wanting to bring Phil home in a couple of weeks, so it would be better to prepare her parents. The thought gave her the courage to go on to say, 'He is nice, though, an' I do like him.'

'Don't be gettin' too serious, sunshine, 'cos one engagement in the family is enough to be going on with.' Molly made for the door, scratching her head and yawning. 'Anyway, yer far too young to be courting.'

'Can I ask 'im to me birthday party? Then yer can see him for yerself.'

'Birthday party!' Molly croaked. 'Who said anythin' about yer having a birthday party?'

'Ah, go on, Mam! Not a real party, just a few friends.'

'Ask yer dad...I'm too tired to think straight.' Molly walked from the room, calling, 'Good night and God bless, everyone.'

'Can I, Dad?'

How can I refuse? Jack asked himself. Jill was courting Steve when she was only fifteen and he couldn't make fish of one and flesh of the other. 'You can certainly ask him along, love, an' a few of yer friends. But don't expect too

309

much, because yer mam's got Jill's engagement party comin' off an' that'll cost a few bob.'

'Ooh, thanks, Dad.'

Doreen didn't need to dwell on her mother's dreams that night—she had plenty of her own. All happy dreams, and Phil was in all of them.

When the knock sounded at half past seven the next morning, Molly looked down in dismay at her scruffy dressing gown. 'Who the heck's knocking at this time in the morning?' she muttered as she walked down the hall. 'The flamin' streets are not even aired yet.'

'I'm sorry to bother yer so early, Molly,' Ellen Clarke fussed, 'but I told Tony I'd open up this morning so he could get to the abattoir.'

'Yer surely haven't given me the fright of me life just to tell me that?' Molly tutted. 'I thought someone was dead.'

'Our Gordon wasn't a bit well last night...he had a real temperature an' I didn't like leaving him. So I was wonderin' if yer'd do me a favour and nip up to Corker's when yer've got time and pass his message on to his mam? I feel mean not goin' up to see her meself, but there's no way I could 'ave left our Gordon, not the way he was.'

'Yeah, of course I'll tell her,' Molly assured her. 'I'll slip up as soon as I've got Ruthie off to school. But what about Gordon? Who's lookin' after him while you're at work?'

'I'm keepin' our Phoebe off school, she'll look after him. He's not nearly so bad today, just a sore throat, no temperature.'

'You poppy off to work and don't worry. I'll see Mrs Corkhill an' I'll also keep an eye on Gordon.'

'Thanks, Molly, yer a pal.' Ellen waved as she hurried away. She was lucky to have a neighbour like Molly Bennett...salt of the earth, she was.

Chapter Eighteen

'What a ruddy mess yer makin',' Molly joked to one of the workmen busy laying electricity cables. 'When yer get down to our 'ouse I'll have a brush an' shovel at the ready, so yez can clean up after yerselves.'

The workman laughed, a grimy hand pushing his cap to the back of his head. 'As long as yer keep us supplied with cups of tea, I'll personally make sure they wipe their feet every time they pass your house.'

'How long before yer down to me?'

'I'd say about two weeks...three at the most.'

'Ooh, the gear! We'll have 'leccy light for me daughter's engagement party!' Molly moved her shoulders up and down to show her pleasure. 'We won't know we're born, will we? Just think, no more standin' on a chair to light the gas, an' no more ruddy gas mantles! Plus, we'll be able to see what we're saying.'

'I like me tea with two sugars,' the man called as Molly made to walk away. 'An' strong enough to stand the spoon up in.'

'Oh, aye, gettin' cocky now, are yer?' Molly laughed. 'Yer'll get what yer given and like it.'

She was in a happy frame of mind as she walked to Corker's. She wouldn't know herself when they had electric light. No more sore eyes trying to read or sew by gaslight. And if her ma was to be believed, the electric meter didn't take any more coppers than the gas had.

Molly lifted the knocker and gave a light rap. And while she waited for an answer she gazed across the street to the Bradley house. No improvement there...the raggedy curtains were still pulled across windows that had never seen a chammy leather, and the windowsills were filthy.

'Hello, Molly.'

Molly's mouth gaped. 'Corker! What the 'ell are you doin' home? I've come up to give yer mam this message yer sent, an' here yer are!'

'Come in.' Corker stood aside to let her pass. 'I just got back to the ship after ringin' Maisie from a phone box, an' the Captain said I could have three days' leave.' He followed her down the hall. 'I didn't ring again because I was rushing around, ready to get the night train.'

'Hiya, Mrs Corkhill.' Molly made straight for the roaring fire and spread her hands out in front of the warmth. Although it was March and the worst of the winter was over, there was a cold wind out. 'I did pass the message on to Ellen, but she couldn't come last night because young Gordon wasn't well. If I'd known, I'd have come meself.'

Corker took hold of Molly's arm and pulled her around. There was concern on his face as he asked, 'What's wrong with the little feller?'

'Ellen said he had a temperature and she was frightened to leave him. But when she knocked this morning she said he was a lot better.'

'Has she gone to work an' left him?'

'No, Phoebe's stayed off school. An' I said I'd keep an eye out for them.' Rubbing her hands, Molly smiled at Mrs Corkhill. 'Made up to have yer son home, eh?'

'I was beginning to think he'd run off. One letter I've had from him since he went away...just one!' Mrs Corkhill craned her neck to look up at the son she adored. 'I've been worried sick about yer.'

'Now, Ma, what could happen to me?' Corker placed his two huge hands around her waist and lifted her up as easily as he would a china doll. 'D'yer not think I'm old and ugly enough to look after meself?'

'Put me down, yer daft beggar.' Mrs Corkhill pushed against his chest, pretending to be angry with him. 'One lousy letter in all that time.'

'Ma, there's no pillar boxes in the middle of the ocean.' Corker put her down gently. 'An' yer know I'm no good at letter-writing... I can't spell an' I never know what to write about.'

'That's a poor excuse.' Mrs Corkhill gave Molly a sly wink as she bustled towards the kitchen. 'Yer don't deserve it, but I suppose I'd better make yer something to eat.'

'Bacon and egg, with some fried bread, Ma.'

Corker licked his lips. 'And plenty of bacon fat to dip me bread in.'

'So, yer've only got three days, Corker?' Molly asked as they heard the gas plop under the frying pan. 'Not long, is it?'

'Only two days really, today and tomorrow. I'll have to travel back on Friday morning. I caught the night train last night so I could have the extra day, but I wouldn't like to do that again, the journey seemed endless.'

'Ellen will get a surprise,' Molly said. 'Will you call in the shop and let her know?'

Corker nodded, then looked towards the kitchen where the bacon could be heard sizzling in the pan. In a low voice he said, 'I want her to ask for the day off tomorrow so we can go an' see Nobby.'

Molly's brow shot up in surprise. 'Why d'yer want to waste one of yer days goin' all the way to Winwick?'

'Not now.' Corker put a finger to his lips. 'I'll tell yer another time.'

Mrs Corkhill popped her head around the door. 'Nearly ready, son. Will yer set the table for me?'

Molly moved towards the hall. 'I'll make meself scarce so yer can eat in peace. D'yer want me to ask our Jill to sit with Ellen's kids tonight, so yez can go out?'

Corker chuckled. 'You're a mind-reader, Molly Bennett.'

'Call in to ours when yer've got a minute, I've somethin' to tell yer about the Bradleys. Me an' Nellie have done a bit of detecting work.'

314

'I was asking Ma about them when yer knocked.' Corker saw his mother coming from the kitchen with a plate in her hand and he jumped up. 'Hang on a minute, Ma, while I get the cloth.'

'Have you seen anythin' of the Bradleys, Mrs Corkhill?' Molly asked. 'Not been botherin' yer, have they?'

'Molly, me door's firmly closed an' I keep meself to meself. They haven't been near me since the last little do, but I know the neighbours are plagued by them. Living right opposite, I can't help but see and hear things. Still, as long as they leave me alone I'm not going to get involved.'

'Quite right, sunshine.' Molly was staring at the plate of bacon, eggs, tomatoes and black pudding. It looked so appetising she could feel her mouth watering. 'I'm going before I ask for a drippin' buttie.'

'Yer can have one, lass, I've got some dripping in.'

'No, thanks, Mrs Corkhill, me eyes are bigger than me belly. It's not long since I had me breakfast, so I can't possibly be hungry.' Molly wrapped her coat closely around her body. 'I'll be on me way, but I'll see yer tonight, eh, Corker?'

'You will that, Molly me darlin'.' Corker had made a bacon sandwich and it was halfway to his mouth when he said, 'I'll pick Ellen up, then we'll give yer a knock.'

'I'll see you to the door, Molly.' Mrs Corkhill wiped her hands down the front of her pinny.

315

'When my son's got a plate of food in front of him, not even the King could take his mind off it.'

When Molly reached the end of the terrace she hesitated, debating whether to slip around and see her parents, or call to the Clarkes first to see how Gordon was. After dithering for a moment, she muttered aloud, 'Me ma first, then Gordon.'

Bridie's face lit up when she saw her daughter. 'Now this is a pleasant surprise, so it is. Yer da will be happy to have someone to talk to...he was just complainin' that he's fed up talking to the flowers on the wallpaper.'

Molly gave her mother a peck on the cheek before breezing through to the living room. 'Top of the mornin' to yer, Da!'

Bob laid down the morning paper, a smile creasing his face. 'Hello, lass, it's good to see you.'

'I can't stay long, but I've always got time for a cup of tea.' There was tenderness in Molly's eyes and sadness in her heart. Her da had aged so much since his heart attack. His face was pale and lined, and he seemed to have shrunk in size. He didn't half miss going out to work, and the camaraderie of his workmates. He was always restless these days, fretting because the doctor had told him he mustn't do anything strenuous, and Bridie made sure he did as he was told.

'Sure, I don't need the house to fall in on me before I take a hint, so I don't.' Bridie headed for the kitchen. 'One pot of tea coming up.'

'Pour me the first cup, Ma, yer know I don't like it too strong.' Molly settled herself on a chair near the fire. 'How yer diddling, Da?'

'Plodding on, lass, just plodding on. I get fed up sometimes, being so inactive, but still, I mustn't complain.'

'Why don't yer get yerself a hobby to while away the time?'

'Hobby? What sort of hobby, lass?'

'I dunno, but there must be somethin' yer can do.' Molly pondered for a while, then her face lit up. 'I know, yer could make a rug! I can get yer a piece of sacking an' me ma must have an old coat she could cut up. If she hasn't, I have! All me flamin' coats are as old as the hills.'

Bob shook his head. 'That's not for me, lass, that's woman's work.'

'Are you kiddin'? Jack's better at the old hook than I am! When I was makin' the rugs in our bedrooms, he did more work on them than I did!'

'Now isn't that a good idea?' Bridie came through carrying a tray. She too worried about her husband having nothing to occupy his mind, but she'd never have thought of rug-making in a million years. She threw Molly a look of gratitude as she set the tray on the table. 'We could do with one for the side of the bed, save puttin' our feet on the cold lino. But instead of using old rags I'll buy some wool and make a nice colourful one.'

'Oh, aye? And what will you be doing while I'm slaving away?'

'Sure, won't I be sitting at the other end of the sack, helping yer with it? It'll be a joint venture, so it will.'

'That's what Jack and I did.' Molly leaned forward to gaze into her father's face. 'One each end, an' we met in the middle.'

'Okay, I know when I'm beat.' Bob gave a deep sigh, but he wasn't displeased. After all, if Jack did it, why couldn't he? Jack was certainly no sissy boy. 'With two of yer against me, I don't stand a snowball's chance in hell.'

'Right!' Molly said triumphantly. 'I'll ask Tucker for a clean sack when he delivers me coal...he's due tomorrow.'

'Here's your tea, lass.' The two conspirators smiled at each other. 'An' there's some ginger snaps on the plate, help yerself.'

'Ooh, me favourites.' Molly made a dive for the plate. 'Yer don't mind if I dunk them, do yer, Ma?' Without waiting for a reply, she dipped the biscuit into her tea. 'No, I thought yer wouldn't.'

'In the name of God, Corker, are you following me, or is it the other way around?' Molly looked up at the big man, who had opened the Clarkes' door in answer to her knock. 'Yer keep poppin' up like a flamin' jack-in-the-box.'

Corker roared with laughter. 'Just keepin' an eye on yer, Molly me darlin', making sure yer don't get up to any mischief.'

'Fat chance of that, Corker! Can yer imagine me having a fancy man on the sly?'

'Well, now, I dunno.' Corker kept his face

318

straight while he stroked his beard. 'Yer a fine figure of a woman, Molly Bennett.'

'Perhaps I should buy a new mirror, Corker, because the one we've got makes me look more like Patsy Kelly than Loretta Young.' A grin crossed Molly's face as a picture of the American comedienne flashed through her mind. She was no oil painting, was Patsy Kelly, but she was one of Molly's favourite film stars. If she was in a picture then you were bound to get a laugh. 'Anyway, Corker, standin' here isn't goin' to get me work done. How is Gordon?'

'Phoebe said he'd done nothin' but whinge since Ellen went to work, but he seems to have perked up a bit now. His throat is inflamed and it's probably sore, so it's only natural he'd want his mam here to mollycoddle him.'

'He'll be more than happy to have you around...thinks the world of Sinbad, does Gordon. Anyway, d'yer want me to stay with him for an hour while you get about yer business?'

Corker shook his head. 'I'm just making him some porridge, nice and thin so he'll have no trouble swallowing it. Then he should sleep for a couple of hours. But I'd be grateful if yer'd slip in this afternoon, just to make sure he's all right. It could be tonsillitis he's got, but we'll wait till Ellen gets home, see what she says.'

'Are yer callin' to the shop to let her know yer home?'

'Yeah. I want to have a word with Tony, see if she can have the day off tomorrow.'

'What on earth d'yer want to go to Winwick

for? It'll only be a waste of time... Nobby won't even know yez.'

'I have my reasons.' Corker turned his head when the sound of a wail reached his ears. 'I'd better get back to him. But if you an' Jack can come for a drink tomorrow night, I'll tell yer what they are. Yer know what Ellen's like, if I leave it to her we'll never get anywhere. She's frightened of what people will say, but me, I couldn't give a monkey's uncle what anyone thinks. Except for me friends, that is. An' as I count you and Jack, and Nellie and George, as me best friends, I want to be open an' above board with yez.'

Ooh, Molly thought, it sounds very mysterious. She would have loved to question him further, but she could see he was on pins to get back to the sick boy. Patience wasn't one of her virtues, but this time she had no option but to keep her curiosity in check. 'I'll give Nellie the eye-eye an' we'll see yer tomorrow night, then, Corker. But in the meantime, I'll ask Jill and Steve to sit with the kids tonight.'

'Thanks, Molly. If Gordon's no better, I'll let them know, 'cos Ellen won't want to leave him. But I'm crushing two aspirin into his porridge, so that might do the trick.' He held up his huge hand. 'See, I'm keeping me fingers crossed.'

'An' I'll cross everythin' I've got...see if that helps.' Molly smiled as she turned away. A sick child was no laughing matter, but she could imagine Jack's face if she was cross-eyed when he came in from work.

320

Ellen was shaking visibly as they walked up the path to Winwick Hospital for the Insane. The place itself was enough to unnerve her, without the added dread of seeing Nobby. Even the pressure of Corker's hand on her elbow did little to relieve her tension.

'Ellen, love, it'll all be over in an hour, so stop worrying.' There was tenderness and sympathy in Corker's voice as he looked down from his great height. 'It's somethin' we've got to do, and the sooner we get it over with the better.'

'Corker, yer've no idea how awful I feel. Even the sound of his name makes me want to shrivel up inside.'

'But he can't harm you, love.' Corker squeezed her elbow. 'I'll make sure he never hurts you again.'

'Promise yer won't leave me alone with him?'

'I promise.' Corker pushed the door open and stood aside to let Ellen through. 'We'll ask to see Nobby first, then you can stay in the corridor while I have a word with one of the doctors.'

A male nurse led them down stark corridors, passing doors through which maniacal laughter, screams and animal noises came. If it hadn't been for Corker's restraining arm across her shoulders, Ellen would have turned and fled. She had sympathy for those forced to live out their lives in such dreadful surroundings, for no one chose to be mad. But the deep scars left on her mind by the years of brutality and humiliation heaped on her by her husband were too raw for her to forgive him.

The nurse unlocked a door and swung it open. 'I'm afraid Mr Clarke isn't in a very good mood today,' he said softly. 'Would you like me to stay in the room?'

'That won't be necessary,' Corker said gruffly.

The nurse sized up the giant of a man and mentally agreed. Here was someone who could lift Nobby Clarke up with one hand if the occasion arose. Pity he didn't work here, they could do with someone like him. Especially when Nobby was in one of his violent moods. He was a bad bastard, was Nobby Clarke, disliked and feared by all the staff. 'I'll have to lock the door...rules, you understand. But I'll only be outside, so knock when you're ready to leave.'

Corker waited till he heard the key turn, then led Ellen towards the man sitting in a chair with his back to them, looking out of the barred window. The room was small and cheerless, the only furniture a small iron bed, a square, heavy table, and the chair Nobby was sitting on. When Ellen looked at him questioningly after glancing around for somewhere to sit, Corker nodded to the wide ledge of the window.

'Hello, Nobby.' Corker waited for Ellen to sit, then lowered himself into the narrow space beside her. 'How are yer?'

Nobby gazed from one to the other, no sign of recognition in the deep-sunken eyes. Seconds turned into a minute, and Ellen could feel the fear building up inside her. She clasped her hands nervously as the unblinking eyes fixed on her, and the words 'we shouldn't have 'come' repeated themselves over and over in her mind.

Then suddenly, without warning, Nobby gripped the arms of his chair and lunged towards Ellen until their faces were almost touching. She could see the saliva trickling from his mouth as a flow of obscenities was screamed at her, and the venom sparking from his eyes was so strong she thought she was going to faint with fear. A cry left her lips as she fell back against the window, trying to put as much distance between them as she could.

'What the hell!' Corker jumped to his feet, pushed Nobby back into his chair and stood in front of him, shielding Ellen from the onslaught. He cursed himself for being caught off guard, but the attack had come out of the blue and he wasn't prepared. He felt like taking Nobby by the throat and shaking him like a rag doll for forcing Ellen to listen to some of the worst language Corker had ever heard. But as he gazed down into the grinning, slobbering face, he asked God to forgive him for the evil thoughts running through his mind. Taking a deep breath, he said softly, 'You haven't changed, have yer, Nobby? You always were a bastard.'

Making sure he was blocking any movement Nobby might make, Corker turned his head. 'Are you all right, love?'

Ellen cleared her throat. 'Can we go now, please?'

'Go an' knock on the door.'

Only when the door had been opened and

323

Ellen was safely in the corridor did Corker move. Without a backward glance, he strode from the room with Nobby's hysterical laughter ringing in his ears.

'I'd like to see one of the doctors in charge,' Corker said, as the nurse turned the key. 'I want some information.'

'I'm afraid all the doctors are busy. If it's information about Mr Clarke yer want, perhaps I can help.'

But Corker was adamant. 'My ship sails tomorrow so I've no time to spare. It's urgent that I see a doctor, and I want to see him now.'

'If you'll wait here, I'll see if I can find one.' As he walked away, the nurse hung a bunch of keys on a belt around his waist. 'I'll be as quick as I can.'

Ellen gazed up at Corker. 'Couldn't you leave it until another time. I feel as though I'm goin' to be sick.'

'No, love, it's got to be now. If we keep putting if off we'll never get ourselves sorted out. And it would mean another trip up here...I'm sure yer don't fancy goin' through a scene like that again, do yer?'

Ellen shivered. 'I'll never come here again.'

'That's settled then. We'll get it over with once and for all.'

Ellen and Corker were already in the snug bar when Molly and Nellie came in, followed by Jack and George. 'You're quick off the mark, aren't yer, Corker?' Molly eyed the drinks lined

324

up on the table. 'Don't hang around, do yer?'

'Life's too short to hang around, Molly me darlin'.' Corker's smile of welcome covered the four arrivals. 'Sit yerselves down an' take the weight off yer feet.'

The conversation between the men went from Corker's last trip to the latest news from Europe. And all the while Molly was getting more impatient. Ellen was always quiet, but tonight she was very nervous and withdrawn. Every time Molly caught her eye, she would look away quickly, as though she was afraid of being questioned. She hadn't called in tonight on her way home from work, and that in itself was unusual. In the end, Molly decided to take the bull by the horns, even though she knew Jack would give her cow eyes. 'How did yez find Nobby?'

Ellen's head dropped and she gazed at the glass in her hand. This was going to be more upsetting than the visit to Winwick. She'd asked Corker not to mention anything, but he'd said that the Bennetts and the McDonoughs were their friends and it was only right they were told.

'No change.' Corker went on to explain in detail what had happened. Then he waited until the various views had been aired before saying, 'I had a word with one of the doctors.'

'Oh, aye?' Molly leaned forward, her eyes bright with interest. 'What did he have to say about Nobby?'

Corker took a long swill of beer before answering. 'The reason I wanted to see the doctor wasn't really to ask about Nobby's health. I wanted to know if there was any chance of him ever gettin' out of there and comin' home.'

'There isn't, is there?' Nellie sounded shocked at the idea.

Corker shook his head. 'No. We'd already been told that, last time we were there, but I wanted to make sure.' Corker put his glass down and reached to take one of Ellen's hands in his. 'Yer see, I want Ellen to divorce him an' marry me.'

Four mouths gaped and four glasses were set down as four heads tried to marshal their thoughts into some sort of order. Molly was the first to recover. 'Can she get a divorce from him?'

Corker scrutinised each face for disapproval, but found none. Shock and surprise, yes, but no disapproval. 'The doctor seems to think so. In his words, if Ellen can produce proof that her husband is insane, with no possibility of him ever returning to a normal life, she should have no problem in gettin' a divorce on those grounds.'

'That's a blessing, isn't it, girl?' Nellie patted Ellen's arm. 'I'm not goin' to be a hypocrite an' say I'm sorry for Nobby, 'cos I'm not. He gave you an' the kids a dog's life...yer better off without him.'

'Nellie's right,' George said. 'Although I shouldn't say it under, the circumstances, I couldn't stand the man. No one who knew him had a good word to say about him.'

'I hope God's not listening in to this conversation,' Molly said. 'We're all being very uncharitable. But as Nobby only has himself to blame for where he is, I think God would understand when I say it's good riddance to bad rubbish.' She quickly made a sign of the cross. 'I'll say an extra prayer tonight, just in case.'

Corker was watching Jack's face. 'What about you, Jack?'

'I think Molly's right in saying we're uncharitable...we should all feel pity for someone who's locked up in a madhouse.' Jack gazed at Ellen's bowed head as he remembered the sounds that used to come from the house next door when she was being subjected to beatings. How she used to walk down the street with her eyes to the ground, her pride and dignity having been knocked out of her over the years. And the kids in their dirty, raggedy clothes, hair alive with fleas because Ellen couldn't afford to keep them clean. Like their mother they were terrified of their own shadows. 'But we all know what Nobby was, and I agree with Nellie. We'd be hypocrites to pretend he was anything but a violent, evil man.' Jack put a finger under Ellen's chin and raised her head. 'You go for your divorce, Ellen, an' I wish you an' Corker the best of luck...yer both deserve it.'

'I'll say they do!' Molly felt as though a weight had been lifted from her shoulders. Jack was a bit straight-laced, didn't believe in divorce, and she'd been afraid of his reaction. Ellen was in a bad enough state as it was without anyone going all religious on her.

'I'm made up for yer, girl.' Nellie nodded her head along with her chins. 'Yer've got a good man in Corker.'

'Just one thing, though.' Molly grinned. 'Don't get married this year, eh? All me money's spoke for with our Jill's engagement party.'

'Molly, it takes at least two years for a divorce to come through.' Corker was relieved the ordeal was over. He wanted his friends' approval, and he'd got it. 'Plenty of time for yer to save up.'

Nellie preened herself. 'Can I be a brides-maid?' She started to shake with laughter. 'Yer'd have no need to buy me a bridesmaid's dress, a barrage balloon would do.' Her cheeks moved upwards to cover her eyes as her tummy shook with laughter. 'That's about the only bloody thing that would fit me.'

Chapter Nineteen

Victoria Clegg shivered and pulled her rocking chair nearer the fender. The dying embers in the grate weren't giving out much heat, but it wasn't worth putting more coal on because the play she was listening to on the wireless would be finished soon and then she'd be off to bed. In fact she'd put the gaslight out half an hour ago, at her usual time for climbing the stairs, but then she'd found herself so gripped by the murder mystery she knew she wouldn't get off to sleep for wondering who the murderer was. She wasn't even tired now, because the plot was so exciting it had her gripping the arms of the chair.

'Well!' She spoke to the empty room as the music heralded the end of the play. 'I'd never have guessed that! Fancy him being the murderer! I could have sworn it was the brother, he had a real sinister voice.'

Victoria pushed her chair back and made her way to the sideboard where a candle was standing on a saucer ready to be lit. 'Now where did I put that box of matches?' She ran her hand over the shiny surface. 'I'm sure I put them on here, but they seem to have disappeared.' With her left hand she made a thorough search between the two brass candlesticks, the statue of the Whistling Boy, and framed photographs of her parents. All to no avail. Then she remembered that the same thing had happened once before and she'd found the matches on the ledge of the window that overlooked the yard.

'I'm getting forgetful in me old age.' Victoria had lived in the house for over eighty years and could find her way blindfolded, so it was easy for her to skirt the table and chairs without bumping into them. 'I just hope they're here...I'll be in queer street if they're not.' She put her hand on the ledge under the closed curtains and ran it along, parting the curtains slightly as she did so.

'Success!' Victoria sighed with relief as her hand came into contact with the box of Bryant and May. 'I'd lose me head if it wasn't stuck on.' She glanced up at the sky. 'It's a nice clear night. We'll have summer on us before we know it.'

She was about to close the gap in the curtains when her heart jumped. On no, not again! Her eyes screwed up, she moved closer to the window. It is, she cried silently...there's a man on the top of the wall! Glued to the spot with fear, she saw him swing his leg over and drop into her yard.

'Oh, dear God, help me, please!' Her mind was telling her to run but her feet refused to move. It was only when she saw the figure creeping stealthily up the yard that she was galvanised into action. 'I've got to get out. Whoever it is out there, they're up to no good.'

Her breath coming in short gasps, she ran from the room as quickly as she could, down the hall to the front door. The bolt was a bit stiff and she cursed the stroke that had taken away the use of her right arm. When the bolt creaked back, she sighed with relief and flung the door open. In her eagerness to get away from the house she almost fell off the front step. Her intention was to knock at the Watsons' next door, but the house was in darkness. Oh, dear God, they're in bed!

Her heart beating fifteen to the dozen, Victoria looked up and down the street. The pale-yellow glow from the streetlamps showed that there wasn't a soul in sight, and her panic grew. She couldn't think straight, her head was in such a whirl. But even in her fuddled state she knew she had to get help...there was no way she could go back into that house on her own. Then came the most welcoming sound she'd ever heard, the raised voices of people coming out of the pub in the corner.

Stumbling over the cobblestones in her slippers, she crossed the road and ran towards the voices. As she neared them, she heard one she recognised. 'Oh, Molly, thank God it's you. Help me, please!'

Philip Bradley was yawning as he turned into the entry. He felt so weary he could have gone to sleep on his feet. Working from eight in the morning till ten at night was no joke...it was all bed and work. And as if that wasn't bad enough, the foreman had asked him to work all day Saturday and Sunday. They were mad busy in their workshop, couldn't get the orders out quick enough. Still, the extra few bob in his wage packet would come in handy. He badly needed a new pair of working shoes, the ones he was wearing were nearly falling off his feet.

Higher up the entry he could see the outline of someone sitting astride a wall, but being so deep in thought, it didn't register at first that it was an unusual sight to see at this time of night. Then his brain became alert and his tiredness fell away. He'd know that figure anywhere...it was his so-called-brother. What the hell was he up to now?

Phil quickened his pace but the figure had disappeared before he could reach it. There were two back doors close to each other and he

331

wasn't sure which yard his brother had entered. There was no doubt in his mind that it was his brother, he wouldn't put anything past the thieving beggar. If he knew which yard he was in, he'd go after him...stop him from robbing some poor soul.

Then Phil heard the sound of a bolt being drawn, slowly, so it wouldn't make a noise. Making it easy for a quick getaway, Phil thought darkly. He rubbed his chin, considering what action to take. Perhaps he'd be wise not to get involved...he might end up in trouble himself. But he couldn't just walk away knowing someone was going to be robbed, could he?

'To hell with it,' Phil muttered, laying his rolled-up overalls on the ground. 'This is one time he's not gettin' away with it. I'll break his bloody neck for him before I'll stand by and let him ransack someone's home.'

'Miss Clegg!' The friends gathered around the distressed woman as Molly put her arm across her shoulders to steady her. 'Just take it nice an' easy, sunshine, an' tell us what's wrong.'

'There's...a...a...man in me yard.' Victoria gulped in the fresh air and tried to calm herself. No one could harm her now, her friends would see to that. 'I saw him on the wall, then he was creeping towards the house.' She started to sob, 'I think he was goin' to break in.'

'Is he still there?' Corker boomed.

Victoria nodded. 'I think so. He didn't see me because me light was out. I ran out the front...I was so frightened.'

'Right! We'll catch the bugger.' Corker took command. 'Jack, you go in the front, and me an' George will nip around the back. Between us we'll have him dead to rights.'

'I'm comin' with yez,' Nellie said, hurrying after the men. 'I'm not missin' this.'

'I'll give our Tommy a shout,' Molly called, 'just in case we need him. Yer never know, there might be a gang of them.'

'I'll stay with Miss Clegg.' Ellen took the old lady's arm. 'Come on, love, we'll walk up to our house.'

Brian Bradley pressed lightly on the kitchen window and a sly smirk crossed his face when it moved at his touch. This was going to be a doddle. There was enough gap between the top and bottom frame to slide his knife in and force the catch. Once he was inside the house there'd be no problem, because he'd seen the light being put out half an hour ago, which meant that the old lady had gone to bed. He'd hung around until now, giving her time to fall asleep.

He slid the knife between the frames and moved it along until he found the catch. Good...it was moving. Another minute and he'd be inside the house. Then he felt a pair of hands encircle his throat and his blood ran cold. His eyes wide with fear, he tried to turn his head but fingers tightened on his windpipe, threatening to cut off his air supply.

'Don't say a word,' a voice hissed, 'and don't try anything or I'll throttle yer. Now, turn around and get back out.'

More terrified than he'd ever been in his life, Brian dropped the knife and allowed himself to be frogmarched down the yard. 'Open the door,' the voice hissed, adding pressure to his throat. 'An' if yer know what's good for yer, yer won't make a sound.'

Once out in the entry, Brian heard the door being closed at the same time as he was flung face forward against the opposite wall. He yelped with pain when his nose came into contact with the bricks, and he felt blood spurt out and run down over his mouth. But the pain wasn't his biggest worry. Uppermost in his mind was the need to escape. He had to get away or he'd be in real trouble. Holding his nose, he bent over and tried to make a dash for it. But he'd only taken two steps when he was caught by the scruff of his neck. 'Oh no you don't!'

Once again he was flung against the wall, but this time he was facing his adversary. His mouth gaped in surprise. 'You!'

'Yes, me.' Phil pushed him back against the wall when he tried to step forward. 'An' yer better get yer hands up because I'm goin' to give yer the hidin' of yer life.'

'Don't be so bleedin' daft! Just wait till I tell our dad what yer've done. He'll kill yer.'

'He's not "our dad", he's *your* dad. Yer've always had great delight to throwin' that at me, haven't yer? Thought it hurt me when yer called me a bastard and laughed behind me back. Well, I'll tell yer now, I'd rather be a bastard than a Bradley.' Phil had never before felt such an overpowering rage. He'd always known that the whole family lived on their wits...robbing and deceiving decent people was a way of life to them. But what he'd witnessed tonight had brought home to him exactly how bad they were. If he hadn't come along, some poor family would have come down in the morning and found their home looted.

The brief lull brought a crafty look to Brian's eyes. He's bluffing, he thought. He wouldn't dare hit me, me dad would kill him and he knows it. 'Come on, let's go home before someone comes an' finds us,' he coaxed. 'Don't worry, I'll tell me dad it was all a mistake...say yer thought I was someone else.'

He doesn't understand, Phil told himself. None of them do. They haven't the faintest idea of the suffering and humiliation they've caused me. And as the thin, wheedling voice continued, the grievances that had been building up over the years exploded like fireworks in his head. He'd never had a close friend in his life because of them. When he was a kid none of the mothers in the street would allow their children to play with him because he was a Bradley. And at school he became a loner...afraid to make friends because he'd be too ashamed to invite them to his home. Even now, when he should be enjoying life, he was reduced to using the back door because he couldn't hold his head up in the street. The same street where the girl he'd fallen for lived. And because of his family, that girl was out of his reach.

The thought of Doreen was the last straw. Filled with a blinding rage, Phil reached forward and grabbed Brian by the front of his shirt. 'Put up yer fists and fight...unless you're the coward I take yer for.'

'Gerroff!' Brian tried to push the hands away. 'Bleedin' mad, that's what yer are. If yer think I'm fightin', yer've got another think comin'.'

'Please yerself, but don't say I didn't warn yer.' Phil drew his arm back, curled his first and let fly. He heard the blow land and Brian's scream of pain. But he was too incensed to feel pity. 'That's for the poor bugger whose house yer were goin' to rob. An' this one,' he drew his arm back again, 'is for me.'

But before Phil could throw the punch, his arm was held in an iron grip and a voice said, 'That's enough, son.'

'Leave go, he's only gettin' what he deserves.'

'Maybe so, but I said that's enough.' Corker pulled Phil out of range of his brother, then released his arm. 'Now, explain what's going on.'

When Phil turned he was amazed to see so many people in the entry. 'How long have yer been here?'

'Not long enough to know what you two 'ave been up to.'

'He was tryin' to break into that 'ouse, mister,' Brian whined. 'I tried to stop him an' he hit me.'

'Is that true?' Corker asked.

Phil looked down at the ground. 'If he says so.'

'It most certainly is not true!' Miss Clegg had slipped Ellen's restraining hand and, after

336

telling her neighbour to go home and see to the children, Victoria had hurried down the entry. When she heard what was being said, she pushed her way between Molly and Nellie. 'It wasn't him, it was that one there.' She pointed an accusing finger at Brian. 'I saw him as plain as daylight.'

The Bradley lad, Molly thought. I might have known. She heard loud footsteps running down the side entry and put her fingers to her lips when Tommy and Doreen appeared. 'Sshh, be quiet.'

Miss Clegg wasn't finished with the hapless Brian. 'And it was him who stole Malcolm's bike last year and hid it in my yard.'

'Where do you come into it, son?' Corker looked puzzled. 'Why would yer take the blame for somethin' he did?'

'He's our Phil, me brother,' Brian shouted. 'An' he was breakin' into the old lady's 'ouse with me.'

Molly heard Doreen's gasp, then her muffled, 'Phil!'

'D'yer know him?' There was no reply to Molly's question... Doreen had taken to her heels and fled. 'What's biting her?' Then the penny dropped. Tall, blond, handsome and his name was Phil. This was the boy Doreen had fallen for! The smashing dancer she'd met at Barlows Lane. The one she wanted to ask to her birthday party. Well, that romance would be short-lived. She wasn't going to take up with one of the Bradleys, not if Molly had anything to do with it.

Corker was weighing Phil up. There was something not right about the whole set-up but he couldn't figure out what. 'Is it true, son? Were you breaking in to Miss Clegg's?'

'No, sir.'

Jack, who had come through the house, was leaning against the yard door taking it all in. This was a queer business, without a doubt. But he was inclined to believe the blond lad, although he didn't know why. Perhaps it was because he'd addressed Corker as 'sir'. That one word showed respect, and the lad went up in Jack's estimation. He moved forward, and in doing so nearly tripped over something on the ground. He bent down to see what it was and picked up the overalls. 'Who do these belong to?'

'They're mine, sir. I was on me way home from work.'

'He's a bleedin' liar,' screeched Brian. 'Don't believe him'

'If I were you, I'd keep me mouth tightly closed,' Corker warned. 'You're in enough trouble without adding to it.' He glanced at Phil. 'You are one of the Bradleys, aren't you?'

'I live with them.' Phil straightened up and met Corker's gaze head on. 'But Mr Bradley is not my father.'

'I heard there was another son. You go to work, don't you?'

When Phil nodded, Corker asked, 'Can yer tell us why yer were knocking hell out of yer brother?'

'I might live with the Bradleys sir, but I

338

don't live *like* them. I am not a thief. I caught Brian attempting to break into that house, an' I stopped him.'

'Well, this is a fine kettle of fish,' Nellie whispered as she gave George a dig in the ribs. 'What happens now?'

'If yer'll give yer mouth a rest,' her husband whispered back, 'we might find out.'

'I heard that, Nellie, an' I confess I haven't got a clue what to do now.' Corker twisted the end of his beard. 'We should take young feller-me-lad here to the police. But they'd think we were havin' them on if we told them his brother stopped him from breaking into a house.'

The word 'police' brought forth a wail from Brian. 'It won't do yez no good goin' to the police... I didn't break in, didn't steal nothin'. Just let me go home! He's broke me bleedin' nose an' it needs seein' to.'

'Oh, I'll take yer home all right.' There was a threat behind Corker's words which wasn't lost on those listening. 'But what about you, young Phil? You won't be welcomed with open arms, will yer?'

'I am never welcome.' There was bitterness in Phil's voice. 'I don't fit in, yer see. But the parting of the ways had to come sometime, so it might as well be tonight.'

'Have you anywhere to go, son?' Corker asked. 'A relative or friends?'

Phil shook his head. 'The Bradleys were disowned by their relatives years ago, and I haven't any close friends. But don't worry, I'll be all right. I've got a couple of mates

339

in work, one of them will put me up until I sort meself out.'

Miss Clegg touched his arm. 'Come in with me and I'll make you a cup of tea.'

'No, I won't bother yer...you've had enough trouble for one night.'

'Molly, tell him he's got to come in... I want him to.'

'You heard what the lady said, yer've got no choice.' Molly turned her head and gave Corker a knowing nod. 'Me an' Nellie will go in with Miss Clegg while you men take the queer feller home.'

'Good idea, Molly. Come on, Jack, and you, George. We'll have a few words with this lad's family.'

'Will yer do me a favour, sir?' Phil hung his head in embarrassment. 'Will yer explain to me mam an' tell her I'll be all right? I'll write to her when I get meself settled somewhere.'

Corker nodded, then took hold of Brian's arm. 'Come on, let's get it over with.'

Molly handed Phil a cup of tea. He looked so dejected she found herself feeling a stir of pity for him. 'Are yer hungry, son?'

'No thanks.' Phil took the cup and gave a faint smile. 'I've caused enough trouble as it is.'

'Make him a sandwich, please, Molly.' Miss Clegg was back in her chair beside the roaring fire Nellie had built up. 'The poor lad said he's been working from eight this morning, he must be starved.'

340

'Have yer got anythin' in for a sandwich?'

'There's some corned beef on a plate in the larder.' Victoria couldn't take her eyes off Phil. She could see the suffering on his face and her heart went out to him. 'And plenty of bread and butter.'

When Molly went out to the kitchen, Nellie followed. 'I'll rinse me hands, they're all mucky.'

Molly opened the larder cupboard and smiled when she saw the plate covered with a hand-made doily. 'She does everything nice, does our Victoria. Considerin' she's only got the one good hand, it doesn't stop her doin' things proper.'

'What d'yer think of him?' Nellie whispered. 'He seems like a nice lad to me...yer wouldn't think he was one of the Bradleys.'

'Just what I was thinking.' Molly cut a slice off a cottage loaf. 'But looks can be deceiving, so yer can't really tell.'

'Victoria's taken a fancy to him.' Nellie shivered. 'That blinkin' water's freezing, I've got goose pimples on me goose pimples.'

Molly handed her a plate with two thick sandwiches on. 'Take that in, will yer? I'll make another just in case...he's a big lad.'

'Nice-lookin' feller, too!' Nellie sighed. 'Bloody shame he's mixed up with that family.'

Molly thought of Doreen, but for once she didn't share her daughter's secret with her friend. Least said the better. 'After what he did tonight, I don't think he likes them any more than we do. When all's said and done, we can choose our friends but we can't choose our family.'

341

'Aye, yer right there, girl.' Nellie was thoughtful as she carried the plate through and set it down in front of Phil. 'There yer are, son, get them down yer.'

'Thank you.' Phil felt more like flying than eating, and when he took a bite the bread tasted like sawdust in his mouth. He was worried sick. Where could he go? One of his workmates would take him in, but what excuse could he make when he turned up on his doorstep at this time of night? He couldn't tell the truth, he'd be too ashamed.

'Here yer are, eat them all up.' Molly topped up the sandwiches on his plate. 'Yer a growing lad.'

'I couldn't eat all that, I seem to have lost me appetite.' He looked briefly into Molly's face before turning to Victoria. 'I can't tell yer how sorry I am about what happened. My so-called brother needs horse-whippin'...but the one really to blame is his father. He's the one that taught Brian and the two girls to steal. Ever since they were old enough to walk, he's encouraged them to lie, cheat and rob. They think nothin' of it, because that's how they've been brought up.' He put his half-eaten sandwich back on the plate. 'But I'm not makin' excuses for Brian, because there is no excuse...he's old enough to think for himself.'

'You're right there!' Nellie said. 'You were brought up with them, but yer haven't turned out like them.'

'Life might have been easier if I had.' The despair in Phil's voice wasn't lost on his

342

audience. 'Many's the hiding I've had when I was a kid because I wouldn't steal from the local shops.' He shook his head to dispel the memories. 'Yer've been very kind to me, considerin' what happened. Most people would have sent me packing.'

'Never mind sending you packing, I'm grateful to yer!' Miss Clegg nodded her head to emphasise how she felt. 'If it hadn't been for you, heaven only knows what that...er...yer brother might have got up to.'

'I'm just glad I was there.' For the first time, Phil noticed the limp arm hanging down by the old lady's side. Oh my God, he knew his brother was bad, but he never dreamed he'd stoop so low as to rob from someone like her. She was a lovely old lady, too! Look how kind she was being to him...a complete stranger and an unknown quantity at that.

The mixture of tiredness, shame, humiliation and anger, followed by more kindness than he deserved, suddenly became too much for Phil to bear. He could feel tears welling up behind his eyes and knew if he didn't move he'd end up making a fool of himself. 'I'd better be on me way.' He pushed his chair back and stood up. 'You've all been very kind and I want yez to know I appreciate it.'

'But you haven't eaten anything,' Miss Clegg cried, looking to Molly and Nellie for support. 'Have another sandwich and a fresh cup of tea.'

He shook his head. 'Honestly, I'm not hungry.'

343

Miss Clegg clutched his arm. 'But where will you go?'

'I'll be all right, I'll go to me mate's. But I'll have to put a move on or he'll be in bed before I get there.'

'And if he is in bed, it means you walking the streets! Oh, no, we can't have that. You can stay here for tonight.' When she heard the gasps from Molly and Nellie, Miss Clegg's face took on a determined look. She had taken a liking to the boy and she wasn't having him walking the streets with nowhere to go. After all, it was through helping her that he'd been put in this position. 'I've got a spare bed upstairs, and I've always kept it aired.'

Molly opened her mouth to object but Phil cut in before she could speak. 'No, but thanks all the same, Miss...er...Mrs...?'

'Miss Victoria Clegg, dear.'

There came a knock on the front door and Molly dashed to open it. She was frightened by the turn of events. The lad seemed nice enough, but you could never be sure.

'How did yez get on?' Molly closed the door and followed the three men down the hall. 'Was there any trouble?'

'None to speak of.' Corker raised his bushy eyebrows at the sight of Phil. 'Still here, lad? I thought yer'd be on yer way to yer mate's house by now.'

'I'm just going.' Phil didn't want to leave without knowing how his family had reacted but didn't think he had the right to ask. It was the old lady who solved the problem for him.

344

'I've said he can stay here for the night, save traipsing around at this late hour.' Miss Clegg, usually so meek and mild, stuck to her guns. 'I've got a perfectly good bed upstairs, he's more than welcome to it.'

'But yer not used to having anyone in the house, Victoria, yer set in yer ways.' Molly tried to talk her out of it. 'Phil's got to get up early for work an' he'll need somethin' to eat before he goes out. You don't get up until nine o'clock...who's goin' to see to him?'

'There's something else to consider,' Nellie said, 'what about if the Bradleys find out he's here an' come down makin' trouble? Yer wouldn't like that, would yer?'

Corker cleared his throat. 'Ladies, can I butt in? I think Miss Clegg's offer is a sensible one. It's too late now for the lad to be lookin' for somewhere to kip. An' yer don't have to worry about the family, they're not likely to find out he's here.'

'Even if they did, they wouldn't dare show their faces.' Jack chuckled. 'Corker put the fear of God into them.'

Molly could feel herself relaxing. If Corker could see no harm in the lad staying, then it must be all right. He was a good judge of character, was Corker. 'What happened?'

This time the chuckle came from George. 'Yer'd better ask Corker. Me an' Jack never opened our mouths. We were dumbstruck.'

'Sit down, lad.' Corker waited until Phil was seated. 'Do yer mind us discussing yer family?

I might as well warn yer, we've nothin' good to say about them.'

'Nothin' yer say about me family can hurt me. And there's nothin' yer can say that I haven't said meself a thousand times over.'

'Well, after the screaming and shoutin' when they saw the mess yer'd made of yer brother's face, I gave them an ultimatum. They're to be out of that house, lock, stock and barrel, within a week. If they're not, I go to the police and report Brian for attempted burglary.'

'Good for you!' Nellie's push would have felled a lesser man than Corker. 'The whole street will put the flags out when they go. In fact, we'll have a party to celebrate.'

'But will they go?' Molly asked. 'Once they know you're away, Corker, they'll get cocky an' stay put.'

'But they don't know I'm goin' away, Molly, me darlin'. I told them a little white lie. Said the ship's in dry dock for repairs and I'll be working aboard for a week, then coming home on leave.'

Phil, a frown on his handsome face, asked shyly, 'Did yer manage to speak to me mam?'

Corker nodded. 'She ran down the street after us, askin' where yer were. She seemed quite concerned, so I gave her yer message.'

'She's not all bad, me mam. It's that husband of hers that's made her what she is.'

When Corker stretched his arms he seemed to fill the entire room. 'It's gettin' late, time to turn in. I'll nip over an' make sure Ellen's all right, then I'm off home to put me head down.

I've got to catch an early train, so I'll have to be up bright an' early.' He held out a hand to Phil. 'Get a good night's sleep, son, things will look better in the morning. And I wish yer well for the future.'

Phil shook the huge hand. 'Thank you.' His eyes took in those looking on with interest. 'All of you. You don't know me from Adam, but yer've been good to me and I won't forget it in a hurry.'

Chapter Twenty

'What on earth's goin' on here?' Molly shook her head in despair as she took in the scene. As though there hadn't been enough upset for one night without coming home to find Doreen with her head in her hands, sobbing her heart out. Her eyes accusing, Molly demanded, 'Have you been upsettin' her, Tommy?'

'Mam, I haven't done nothin'!' Tommy huffed in disgust. Why was he always the first one to get the blame? 'She came in cryin' about half an hour ago an' she hasn't stopped since. We've asked her what's wrong but she won't tell us.'

'Tommy's right, Mam.' Jill was sitting opposite her sister, looking concerned. 'We've asked and asked, but she just tells us to leave her alone.'

Jack stood beside his daughter, stroking her hair, 'What's wrong, love? Come on, tell yer

347

dad.' But the only response he got was a sniff, a sob and a shake of the head.

'It's all right,' Molly said wearily, slipping her coat off. 'I'll see to her.' She patted Tommy's head. 'Off to bed, son, or yer'll never get up in the mornin'.'

'But what's up with her?' Tommy and Doreen were often at each other's throats, fighting like cat and dog, but when one of them was in trouble the other would rush to their defence. 'Is she sick or summat?'

'No, of course she's not! Now poppy off, there's a good boy.'

Reluctantly, Tommy stood up. 'Good night and God bless.' He lowered his head to whisper in his sister's ear. 'Good night, sis.'

A muffled 'Good night' satisfied him and he made his way upstairs, wondering what made girls tick. He was blowed if he could understand them.

Molly waited until the sound of his footsteps had faded before closing the door. 'Come on, Doreen, let's be having yer.' She put her hands on her daughter's shoulders and pulled her into a sitting position. 'There's no need to carry on like this, it's not the end of the world.'

'But you don't understand,' Doreen sobbed as tears ran down her cheeks.

'Yes, I think I do, sunshine.' Molly turned to her husband and indicated the chair Tommy had vacated. 'Sit down, Jack.' She gathered her daughter to her and hugged her tight. 'I was young meself once, remember?'

'Will someone tell me what's going on?' Jack

asked, looking bewildered. 'Or is it a secret?'

'Mam?' Jill asked softly. 'Do you want me to go to bed?'

'No, I think it's best if it all comes out now.' Molly pressed Doreen's head to her breast. 'Yer bound to find out sooner or later, so better get it over with.'

Jack was mystified by his wife's words. 'Get what over with?'

'Yer know this bloke our Doreen's been seeing at the dance in Barlows Lane? The one she asked you if she could bring to her party?'

Doreen sprang from her mother's arms. 'You know?'

'I put two an' two together, love, an' came up with the answer. It didn't take much to figure it out...tall, blond, handsome, and his name's Phil. It was too much of a coincidence.'

Jack was flabbergasted. 'Yer not saying...?'

Molly drew her daughter close again. 'Yes, Phil Bradley.'

Jill had stayed in to listen for Ruthie, so she'd missed the shenanigans in the entry. Now there was surprise written on her face and sympathy in her voice, 'Ah, you poor thing, why didn't you tell me?'

Doreen hid her face in her mother's shoulder. 'I don't want to talk about it. He's a liar an' I never want to see him again.'

'There now,' Molly crooned. She could feel the dampness of her daughter's tears through the thin material of her dress. 'Don't take on so. Dry yer eyes an' we'll talk about it.'

'I don't want to talk about it...I hate him!'

349

'Now, now! Hate is a very strong word, love.'
Jack wished there was some way to comfort his
daughter, but with the situation as it was, what
could anyone say? 'He didn't strike me as being
a lad who would lie.'

'Well he did... He told me he lived down by
Barlows Lane.'

Molly's mind was ticking over. 'Does he know
where you live?'

'No... Oh, yes, he does! That makes him more
of a liar! Last Tuesday he asked me where I
lived.'

'Was that before or after he told you he lived
in Fazakerly?' Molly asked, trying to build up a
picture. Like Jack, she wouldn't have taken Phil
Bradley for a liar.

'What difference does it make?' Tears were
pouring down Doreen's face. 'A lie is a lie,
isn't it?'

'People tell lies for different reasons.'

'Oh, he had a good reason,' Doreen sniffed.
'He's crafty, he is. He knew I wouldn't touch
him with a bargepole if he'd said he was one
of that horrible family.'

'Perhaps that's why he told a little white
lie.'

'I don't care... I hate him!'

'Never mind, Doreen, you'll soon get over
him.' Jill couldn't think of anything else to say.
'You'll meet someone else.'

Doreen looked at her blankly. She doesn't
understand...none of them do! I was crazy about
him! I've thought of nobody else since the night
I clapped eyes on him, and I thought he felt the

350

same way about me. I'd have gone to the ends of the earth for him, and this is how he pays me back. He's humiliated me, made me look a right fool in front of my family, and I've got to face Maureen yet! Talk about getting my eye wiped! Deep down, though, it was the thought of never seeing Phil again, not what people might say, that was breaking Doreen's heart. But she had too much pride to admit that to anyone. And while she'd been crying her heart out, she'd made a promise to herself. Never again would she be hurt by a boy. She'd play the field in future...love them and leave them.

'Oh, I'll get over him.' She ran a hand across her eyes. 'It was just the shock of seein' him tonight, that's what upset me.'

Molly and Jack exchanged glances. They were brave words she'd spoken, but neither of them believed her. They remembered how alive her face had been when she spoke of him, the excitement in her eyes when Jack said she could invite him to her birthday party. These signs had told them that this boy was someone special. Now she was hurting inside and their hearts bled for her. 'He's not a bad lad, yer know, love,' Jack said. 'Me an' yer mam took quite a liking to him.'

'He's a liar!' The words shot from Doreen's mouth. 'An' I never want to see him again.'

'We're not the only ones who took a liking,' Molly told her. 'Miss Clegg did too. He's sleepin' over there tonight.'

'More fools you! He's taken you in like

351

he took me in.' Doreen scraped her chair back and stood up. 'I'm goin' to bed, an' I don't want to hear Philip Bradley's name again, ever.'

Victoria Clegg sat up in bed, putting her hairnet on. It wasn't an easy task with just the one hand, but tonight she didn't get impatient like she normally did. She felt happier than she'd felt since her parents died, many moons ago. It was a lovely feeling knowing there was someone sleeping in the next room, that she wasn't all alone. Funny how things worked out. They said God moved in mysterious ways, well He certainly had tonight. Who would have thought that a common criminal—because that was what the young lout was—would have brought her a welcome visitor? Victoria smiled as she blew out the candle on the bedside cabinet and snuggled up under the bedclothes. She'd set the alarm clock for six o'clock so she would have plenty of time to cook Phil a proper breakfast. He'd get a surprise, because before he'd gone to bed he'd thanked her for her kindness and said she wasn't to worry, he'd let himself out quietly in the morning. He'd given her a kiss on the cheek and she'd swear she'd seen tears in his eyes.

'He's a nice boy,' Victoria muttered as she turned on her side and pulled the clothes up to her chin. 'I don't care what anyone says.'

It was Molly's turn to take Ruthie and Bella to school, and after she'd seen them safely inside the gates she hurried home. Her first port of call was to be Miss Clegg's, but she decided to give Nellie a knock first and ask if she'd come with her.

'Bloody 'ell, girl, I haven't even washed me face yet!' Nellie's hair was hidden under a mob cap which had slipped to the side of her head, making her look comical. 'I'm cleanin' the grate out.'

'Nobody will notice what yer look like...just rinse yer hands.'

'I dunno,' Nellie clicked her tongue, 'no rest for the wicked.'

'Don't yer want to know if Miss Clegg's all right?' Molly stood by the kitchen door as Nellie ran water over hands covered in coal dust. 'She's been on my mind all night.'

'Of course I want to know how things are over there! But couldn't you 'ave called there first, save me goin' out?'

'How soft you are, Nellie McDonough! Yer want to know what's goin' on, but yer can't be bothered gettin' off yer fat backside to find out!'

Nellie's grin transformed her face. 'I'll thank you not to be so personal, an' leave my backside out of it.'

Molly grinned back. 'Nellie, it would be very hard to ignore your backside. It's like the back of a bus.'

'I'll treat that remark with the contempt it deserves.' Nellie threw her mob cap on the draining board and ran her fingers through her fine, mousy-coloured hair. 'Will I do like this, girl? I don't fancy gettin' meself all dolled up when I've got work to come back to.'

'You'll do.' Molly tried to suppress a giggle. 'Claudette Colbert you ain't, but I'm not too proud to be seen out with yer.'

'Hark at her! Who d'yer think you are... Maureen O'Sullivan?'

'Don't be silly, my hair's not as dark as hers.' Molly tapped a finger on her chin. 'I'd say I'm more a Greta Garbo.'

Nellie slipped her arms into her loose edge-to-edge coat. 'There's no flies on you, is there, girl? An' d'yer know why? They're all buzzing around the midden outside, enjoyin' yesterday's leftovers.'

Molly waited until Nellie banged the door behind her, then linked her arm. 'One of these fine days I'll get the last word in.'

'Yer'll have to be up early to do that, me old cock sparrer. Either that or catch me when I'm asleep.'

A smiling Victoria opened the door to them. 'Good morning, ladies.'

'You look very happy this morning.' Molly was surprised to see a fire roaring up the chimney. 'It's early for you to be up and dressed, and with the fire lit.'

'I was up at six to make Phil breakfast.' The old lady looked very pleased with herelf. 'Couldn't have him going to work on an empty tummy, now could I?'

'Keep yer eye off him, yer brazen hussy.' Nellie chucked her under the chin. 'He's too young for yer. Yer'd be had up for cradle-snatchin'.'

'More's the pity! If I was seventy years younger I'd be chasing after him.'

Molly couldn't get over the change in Victoria. She'd never seen her so animated, happy and self-assured. She looked ten years younger, too. 'How did yer get on with him?'

'Marvellous! He's a nice, decent, considerate boy. Before he went to work he insisted on raking the grate out, lighting the fire and filling the coal scuttle.'

'It was the least he could do, seein' as yer gave him a bed for the night.' The words sounded churlish even to her own ears, and Molly wished she could take them back. 'It was thoughtful of him, though, I'll grant yer that.'

'Pity he's leavin' the street.' Nellie winked at Victoria. 'Yer could do with a handyman.'

'He isn't leaving the street...not yet anyway. I've asked him to come back tonight and stay until he gets himself sorted out.'

The silence was so profound you could have heard a pin drop. Molly and Nellie gazed at each other, wide-eyed. Then Molly asked, 'Victoria, are yer sure that's wise? After all, yer hardly know the lad.'

Victoria's hand fluttered to her throat. 'You're my best friends and I know you both mean well. But give me a chance to explain.' She smiled nervously. 'I've lived on my own now for over fifty years. They've been lonely years, more lonely than anyone could imagine. In fact, there have been times when I've prayed for the good Lord to take me. Oh, I know I shouldn't complain, not when I've got friends

355

and neighbours like yourselves. But it's not the same as having your own family. There's no sense of belonging. I have neither kith nor kin to call my own, and the wireless is a poor substitute for a real-life, flesh-and-blood companion. The days drag and the nights seem endless.' She gazed from one to the other. 'Last night I slept easy, knowing I wasn't alone in the house...that if I called out, someone would hear. And this morning I had someone to talk to, make a fuss of. So don't condemn me for being a selfish old woman who wants a little brightness in her life.'

'I'm goin' to cry.' The remark was unnecessary as the tears were already flowing from Nellie's eyes. 'Look what yer've gone an' made me do...bawlin' like a flippin' baby.'

Molly was silent, lost for words. She hadn't realised how lonely the old lady was, because Miss Clegg had never bared her soul before. But what she'd said was true...being on your own all the time was a lonely life for anyone. Especially someone like Victoria who was housebound. The neighbours took it in turns to bring her a hot dinner every day, and did her shopping. But that only amounted to an hour a day...the other twenty-three she spent in solitude.

'Nobody is condemning yer, Victoria! You're the least selfish person in the world.' Molly finally found her voice. 'It's us that's selfish for not realising how lonely yer were. But we do care for yer, an' that's why we want to make certain yer doin' the right thing.'

'I know that, Molly, and I'm grateful to you.

356

But I know what I'm doing, so you don't need to worry.'

'Are yer sure he's coming back tonight?'

'I had a job persuading him...he was worried what people would think about me taking a Bradley in. But in the end he promised, and I don't think he's the type to break a promise.'

'In that case yer'll need some food in. Tell me what yer want an' I'll get it for yer when I go to the shops.' Molly glanced sideways. 'Will yer stop snivellin', for heaven's sake!'

'I can't help it.' Nellie lifted the skirt of her dress to wipe the tears away and revealed the elasticated legs of her pink fleecy-lined bloomers, and the six inches of bare leg between the bloomers and her rolled-down stocking tops. 'I've always been a sucker for a sad story.'

Molly saw the twinkle in Victoria's eyes and burst out laughing. 'Have yer ever in yer life seen anythin' like that? Honest to God, I'm ashamed to take her anywhere.'

'When we go to the shops I'll walk behind yer,' Nellie sniffed, 'then no one will know we're together. The last thing I would want to do is embarrass yer.'

'Ah, poor little Orphan Annie.' Molly put an arm across her friend's shoulders and hugged her. 'Yer me best mate an' I love every inch of yer. If yer came to the shops with me in yer nuddy, yer wouldn't embarrass me.'

Nellie chuckled. 'No one would know I 'ad no clothes on, girl! I've got that many wrinkles, folds and creases on me body, no one would be

357

any the wiser. They'd just think me coat needed ironing.'

'Oh, she's in one of her funny moods now, Victoria. I won't be able to get any sense out of her. Just tell us what yer want from the shops an' we'll be on our way.'

Victoria was smiling as she reached for her purse. It was a long time since she'd felt so light-hearted. These two friends were always guaranteed to make her laugh. But the glow in her heart came from the knowledge that, like the other women in the street, she'd be setting the table tonight for someone coming home from work.

Molly gazed around the table. She'd never known her family be so quiet. Mind you, with Doreen having a face on her like a wet week, it was enough to put a damper on anyone's spirits. She was dying to tell Jack about Miss Clegg's lodger, but was afraid to mention Phil's name in case it brought on another crying match. She'd just have to bide her time and hope her daughter was going up to Maureen's.

Jack wiped a piece of bread over his plate to soak up the gravy. 'I really enjoyed that, love.' He pushed his chair back and undid the top button of his trousers. 'I'm bloated now...me eyes are bigger than me belly.'

'I feel full meself.' Molly patted her tummy. 'It's the suet dumplings that do it, they don't half fill yer up.'

'I'll wash up, Mam,' Jill started to stack the

empty plates. 'Steve's not coming till eight o'clock.'

'Yer a pal an' a half, sunshine.' Molly smiled her appreciation. 'I've had a busy day, with one thing an' another, an' me feet are givin' me gyp.'

'I'm goin' up to Ginger's,' Tommy said. 'I won't be late, Mam.'

'See yer not! It was all hours when yer got to bed last night.'

'Okay, boss!' Tommy took one look at Doreen's glum face and couldn't get out of the house quick enough. Flippin' girls! They could be a right pain in the neck sometimes.

Jack puffed on his newly lit cigarette, then in all innocence asked, 'How did Miss Clegg get on with young Phil?'

Doreen's chair crashed back as she sprang to her feet. 'I'll help Jill with the dishes.'

Molly gave Jack daggers and tutted. 'Have yer not got the sense yer were born with?'

'I never thought,' he grimaced. 'Anyway, his name is bound to crop up sometime, she'll just have to get used to it.'

Molly kept her voice down. 'He's bound to crop up in person, never mind his name! Victoria's asked him to stay with her until he can find himself digs.'

'Go 'way!'

'Yeah, honest!' Molly briefly related all that Victoria had said. 'An' after listening to her, I don't blame her for wanting company. I wouldn't be in her shoes for a big clock, sitting on yer own day an' night, it's enough to send yer round the bend. Yer should see the difference it's made to her, knowing he's coming tonight. She's over the moon...runnin' around like a spring chicken.'

'Let's hope she doesn't live to regret it.' Jack watched a smoke ring rise to the ceiling. 'If she gets used to him being there, it'll come as a blow when he finds himself digs.'

'Well, that's a bridge we'll cross when we come to it. In the meantime I'm all for her bein' happy. And I know it sounds daft, but I've got a feeling it was meant to be...you know, like fate stepping in.'

Jack chuckled softly. 'You an' your romantic notions. A happy ending and you're in yer applecart.'

'I just hope he doesn't let her down...but yer know, I don't think he will. From what she says, he should be working overtime tonight until ten o'clock, but he told her he'll finish at eight so she won't have to stay up late.' Molly glanced towards the kitchen then leaned forward. 'I'm slippin' over about nine o'clock, just to make sure.'

'Don't yer think you'd be better keeping yer nose out of it? Miss Clegg might think yer interfering.'

'No she won't... I told her I'd slip over and she seemed quite pleased. I won't stay, just make sure she's managing.'

Jack was about to say something when Doreen came into the room and put an end to the conversation. She plonked herself down on the couch and reached for the unopened *Echo,* a sure sign that she had no intention of going out. Normally, Molly would have asked, but the look on Doreen's face told her questions wouldn't be welcomed.

Even Jill was affected by the heavy atmosphere. Combing her long blonde hair in front of the mirror, her eyes met her mother's and she pulled a face. 'I think I'll go up to Steve's, save him calling for me. We're going back to his house anyway, to have a game of cards with his mam and dad.'

'Well, keep yer eye on that mate of mine or she'll rob yer blind.'

'I'll tell her you said that,' Jill replied with a grin. 'Not that it makes much difference, seeing as we only play for matches.'

When Jill had left, the air hung heavy and the minutes seemed to drag. Molly tried a few times to engage her daughter in conversation but it was such heavy going she gave it up as a bad job and sat watching the hands of the clock creep slowly around to nine o'clock. *Another night like this and I'll be telling her to pull her socks up. We can't have the whole family suffering because of a romance that never got off the ground in the first place!*

'D'yer want some of the *Echo?*' Jack lowered the paper Doreen had finally relinquished in exchange for a magazine. 'I'm finished with the first few pages.'

'No, ta, I think I'll go up to Nellie's for half an hour, stretch me legs.' When she saw Jack's brows shoot up, Molly stared at him until he got the message.

It was Phil who answered the door to Molly's knock. He looked embarrassed and uncertain, so she just stepped into the hallway. 'It's all right, son, Miss Clegg knows I'm coming.'

It was a comfortable, homely scene that met Molly's eyes. Two armchairs were drawn up to the hearth and a fire burned brightly in the grate. 'Well, this is nice and cosy.' Molly planted a kiss on the wrinkled cheek. 'Ooh, yer all warm and cuddly.'

'Me and Philip have been having a good conversation.' Victoria pointed to the couch. 'Sit yourself down, Molly, but take your coat off first or you won't feel the benefit of it when you leave.'

'A real bossy-boots, isn't she?' Molly smiled at Phil as she handed him her coat. 'Put it on the hall stand for us, there's a good lad.'

'He was asking me if I knew a young girl called Doreen.' There was a mischievous glint in the faded eyes. 'She's slim, got long blonde hair and is lovely to look at. Do you know anyone answering that description, Molly?'

Phil hung his head, but not before Molly had seen his face turn the colour of beetroot. 'He knows who she is, 'cos you've already told him, haven't yer?'

Victoria nodded. 'I didn't think it would do any harm.'

'The harm has already been done.' Molly looked at the bowed head. 'You're not very popular in our 'ouse, son.'

'I didn't expect to be.' There was a cynical

smile on Phil's face when he looked up. 'It's the story of my life.'

'You lied to her, and that's what's upset her.'

'I don't know why I lied to her, it was on the spur of the moment. I knew if I told her the truth she'd have sent me packin' and I'd never have seen her again. It would have had to come out in the end, but I never expected her to find out the way she did.' Phil looked down at his clasped hands. 'I don't blame her for bein' upset and not wantin' to see me again, Mrs Bennett.' He raised his head and gazed into Molly eyes. 'I don't suppose she'd see me, just so I can explain, would she?'

'Right now your name is muck in our house, son.' Molly saw the hurt on his face and groaned inwardly. She couldn't help feeling sorry for him. He was everything Doreen had said he was...tall, handsome, and nice. And she'd swear he was as honest as the day was long. To condemn the lad just because his name was Bradley wouldn't be fair. 'She might come around when she's had time to think it over, but I wouldn't bank on it. She's as stubborn as a mule, is our Doreen.'

'Would yer put in a good word for me, Mrs Bennett?'

'Not yet, son, not with the mood she's in. If I mentioned your name she'd clock me one.' Molly grinned. 'But who knows what the future holds? She could change her mind tomorrow for all I know. After all, she's only a kid.'

'She'll be sixteen soon,' Phil said softly, 'I

remember her telling me.'

'Well, I wouldn't be shining me shoes if I were you. Apart from being stubborn, my daughter's got her pride. She thinks yer've made a fool of her, and even if she wanted to, she wouldn't give in.'

'Perhaps if I had a word with her?' Victoria had been listening intently, her face sad. 'She might take notice of me.'

'No, Victoria, leave things as they are for now. If she's goin' to come around, she'll do it in her own time. If I see any sign of her having a change of heart, I'll stick my twopennyworth in. More than that I can't promise, so yer'll have to wait and hope for the best, Phil.'

Chapter Twenty-One

While Jimmy Cookson untied the knot at the back of his leather apron he kept a watchful eye as Phil Bradley hammered into shape a rod of molten iron. Rivulets of sweat ran down the lad's face as he brought the hammer down time and again, determined to finish the shaping before the rod cooled. He was a real grafter was Phil, the best apprentice Jimmy had ever had. He never downed tools the second the dinner hooter sounded, like the rest of the workers in the furnace room. In fact, he seemed to thrive on hard work, and he turned out as good a job as many of the skilled workers who'd been in the trade for years.

Jimmy rolled his leather apron up and threw it down at the side of the furnace. It was so hot in here, he'd be glad to get out and breathe in some fresh, cool air. 'Come on, lad, dinnertime.'

'Okay.' Phil grinned as he wiped the back of his hand across his forehead. 'I'm coming.' He had a lot of respect for the older man, who had always shown patience and good humour whilst teaching him the skills of the trade. He was a hard task-master...believed in giving a good day's work for a day's pay. But as long as you pulled your weight he was easy to get on with. He was twenty years older than Phil, married, with three children. But despite the age gap, he and Phil got on well together. It was to Jimmy that Phil would have gone to for help if Miss Clegg hadn't taken him in two nights ago. He had no doubt he would have been made welcome, but was nevertheless relieved that the situation hadn't arisen. You couldn't turn up on someone's doorstep without an explanation, and the whole sorry story would have had to come out. That was the last thing Phil wanted. They were good mates, him and Jimmy, and he wanted it to stay that way.

Every dinnertime they would go together to the local chippy to buy a pennyworth of chips, liberally sprinkled with salt and vinegar, to eat with the bread and butter they brought from home. 'It's a damn sight cheaper than the missus havin' to buy somethin' to put on me bread,' Jimmy had said that first day, and now it was a daily ritual.

As they turned out of the factory gates, Jimmy was holding forth with his very strong views on Hitler. 'He's a bugger up the back, that one!'

'Phil!'

Both heads turned to see a woman waving to them from the opposite side of the road. She pointed to the small battered suitcase by her feet and beckoned. 'It's me mam,' Phil said. 'I wonder what she wants?'

'Only one way to find out, son, go an' ask her.' Jimmy waved a hand in greeting, then added, 'I'll go on ahead.'

'Hello, son.' Fanny Bradley was wringing her hands, looking nervous and agitated. 'How are yer?'

'I'm all right, Mam.'

'I brought yer some clothes.' She touched the suitcase with her toe. 'I was worried yer had nothin' to change into.'

'Thanks, Mam! I need a change, I've had these clothes on for three days now.'

'Are yer sure yer all right? Have yer got somewhere to stay?'

Phil looked down at the ground. He was afraid to tell her the truth in case his stepfather came down and created trouble for Miss Clegg. 'Yeah, I'm staying with one of the men I work with. It's only temporary, until I can find lodgings.'

'I'm sorry for what happened,' Fanny said, then added defiantly, 'but yer should have kept out of it.'

There was sadness on Phil's face as he gazed at the woman who had brought him into the world. She claimed she was sorry for what happened but laid the blame at his door. There was no pity in her for the old lady whose house would have been burgled if he hadn't happened on the scene. As far as she was concerned, if Phil had turned a blind eye there wouldn't have been any trouble.

'No, Mam, I couldn't have kept out of it. If it happened again I'd do the same thing. That's the difference between me an' the rest of the Bradleys.' He stooped to pick up the case. 'I'll have to go now, we only get half an hour for dinner. But I'm grateful to yer for bringing me things. And when I get meself settled I'll let yer know.'

Fanny put a restraining hand on his arm. 'We're movin' in a few days to a little house in Huyton. I'll be glad to get away from that street, the neighbours are a bleedin' miserable lot.'

'It's not the neighbours, Mam! Can't you see, it's that man you're married to...he's pulled yer down into the gutter.' Phil sighed. He was only wasting his breath. Whatever she saw in the Bradley man was beyond comprehension, but she bowed to his every whim. She agreed with him in everything he did, even the lying, cheating and stealing. He was never wrong in her eyes, and she'd stick by him through thick and thin. Phil switched the case to his other hand. His head and his heart were filled with mixed emotions. You were supposed to love and respect your mother, and he'd tried hard to do

367

that. But now he asked himself how he could love someone who didn't love him enough to protect him from the evil of the man she'd married. Who blamed him for doing what any self-respecting, God-fearing person would have done.

'If yer let me have yer new address some time, I'll write to yer when I get meself sorted out.' Even now Phil found it hard to walk away from her. It wasn't the love of a son for his mother that held him back, it was sadness for a woman who didn't know right from wrong. 'Look after yerself.'

'I'll come down an' meet yer outside work one day,' Fanny said, 'see how yer gettin' on.'

Phil nodded and turned away. He walked a few steps, then stopped. There was something that had preyed on his mind since he was old enough to understand that Tom Bradley wasn't his father...perhaps now was the time to ask the question that had plagued him over the years. He turned to face his mother. 'Mam, who was my real dad?'

Fanny lowered her eyes as her face drained of colour. 'What d'yer want to know for? What difference does it make who he was?'

'You don't understand, do yer, Mam? Everyone has a right to know who their father is, in my case more so than most. D'yer think it's been easy for me over the years, people thinkin' Tom Bradley's me father? I hate that man, and there's been times when I've hated you for marrying him.'

Fanny screwed up her eyes as the words

brought reason to a mind and heart where for years there'd been none. She could see herself as a young girl again, with a boy she'd been crazy about. He was tall, blond, handsome and full of fun. She opened her eyes to see the image of that boy standing before her...her son. And at that moment she knew how much she'd failed him.

'Mam, I want an answer. I think I'm entitled to know who my real father was. What he was like and why you didn't marry him. I don't want to seek him out or cause trouble, I just need to know something about him.'

'If yer look in the mirror, yer'll see yer father. You're the spittin' image of him.' Fanny spoke softly, her head bent so she didn't meet his eyes. 'We were courtin' for a year, and were goin' to get married when I was eighteen.'

There was a long silence, then Phil asked, 'What happened?'

'He worked down at the docks and there was an accident.' Fanny's voice faltered as she was forced to relive something from her past that was so painful she'd blotted it from her mind years ago. 'He...he was killed.'

Phil dropped the case and put a hand on her arm. 'Mam, are yer tellin' me the truth?'

'Yes!' she cried. 'If I never move from here, it's God's honest truth! I know I haven't been the best mother in the world to yer, but I wouldn't lie about a thing like that!'

'Did you love him?'

'We were crazy about each other. I was devastated when he died, thought I'd never get over it. Then, a month after he was buried, I found out I was expectin'.'

'So you married Tom Bradley? Did he know you were pregnant?'

Fanny nodded. 'Yeah, I told him.' Her eyes were pleading for understanding. 'I was so ashamed...never thought anyone would have me with an illegitimate baby. When Tom asked me to go out with him, I refused and told him why. Then he asked me to marry him, said if we got married quick, no one would know it wasn't his baby.'

For a while Phil couldn't speak, he was dumbfounded. Then he found his voice. 'Mam, I'm sorry, it must have been terrible for yer. But I'd be tellin' lies if I said yer did the right thing. I'd rather have been illegitimate than have Tom Bradley for a father.'

'Don't you say anythin' against him, he's been good to me!' Fanny's voice rose. 'How many other men would 'ave married me? Just you tell me that!'

'I'm not goin' to argue with yer, Mam. It's your life to do with what yer will. Just don't expect me to be grateful to a man who has turned his children into thieves and pulled you down to his level. You might think you owe him something, perhaps yer do, but I don't owe him a thing. Not for all those years of misery he caused me.'

'Ay, don't you be forgettin' he put a roof over yer head,' Fanny said hotly. 'If he hadn't married me I'd have been walkin' the streets, because me family would have disowned me.

370

An' you'd 'ave been born in the bleedin' workhouse, so just think on.'

'You think that would have been worse, do yer, Mam?' Phil closed his eyes, sighing at the futility of arguing with her. She was quite happy and content with the life she led, could see no wrong in the man she'd married. He could try to reason with her until kingdom come, it wouldn't change her. And for good or bad, she was his mother and he didn't want to part with ill feeling between them.

'I'll have to go, Mam.' Phil had spotted Jimmy approaching the factory gates, and even from that distance he could see the steam rising from the newspaper parcel his workmate was carrying. 'Me mate's back with our chips. If I don't put a move on they'll be stone cold.'

'I'll come down again an' see yer, son.' Fanny was torn. She had feelings for her son and hated to see the hurt in his eyes. But she was under no illusions...if she had to choose between him and Tom Bradley, her son would be the loser. 'When we get settled in our new 'ouse.'

'Okay, Mam, I'll see yer.'

Fanny watched him walk away, swinging the scruffy case. In her heart she admitted she hadn't been a good mother to him, that he deserved better. But there was one decent thing she could do for him now. 'Phil!'

He turned. 'I'm sorry, Mam, but I've really got to go.'

She walked towards him. 'Would yer like to see a photo of yer dad?'

Phil's mouth gaped. 'Yer mean to tell me

yer've got a photo of him? All these years, an'
yer've never let on?'

'I haven't looked at it for years...kept it hidden
away in case, er, in case someone saw it. It was
taken about a month before he died. We'd gone
to New Brighton fair with a gang, and someone
took the snap of us together.'

There was no sign of Jimmy when Phil
glanced over his shoulder. He was probably
sitting in their usual place, pouring tea into
his chipped enamel cup before making his
doorstep-thick chip butties. He'd be wondering
what was keeping his mate, but what Phil was
hearing from his mother meant more to him
than a king's banquet. For the first time in his
life he was learning about his real father, his
own flesh and blood, and he was filled with
an overwhelming desire to know more. What
did he look like? Was he a good man? Oh,
there was so much he needed to know about
the man who had fathered him. 'Will yer let
me see the photo, Mam?'

Fanny nodded. 'I'll meet yer here tomorrow,
same time. An' yer can keep the photo.' She
dropped her head and gazed at the cracks in
the pavement. A heavy sadness descended on
her as she realised she wasn't only letting her
son down, but also the man she'd loved so
much...his father. Fanny shivered. For some
reason she couldn't put her finger on, she
had a feeling the day wasn't far off when
this handsome lad would walk out of her life
forever. Before that happened she had to put
the record straight between them. 'It's only

right yer should have it...it's what he would have wanted.' With a catch in her voice, she told him, His name was Bob Mitchell, an' he was a fine, upstanding man. He was as honest as the day is long, always had a smile on his face and was liked by everyone. And I can tell yer this, he'd have been right proud of you, son.'

Phil opened the front door the next morning and stepped into the street, at the same time as the door opposite opened and Doreen appeared on the top step. Their eyes locked and for several seconds they were frozen in time. Phil was willing her to smile, to show some recognition, but Doreen dropped her gaze, banged the front door and took to her heels without a backward glance. With a heavy heart, Phil watched her slim legs cover the ground quickly as her long hair bounced around her shoulders.

'Well that's put an end to any hopes I had,' he murmured softly as he closed the door behind him. 'She's made it clear she doesn't want anything to do with me.' His steps were heavy as he walked down the street. He should have expected her rejection, he supposed, because she had every right to be angry. But there'd been a tiny flame of hope in his heart that she'd give him a chance to explain. In the last few minutes she'd extinguished that flame.

Victoria had come to expect a smile on Phil's face when he came in from work. He was a pleasure to have in the house, and his presence gave a whole new meaning to her life. The days didn't drag now that she had something to look forward to. There was a song on her lips as, with her one good hand, she made the beds, washed the dishes and dusted around. But her favourite job was setting the table for two. No more sitting with a tray on her knee, in front of the fire to eat her meal alone. But as soon as Phil walked through the door that night she sensed a change in him. He had a permanent smile on his face and when he talked there was excitement in his voice. She was curious, but didn't pry. If there was anything he wanted her to know, he'd tell her in his own good time.

'I enjoyed that, Miss Clegg.' Phil laid down his knife and fork. 'Yer can't beat steak an' kidney in a nice thick gravy.'

There was pleasure on Victoria's face as she reached for his plate. 'The kettle's boiled, I'll make yer a nice cup of tea.'

'You stay where yer are, Miss Clegg, I'll make it.' Phil took the plate from her. 'You spoil me too much.'

Victoria sat at the table, listening to him bustling around in the kitchen. 'I'll use this water to wash the few dishes, save botherin' later,' he called. 'It won't take a minute to stick the kettle on again.' It hadn't taken him long to get used to the layout and he knew where to put his hand on what he wanted. He was a tidy boy and Victoria knew everything would be put away where it should be.

'Here we go!' Phil came in carrying two cups of tea and set one in front of her before sitting down. 'Have yer had a good day, Miss Clegg?'

Victoria grinned as she tutted. 'You can't keep on calling me Miss Clegg, it sounds so formal!'

'What else can I call yer?' Phil leaned across the table. 'I can't call yer Victoria, it wouldn't be proper.'

'You could call me Auntie.' There was a shy smile on her face. 'It sounds more friendly.'

'You wouldn't mind?' Phil beamed when she shook her head. The day that had started off badly, with Doreen ignoring him, was turning out to be one of the best days of his life. His mother had been waiting for him outside the factory gates as she'd promised, and she'd given him something he would treasure all his life. And now here was Miss Clegg treating him like one of her family. 'Auntie Victoria...it's quite a mouthful, isn't it?'

'My parents used to call me Vicky...how about Aunt Vicky?'

'Aunt Vicky.' Phil rolled it around his tongue and liked the sound of it. He stuck out his hand. 'How d'yer do, Aunt Vicky?'

As Victoria reached across the table she thought how easy this boy was to live with. He'd only been here a few days but she felt she'd known him all her life. She took his hand, roughened by the years of handling iron, and squeezed. 'I'm very happy to meet you.'

'Seeing as we're practically family now, I've got somethin' to show yer.' He reached into his top inside pocket and produced a photograph. Rounding the table, he placed it in front of her. 'That's me real dad.'

Victoria stared at the old sepia-coloured photograph, creased and faded with age. Her eyesight wasn't what it used to be so she picked the snap up and held it closer. 'You're the image of him!' She gazed at Phil with wonder. 'It's like looking at the same man!'

Phil's chest expanded with pride. 'That's just what me mate in work said.'

'Who's the woman with him?'

'That's me mam.' His face clouded. 'Yer wouldn't think to look at her now that she used to be so pretty, would yer?'

Victoria didn't trust herself to speak. When all was said and done, the woman was still his mother. And the photograph showed she'd been quite a beauty when she was young. But what on earth had possessed her to allow the man she'd married to change her into what she was today?

'Me dad was courtin' her for a year an' they were goin' to be married. That photo was taken on a day out at New Brighton.' Phil took the photograph from her hand before returning to his seat opposite. Without taking his eyes off the face of the man he would give anything to have known, he slowly told his Aunt Vicky the story of how he came to be part of the Bradley family.

And as she listened, her eyes glistening with tears, Victoria's heart went out to the boy she'd have been proud to call her son. He certainly didn't deserve the cruel hand fate had dealt him.

When he'd finished telling her all that had

been said, Phil sat gazing at the photo he held in his hands. 'She said he was a smashing man. Kind, full of fun and liked by everyone.'

'I'm sure he was...he must have been very special to have fathered a fine boy like you. And I'm sure you feel more settled in yer mind, knowing who he was and why he and your mother were never married.'

'Yer don't know the half of it! Honest, Miss...er... Aunt Vicky.' A wide smile stretched his handsome face. 'It'll take me a time to get used to callin' yer that, but I'll get there! Anyway, to get back to what I was sayin', I feel as though a heavy weight has been lifted off me shoulders. It's a marvellous feeling to be free of the Bradleys at last. For the first time in me life I know who I am. I'm not a nobody... I'm the son of Bob Mitchell.'

The sound of the door knocker had Phil shoving the photo back in his pocket as he stood up. 'I'll go.'

'It'll only be Molly, come for her pan back.'

And Victoria was proved right. 'Hiya, sunshine!' Molly breezed in, bringing a draught of cold air with her. 'All nice and cosy, eh, as per usual.'

'We're ahead of ourselves tonight.' Victoria was looking so smug she might as well have stuck her tongue out and said 'so there!'. But Victoria didn't do things like that so she contented herself by adding, 'Phil's already washed the dishes and tidied everythin' away.'

'You're too bloody good to be true!' Molly took the sting out of her words by rewarding

377

him with a sunny smile. 'I could do with yer in our house.'

'I don't think yer daughter would be too happy about that.' Phil pulled a face. 'She cut me dead this morning.'

Molly looked surprised. 'Where did yet see her this mornin'?'

'We both came out of the house at the same time. She looked at me as if I was somethin' the cat had dragged in, then legged it hell for leather down the street.'

'She's been in a right mood for the last few days. Got a face on her like a wet week and snaps yer head off if yer so much as look sideways at her.' Molly perched on the arm of the couch. She didn't want to get comfortable or she'd never budge. 'Me ma says she takes after me, but I can't remember bein' as moody as she is.'

'You've got to make allowances for her, Molly, she's at an awkward age,' Victoria said. 'Too old for a doll's pram, but not old enough to go out and do what she wants.'

'Then all I can say is, I hope she grows up ruddy quick. She sat at the table tonight with a right miserable gob on her, an' it puts a blight on the whole family.'

Victoria had been at the window this morning waiting to wave to Phil as he passed, and she'd witnessed what had taken place. Not for the world would she tell him, in case she embarrassed him. Or, worse still, he'd think she was being nosy. But after what she'd seen with her own eyes, and with what Molly was telling them now, she thought she knew what might be ailing Doreen. Perhaps a little push in the right direction wouldn't go amiss. 'Show Molly your photograph, Phil.'

'Aw, Aunt Vicky! Mrs Bennett wouldn't be interested!'

Molly's brows shot up in surprise. Aunt Vicky! Well I never!

'Of course she'd be interested!' Victoria wasn't to be put off. 'Go on, show it to her.'

Phil reached into his pocket as he crossed the room. 'Guess who that is?'

Molly glanced casually at the snap, then bent her head for a closer look. 'I can't see a thing in this light.' She went to stand by the table, under the gas lamp. For several seconds she stared at the photograph, then turned to Phil. 'This is uncanny! The feller on this looks like you, but I know it can't be 'cos the snap's donkey's years old!'

'Nineteen years to be precise.' Phil was looking over her shoulder. 'His name was Bob Mitchell, he's me dad.'

'Well, I'll be blowed!' Molly's eyes were drawn to the face staring up at her. She couldn't get over the likeness. 'He's a handsome man.'

'He was.' There was a catch in Phil's voice. 'He's dead.'

Victoria could see the questions in Molly's eyes and could hear the pain in Phil's voice. Perhaps it wasn't fair to ask him to go over the story again so soon, he must be hurting terribly inside. But Victoria had a feeling that only good could come out of Molly knowing the truth.

'Sit down properly, Molly, and I'll make you a cuppa while Phil tells yer about his dad.'

'Will yer try and put a smile on yer face?' Maureen took the two cloakroom tickets from the girl behind the counter and put them in her purse. 'Honest, I don't know why yer agreed to come out with Mike an' Sammy if yer feel as miserable as yer look.'

Doreen took a deep breath and forced a smile. 'I'm all right! If I go around with a permanent smile on me face everyone will think I'm doolally.'

'Don't be sarcastic, Doreen,' Maureen said, 'there's no need for it. All I'm askin' yer to do is make an effort, otherwise we're all in for a miserable night.'

Doreen slipped her hand through her friend's arm. 'If yer see me without a smile on me face, give me a kick.'

'Don't tempt me.' As they neared the entrance to the dance hall, Maureen saw Mike and Sammy waiting and she walked towards them. 'We're ready if you are.'

Bowing from the waist, Mike opened the door and the strains of a tango reached their ears. 'How about it, Doreen?'

'Yes, okay.' Doreen passed her handbag to her friend. 'Put this down for us, kid.'

Maureen's eyebrows were raised when she took the bag. 'That's one kick I owe yer so far.'

'What did she mean by that?' Mike asked as he whisked Doreen across the floor. 'Have you two 'ad a row?'

'No! It's just one of her little jokes.' Doreen forced a smile as she looked into his face. 'If she ever kicked me I'd kick her back.'

The music came to an end and Mike pulled a face. 'We came in at the tail end.'

'Never mind, there'll be another tango later.' Doreen glanced around the room for sight of her friend. 'There they are, near the stage.'

The next dance was a quickstep and Mike was surprised when Sammy claimed Doreen. They'd been going out as a foursome for nearly a year now, only once a week to a dance, and although nothing had ever been said, it was usual for Mike to partner Doreen and Sammy her friend.

On the surface there was no romantic attachment but Mike was very keen on Doreen and was living in hope. He was only waiting for a sign of encouragement from her and then he would declare his feelings. So far she had never given that sign.

Sammy performed a set of intricate steps before slowing down. 'D'yer still go to Barlows Lane, Doreen?'

Doreen kept her eyes averted. 'No, we haven't been for weeks.'

'So yer don't see that big blond feller now? What was his name, er, Phil, wasn't it?'

Doreen ground her teeth together. It was bad enough having Phil on her mind all the time without talking about him. 'No, I haven't seen him.'

'I thought yer fancied him.' Sammy wasn't going to let it drop. 'It seemed that way to me.'

381

'Well yer were wrong.' May God forgive me, thought Doreen, but I've got to shut him up. If he mentions Phil's name again I'll burst out crying. 'Are we goin' to dance, or just walk around the floor?'

His curiosity satisfied, Sammy picked up the tempo. He was a good dancer but his arms weren't the arms Doreen wished were holding her. The mention of Phil's name had brought back the longing and the pain, and she was sorry now that she'd agreed to come to the dance at Blair Hall. But she couldn't blame her friends for the way she felt, and it wouldn't be fair to spoil their enjoyment. So for the rest of the night she hid her feelings well. She laughed, joked and danced every dance as though she was thoroughly enjoying herself and didn't have a care in the world. She even fooled Maureen, and her friend wasn't easily fooled. But no one would ever know what the effort cost her. Inside she was heartbroken. She couldn't wait for the evening to end so she could crawl into bed and cry her grief away.

Chapter Twenty-Two

Molly laid the donkey stone down at the side of the bucket before sitting back on her heels. It was a beautiful spring day, the sky a bright blue with white fluffy clouds bouncing in the warm breeze. It was a day to enjoy a stroll through the park, not to be scrubbing the front step. Pushing a strand of hair out of her eyes, Molly's thoughts wandered. If only the world was as peaceful and serene as the weather, life would be perfect. But during the last month or so there'd been nothing but bad news, bringing the threat of war nearer each day. First it was that strutting madman Mussolini invading Albania. Then Chamberlain signing a pact with France, vowing to go to their assistance if they were attacked. He'd also pledged to help Denmark, Switzerland and Holland if they were invaded by the German troops massed on their borders.

'Aye, it's a great life if yer don't weaken,' Molly muttered as she reached into the bucket for the floorcloth. She'd held out as long as she could, hoping for a miracle, but the threat of war was becoming more of a reality with each passing day and she couldn't pretend otherwise. In the last week the Territorial Army had been doubled and the Government had voted to conscript men of twenty into the forces. Only an imbecile could ignore those signs. 'Bloody men!' Molly vented her anger on the floorcloth she was wringing out. 'If it was left to women, there'd be no wars.'

'What 'ave I told yer about talkin' to yerself?' Nellie had crept up on her silently. 'One of these days some tall men in white coats will come and put yer in a straitjacket and cart yer away.'

Molly grinned as she wiped the step over. Nellie was just the tonic she needed to cheer her up and take her mind off the troubles in the world. 'Will they be handsome men?' She threw the cloth back into the water. 'And will they torture me until I give in to their lust for me body?'

'It's only them sheikh fellers who ride camels in the desert that do that, girl, an' yer won't find many of them livin' in a two-up-two-down in Walton. I should know, I've been lookin' for one long enough.'

'No luck, eh, Nellie?'

'Well, it stands to sense, doesn't it, girl?' Nellie's face was deadly serious as she leaned back against the wall, folding her arms across her tummy. 'I mean, where the 'ell would they pitch their tent around here?'

Molly struggled to her feet and picked up the bucket. 'I think it's you the men in white coats will be after. Yer definitely not right in the head.' She put her face close to her friend's and grinned. 'Come in an' I'll make yer a cup of tea, eh?'

'Thought yer'd never ask.' Nellie followed her down the hall. 'If the men in white coats come, let me open the door. If they're nice-lookin' I'll invite them in. If they're as ugly as sin, I'll tell them we gave ourselves up last week.'

'Yer know, I'm glad you're away with the mixer,' Molly said as she emptied the dirty water down the sink. 'Everyone else I know is sane, wouldn't know a joke if it jumped up an' hit them in the face.'

'Ay, just you watch it, missus! Don't forget that a week on Saturday my son is gettin' engaged to your daughter...I'm practically one of the family now.'

'May God preserve us!' Molly struck a match under the kettle. 'Yer know, I have nightmares about that. I don't know how I'm goin' to live with the shame.'

'Shut yer cakehole an' get that tea made.' When Nellie poked her tongue out it seemed such a little thing in her chubby face. 'I'm goin' to sit on yer posh couch, just for spite.' When she turned at the door there was a twinkle of mischief in her eyes. 'I might even put me feet up on it.'

When Molly carried the cups through, Nellie was sitting perfectly still, staring into space. 'You've gone quiet! Two whole minutes without a word...that must be a record!'

'I was thinkin' about our Steve. It only seems like yesterday that he was playin' ollies in the gutter, an' here he is gettin' engaged to be married.'

'I know...makes yer realise how old we're gettin'. But I'm really made up for them, they're the happiest couple I've ever seen.' Molly was so wrapped up in her thoughts she forgot one of her own rules and rested her feet on the spindles of her chair. 'They sat at this table last night counting their money to make sure they had enough for the ring. They're so young in one way, yet in another they're very grown-up. When they look at each other yer can see the love shining in their eyes, an' it makes me want to cry.'

'Let them be happy while they can,' Nellie said. 'With the state the world's in, only God knows what's goin' to happen.'

'I know, it doesn't bear thinkin' about, does it, Nellie?'

'Then don't let's think about it, kid! We've got the engagement party to look forward to next week. And because it's their birthdays as well let's give them a do they'll never forget...a real knees-up, jars out. What d'yer say, eh, girl?'

'Right! To hell with bloody Hitler and his toadies.'

'That's the spirit!' Nellie had been biting so hard on the inside of her cheek to keep the laughter at bay, she could taste blood in her mouth. 'D'yer know yer breaking the eleventh Commandment?'

Molly frowned. 'What's the eleventh Commandment when it's out?'

Nellie bowed her head and put her hands together as though in prayer. 'Thou shalt not put thy feet on my spindles.'

Molly opened her mouth in horror, jerked her feet back, looked at Nellie's solemn face, then doubled up with laughter. 'I'm always tellin' the kids off for it, then go an' do it meself! I'd never hear the last of it if they found out.'

'What do I get for keepin' me trap shut, kiddo?' Nellie spoke out of the side of her mouth like Edward G. Robinson when he'd played the role of a gangster in a film she'd seen. 'What's it worth to yer?'

'Another cuppa,' Molly stretched out her hand for the empty cup, 'and if yer behave yerself, I might even run to a ginger snap.'

Nellie couldn't be bothered making the effort

386

to get off the couch, so she followed Molly with her voice. 'Who's comin' to the party, kid?'

'Ooh, don't mention it, Nellie! I'm havin' sleepless nights just thinkin' about it.' Molly handed over the refilled cup. 'I've got the young ones sorted out, that's one blessing. Ellen's four, our Ruthie an' Bella are havin' their own party in Ellen's house, with Mary supervising. I feel a bit mean about not invitin' Mary an' Harry to the party, but Mary understands the house will only hold so many an' she's quite happy to look after the kids. I mean, I don't know how I'm goin' to fit everyone in as it is! There's your crowd, that's five before we start! Then me ma an' da, Maisie an' Alec, Tommy an' his mate, Doreen an' her three friends an' Victoria and Ellen! An' that's not countin' meself, Jack and our Jill!'

As Molly was speaking, Nellie was ticking the names off on her fingers but gave it up as a bad job when more than two hands were needed. 'Bloody hell, girl! That's over twenty!'

'I know that, soft girl, I can count! If it's a day like today it'll be all right, the young ones can dance in the yard. But if it's raining, then all I can say is God help us!'

Nellie squinted. 'Is Phil comin' with Victoria?'

'Uh, uh! That would put the cat amongst the pigeons...spoil it for the lot of us. I've explained to Phil, an' he says he understands. He probably wouldn't come even if I invited him, 'cos he knows he'd get the cold shoulder.'

'Your Doreen's stickin' to her guns, isn't she? Me, now, I think he's a crackin' lad!

387

An' he's marvellous with Victoria! Pays his whack every week even though she's told him she doesn't want it. An' he practically carries her around...won't let her lift a finger when he's home. She thinks the sun shines out of his backside!'

Molly nodded. 'I know! Now I'm goin' to tell yer somethin' on the quiet, Nellie, so keep it to yerself. I think our Doreen's cuttin' off her nose to spite her face. She goes out nearly every night with Mo, and a couple of times a week they go dancin' with Mike and Sammy. She lets on she's havin' the time of her life, but I've a sneaking suspicion she's still carrying a torch for Phil.'

'Aye, well, she's only young. Happen she'll come to her senses one of these days.'

'It would serve her right if she left it too late an' he found himself another girl.'

'I'm surprised he hasn't got one!' Nellie shuffled to the edge of the couch. 'Fine-lookin' feller like him, there must be plenty have their eye on him.'

'He never goes out to meet any. Works late nearly every night and then sits talking to Victoria until it's time for bed. The pair of them get on like a house on fire.' Molly could see her friend struggling and went to give her a helping hand. 'Grab hold an' I'll pull yer up.'

'Don't know what I'd do without yer, girl.' Nellie grinned up into her face. 'Of course, I could sit here all day.'

'Not on yer ruddy life, sunshine! Yer can just poppy off while I get meself washed and changed. I'm goin' to walk round to Ma's...get a bit of fresh air.'

'I'll come with yer.' Nellie made for the door. 'I'll nip home an' swill me face, comb me hair, an' be back in ten minutes.'

'Oh, gawd!' Molly groaned. 'I can't get rid of yer, can I?'

'Ay, just watch it, missus! Remember, I'm family now.'

'Yer won't let me forget it, will yer?' Molly smiled as her friend swayed down the hall. Softly she added, 'I wouldn't want to, either. The best friend in the world, yer are, Helen Theresa McDonough. Just seein' yer brightens me day.'

'Oh, sunshine, it's beautiful!' Molly gazed at the ring nestled in the padding of the small square box. It was a cluster, with a diamond in the centre surrounded by garnets. It was a very pretty ring, and as Molly moved the box she gasped as the diamond changed colour in the light from the gas lamp overhead. 'It's gorgeous.'

'It certainly is.' Jack was inspecting it over his wife's shoulder. 'You've done her proud, Steve.'

'Come on, Mam, let's have a dekko.' Doreen was inching her mother out of the way. 'Yer not the only one in the house, yer know.'

When Molly and Jack stepped back, their arms around each other's waists, Doreen and Mo moved in for a closer look. 'Ooh, it's lovely, our kid!'

'It certainly is,' Maureen agreed, 'one of the prettiest I've ever seen.'

'Try it on,' Doreen coaxed, 'let's see it on yer finger.'

'Uh, uh!' Jill's hair swayed around her shoulders. 'I'm not putting it on until we get engaged. Steve's taking it home with him and he's not going to let me see it again until the big day.'

Doreen tutted, 'What harm would it do to let us see it on yer?'

'No, don't do it!' Maureen knew she'd get a sly look from her friend but she threw caution to the winds. 'I think it's dead romantic...like yer see in films.'

Ruthie, hopping from one foot to the other, had a pain in her neck from trying to see into the box. Jill's my sister as well, she thought, and they've forgotten all about me! Near to tears, she pulled on Molly's skirt. 'Ah, ray, Mam! What about me?'

'Oh, I'm sorry, sweetheart!' Molly scooped her up. 'There yer are, now yer can see what all the fuss is about.'

Ruthie ran her fingers over the stones, a look of wonder on her pixie-like face. 'It's lov-er-ly, our Jill. The most bootiful ring in the whole world.'

'Thank you, love.' Jill kissed the rosebud mouth before snapping the box closed. Then she handed it to Steve. 'Here you are, you take it.'

Feeling ten feet tall and bursting with happiness, Steve pocketed the box. 'We'll go an' show me family, then yer won't see it again until the day I put it on yer finger.'

Ruthie sighed with pleasure and went back to her picture book...where the fairy princess looked just like their Jill, and the handsome prince bore a remarkable resemblance to Steve.

'Oh, it's a real beauty, girl!' Nellie was lifting the ring from its cushion when Steve smacked her hand.

'No one's touching it until I put it on Jill's finger.' He was adamant. 'An' before yer ask, Mam, the answer is no, Mrs B wasn't allowed to take it out.'

'Ay, if he starts puttin' his foot down like that when yer married, girl, stamp on it.' Nellie's face creased. 'He's just like his dad, the strong he-man type.'

'What!' George gaped. 'I'm terrified to open me flamin' mouth, let alone put me foot down!'

'There, d'yer hear the way he shouts at me? Now yer know what I've got to put up with.' Nellie's face was straight but her shaking tummy gave her away. 'He started that just after we got married, an' I thought, aye, aye, I'm havin' less of that! So I put me foot down with a firm hand.' She gave Jill a broad wink. 'It did the trick...he's been as good as gold since.'

The house was bursting at the seams and the roof seemed to lift when a rousing cheer went up as a blushing Steve slipped the ring on Jill's finger. Everyone had a drink in their hand

391

to toast the happy couple, and after taking a sip, they all surged forward to offer their congratulations.

Molly was the first to reach her daughter, and she enveloped her in a bear-like hug. 'Oh, I'm so happy for yer, sunshine. This is the best day of me life.'

'Then why are you crying, Mam?'

'Because I love you so much.' Molly sniffed and laid her head on her daughter's shoulder. 'An' yer couldn't have picked a better man...I love him as one of me own.'

'And I love you, Mam.'

The words threatened to bring on a fresh outburst, and Molly, mindful that this was supposed to be a happy occasion, gave a tearful smile before turning away and walking into the comfort of Jack's outstretched arms.

Nellie, waiting to get near her son's fiancée, made herself a promise that she wasn't going to get sentimental. But when she finally stood in front of Jill it was a promise she found hard to keep. Her future daughter-in-law was everything any mother could wish for. She was as pretty as a picture and had a kind and caring nature. Nellie would have welcomed her into the family no matter who she was. But she was her best mate's daughter, and today was the day the two families were joined together. The day the two friends had hoped for since the children were little. Nellie opened her arms wide. 'Come here, girl, an' give yer future ma-in-law a kiss.'

Jack patted Molly's back as she buried her head in his shoulder. 'Come on, love, there's no need to carry on like this.'

'I can't help it,' she sobbed. 'I love them both to death.'

Jack chuckled. 'Why is it that when women are happy they cry?'

Molly pulled away, wiping the backs of her hands across her face. 'I know, we're crazy, aren't we?' She held out her hand. 'Be a pal and lend us yer hankie.'

'I can't help yer there, love, I haven't got one on me.'

'I'll nip up and get one... I can't keep sniffing all night.' Molly stood on tiptoe to kiss his cheek. 'Yer a smasher, Jack Bennett, an' I'm crazy about yer.'

There was laughter in Jack's brown eyes. 'Shall I come upstairs with yer to look for a hankie?'

'Behave yerself, we've got company.' Molly grinned as she pushed through the crowd and made her way upstairs. If ever anyone was lucky, it was her. She had a husband and children she adored, and now her family was to be extended to include the McDonoughs. Definitely a cause for celebration. She'd make herself presentable, then go down and have the time of her life.

She walked into the bedroom and came to an abrupt halt. 'What are you doin' up here?'

Doreen moved quickly away from the window, guilt written on her flushed face. She'd built her hopes on Phil coming to the party with Miss Clegg and had been filled with disappointment when the old lady walked in on her own. It would have been an ideal time to make it up with him without having her pride dented. And she wanted more than anything in the world to make it up with him. Suddenly she had no heart for a party and had come upstairs to try and get a glimpse of him. It would have been a comfort to know he was at home and not out enjoying himself with another girl. 'I, er, I was in our bedroom an' I thought I heard a knock on the door. I came in here to look out of the window, see if I could see anyone. But I must have been hearing things 'cos there's no one there.'

Molly opened her mouth, then closed it again. In a flash she knew what Doreen was doing looking out of the window...she was watching the house opposite, hoping to catch a glimpse of Phil. Stupid girl, Molly thought. All she has to do is give him a smile and he'll be over like a shot. 'Yer imagining it...I didn't hear no knock. Now get downstairs and entertain yer friends.'

Doreen passed her without a word, and for a while Molly stood looking at the spot where her daughter had stood. Then, with a sigh, she pulled open a drawer in the dressing table and took out a hankie. 'She's a silly article. Her pride will be her downfall.'

Phil stepped away from the window and flattened himself against the wall. He'd nearly got caught out there! He'd been watching the Bennetts' house, wondering how the party was going and wishing he was there. He wasn't worried about being seen, thought they'd all be too busy enjoying themselves to look out of the window. But he'd got the fright of his life when he saw

394

the net on the bedroom window move and the shape of someone standing behind it.

'Serves me right if they saw me,' he muttered as he fell into the chair and picked up the evening paper. 'It's a pity I've got nothing better to do.'

He was engrossed in the latest news from Europe when there was a knock on the door. Lowering the paper, he sat for a while, a puzzled expression on his face. The only visitors Aunt Vicky ever had were Molly, Nellie or Mary, and it wouldn't be them, not tonight. And it certainly wouldn't be for him.

When the knock came again, Phil laid the paper aside. He'd better open the door in case it was his adopted aunt...she hadn't taken a key with her because she said she wouldn't be staying long.

The breath caught in Phil's throat when he saw who was standing on the bottom step. 'What the hell are you doin' here?'

'Hello, son.' Tom Bradley was chewing on a matchstick, a sly grin on his sallow face. 'Just thought I'd call an' see how yer are.'

'Don't you ever call me "son". I never have been your son, never want to be and never will be.' Phil was beside himself with rage. How had this man found out where he was! And why had he travelled all the way from Huyton to see him? 'You're not welcome here, so just clear off.'

Tom took the matchstick from his mouth and began picking his teeth with it. He eyed Phil up and down, his lip curled. 'Landed on yer bleedin' feet here, haven't yer? The old lady got money, has she?'

Phil made a fist of his hand. Oh, how he'd like to smash the sneering face in. Get his own back for all those years of suffering and humiliation. But he wasn't about to bring trouble to the home of the woman who had been good to him. 'Are yer going to leave while yer all in one piece, or do I have to make yer?'

'Now, there's no need to take that attitude.' Tom Bradley's smile would never be anything but a sneer. He wasn't capable of genuine warmth or sincerity. 'Yer ma was worried about yer, so I said I'd come an' put her mind at rest.'

'Now you know I'm all right yer can clear off. And don't bother comin' back again.' Phil picked his words carefully. It was obvious his mother hadn't told Bradley that she'd been down to his works to see him, and he didn't want to get her in trouble. In any case, she couldn't have told where he lived because she didn't know! 'Just out of curiosity, how did yer know I was here?'

'Didn't think we'd find out, did yer?' Bradley bared his yellow teeth in a snarl. 'It was easy, really, our Brian followed yer home from work.'

'They say small things amuse small minds, and minds don't come any smaller than Brian's.' Phil put his hand on the latch, ready to close the door. 'Now get on yer bike and don't ever come back again. In fact, I'm surprised yer've got the nerve to show yer face around here, seeing as how yer were run out by the neighbours for stealing. But I promise yer this...if I catch yer within a mile of this street, so help me, I'll flay the livin' daylights out of yer.'

'Now don't be so hasty.' Tom put his foot on the top step so Phil couldn't close the door. 'There's no need for talk like that. Yer don't want to upset yer ma, do yer?'

'Leave me mam out of it.'

'But yer ma's the reason I came! Yer see, she misses yer few bob every week an' I think it's only right and proper that yer should turn somethin' up. Just a few bob a week to help out, that's all I'm askin' for. After all, she is yer mother.'

Phil couldn't believe the man's bare-faced cheek. 'An' although you're a pathetic excuse for one, you're her husband! It's your responsibility to look after her.' He gave a bitter laugh. 'What's wrong, can't yer take care of yer own family? Not enough easy pickings from the people of Huyton, is that it?'

'Yer've no bleedin' right to talk to me like that! After all the years I gave yer a roof over yer head? Ungrateful soddin' bastard, that's what yer are. All we're askin' for is a few measly bob. Yer've hopped in lucky here... I bet yer don't have to hand over a penny.'

'Whether I do or not is none of your business. Nothing in my life has anythin' to do with you now, thank God. So push off before I kick yer the full length of this street. An' don't think I won't, because nothin' would give me greater pleasure.' He moved forward

397

and Bradley stepped back, a look of fear on his face. 'Get going, now!'

Tom Bradley backed a few steps, out of harm's way. 'I'll go, but yer haven't seen or heard the last of me. There's more than one way of skinning a cat, as yer'll find out to yer sorrow.' He didn't wait to see the reaction his words brought, but took to his heels and fled down the street. He made a comical figure as he covered the ground, but Phil knew there was nothing remotely amusing about Tom Bradley. He was cunning, evil and dangerous. He didn't care who he hurt and he was capable of causing untold harm.

As he picked the paper up and sat down, Phil's anger turned to worry. Not for himself, but for the woman who'd given him shelter, made him feel as though he was part of a family. She was the grandmother he'd never had, and her friends, Nellie and Molly from over the road had taken him to their hearts and treated him as though he was one of them. Even the neighbours had a smile and a greeting for him.

Phil gave a deep sigh as he scanned the front page of the paper. He saw the printed words but couldn't concentrate on their meaning. His mind was full of what Tom Bradley had in store for him. Not for one moment did he doubt the man's threat. One way or another he'd get his own back. And in his quest for revenge he'd wreck the life Phil had made for himself and ruin his chance of happiness.

He closed his eyes as thoughts whirled around

in his head. What would happen if Bradley came one day when he was at work? It was the sort of thing the devious devil would do. He wouldn't harm the old lady, he was too crafty for that, but he could put the fear of God into her.

'There's nothin' else for it, I'll have to warn her.' Phil spoke to the empty room. 'It wouldn't be fair not to, after she's been so good to me.' His eyes on the ceiling, he wondered how he could tell her without alarming her. I could tell Molly and Nellie...ask them to keep an eye open. They'd spread the word to the other neighbours and if Bradley showed his face he'd soon be sent packing.

But was it right to expect other people to get involved in his problems? Phil sighed. The best thing he could do to spare the old lady any trouble was to get out of her life. The thought saddened him, because he'd grown to love the frail, gentle woman, but what else could he do? He'd be out of his mind every day at work, wondering when Bradley would strike...and how.

This time the sigh came from deep within him. Just when he was beginning to value the warmth of happiness and real friendship, it was to be snatched from him. The day his mother had married Tom Bradley, she'd put a jinx on her son, and it seemed he was going to suffer from it all his life.

Phil idly turned the page of the newspaper and found himself looking into a man's face. It caught his attention because it was a full-page photograph of a moustached soldier whose finger seemed to be pointing directly at him. Across the top of the page, in big letters, were the words YOUR COUNTRY NEEDS YOU.

Chapter Twenty-Three

'I'm sorry I wasn't here for yer party, princess, but I'm afraid it couldn't be helped. Yer know I'd have been here if it had been humanly possible.' Corker's huge frame seemed to fill the small room. He'd come straight from the ship, his canvas bag slung over his shoulder and a huge grin on his weatherbeaten face. 'Me favourite girl an' I have to go and miss her big day.' He lowered his bag and stood it next to the sideboard, making sure it was safe and couldn't topple over. Then he held his massive arms wide. 'Come an' give yer Uncle Corker a big kiss.'

Jill stood on tiptoe to fling her arms around his neck. 'We were hoping you'd make it, Uncle Corker, but I understand.' She gave him a kiss on the cheek, her nose wrinkling as the coarse hairs of his beard tickled her skin. 'We missed you, didn't we, Mam?'

'We sure did...we could have done with yer here to play yer concertina. It was a really good do, though, even if I do say it meself.' Molly looked on, happy to see the man she counted as one of her best friends. 'It was a party an' a half, an' that's a fact. We made so much noise it's a wonder the neighbours didn't complain.' She chuckled. 'Mind you, Mrs Connelly next door is as deaf as a doorpost, she probably didn't hear a sound. And with Ellen being in here I didn't have to worry about the neighbours the other side.'

'I've still got a hangover from it,' Jack chuckled. 'It was three o'clock before we managed to get rid of everyone...they were havin' such a good time we literally had to throw them out.'

'And four o'clock before we got to bed.' A smile hugged the corners of Molly's mouth. 'I made them all stay up until the mess was cleared away. Yer should have seen the place, it looked as though a bomb had hit it. I didn't fancy the idea of comin' down to face it, so I made them all get stuck in an' tidy up.'

'We'll have another little celebration before I go back, eh, princess? Just a few drinks down at the pub so I won't feel left out.' Corker bent to loosen the ties on his sailor's bag. 'I've brought a little present for you and Steve...somethin' for yer bottom drawer.' Using both hands he brought out a large, bulky parcel which he placed carefully on the table in front of Jill.

'Don't open it now, wait until I've gone. And be careful when yer unwrapping it, there's breakables inside.'

'Ah, can't I open it now?' Jill's face was aglow with happiness and excitement. 'Please?'

'I'll be gone in a minute an' yer can open it then.' Corker ruffled her blonde hair as he gazed down into the vivid blue eyes. 'It comes with love and my best wishes.' Turning his head slightly, he winked at Molly. 'And yer can tell Steve he's the luckiest lad alive to have landed you! If I'd been twenty years younger I'd have given him a run for his money.'

'Oh, Uncle Corker, I can't tell him that!' Jill's long, slender fingers were running over the parcel, trying to guess by the shape what was inside. 'I can't wait to see what it is.'

Corker's massive hand covered hers. 'That looks a very pretty ring, let's have a gander.'

Jill slipped her hand from his and held it aloft, her fingers wiggling for greater effect. 'It is pretty, isn't it?'

'It certainly is! But it's not as pretty as the girl wearing it.' Corker pulled the draw cords on his bag and tied them before swinging it over his shoulder. 'I better be on my way an' see how me ma is.'

'She's fine, Corker,' Molly told him. 'Me an' Nellie went up to see her yesterday. She said she was expectin' yer home any day.'

'It was a load off me mind when Ellen wrote that the Bradleys had done a flit.' Corker's laugh ricocheted off the walls. 'They've saved me a job!'

'Aye, it was good riddance to bad rubbish,' Jack said. 'They were a bad lot.'

Molly's head jerked up and down in agreement. 'Yer can say that again! How young Phil turned out to be such a good lad, livin' with that family, is a mystery. Yer know he's still with Victoria, don't yer?'

Corker nodded. 'Aye, Ellen's kept me up to date with the news. She said Miss Clegg's over the moon with him. And it doesn't surprise me one bit. I'm a pretty good judge of character, and I'd have bet me bottom dollar on him being a good 'un.'

'We've got loads to tell yer, Corker, but I know yer on pins to get home so we'll leave it until yer've got more time.'

'Like twenty-four hours.' Jack stood up and thrust his hands in his trouser pockets. 'Yer'll need that long when Molly and Nellie start gabbing...they'll talk the ears off yer.'

'Hey, just watch it, me laddo!' Molly put both hands on his chest and pushed him back in the chair. 'I'll see Corker out.'

The big man planted a kiss on Jill's head. 'Congratulations, an' I hope yer like the present.'

Preceding him down the hall, Molly asked over her shoulder, 'Does Ellen know yer home?'

'Not yet. I'll give a knock now when I'm passing, but I won't go in. I'll go home first and see me ma, have somethin' to eat, get washed and changed, then come back.'

'She's a different woman these days, Corker, thanks to you. She didn't half enjoy the party an' really let herself go.' Standing on the top step, her eyes level with his, Molly said, 'An' the kids have never stopped talkin' about their party, they had the time of their lives. It was a pleasure just looking at the sheer enjoyment on their faces. I don't think they'd ever had a party before.'

'They hadn't!' Corker's sigh came straight from his heart. 'But the bad days are behind them now, an' I'll make sure they never come back.'

'Good for you!' Molly said, giving him a broad wink. 'I think yer a crackin' man, Jimmy Corkhill, an' Ellen's a lucky woman.' She watched as he walked the few steps to the house next door. 'Ta-ra, Corker, see yer tomorrow.'

In her eagerness to see Jill's present, Molly banged the door without thinking. Too late she remembered that Ruthie was asleep upstairs, 'Oh, yer stupid article,' she scolded herself, 'yer'll have gone an' woken her up now!' With a hand covering her mouth, she stood for a few seconds at the foot of the stairs, dreading the shout that would tell her she'd woken the child. But there wasn't a sound and she breathed a sigh of relief. 'Thank God for that!'

'Mam, look what Uncle Corker's brought us.' Jill was staring wide-eyed at the array of china and cloths spread out on the table. Picking up a cup, she handed it to her mother. 'Me dad said it's real china.'

'I can see it is, sunshine!' Molly pulled out a chair and sat down. 'It's beautiful!'

'There's six of everything, Mam! A full tea service and dinner plates to match. And look at these.' Jill spread the cloths out for her mother's inspection. 'A sideboard runner, a tablecloth and matching serviettes...all hand-embroidered!'

'Corker doesn't do things by halves, does he?' Jack was standing behind Molly's chair, a hand

404

on her shoulder. 'Those cups and saucers are fit for a king.'

'Oh, I won't use them for every day, they'll go away for special occasions.' In Jill's mind was the vision of a glass display cabinet she'd seen in George Henry Lees. Just the thing for showing off the beautiful china spread out before her. 'Mo bought me a teaset, that can be for everyday use.' She glanced at the clock on the mantelpiece. 'Steve will be here soon... I can't wait to see his face when he sees this lot!'

Molly turned her head and looked up into Jack's face. 'Times have changed, haven't they, love? We didn't get anythin' like this when we got engaged, did we?'

Jack smiled down at her, his eyes soft and tender. 'If my memory serves me right, we got towels, towels, and more towels! I can even remember you saying we'd got enough to open a stall at Paddy's market.'

Molly gurgled with laughter. 'Yeah, an' I can remember you saying that they probably came from Paddy's market in the first place!'

Jack cupped her face in his hands. 'We didn't have much in those days, but it never stopped us from having a wonderful life together, did it? We had each other and that was enough.'

Her presents forgotten for the moment, Jill rested her arms on the table and watched the show of affection. They were never soppy, her mam and dad, at least not in front of the children. But they showed their love for each other in so many ways. Like now, you could almost touch the emotion that was flowing between the two of them. And that's how it was going to be with her and Steve. They'd be just as much in love after twenty years of marriage as her mam and dad were.

When Corker stepped off the tram the next night, he happened to glance at the row of shops facing him and glimpsed a figure lurking in one of the doorways. He wouldn't normally have thought anything of it, but it seemed to him that whoever was there had sought the safety of the doorway when they'd seen him get off the tram. He hesitated for a few seconds, telling himself he was imagining things. It was probably just some lad waiting for his girlfriend. But curiosity got the better of him and he walked slowly towards the shop. He was a couple of strides from it when a figure darted out and started to run in the opposite direction. 'It's the Bradley boy,' Corker muttered, quickening his step. 'What the hell is he doin' around here?'

Brian Bradley fled around the corner of the nearest street, Corker in hot pursuit. But when the big man turned the corner, there was no sign of him, the street was deserted. 'My God, he was quick!' Corker stroked his beard, knowing it was useless to carry on. The entries running along the backs of these houses were like a maze, easy to get lost in. It would be like looking for a needle in a haystack.

He turned and retraced his steps. If he'd had time he would have continued the chase, but he was late as it was...he should have picked Ellen up half an hour ago to take her to the pub on the corner, where they'd arranged to meet up with their friends for a few drinks to celebrate Steve and Jill's engagement. By rights, Jill shouldn't be allowed in the pub because she was only seventeen, but a quiet word in the manager's ear had worked wonders. Particularly when it came from the man who spent more money there when he was home on leave than the rest of the customers did all the year round.

Hurrying now to make up for lost time, he told himself he should have listened to his conscience and kept away from the pub where he knew his shipmates would be congregated. His common sense should have told him that the one drink he'd promised himself was impossible. It always led to another, then another, as each man insisted on buying his round. The trouble was, when you'd had a few drinks you lost all sense of time. As he neared the Clarkes' house, Corker felt in his pocket for the packet of Victory V lozenges. He popped one in his mouth and sucked furiously, hoping it would take away the smell of drink. There'd be merry hell to pay if Ellen knew he'd been knocking the pints back while she was patiently waiting for him. She wasn't the size of sixpennyworth of copper but she could certainly stick up for herself. She could get into a right little paddy when she was annoyed. Still, Corker consoled himself as he rapped on the door, I've got some news that will please her.

'Here's wishin' yer both all the luck in the world.' Corker raised his glass and smiled at the young couple. 'May yez always be as happy as yer are now, and never know what it is to want.' He drank deeply, then wiped the froth from his moustache with the back of his hand. 'And may I say that yez make a real handsome couple.'

'I'll drink to that!' Nellie was perched on a stool, her legs wide apart and showing her knickers. 'Mind you, with me as his mother it's only natural that our Steve's good-lookin'.'

'I'm saying nothin'.' Molly raised her brows and hoped the expression on her face was one of scorn. 'But then, I don't have to, do I? I mean, yer only have to look at our Jill to know who she takes after.'

Nellie bristled. What could she say to beat that? But she couldn't let her friend get one over on her. 'Funny yer should say that, girl! I've always thought your Jill resembled Tucker, the coal man.'

Bridie gasped, 'Sure, now, that's not the kind of talk yer should be usin' in front of the young ones. 'Tis ashamed of yerselves yer should be, the pair of you.'

'Ay, don't be blamin' me, I haven't said anything!' Molly could see the laughter in everyone's eyes and knew that out of respect for her mother they were trying hard to contain it. She was trying herself, but she couldn't keep it from bubbling over. 'I mean, I could have said I've always thought Steve looked like Mr Henry, the rent man! But I didn't say it, did I?'

Even Bridie joined in the roar that followed. Dabbing at her eyes with a wisp of a hankie, she croaked, 'Molly me darlin', you'll have a lot of explainin' to do when yer get to the pearly gates, so yer will.'

'Oh, she's not goin' up there!' Nellie feigned a look of surprise. 'She's comin' down below with me! Where I go, me mate goes! I've got two shovels ready, 'cos bein' new arrivals, the Devil is bound to put us on stokin' the fires.' She turned to Molly, 'Ay, girl, I wonder if the Devil is one of Tucker's customers?'

Every head in the pub turned when Corker's laugh boomed out. 'Why d'yer ask, Nellie? D'yer think yer can get him a discount?'

Molly threw her hands up. 'Nellie Mc-Donough, yer can just forget about that! I mean, that's taking friendship a bit too far.' She jabbed a stiffened finger in the air, 'I have every intention of goin' up there, so if yer want to come with me yer'd better start mending yer ways.'

Bridie didn't know whether to laugh or cry. 'May the good Lord forgive the pair of yer.'

Corker, sitting next to her, patted her hand. 'Oh, I'm sure He will, Bridie me darlin'. After all, it's well known He has a good sense of humour.'

'He'll need it,' Bob said drily, 'if these two ever make it up there.'

Jill and Steve sat holding hands, enjoying the banter. Being engaged was still a novelty to them and they were as happy as two people could be. 'Are you all right, sweetheart?' Steve leaned sideways to whisper in her ear. 'Enjoyin' yerself?'

'Oh, yes!' their eyes locked and sent a thrill like an electric shock through their whole bodies. Jill turned away quickly and glanced around the table to see if they were being watched. Satisfied that the company were deep in conversation, she whispered, 'I love you, Steve McDonough.'

Steve groaned. 'An' I love you more than words can say. I want the next few years to fly over, so I'm out of me time and can afford to get married. Then we'll have our own little house an' yer'll be there every night when I come in from work.'

Their dreams were interrupted by Molly. 'Wake up, you two! Uncle Corker's been talkin' to yer but yer were miles away, in another world!'

'Sorry, Mam, we were only talking.'

'Well, he's gone to the bar now, but I told him yer didn't want another drink 'cos I think yer've had enough.'

'I have.' Jill laughed nervously. 'I feel tiddly now.'

'Yer've only had one glass of sherry!' Steve put his arm across her shoulders. 'I'm glad you don't drink much... I hate to see a woman drunk.'

Corker came back with a tray of glasses and set them down. 'You can help yerselves, folks.' He took his seat next to Ellen, a thoughtful expression on his face. Should he tell her the news now? She'd had her coat on when he'd called for her and had come straight out, not giving him a chance to tell her where he'd been that day. But she got embarrassed so easily, she might not take kindly to discussing their business in front of their friends. Still, they had to find out some time, it might as well be now. 'I went to see a solicitor today, love.'

Ellen could feel the colour drain from her face and hoped that no one would notice in the dark, smoke-filled room. Filled with apprehension she said softly, 'Oh, yes?'

'Yes, one of me mates recommended a bloke in Dale Street. I explained about Nobby, and what the doctor had told us, an' he said that under the circumstances he couldn't see any reason why you wouldn't be granted a divorce.'

There was silence around the table for a few seconds, then Molly said, 'That sounds hopeful, doesn't it, Ellen?'

When Ellen didn't speak, merely nodded, Corker went on. 'He said it would take about two years, so the sooner you apply the better.'

Out of the corner of her eye, Ellen could see Bridie's lips set in a thin, straight line. She knew that the older woman objected strongly to divorce on religious grounds, and she wished fervently that Corker had waited until they were on their own before bringing the subject up. 'We'll talk about it later, shall we?' she said quietly. 'This is hardly the place.'

Molly and Nellie exchanged glances which said that Corker was going to need some support in persuading Ellen to make a move. 'Don't take too long talkin' about it,' Nellie said. 'Get it over an' done with.'

'The sooner yer set the wheels in motion, the

411

better yer'll feel. It'll be a load off yer mind.'
Molly gave Jack a sharp dig in the ribs. 'Don't
you agree, Jack?'

'Yes I do! If I were you, Ellen, I'd go with
Corker and see this solicitor bloke.'

'I agree with me dad.' Jill surprised herself
and everyone else by the strength of her feelings.
She'd never hated anyone in her life before.
Never thought it possible to dislike another
human being as much as she did Nobby Clarke
for the way he'd treated Ellen and the children.
'You go with Uncle Corker, he'll know what
to do.'

Ellen's face was set, and seeing that she wasn't
going to be drawn, Corker changed the subject.
'By the way, have any of yez seen anything of
the Bradley family since they left? Do they ever
come around?'

'You're joking, aren't yer?' Molly grimaced.
'They wouldn't 'ave the nerve to show their
faces...the neighbours would flay them alive.'

Jack looked interested. 'Why Corker?'

'No reason, I just wondered.' Corker decided
to keep quiet about what he'd seen. After all, it
was possible he'd been mistaken, but he didn't
think so. If the lad had nothing to hide, why
had he scarpered like that?

The bell behind the bar sounded. 'Time,
please,' Les called, putting the towels over
the pump handles. 'Drink up an' let's be
havin' yer.'

They were walking up the street when Corker
said casually, 'I'll have to call in an' see Miss

Clegg while I'm home. I suppose it's too late now, she's probably in bed.'

'No, look,' Molly pointed, 'the light's still on. Since Phil's been there she doesn't go to bed so early.'

'I wonder if she'd mind if I knocked now? I mightn't get another chance before I go back.'

'She'd be made up to see yer,' Nellie told him. 'She loves visitors.'

'Right, I'll slip over for five minutes.' Corker took his hand from Ellen's elbow. 'Put the kettle on, love, an' I'll be back before it's boiled.' His long legs covered the cobbled street in a few strides. 'I'll bid yez good night, folks.'

The chorus of 'good nights' was fading when he lifted the knocker and rapped softly, not wanting to frighten the old lady. He would have left it until tomorrow, but Phil would be at work then and it was him that Corker wanted to see. There was a question niggling at the back of his mind which Phil might be able to answer.

It was Phil who opened the door, and when he saw Corker his eyebrows shot up in surprise. 'Hello, Mr Corkhill! We couldn't make out who'd be knockin' this time of night.'

'I know it's late, son, but when I saw the light was still on I thought I'd call an' see how Miss Clegg is.'

'Come in, she'll be glad to see yer.' Phil let Corker pass then closed the door. He was tall himself, had never had to look up at a man before, but he felt dwarfed by the size of the

413

big man. 'We're just havin' our supper.'

'I've just had mine,' Corker chuckled, 'six pints of ale.'

'Well I never!' Victoria's hands fluttered. 'This is an unexpected pleasant surprise.'

'It's only a quick call, just to see how yer are.' Corker held his cap in his hand, his fingers running back and forth along the shiny peak. 'I must say yer looking well...the picture of health!'

'I'm fine, Corker. Phil looks after me, makes sure I keep warm and eat all me dinner.' She pointed to a chair. 'Won't you sit down?'

'No thanks, me darlin', I won't keep yer from yer supper. I'll come in one day and we'll have a good old natter.' Corker turned to Phil, who was standing by the door. 'I'm glad she's got you here to keep an eye on her. You're doin' a good job, too, from the looks of things...she looks great.'

Phil blushed. 'It's her that looks after me, not the other way around. I've never been so well fed in all me life.'

'I can see yer like two bugs, snug in a rug.' Corker twisted the end of his moustache, bringing it to a point which defied the laws of gravity. 'I believe yer family moved out?'

Phil nodded. 'I think it was a case of goin' before they were pushed.'

'He's seen his mam, though, haven't you, Phil?' Victoria's eyes were bright. 'She met him outside the factory, and guess what? She told him all about his real dad, and even gave him a photo!'

414

'Really? Well, that was a turn-up for the books, wasn't it?' Corker smiled to ease the boy's embarrassment. 'Yer'll have to tell me all about it when we've more time.' He hesitated for a second, then asked, 'Have yer seen anythin' of the rest of the Bradleys...do they ever come around here?'

'No.' Phil lowered his eyes but wasn't quick enough to hide the guilt written in them. He'd never told Aunt Vicky about Tom Bradley's visit because he didn't know how to do it without frightening her. It had been on the tip of his tongue dozens of times, but her trusting eyes and her gentle frailty kept him from speaking the words. 'I don't want to see them, either! They can rot in hell for all I care.'

'Aye, well, happen they'll do that eventually.' As Corker put his cap on, he was thinking that the lad wasn't telling the truth, was keeping something back. 'Anyway, I'll be on me way an' leave yez to eat yer supper in peace.' He dropped a kiss on the fine, snow-white hair. 'Now I know yer all right, I'll sleep easy in me bed tonight.'

'You will call again, won't you, Corker?' Victoria asked eagerly. 'It's always a tonic to see you.'

'Have no fear, me darlin', yer'll be sick of looking at me by the time I go back. Like the proverbial bad penny, I'll keep turning up.'

Phil opened the door and stepped back to let Corker pass. The fluttering in his heart and tummy was an indication of the apprehension he felt at having to admit he'd told a lie. But better that than living with the knowledge that he was no better than the Bradleys.

'Can I have a quiet word, Mr Corkhill?' Phil pulled the door to behind him. 'I didn't tell the truth in there because I didn't want to upset Aunt Vicky. But me dad did call here one night...it was the night of Jill's party, thank God, so she wasn't in.'

'I thought there was something, son, because yer not a very good liar. It was written all over yer face.' Corker's heart was gladdened by the boy's admission, it showed that his judgement about him had been right. 'What did he want?'

'He was after money. Wanted me to cough up a couple of bob a week...said it was me mam's idea. But I know she hadn't sent him because I'd seen her a few times. I didn't tell him that, though, 'cos she must have kept quiet about it.'

'The cheeky sod!' Corker exploded. 'I hope yer told him in no uncertain terms where to go to!'

Phil nodded. 'I sent him packing with a flea in his ear. But I'm worried, Mr Corkhill, 'cos he threatened to get his own back.'

'Huh! I wouldn't worry about that, he was just tryin' to sound tough. He can't do yer no harm, son.'

'You don't know him like I do, he's a sly, crafty beggar. I'm not afraid for meself, he doesn't scare me one bit. But I'm worried about Aunt Vicky...I wouldn't put it past him to get at me through her.' There was a catch in Phil's voice. 'She's been so good to me I'd go mad if I brought trouble to her door. I'm worryin' meself sick every day in work in case he comes...she's so inoffensive and trusting, she'd probably let him in.'

Corker took his cap off and ran his fingers through his hair. The lad was right: Victoria was of the old school where you didn't keep people standing on your step, you invited them in. 'I don't want to add to yer troubles, son, but yer've been honest with me and I'll be honest with you. When I got off the tram tonight I saw your Brian lurking in one of the shop doorways. I went after him, but he legged it down a jigger an' I lost him.'

A groan of anguish left Phil's mouth. 'Oh, no!'

'I'm afraid so! I was suspicious, that's why I tried to nab him, but he was too quick for me.'

'D'yer know, Mr Corkhill, for the first time in me life I'm beginning to get a bit of pride in meself. Aunt Vicky can be thanked for that...she treats me as though I am somebody. But talk about yer past coming back to haunt yer, well, that's goin' to be my lot in life from the looks of things. I'll never be free of my past.' Phil opened the door a little and glanced down the hall before continuing. 'The best thing I can do is get out of her life. They'll leave her alone if I'm not here.'

'And break the old lady's heart? That's not the answer son, 'cos she's the one would get hurt the most. Anyway, I'm blowed if I'd let the buggers run me out!' Corker could feel his anger rising. 'Don't you do anythin' until we've had a chance to talk it through. We'll come up with something, so don't worry. But for heaven's sake, don't say anythin' to Miss Clegg about leavin', 'cos it would only upset her.' Putting his cap back on, he said gruffly, 'Come over to the Clarkes' house tomorrow night after yer've had yer dinner. You can always make some excuse...say I've promised to lend yer a book.'

'Okay. An' thanks for bein' so understanding, Mr Corkhill, I appreciate it.'

'Think nothin' of it, son,' Corker said as he stepped into the street. 'I'll see yer tomorrow, God willing.'

It was two o'clock in the morning before Corker slipped the front door key into the lock. The house was silent and in darkness. He took his shoes off before climbing the stairs in case he woke his mother. It had been a long day and his whole body felt heavy with tiredness. But his mind and heart were at ease. At last Ellen had agreed to go with him to see the solicitor about setting the wheels in motion for her divorce from Nobby. It was going to be a long two years of waiting, but he didn't mind that. After all, what were two years? Hadn't he been in love with her for the last twenty?

Chapter Twenty-Four

Jack barely had time to get the key out of the lock and push the door open before Molly was upon him, blocking his entrance. With her face aglow and hopping up and down with excitement, she told him, 'Monday mornin' the electric gets switched on...isn't that the gear?'

'It certainly is!' Jack was pushing her slowly back along the hall so he could get near the hall stand to hang his cap on one of the hooks. 'I'll be able to patch up the wallpaper then, get the room back to normal.' He sidestepped to try and squeeze past her but she stood firm. 'Molly, can me an' Tommy get in, please, we're both starving! I felt ashamed of meself on the tram, the way me belly was rumbling.'

'Mine too!' Tommy followed them into the room. 'I could eat a flippin' horse.'

'Well, it does me heart good to see yez so thrilled at me news.' Molly stood with her hands on her hips, shaking her head in disappointment at their lack of enthusiasm. 'Typical flamin' men! All yez can think about is yer ruddy tummies! I bet if I told yer a long-lost relative had died and left us a fortune, it wouldn't raise a flicker of interest! Yer'd still stand there gawpin', asking "Is me dinner ready?"'

'I wouldn't, yer know,' Jack laughed, 'I'd die of shock! Who do we know that's got more than two ha'pennies to rub together?'

'Well, if it was a whole lot of money, say a thousand pounds, I'd go without food for a week.' Tommy's voice was still in the process of changing from boy to man, and varied from a high squeak to a low growl. 'But as that's unlikely, can I ask what we're havin' for dinner?'

'What are those things stickin' out at the end of yer legs?' Molly asked, pointing to the floor. 'Those flamin' big clodhoppers.'

Looking puzzled, Tommy gazed down the length of his body. 'Yer mean me feet?'

'Yeah, right in one go! Except a pig was running around on these last week. And d'yer know what? I'm sorry they killed the pig, 'cos it would probably have been more enthusiastic about gettin' the 'leccy on than you two!' Just then a deep rumble from Jack's tummy filled the air and the sound had Molly biting on her bottom lip. The poor beggars must be starving. If she'd had the sense to leave her news until they'd had their dinner, she might have got the reaction she was hoping for. 'Pigs trotters, with lots of carrots and barley.'

'Mmm!' Tommy licked his lips while rubbing his hand in circles over his tummy. 'Let's be havin' them, Mam, me mouth's watering.'

'Where is everyone?' Jack called as Molly went into the kitchen. 'I saw our Ruthie playin' hopscotch in the street with Bella, but where's the other two?'

'Jill's upstairs getting changed, an' our Doreen's out here fiddling with her hair...as per usual.' Steam was rising from the plates Molly carried through, her hands protected by a tea towel. 'She borrowed Mary Watson's curling tongs, 'cos she reckons they're better than ours, and she's heating them on the gas ring. Said she fancies a pageboy bob like Joan Crawford.'

She pulled out a chair, and curling a strand of hair around her finger, watched father and son dig forks into the meat of the trotters and pull it from the bone. Not that there was ever much meat on a pig's trotter, but what there was was tasty. 'Corker an' Ellen called today, after they'd been to see the solicitor.'

'Oh, aye. How did they get on?'

'Yer know what Ellen's like, yer've more chance of getting blood out of a stone than gettin' anythin' out of her. But Corker seemed pleased they've got the ball rolling.' Molly was thoughtful as she watched Tommy gnawing at the bone, grease running down his chin. 'If I tell yez something, it's to go no further than these four walls, d'yer hear me, Tommy?'

'I might be daft, Mam, but I'm not Mutt and Jeff!' Tommy put the bone down and wiped a hand across his chin. 'An' I'm not a girl...I've got more to do than go around tellin' tales.'

'Aye, well, just think on,' Molly warned before telling them about Phil's visit from Tom Bradley.

In the kitchen, Doreen pricked her ears. She stood gazing into the spotted mirror she had propped up on the wooden draining board, the curling tongs in her hand forgotten as she strained to hear what was being said. She hadn't

421

set eyes on Phil since the morning she snubbed him...an action she bitterly regretted. But he was never out of her thoughts, and if she only had the chance, she'd pluck up the courage to tell him how sorry she was. Every morning when she opened the door to go to work, she prayed that his door would open too. She'd gone over in her mind what she would do...give him a smile or a nod, anything to break the ice and encourage him to make a move to patch things up between them. But the opportunity hadn't come along. He was either leaving early for work or using the back door. The only sight she'd had of him was a shadow through the window of the house opposite.

She heard her mother saying, 'Phil's comin' over to Ellen's tonight, an' Corker's asked me and Nellie to be there. We're going to think of some way of scaring the Bradleys off, so Phil won't have to leave.'

'What time are yer goin'?' Jack asked. 'I might come with yer.'

'Not until about nine o'clock, 'cos young Phil works late every night.'

Doreen put the tongs back on the gas ring, and as she waited for them to heat her mind was ticking over. How could she wangle things so that she was in the street when he crossed to Ellen's?

'Where are you goin' tonight, Doreen?' Molly bawled. 'Will yer stay in an' listen for Ruthie?'

'I was goin' for a walk with Mo...she'll be here soon.' Doreen kept her voice steady. This might be just the break she needed, but it wouldn't do to let her mother know she'd been listening. 'I'll see what she says.'

'Aye, well, at the moment I'm just askin' yer to volunteer,' Molly yelled back, 'but if yer refuse then it won't be a request, it'll be an order.'

This was one order Doreen didn't mind, and one that she wouldn't disobey.

'I know it's early, but I'm goin' up to Ellen's for a little natter. I've been stuck in the house all day, talking to meself, so it'll do me good to get out for a while.' Molly ran a comb through her hair before pinching her cheeks to put some colour in them. She never bothered with make-up unless she was going somewhere special. 'You can follow on when yer've finished readin' the *Echo*.'

'What about Nellie?' Jack peered over the top of the paper. 'Is she callin' here for yer?'

'No, we arranged to meet in Ellen's.' Molly glanced in the mirror and patted the blonde hair that was now liberally sprinkled with grey. 'I'll have to get meself a perm one of these fine days.'

'I don't know why yer don't mug yerself, yer can't be that hard up.'

'Jack Bennett, yer haven't got a bloody clue! Three birthday presents I've had to buy in the last three weeks, then on top of that was the engagement party. That cost me a small fortune... I still owe Maisie money for stuff I got on tick!' Molly huffed with temper. 'Honest to God, if men had to manage the housekeeping,

423

they wouldn't know what had hit them! If you think yer can do any better, be my guest an' take over for a week...see how yer like it.'

Seeing the look of hurt bewilderment in her husband's eyes, Molly's temper died as quickly as it had risen. What was she shouting at him for? All he'd wanted was for her to treat herself to a perm. He never asked for anything for himself, it was always her and the children he thought of. Crossing to his chair, she knelt in front of him. 'I'm sorry, love, I don't know what got into me. Must have got out of bed on the wrong side this morning.' She stroked his cheek with a finger. 'I love you, Jack Bennett, an' I wouldn't swap yer for all the money in the world.'

But the frown on Jack's forehead wouldn't be stroked away. 'I didn't know you'd had to get things on tick.'

'Oh, don't take any notice of me...a few bob, that's all I owe Maisie. I can finish it off this week.' She grinned. 'Yer know what I'm like for exaggerating.'

'I'll believe that when I come home one night to find yer've had yer hair permed.'

'Okay, boss!' Molly raised her chin and puckered her lips. 'Give us a kiss an' tell me how much yer love me.'

Jack raised his hand, holding his thumb and forefinger an inch apart. 'About that much.'

'You skinny beggar!' Molly made a fist of her hand and shook it in front of his face. 'How much did yer say?'

'Yer strike a hard bargain, Molly Bennett,'

Jack chuckled as he stretched his arms wide. 'Does that much satisfy yer?'

'Mmmm, I don't know.' Molly wagged her head from side to side. 'Give us a kiss first, then I'll tell yer.'

She gazed into eyes the colour of melted chocolate, and as his lips covered hers, her heart did a double somersault. To think that after twenty years the spark of love and passion was as strong as ever. How well and truly blessed they were.

A noise caused Molly to break away. 'Here's one of the girls.' Using Jack's knee as a lever, she pushed herself up. 'I'll slip out the back way, love, see yer later.'

As she walked up the entry, Molly crossed her arms over her tummy and hugged herself. One in a million, her husband was. She really shouldn't have lied to him about only owing Maisie a few bob when it was more like a few pounds, but he'd have worried if she'd told him the truth. He didn't like debt, always said if yer couldn't afford it then do without. He didn't mind her getting cheques off the club woman, that was only a few bob a week, but he drew the line at anything else. That was why, over the years, she'd never told him when she'd bought anything on the never-never. No point in worrying him...what the eye didn't see, the heart wouldn't grieve. And anyway, she had more sense than to get up to her neck in debt.

Molly dropped the latch on the Clarkes' door and walked up the yard. After a quick rap, she opened the door, calling, 'It's only me, Ellen!'

It was Corker who answered, his deep voice booming. 'Come in, Molly me darlin'.'

Molly stopped on the threshold of the living room. What a difference from this time last year, when the room had been cold and cheerless. The wallpaper had been dirty and torn, the lino ripped and the furniture scuffed and broken. Now the walls and lino were brightly coloured and the furniture, bought from a second-hand shop, was polished until you could see your face in it. And you could feel the warmth, happiness and love in the atmosphere.

Corker was sitting in a rocking chair with Gordon in his lap, and a book open in his hands. Peter, who considered himself too big to sit on a knee, was standing at the side of the chair, as close as he could get to the gentle giant they all adored. The two girls, Phoebe and Dorothy, sat at the table leaning on their elbows, their eyes wide with wonder. It was obvious to Molly that she'd walked in while Corker was in the middle of telling them a story.

'Go on, Sinbad,' Peter pleaded, 'what happened next?'

'Yeah, don't stop, Sinbad!' Gordon's eyes huge in the thin face. 'Did the baddie get killed?'

'Hush, now, where's yer manners?' Corker chided softly. 'Can't you see we've got a visitor?'

Seeing the dismay on the faces of the children, Molly said quickly, 'Don't let me interrupt. I'll just sit here quietly and listen.'

'Ellen will be down soon, she's just getting changed.' Corker smiled before lowering his eyes to the book of fairy tales. 'Where was I now? Oh, yes, the captain of the King's galleon was waving his cutlass in the air and shouting...'

Corker's voice faded as Molly's mind drifted from the fairy story in the book to the real-life fairy tale that was happening to these children. After years of terror and misery, their lives were only just beginning.

The first thing Phil noticed when he opened the front door was the sight of Doreen and Mo sitting on the step opposite. It threw him for a while, then he decided it wasn't worth risking another snub, so he reserved his smile for Doreen's friend. 'Hiya, Mo!'

Maureen waved. 'Hiya, Phil! Long time no see.' She gave Doreen a sly dig to remind her that this was her big chance, but Doreen was tongue-tied. She was willing him to look at her so she could give him the smile she'd been rehearsing for the last hour, but his eyes never turned her way. And she was too afraid to call a greeting in case he ignored her.

'I give up.' Maureen sounded disgusted as Ellen's door opened and Phil disappeared inside. 'Why the hell didn't yer open yer mouth...or even wave? Yer've had me sittin' on this step for nearly an hour, waitin' for him, an' what happens when he finally shows? Sweet Fanny Adams, that's what happens!'

'I couldn't, Mo! I'd have died of shame if he'd looked through me as though I wasn't here.'

'Well, you just listen to me, Doreen Bennett! If I was as crazy about a bloke as you are about Phil, I'd have made sure he noticed me. I'd have fainted at his feet, then he couldn't help but notice me.'

'It's easy for you to talk, you're not in my shoes!' Doreen was so disheartened she was near to tears. 'If he'd looked at me, I would have smiled or said somethin'.'

'Oh, I give up.' Maureen scrambled to her feet and brushed the back of her skirt. 'Let's go in an' listen to the wireless... Victor Sylvester and his band are on at half nine.' She linked her arm through her friend's. 'There's bound to be a next time, kid.'

'An' I'll probably mess it up again.'

'Oh, for cryin' out loud! D'yer know, yer've been a right misery-guts for the last few weeks.' Maureen remembered Ruthie asleep upstairs and kept her voice low as they walked towards the living room. 'I've a good mind to wait for him an' tell him how yer feel.'

'Don't you dare!'

'Oh, I dare all right! An' d'yer know why? 'Cos I'm fed up looking at yer walking around like a wet week...a real string of misery. Even when we go out with Mike an' Sammy, yer don't try to look as though yer enjoying yourself. In fact, I don't know why Mike puts up with yer...yer treat him somethin' shocking.'

'He doesn't have to put up with it.' Doreen's voice was spirited. 'He can find another girl for all I care.'

'He'd be doin' himself a favour if he did. He's

too nice for you to mess around with.' Maureen glanced at the clock on the mantelpiece and switched the wireless on just as Victor Sylvester's band began to play 'Blue Moon'. Her frown disappeared and her pretty face lit up. With her dark bobbed hair swinging, and her slim body swaying from side to side in time with the music, she said dreamily, 'Ooh, lovely, this is me favourite slow foxtrot.'

Doreen watched in silence for a while. Her friend was right, she had been a right misery-guts. Because she was unhappy it didn't mean she had to make her best friend suffer for it. She jumped up and held her arms out. 'Come on, kid, let's shake a leg. I'll be the man.'

Jill tapped her fingers on the table as she watched her sister combing her hair in front of the mirror while performing the difficult task of eating a piece of toast with no hands. It was the same ritual every morning. No matter how many times she was called, Doreen would stay in bed until the last minute and then have to dash like mad to catch the tram that would get her to work on time. Most mornings she was running out of the door while still struggling into her coat. Rushing around like that would be no good for Jill, she liked to move at a slower pace. Even though she didn't have to be at the office until nine, she got up at the same time as her sister so she could take things easy. She enjoyed sitting with her mother for a quiet cup of tea and a natter before starting to get ready. 'How did you get on at the Clarkes' last night, Mam?'

429

Molly sat down heavily and rested her elbows on the table, glad of the chance to sit for a few minutes and calm herself down. It was all go in the mornings...seeing to breakfast and carry-out for Jack and Tommy, then as soon as they were out of the door she had to start all over again for the girls. By the time she got around to waking Ruthie up, she felt as though she'd done a hard day's work. In fact, as she often said to Nellie, looking after a family was the toughest job in the world.

Wiping a hand across her brow, Molly sighed. 'Unless they show their faces around here, there's nowt much we can do, 'cos Phil doesn't know their proper address. All he knows is that they live on one of the new estates in Huyton. So all we can do is spread the word in the street, an' if they do show up, someone is bound to see them and we'll all get together and send them packing.' She happened to catch sight of Doreen's reflection in the mirror and noted the comb hovering in mid-air as her daughter listened intently to what was being said. She wants her bumps feeling, that one, Molly thought. Does she think we're so stupid we don't notice the number of times she goes to the window in the hope of catching sight of Phil? She's hankering after him but is too flaming proud to hold out an olive branch. It would only take a smile or a wave and he'd be over like a shot. Every time he saw Molly he asked after Doreen, making no secret of the fact that he was smitten with her. The sooner they kissed and made up the better. The whole family were fed up seeing her looking glum and would be glad when the smile was back on her pretty face.

'Hadn't you better be makin' tracks, Doreen?' Molly asked. 'You'll miss the tram if yer don't put a move on.'

'I'm off now.' Doreen threw her comb into her handbag and made for the door. 'I'll see yez tonight...ta-ra.'

Molly waited until she heard the front door close, then pulled a face. 'Honest to God, I feel like giving her a good shake! I thought I was stubborn, but she takes the biscuit. She's eating her heart out but won't give an inch. An' he's such a nice bloke, it's a crying shame.'

'I wish there was some way we could get them together,' Jill said. 'When me and Steve fell out, it was our Doreen who got us back together again. Remember how she tricked us both into going to the Grafton without telling either of us the other one was going?'

Molly smiled as the memory came flooding back. 'Yeah! She did a good job there, the crafty little madam. Planned it like a military operation.'

'Couldn't we do something like that?'

Molly glanced at the clock and pushed her chair back. 'We'll talk about it another time...right now I've got to see to Ruthie. It's my turn to take her an' Bella to school. I'll be glad when she'd old enough to go on her own. I feel more like flying than walkin' all that way.'

'Now, Mam,' Jill said, 'remember what you're

431

always telling us about wishing our lives away?'

Molly turned at the door, a huge grin on her face. 'I know. I'm fond of givin' other people advice but refuse to follow it meself I'm what polite people would call contrary...but if yer weren't polite, like me mate Nellie, then yer'd say I was just plain bloody awkward.'

'Can yer throw us a bag of nutty slack in as well, Tucker?'

The coalman took his jacket off and threw it on the long wooden seat in the front of his cart. Wiping the sweat from his brow with the back of a blackened hand, he blew out a deep breath. 'The weather's beautiful, but no good when yer luggin' bags of coal around.' He gazed up at Molly, who was standing on the top step. 'I'm not gettin' me usual delivery, Molly, so to be fair I'm rationin' me customers to one bag each.'

Molly opened her mouth with the intention of wheedling an extra bag, but her conscience stopped her. Her coalhole was full because she wasn't lighting the fire so much with the weather being warm, so it would be greedy to ask for more. Tucker was right, he had to be fair to all his customers. 'Just give us the bag of nutty slack, then. The coal lasts longer when the fire's banked down with a shovelful of slack.'

Tucker spanked his faithful horse on the rump to signal it was time to move up to the side entry. 'I bet yer glad to see the back of the workmen, Molly.'

'Yer can say that again! We've been in a right

mess for the last few weeks, but today's the big day an' I can't wait. They're still doin' a few little wiring jobs in the house, but they said they'll definitely be finished this afternoon.'

Tucker heard a door opening nearby and grinned when Nellie appeared. 'Look out, here comes trouble.'

'Ay, you watch it!' Nellie wagged a chubby finger. 'Any more cheek out of you an' I'll clock yer one.' Suddenly her face creased and she fell back against the wall, clutching her tummy as her whole body shook with laughter.

'Oh, aye,' Molly said, walking towards her friend, 'what's tickled yer fancy now?'

Nellie shook her head, unable to speak. Then, trying to compose herself, and gulping in air, she spluttered, 'I...I was just thinkin', I'd be wasting me energy givin' him a black eye. Have yer seen the colour of his face? It's as black as the hobs of hell! If he had two shiners, sky-blue pink with a finny haddy border, no one would flamin' notice!'

'Take no heed of her, Tucker.' Molly winked broadly. 'She's havin' one of her funny half-hours. If she doesn't have at least three a day, I worry about her.'

When Tucker winked back, the white of his eyelid showed in sharp contrast to the rest of his face. 'Well, she can laugh the other side of her face now, 'cos by insulting me she's talked herself out of a bag of coal.'

Nellie straightened up. Moving her hands from her tummy to cover her heart, and with a straight face, she struck a dramatic pose. 'Oh, sir, I didn't mean no harm. Won't you take pity on a poor woman with a husband out of work and twelve children to care for?' With a sob in her voice, she stretched her arms wide and fixed a pained expression on her face that would have put Bette Davis' acting in the shade. 'Please, sir,' she begged, 'I'll do anythin' yer ask...even let yer have yer wicked way with me...but don't deprive me poor kids.'

Molly started to clap. 'Yer gettin' better, Nellie! If yer don't end up in films one day, I'll eat me hat. At least, I would if I had a hat.'

The neighing of Tucker's horse had him walking backwards towards the entry. 'I'll throw yer a bag in, Nellie,' he grinned, 'but I want payin' for it. Yer acting was good, but not that good.'

'Ay, hang on a minute,' Nellie called, 'what about havin' yer wicked way with me? Surely that's worth a bag of ruddy coal?'

His hands reaching backwards over his shoulders to grab the ends of a sack, Tucker roared, 'Nellie, yer'd kill me!'

'Yeah, but what a lovely way to die! Just think, yer'd still have a smile on yer face when they were nailing the lid of yer coffin down.'

'In the name of God, she'd get yer hung, this one! Yer never know what she's goin' to come out with next!' Molly tutted. 'Now get in our house, Nellie McDonough, before I die of shame.'

'I only came down to cadge some sugar so I could have a cuppa,' Nellie protested as she was pushed unceremoniously up Molly's steps.

'I'll pay yer back when I go to the shops.'

'Here we go again! Yer like the cow's tail...always on the bum.'

'Well, I like that!' Nellie grunted, swaying down the hall. 'I'll have yer know I wouldn't be askin' if it wasn't for me being so kind-hearted. Mrs Gillespie sent their Betty down to borrow some for her feller's breakfast, an' I gave her what was in the bag, thinkin' I had another full one in the cupboard. Only I was wrong, yer see, 'cos when I got to the cupboard it was like Old Mother Hubbard's...bare.'

'I haven't got much meself,' Molly called from the kitchen where she was filling the kettle. 'The ruddy workmen are drinkin' me out of house an' home.'

'Won't be long now, girl!' Nellie said, shaking her head as she eyed the couch. Thank you very much, she thought, but I'm not getting stuck on you again! A nice piece of furniture you may be to look at, but you should come complete with block and tackle! So she opted for a chair. 'Remember me tellin' yer that George wasn't the least bit excited about gettin' the 'leccy on, an' you said Jack was the same? Well, I'm gettin' me own back on him tonight. I've got a nice little trick lined up for him.'

'Oh, aye!' Molly set the two cups of steaming tea on the table. 'Tell me more.'

Nellie leaned closer. 'Even if I do say it meself, it's a masterpiece, this. So pin yer ears back, girl, and listen to what I've got planned for my beloved.'

Chapter Twenty-Five

Jack let his eyes travel slowly from the naked light bulb up to the moulding in the centre of the ceiling from where the length of flex was suspended. 'Yer mean to tell me they've left us without any light at all? Taken the gas fittings away before they were ready to switch the electric on?'

'I know...it's maddening, isn't it?' Molly had to turn her head away to hide the sparkle in her eyes. 'I played merry hell with the workmen, but they said they couldn't do anythin' about it today, it was late and their knockin'-off time. The foreman said somethin' about a fault on the cable...somethin' like that.'

'Well, I must say it's a pretty kettle of fish. What are we supposed to do when it goes dark? Feel our way around?' Jack reached for the switch on the wall and flicked it up and down several times before grunting, 'Stupid buggers.'

'Oh, it won't hurt us for one night. I've got a couple of candles ready, we'll have to make do with those.' Molly glared at the three girls, who sat around the table, their dinners forgotten as they nudged each other and bit on their lips. If they didn't take those smirks off their faces, sure as eggs they'd give the game away. 'You lot get on with yer dinner or it'll be stiff.' With that, she marched through to the kitchen to get

436

Jack and Tommy's dinner out of the oven. But as she turned the knob on the door of the stove, she allowed a smile to settle on her face for a few seconds. They'd fallen for it hook, line and sinker, just like Nellie had said they would. She couldn't wait to see their faces when she switched the power on. All she had to do was push down the lever at the side of the new meter, like the workman had shown her, and hey presto, the lights would come on. It was as easy as falling off a bike.

'You're up late tonight, love.' Jack smiled at Ruthie as he picked up his knife and fork. 'How come?'

'Me mam said I could stay up a bit later 'cos I've been a good girl, didn't yer, Mam?' Ruthie was swinging her legs backwards to kick the bottom of her chair. 'I came top of the class in sums today.'

'Clever girl!'

'She's always swanking.' Tommy's muffled voice came through a mouthful of potato. 'I bet she doesn't even know her two times table.'

Ruthie stuck her tongue out. 'Yes I do, so there! One two is two, two twos are four, three twos are six...'

'All right, sunshine, we'll take your word for it.' Molly ruffled her youngest daughter's hair. 'Keep yer legs still and stop kickin' me good chairs.' A bright flash took her eyes to the window just as lights flared in the upstairs and downstairs windows of the house opposite. Oh Lord, she groaned to herself, it's getting dusk out and soon every house in the street will be

437

lit up. 'It's only our side that's affected.' She crossed her fingers behind her back as the lie left her mouth. 'The houses across the street are okay.'

'Seems fishy to me,' Jack said, mopping up his gravy with a piece of bread. 'I'm surprised they were allowed to knock off before the job was finished.'

Molly began to collect the empty plates. She'd only let Ruthie stay up late because the child was so intrigued with the new lighting she'd probably have been hopping in and out of bed playing with the switch and spoiled everything. But it was way past her bedtime and the sooner the charade was over, the sooner she could take her upstairs. 'Doreen, you give Jill a hand with the dishes while I get Ruthie undressed.'

Jack had bought the evening *Echo* on his way home from work and he went into the hall to get it from the pocket of his jacket. 'I may as well not have bothered buying this.' He waved the paper in the air. 'I'll never be able to read in this light.'

'Wait till I shake the tablecloth out, then I'll light yer a candle.' Molly suppressed a giggle. 'If yer stand it on the mantelpiece yer should be able to see to read.'

The two older girls were standing at the sink, doubled up with silent laughter. 'Mam, me dad will kill yer for this,' Doreen tittered, 'he'll have yer guts for garters.'

'He'll have to get through you first, 'cos I'll make sure I'm standin' behind yer.'

438

'Don't worry, Mam,' Jill whispered, 'I'll protect you.'

Molly put a finger to her lips. 'Yez know the plan. Doreen, you go upstairs and make sure all the light switches are down...don't forget the landing and the hall. This one's all right, so is the one in the living room. All you've got to do, Jill, when yer hear me striking a match to light the candle, is pull that lever down. Okay?'

'I'll run up now,' Doreen said, tapping Jill on the shoulder. 'I'll only be a tick, then I'll dry the dishes.'

Molly took a deep breath and put on a straight face as she gazed towards the ceiling. If Jack doesn't see the funny side of this, Nellie McDonough, she thought, so help me I'll flatten yer.

'Come on, sunshine, let's get yer ready for bed.' Molly pulled Ruthie's gymslip over her head. 'A quick cat's lick and a promise, then it's up the wooden stairs for you.'

'This is bloody ridiculous!' Jack, holding the newspaper just inches from his face, sounded frustrated and impatient. 'I can't see a flamin' thing!'

'Oh, I'm sorry, love!' Molly heard her daughter's footsteps running down the stairs and winked as Doreen dashed through to the kitchen. 'I went out to get you a candle and forgot what I'd gone for. I must be gettin' forgetful in me old age.' She picked Ruthie up and set her on a chair. 'I won't be a minute, sunshine.'

'Yer know, for two pins I'd come home in me

dinner hour tomorrow and give these workmen a piece of my mind,' Jack called after her. 'I've never heard anythin' like it...leaving folks in the dark! It shouldn't be allowed.'

'I'll come with yer,' offered Tommy, who was sitting on the couch waiting patiently for the dishes to be finished so he could get washed before going up to Ginger's. 'If yer ask me, I think they've got a ruddy cheek.'

In the kitchen, Molly and her two daughters were huddled together, trying to muffle their laughter. 'If I don't go to the lavvy soon, I'll wet meself,' Molly spluttered. 'Yer dad's got a right cob on.'

'An' did yer hear our Tommy, the big he-man?' Doreen's hand was covering her mouth. 'He wants to sort the workmen out! They'd make mincemeat of him!'

'Hush now,' Molly warned. 'Give us that candle and the box of matches. An' don't forget, as soon as yer hear me strike the match, switch on.'

Placing the candle in the middle of an old chipped saucer, Molly carried it through. 'Where d'yer want it? On the hearth or the mantelpiece?'

'Makes no odds.' Jack sounded grumpy. 'It won't make a ha'porth of difference no matter where yer put it.'

'Well, hold the damn thing while I strike a match.'

The match was halfway down the strip of sandpaper when it burst into flame, and at the same instant the room flooded with light.

'What the...?' Jack fell back against the chair, his mouth gaping, his eyes blinking rapidly against the sudden glare. It took a few seconds to adjust to the brightness, then he noticed the figures of his two daughters silhouetted in the light coming from the kitchen. He turned his head to see that the hallway was also well lit. 'They must have found the fault and put it right.'

Tommy opened his mouth to agree, then closed it without saying a word. Frowning, he looked from his mother to the two girls by the kitchen door, then to his kid sister. And it was the look of mischief on Ruthie's face that confirmed his suspicions. 'They've been pullin' our legs, Dad! Can't yer see, we've been had!' He fell forward, and with his head resting on his knees shook with laughter. 'Oh, God, wait till I tell Ginger!'

Jack looked bewildered. 'Will you stop acting daft an' tell me what yer find so funny?'

Tommy turned his head, tears of laughter running freely down his cheeks. 'Ask me mam.' His body shook as a fresh outburst threatened. 'This has got to be the funniest stunt she's ever pulled.'

'Stunt!' Jack blazed at Molly. 'Is he crazy? 'Cos if he's not, then you are about to get yer neck broken.'

Molly beckoned the two older girls over. 'Stand in front of me an' hit him with the poker if he so much as lays a finger on me.' She peered between the two blonde heads. 'It was like this, yer see, Jack. Me an' Nellie were

441

talkin' and sayin' how miserable you an' George were about...'

As Molly's voice droned on, Jack eyed the scene before him. He could see tears of laughter on the faces of his two elder daughters as they stood like sentries protecting their mother. And as he looked, Ruthie came to stand in front of the trio. There was an expression of puzzlement on her pixie-like face that told Jack she couldn't understand why he wasn't amused like everyone else. And when she planted her feet firmly apart, stretched her arms wide like a shield and glared at him defiantly, he had to bite hard on the inside of his cheek to keep a grin at bay.

Molly had stopped talking and her eyes were narrowed to slits. 'I know you, Jack Bennett, it's takin' yer all yer time to keep yer gob straight, isn't it?'

There was silence for a few seconds as they waited with bated breath for his response. Then, when his loud laughter bounced off the walls, they all let loose. 'Dad, yer should 'ave seen yer face,' Doreen spluttered. 'Talk about a picture no artist could paint.'

'Yeah, it was good, wasn't it, Dad?' Ruthie pushed her fringe out of her eyes before scrambling on to his knee. 'Wasn't me mam clever to think of pullin' yer leg like that?'

'Ooh, hang on a minute,' Molly said. 'Before I take any credit, I want to make sure yer dad's laughing an' not having hysterics. If it's hysterics then Nellie can take the blame. If it's funny ha-ha laughter, then I'll sit back an' bask in the glory.'

Jack couldn't control himself. Banging his clenched fists on the arms of the chair, he rocked back and forth. In his mind's eye he could see himself holding the *Echo* two inches from his face, his eyes squinting while he cursed to high heaven. He must have looked a right nit! And holding the candle while Molly struck a match... Oh dear, oh dear, oh dear! He'd never hear the end of this lark.

In the house opposite, Victoria Clegg moved from one foot to the other as she kept watch through the back window for the entry door to open, heralding Philip's arrival. She could smell the pan of stew simmering on the stove in the kitchen and hoped he wouldn't be too long in case it boiled dry. Not that he was any later than usual; he worked overtime most nights. But tonight there were two special reasons she was eager for the sight of the boy she'd grown so fond of. The first was the electric light, which he'd see as soon as he opened the entry door because she'd left the curtains open and the whole yard was lit up. And the second and more exciting reason was the letter she was holding in her hand. When the postman had delivered it this morning she'd been full of misgivings, worrying that it might be from his family, asking him to go back to them. She'd got so used to him now she couldn't bear the thought of losing him. He gave her a reason for living and she'd be devastated if he left her. But as the day had progressed, she'd talked herself out of that possibility. He'd never go back to that family, not Philip, not after what they'd done. So the letter must be from a friend, and this idea delighted her. It would be lovely for him to have friends, people his own age he could go out with. He could even invite them here and she'd make them more than welcome.

Victoria was so lost in thought she missed the opening of the yard door, and before she knew what was happening, Philip was waving to her from the other side of the window. 'I thought I'd come to the wrong house,' he called, his handsome face beaming. 'Proper posh now, aren't we?'

Victoria grinned. 'Yes, you'll have to wipe your nose and your feet before yer come in now.' She moved to the kitchen and as soon as he was in the door handed him the letter. 'This came for you this morning.'

The smile dropped from his face. 'For me? I don't know anyone that would be wanting to write to me.' He scanned the barely legible writing on the envelope and his heart sank. He'd know that childish, spidery scrawl anywhere.

'Aren't you going to open it?'

'Nah, I'll have a look around first, see if I like this electricity lark. If it doesn't come up to scratch, they can take it away and put the gas back in.' He laid the envelope casually on the table, hoping that she couldn't hear the loud beat of his heart. The contents of that letter could only mean trouble, because 'trouble' was Tom Bradley's middle name. 'I'll have a look-see upstairs while yer dishing me dinner up, then I'll wash me hands and read the letter.'

His air of indifference didn't fool Victoria at all, and her misgivings grew. He knew who the letter was from, she could tell, and he wasn't happy about it. If she'd known, she'd have torn the blasted thing up and said nothing.

'How many times have I got to tell yer that yer shouldn't carry anythin' heavy?' Phil came into the room to see her bringing in his heaped plate in her one good but unsteady hand. He rushed to take it from her. 'Aunt Vicky, yer'll be the death of me! One of these days yer'll have an accident.'

'I get so frustrated, not being able to do things.' Tears were not far from the surface. 'I'm hopeless and useless.'

Phil put the plate down and his arms around her shoulders, feeling the frailty of her body through the thin dress she was wearing. 'You are not hopeless and useless...yer do very well considerin'. But I worry about yer trying to do too much.' He stroked the white hair from her brow before planting a kiss. 'Yer the kindest, loveliest person I've ever known in me life, an' I love yer to bits.'

'Oh, Phil.' Victoria buried her head in his chest. 'That's the nicest thing anyone has ever said to me.' She sniffed loudly. 'God was certainly looking after me the day he sent you along.'

'Yer mean He was looking after me!' He patted her shoulder before pushing her gently towards a chair. 'Now, sit yerself down and watch a hungry man lick his plate clean.'

'Aren't you going to read the letter?' Victoria

couldn't keep the words back. 'It might be important.'

'Oh, all right, nosy poke.' With a fixed smile on his face, Phil tore at the envelope. The smile stayed firm when he took out a piece of paper covered in dirty finger-marks and jam and grease stains. Holding it close to his chest, he read and reread the brief but sinister note which had no address on and was unsigned.

Thort I'd let yer know I haven't forgot yer. I'll turn up when yer least expect it so keep lukin over yer showlder.

Phil felt his adopted aunt's eyes on him and held back the sigh that had risen from the very depths of his soul. 'It's only from me mam,' he lied, folding the paper and returning it to the envelope. 'Just to let me know she'll get down to the works one day to see me.'

'That was nice of her.' Victoria sounded relieved. 'She must miss you, you know.'

Phil gazed into the faded grey eyes and felt an overwhelming desire to hold the frail elderly lady in his arms and tell her that she'd shown him more love in the short time he'd been with her than his mother ever had. How could he tell her that the Bradley family didn't know the meaning of the words respect, politeness or compassion? That they never uttered a sentence that didn't contain obscenities or blasphemy? They weren't fit to wipe Miss Clegg's shoes, and although he didn't know right now how he could protect her from them, by God, he would think of a way.

'I'm goin' to tuck into this dinner now before it gets cold.' Phil gave her a cheeky wink. 'If I can move after gettin' this lot down me, an' if yer behave yerself, I'll make yer a nice cuppa. How does that sound?'

Molly brushed the dirt into a small mound in the middle of the yard and reached for the shovel standing by the lavvy door. With two brisk strokes she had the dirt on the shovel and emptied it into the bin. There, that was another little job done.

'Is that you, girl?' Nellie's voice winged its way over the two yards separating them.

Molly grinned as she called back, 'No, it's someone else.'

'Well, whoever yer are, d'yer feel like a cuppa? Or are yer a miserable bugger like me mate Molly Bennett?'

'How can she be yer mate if yer call her a miserable bugger? I don't think I'd like you for a friend.'

'Molly Bennett, shut yer gob an' get yerself up here! I'm dyin' to know how yer got on last night.'

'Then yer'll have to prolong yer dying, Nellie, 'cos I'm not stopping for a gossip until I've swilled the front and washed me windowsill. I've got all me jobs planned out, an' I'm sticking to me routine.'

'Right ho, Sergeant Major!' Although no one could see her, Nellie gave a smart salute. 'I'll see yer in the street in five minutes.'

Molly plunged the bucket in the dolly tub and

brought it out full to the brim with soapy water left over from the washing she'd done earlier. When she'd swilled the front, she'd throw the rest of the water over the yard...no point wasting good suds.

Nellie was waiting outside the front door. 'Throw it, girl, an' I'll sweep the pavement.'

'If yer don't move yerself, Nellie McDonough, I'll throw it over you!'

'Temper, temper!' Nellie moved back, resting her hands on top of the handle of the stiff brush, 'You're not in a very con...convo...convu...'

'Nellie, I think the word yer looking for is convivial,' Molly said, grinning as she threw the contents of the bucket over the paving stones.

Nellie's eyes darted to where the water was running down the pavement into the gutter. Dipping the bristles of her brush in the small pools that had gathered, she then shook the handle and sent the water spraying over an unsuspecting Molly. 'I don't need fancy words to tell yer yer a bad-tempered so-and-so.'

Drops of water were running from Molly's hair, nose and chin. Her pinny was sodden and she could feel the dampness seeping through to her knickers. It wasn't even clean water, either! She didn't know whether to laugh or cry. A sly glance from under her lowered lids showed her Nellie leaning against the wall doubled up with mirth. She felt like joining in the laughter, 'cos it was funny, but she decided she'd get her own back first. 'Right!' Molly picked up the bucket and made for the front door. 'Wait till I fill this an' see if yer still laughin' when I pour it over your head. See how you like it.'

Nellie waddled behind her down the hall, the brush held firmly between her chubby hands. 'Now hang on a minute, girl! Let's be reasonable about this...it was only a joke.'

Molly plunged the bucket into the dolly tub. 'Then yer won't mind if the joke's on you, will yer? So out into the street with yer...go on, on yer way.'

'I ain't movin' an inch.' Nellie planted her feet firmly together. 'If yer want to throw it over me, then yer'll have to do it in here, all over yer nice clean floor.'

Molly lowered the bucket to the floor. 'Yer've got to leave sometime, so I can bide me time.'

'Well, seein' as how it's goin' to be a long wait, can we have a little natter while we're standin' here doin' nothing?' Nellie asked in all innocence. 'Like, for instance, how did yer get on with Jack last night over the 'leccy? An' why didn't yer come down to ours like yer said yer would?'

'Don't think yer can talk yer way out of it, Nellie McDonough, 'cos I'm determined to get me own back on yer.'

'I don't blame yer for one minute, girl! If it was me, I'd want to get me own back on me too!' Nellie held her tummy as laughter rumbled. 'By the way, that water must be filthy, 'cos yer've got dirty streaks all down yer face.'

As Molly reached for the towel hanging from a nail on the kitchen door, she asked herself what she would do without Nellie to brighten up her days. There was never a dull moment when the big woman was around. Holding the end of the towel under the tap, she wet it before wiping it over her face. 'I thought the trick was going to backfire at first, but then we didn't half have a laugh.' She went on to tell her friend in detail what had happened, then listened as Nellie told her it had been the same in their house. 'I intended coming up to yours,' Molly said, hanging the towel back on the nail, 'but young Phil came over, and by the time he left it was too late.'

'What did he want?'

'He went next door first, but the kids told him Corker and Ellen had gone for a drink so he came here. The poor lad was out of his mind with worry about this letter he'd had.'

When Molly explained what was in the letter, Nellie's chins wobbled with indignation. 'The ruddy swine! What that Bradley feller needs is to meet someone like Corker in a dark alley one night...put the fear of God into him.'

'Phil's in a terrible state about it. He's got it into his head that they'll do somethin' to frighten Victoria.'

'I can't see them comin' down here, girl, not if they've got any sense. Everyone in the street has got their eyes peeled for them.'

'I told Phil that, but he said we don't know them like he does. They want him home for his few bob a week, and they'll move heaven an' earth to get Victoria to throw him out.'

'She'll not do that! She thinks the world of him.'

'Aye, well, we'll just have to hope nothing

comes of it. But the letter has certainly upset the lad. Last night he looked as though he had all the troubles of the world on his shoulders.' Molly folded her arms and leaned against the sink. 'One good thing came out of it, though, and that seemed to cheer him up. As I was seein' him to the door, who came in but our Doreen! And surprise, surprise, she actually smiled and said "hello" to him.'

Nellie used her tummy as a ledge to rest her arms on while taking in this latest bit of juicy gossip. 'Go 'way, she never did?'

'Scout's honour! That's as far as it went, like, 'cos she came straight through to the living room. But it's a start. And the lad was as pleased as Punch, I could tell.'

'She could do a lot worse than young Phil.' Nellie nodded knowingly. 'I wouldn't mind havin' him for a son-in-law.'

'That's rushing things a bit,' Molly laughed. 'But I think before the next week is out, they'll be dating.' She put her hands on her friend's shoulders, 'Now, missus, have you got a home to go to?'

'Okay, okay! I don't need a house to fall on me to know when I'm not wanted.' Nellie got halfway to the door, then turned. Delving into her apron pocket, she brought out a tattered purse. 'I nearly forgot to ask, have yer got three pennies for a thru'penny joey? Me gas is likely to go before me ham shank is cooked.'

Molly reached up to the top shelf where she kept her coppers. 'I'll get some change when I go to the shops, I'm nearly out meself.'

'Ta, girl!'

Molly watched her friend sway through the living room, then eyed the full bucket of water at her feet. No, don't do it, she warned herself. Then the mischievous part of her mind egged her on. Go on, she'd do it to you if she was in your place.

Picking up the handle of the zinc bucket gently so as not to make a noise, Molly tiptoed down the hall. Nellie would be almost at her door now. She wouldn't throw the water over her, just aim for the ground around her feet. Grinning at the thought of getting her own back, Molly stepped into the street and came face to face with Nellie.

Shaking her head and sending her chins in all directions, the big woman said, 'Yer didn't really think yer'd catch me out that easy, did yer, girl? God, yer must think I came over on the banana boats!'

'Helen Theresa McDonough, if I had the energy to lift this flamin' bucket I'd empty the whole lot over yer.'

'Tut, tut, temper!' Laughing eyes disappeared as the fat on Nellie's cheeks moved upwards. 'I'll tell yer what, girl, seein' as yer me best mate, I'll help yer out. Now I can't be fairer than this, can I, when I tell yer how yer can get one over on me?'

Molly's eyes narrowed suspiciously. 'How come I've got a horrible feelin' I'm goin' to come off second best again?'

''Cos yer already have!' Nellie walked away chuckling. 'Yer see, girl, the secret is bein' like the bird what got up early to catch the worm.'

'Are you callin' me a worm, Nellie Mc-Donough?'

Nellie turned, a look of mock horror on her face. 'Now would I do a thing like that? After all, we're mates...so if I called you a worm, I'd have to call meself one.'

'Well, with you I could see a resemblance.' Molly was well pleased with herself because she had a feeling that for once she was going to get the last word in. 'I've seen you worm yerself out of more scrapes than anyone I know.'

Nellie held up her hands in surrender. 'You win, girl! I can't think of an answer to that. Mind you, I might come up with one by the time I come to yours for afternoon tea.'

Molly gaped. 'Who invited you for afternoon tea?'

'You did, about half an hour ago.'

'You flamin' liar! I did no such thing, Nellie McDonough!'

Nellie shook her head, a look of sadness on her face. 'It breaks me heart to see yer goin' down the nick, girl. Why don't yer go an' see yer doctor, see if he can give yer somethin' to help yer memory? I've noticed yer gettin' very forgetful lately.' She pecked at her bottom lip. 'I bet yer've even forgot that yer said I'd be getting a cream slice with me afternoon tea.'

Nellie just had time to hop on to the step before the bucket of water was emptied at her feet.

Chapter Twenty-Six

There was a broad beam on Mary Watson's face as she let the net curtain fall back into place. 'They're all off to the pub for a farewell drink with Corker,' she told her husband. 'He goes back off leave tomorrow.'

Harry lowered the evening paper. 'Who d'yer mean by all?'

'The usual gang... Molly and Jack, Nellie, George, Molly's ma and pa, and Ellen an' Corker.' Mary pulled a chair out and sat down. 'There'll be some fun there tonight, 'cos when Molly an' Nellie get together there's no stopping them. This mornin' they had me laughing so much I had a pain in me side.'

'Oh, aye!' The comic duo had given Harry many a chuckle and there was a smile of anticipation on his face when he asked, 'What were they up to?'

'It was only half past nine, I hadn't been back long from takin' the girls to school, and I was washing the front step when Nellie shouted over on her way to Molly's.' To do justice to her impersonation, Mary pushed her chair back. 'I'll have to stand up to tell yer what happened next. Just pretend I'm Molly, opening the door to Nellie.' Mary swept her arm wide to open an imaginary door. 'In the name of God, Nellie, what yer doin' knockin'

454

this time of the morning? I'm sure yer tryin' to haunt me...every time I turn around, there yer are, like me flamin' shadow.'

Mary changed position to indicate she was taking over another personality. Puffing her chest out, she folded her arms, a habit of Nellie's that was familiar to everyone in the street. 'Ay, girl, if your shadow is the same size as me, then I think yer should get yer eyes tested. After all, anyone with half an eye can see I'm a few pounds heavier than you.'

Harry guffawed as he banged his fist on the table. 'A few pounds! More like six stone!'

Mary clutched her tummy and doubled up. 'It's the expressions on their faces that make it so funny.' She pulled a chair out and flopped down. 'Nellie had been up to the corner shop and Maisie had shown her the new vacuum cleaner she's bought. Of course, Nellie thought it was magic and was tryin' to coax Molly up to the shop so she could see for herself the machine that sucks up the dirt. Poor Molly kept saying, "Will yer go away, Nellie?" But once Nellie gets into her stride, there's no stoppin' her.'

'So what happened in the end?'

'Well, I suppose yer could call it a draw. Molly refused point-blank to go to the shop, but after half an hour she ended up askin' Nellie in for a cup of tea to shut her up.'

'You could have gone with them tonight for a drink, yer know,' Harry said. 'I'm here to listen for Bella.'

'No, I'd be the odd one out...a gooseberry. Anyway, I wouldn't want to go without you.

455

When Bella's a bit older, then we'll have plenty of time to go out together.' Mary pushed her chair back and stood up. 'I think I'll nip up to the corner shop though, and treat meself to a quarter of mint imperials.'

Coins jingled as Harry fished in his pocket and brought out a sixpenny piece. 'Here yer are, I'll mug yer to a slab of chocolate.'

'Who's a lovely man, then?' Mary rounded the table and planted a noisy kiss on his cheek. 'I'll slip out the back in case our Bella's still awake an' hears the front door open.'

Mary glanced up and down the entry as she let the latch fall into place. There was no one about except for a solitary man walking towards her. He held her attention because he was walking so close to the wall his clothes were brushing the brickwork. Mary didn't recognise him from Adam and wouldn't have given him a second glance, but there was something shifty about him that aroused her suspicion. A flat cap was pulled so low over his forehead that the peak hid most of his face from view, a white knitted scarf was tied in a knot at his throat and he was carrying what appeared to be a workman's tool bag.

As they drew closer, Mary expected the man to stand aside to let her pass, but with his head buried even deeper into his chest, he barged ahead, forcing her to step out of his path to avoid a collision. Angry now, she spun around, muttering, 'The ignorant so-and-so.' It was then that she spotted the lock of long black hair which had escaped from his cap and was lying on the collar of his navy serge jacket. There was only one man she knew who wore his hair like a gypsy, and that was Tom Bradley. Mary's hand went to her mouth. Oh my God, what was he doing around here? She glanced first to her own back door, then to the side entry a few steps away, wondering which way to turn. Then instinctively her winged feet were taking her down the short entry towards the pub.

'Nellie McDonough, if yer don't stop harping on that vacuum cleaner of Maisie's, so help me I'll throttle yer.' Molly set her glass on the table and appealed to her friend's husband. 'George, do us a favour an' buy her one to shut her up.'

'I've got one and thruppence in me pocket, Molly,' George laughed, 'if that's any good, she's welcome to it.'

'I'll have to do somethin' about her...half past ruddy nine this mornin' she was at me door, I hadn't even made the flamin' beds! An' all she wanted was to talk about Maisie's vacuum cleaner...or as Nellie calls it, "Maisie's new fangled machine".'

Perched on one of the small round stools, Nellie folded her arms. Her voice calm, her face angelic, she spoke softly and slowly. 'When I got out of bed this mornin', I promised meself I wasn't goin' to lose me rag no matter what. Yer see, girl, it's not good for the old ticker! So you go right ahead an' call me all the names under the sun, an' I won't turn a hair. Sticks

457

an' stones may break my bones, but words will never hurt me.'

'If I were you, Molly me darlin', I'd give in.' Corker boomed as he licked the beer from his moustache. 'Yer on a loser with Nellie.'

'I know! Yer'd have thought I'd have learned my lesson by now, wouldn't yer? Twenty years, an' I don't think I've ever once got the better of her. It's a wonder I haven't got an inferiority complex.'

'Haven't got a what?' Nellie gaped. 'The state of her an' the price of fish!' She turned to Bridie. 'Where does your daughter get all these big words from? When I was a baby I got Farley's Rusks to chew on...I think she cut her teeth on a ruddy dictionary!'

'Well now, it would be a dull world if we were all made alike, so it would.' Bridie smiled. 'I think the good Lord was very clever when he matched you two for friends. He gave Molly the gift of the gab, and you the gift of humour.'

Nellie narrowed her eyes at Molly. 'Ay, girl, how come when your ma is dishing insults out she does it in such a nice way no one ever gets offended?'

Before Molly had time to reply, Mary appeared at the table, flushed and out of breath. With a hand to her chest, she gasped, 'Mr Bradley's in our entry.'

'What!' Corker stood up so quickly he sent the table rocking. 'When was this?'

'Just now! I didn't recognise him at first, he's wearing a cap, but it's him all right.'

'I'll come with yer.' Jack was already squeezing

458

past Molly. 'It's about time someone sorted that little weasel out.'

'We'll all come.' Molly jumped to her feet. 'The more the merrier.'

'No, just me and Jack.' Corker waved her down. 'Get a drink in for Mary, there's a good girl. We won't be long.'

Outside, Corker nodded to the entry facing. 'I'll go in this end, you go down the side one opposite your house. I'll wait here till yer get in place.'

Tom Bradley was leaning against Miss Clegg's wall, a hand-rolled cigarette dangling from the side of his mouth, when he saw Corker. Grabbing the bag at his feet, he made to bolt in the opposite direction, until he saw Jack and realised he was cornered.

'And to what do we owe the pleasure?' Corker towered over the sickly-faced man. 'Come visiting, have yer?'

'I've been on a message and was just takin' a short cut to the tram. It's a public entry, isn't it?' Tom Bradley, even though he was quaking in his shoes, decided the best way was to brazen it out. 'Yez don't own the bleedin' place.'

'I'll grant yer that.' Corker sounded quite amiable. 'But I'm sure yer won't mind answerin' a few questions. For instance, what are yer doin' in this particular entry? Why are yer leanin' against this particular yard wall? An' why, if yer only takin' a short cut, have yer been hangin' around for the last ten minutes?' Corker's tone changed as he moved menacingly closer. 'An'

459

don't tell fibs, 'cos I only get mad when people lie to me.'

Tom Bradley changed the tool bag to his other hand. 'I've told yer all I'm goin' to tell yer. If I want to walk down a bleedin' entry, it's got sod all to do with you.'

Corker sniffed and wrinkled his nose. His eyes narrowed, he bent towards the bag. 'Can you smell anythin', Jack?'

'Yeah, I got a whiff of it before. Smells like paraffin to me.'

Tom Bradley started to blink nervously. A frightened man now, he tried to bluff his way out. 'I don't 'ave to stand 'ere wasting me time talkin' to you two! Out of me way.'

'Not so fast,' Corker said. 'Let's see what yer've got in that bag first.'

'Who the soddin' 'ell d'yer think yer are?' Tom Bradley gulped as two hands the size of ham shanks grabbed his shoulders and pressed him back against the wall.

Corker jerked his head. 'See what's in the bag, Jack.'

Jack opened the bag and turned his head away from the strong smell. 'Whew, it stinks!' Gingerly he put his hand in and brought out a bundle of rags. 'They're soaked in paraffin... I wonder what he intended doin' with them?'

'I'll take a guess, shall I?' Corker bent his head until his eyes were on a level with Bradley's. 'Yer were hangin' around until it gets dark, weren't yer? Then yer were goin' to set the rags alight an' stuff them through the old lady's letter box...right?'

460

'No! I wouldn't do that!' Bradley's struggles were useless against the strength of Corker. 'I wasn't goin' to do nothin' like that!'

'What were yer goin' to do with them, then? An' by the way, I'm in no hurry. I can stand here all night if that's what it takes to get the truth out of yer.'

When Bradley was still sticking to his story twenty minutes later, Corker was running out of patience. He was certain the squirt of a man had been intent on causing trouble for Miss Clegg and Phil, but how to prove it? He thought of beating it out of him, but his sense of fair play ruled that out. Someone his size fighting a man he could lift up with one hand just wasn't on. No, a radical solution was needed, one that would put the fear of God into Bradley once and for all.

Corker racked his brains. He knew most of the desk sergeants at the local police station, perhaps they would help. Bradley was known to them, having been brought in several times on suspicion of theft. But they'd had to let him go each time because they'd no proof. He'd never been caught in the act and was too wily to keep knock-off stuff in his own home for the police to find when they searched. They wouldn't be able to arrest him now because they had no proof he intended to commit a crime. Still, the police were Corker's last hope. If Sergeant Murphy was on desk duty, he might think of some way of scaring Bradley so much he'd be afraid to show his face in the vicinity again.

Grasping Bradley by the scruff of the neck,

Corker pulled him none too gently away from the wall. 'Right, it's down to the local nick for you, me laddo. Let's see what the police think of yer cock-and-bull story.' He winked at Jack. 'You bring the evidence along, Jack.'

It was nine o'clock when the two men came out of the police station, cock-a-hoop. 'Thank God for Sergeant Murphy!' Corker chortled. 'He came up trumps.'

'He certainly did...he frightened the livin' daylights out of me an' I haven't done anythin'!' Jack threw his head back and roared. 'Did yer see the look on Bradley's face when he was led away to the cells? He really thinks he's for the high jump.'

'Yeah, the Sergeant played his part well.' Corker nodded to emphasise his feelings. 'I don't know how I kept me face straight when he said he was keeping the bag of rags as evidence. An' I nearly cracked up when he said he was contacting all the police stations to see if they had anything on Bradley. This is one night that little crook won't forget in a hurry.'

'Will they keep him in the cell overnight?'

'Sergeant Murphy comes off duty at midnight, so they'll probably release him just before that. The officer relieving him might not have the same sense of humour as Murphy, so they'll get Bradley out of the way before he comes on.'

'I know we're laughing,' Jack said, 'but it's not a laughing matter, is it? I mean, what would have happened if Mary hadn't spotted him in the entry?'

462

'Doesn't bear thinking about, Jack.' Corker's face was serious. 'An' yer right about it not bein' a laughing matter. That's why I want you to go on to the pub while I call in to Miss Clegg's. I'll make the excuse I've come to say goodbye, but I really want to have a quiet word with Phil. I think it's only right he knows about tonight's little drama. Not that I think Tom Bradley will be back. I'm convinced we've seen the last of him. But it's best if Phil's on his guard.'

'You're missing a lot of drinking time, Corker.'

'I know!' Corker groaned. 'An' it's me last night. Ellen will have me guts for garters.'

They stood outside the pub. 'I'll get a round in, Corker, so don't be long.'

'Fifteen minutes at the outside,' Corker promised. 'And give my apologies to everyone... especially Ellen.' He started to walk away, then turned. 'By the way, tell Nellie if she needs any acting lessons, go an' see Sergeant Murphy.'

'Are you sure yer know what yer doin', lad?' There was a worried frown on Jimmy Cookson's face as he wiped his oily hands on a scrap of rag. 'Have yer given it plenty of thought?'

Phil nodded. 'I'd be gettin' called up next year anyway, when I'm twenty, so I might as well join up now.'

'But there's every chance yer won't be in the first lot to be called up; we're on war work here and that might exempt yer for a while.' The older man could feel his anger rising. There were lots of young lads rushing to

463

enlist, thinking of the excitement and glamour of being in uniform. But there was nothing glamorous about war. He should know, he had been in the trenches in the last lot and had seen many of his friends killed and maimed. And for what? Oh, they'd beaten the Germans, but the cost in lives and suffering was too high a price. No, if there was another war, and the likelihood was looking more certain each day, they'd have to manage without yours truly because Jimmy had had a bellyful last time. 'Joining the army isn't like joinin' the boy scouts, yer know, Phil, yer can't drop out if yer don't like it. And yer can take it from me, boy, it's no bloody picnic!' He threw the rag down in disgust. 'What have yer family got to say about this crazy idea?'

Phil lowered his head, shrugging his shoulders. He'd never told his workmate about his family because he'd been too ashamed. And it was too late now to try and explain, because he'd end up telling Jimmy the real reason he intended joining up. 'There's not much they can do about it. It's my life and I'm old enough to know what I want.'

'Well, yer seem to have made up yer mind, so it's no good me trying to talk yer out of it, even if I do think yer need yer head testin'.' Jimmy gave a deep sigh. 'Yer'd better go an' see Mr Latimer about having tomorrow morning off. And stand well back when yer tellin' him, 'cos he won't be very pleased. There's a few apprentices he'd like to see the back of, but you're not one of them.'

Jimmy was feeling very emotional as he

watched Phil make his way to the glass-fronted office. He was surprised at the depth of his feelings for the lad. Mind you, anyone that couldn't get on with Phil Bradley must be very hard to please. They'd worked together now for five years and never a cross word between them. Funny how you took people for granted when you were with them every day, you sort of expected things to go on forever. But Phil's news this morning had certainly shaken him out of his complacency...it was like a bombshell, knocking him for six. He couldn't have felt any worse if it had been his own son.

Jimmy wasn't a shirker, he never wasted time in work. But because of his concern, he now took the time to watch as Phil knocked on the office door, waited for a second then walked in. The bottom partition of the office was wood, the top half glass. So all Jimmy could see of his workmate was his back from the shoulder blades up. He couldn't see the manager, Mr Latimer, but guessed by Phil's head movements that he was seated behind his desk. After a short while, Mr Latimer shot up like a jack-in-the-box. His face was red and angry, and as his shoulder moved up and down, Jimmy knew he was banging like hell on the desk with his fist.

'I told him he wouldn't like it,' Jimmy muttered. 'Let's hope he can talk some sense into the lad.'

But when a pale-faced Phil appeared at his shoulder, and Jimmy raised his brows questioningly, the lad shook his head. 'He called me all the stupid buggers under the sun, but I told him I'd made up me mind.'

Jimmy sighed. 'So yer off in the morning?'

'Yeah. It shouldn't take long, I'll probably be back here before the dinner break.'

'Where d'yer have to go?'

'There's a recruiting office in Pembroke Place. I can get the tram to London Road, get off the stop before TJ's and just cross over.'

'Will yer promise me one thing, son?'

'Yeah, sure, Jimmy!'

'That yer'll give it more thought before yer commit yerself. Think of all the people and things yer'll leave behind.'

'I'll do that, Jimmy.' Phil found it hard to smile. Hadn't he spent the whole night tossing and turning in his bed, thinking of those he'd be leaving behind? Because of the rotter his mother had married, he was being forced to walk away from the only people who had ever shown him kindness and respect. Like Jimmy here...you could walk to the ends of the earth and never find a better bloke.

And Aunt Vicky... The thought of leaving her made him want to cry. He didn't know how he was going to pluck up the courage to tell her. He certainly couldn't say he was doing it for her sake, so his family would leave her alone. He'd have to find the right words to tell her how much she meant to him. She was his family now, and if she'd have him, he wanted her home to be his home. He'd have to ask Molly and Nellie to help him over that hurdle, and also ask them to keep an eye on the old lady for him. They were two he'd certainly miss...they'd turned out to be really true friends.

But it was a slim, blonde-haired girl with laughing blue eyes and a cheeky grin who was causing him the most heartache. She was his dream girl, he was crazy about her. He'd been filled with hope over the last week as the signs indicated she wanted to be friends again, and each night he'd lain in bed dreaming of a blissfully happy future together.

But it wasn't to be. He'd soon be gone and Doreen would find another bloke and forget Phil Bradley ever existed.

May Tom Bradley rot in the hell he deserved.

Chapter Twenty-Seven

'I'd given you up hours ago!' Jimmy Cookson rested his hammer and gazed at Phil. 'I had visions of them givin' yer a tin hat and a kitbag and sendin' yer off to camp.'

After running all the way from the tram stop, Phil was red in the face and his breathing was laboured. He'd been expecting to be back at work before dinnertime; instead, it was now four o'clock. 'That recruitment office in Pembroke Place was like a madhouse...yer'd have to see it to believe it. I waited an hour to be called over to one of the desks, and I thought it would just be a case of giving me name and address in, then waiting for them to send me a letter to go down for a proper interview. But after the officer I saw took all me particulars down, he handed me the form and told me to take it around to Central Hall in Renshaw Street.' Phil, struggling into his dungarees, was dazed by the speed of events. 'When I got round to Central Hall, that place was chock-a-block too! The form was taken off me by a soldier standing near the door, and I was told to take a seat and listen for me name to be called out. That meant another long wait, then more questions and more forms to be filled in.'

'And what happens now?'

'I'll get a letter in the next week or two to go for a medical. The bloke asked which service I would prefer, the army, navy or air force. I said the army, although I don't really mind.'

'So yer've been and gone and done it, eh?'

'Yep! No turning back now.'

Jimmy shook his head sadly, thinking what a waste it was. 'Have yer had anythin' to eat, son?'

'Yeah, I was that hungry, me tummy thought me throat was cut, so I nipped into the Kardomah for a pot of tea and a round of toast.'

'Then we better get crackin' on this job. It's wanted in a hurry, part of an order that's due for delivery the day after tomorrow.'

Phil went at the job hammer and tongs, trying to rid himself of the doubts racing through his mind. One voice was telling him he was crazy, while another answered that under the circumstances it was the best thing he could do. With him away, Tom Bradley would have no reason to be turning up like a bad penny.

His biggest worry was telling Aunt Vicky. He dreaded breaking the news to her because he knew she'd be hurt and upset. So even while he was calling himself a coward for putting the deed off, he made up his mind not to say a word until the letter came asking him to attend a medical.

'If you two don't put a move on, it'll be time to come home before yez get there,' Molly said, walking to the door with Doreen and Mo. She eyed them up and down as they stepped into the street and had to admit they looked very attractive. But she wouldn't tell them that, 'cos their Doreen was big-headed enough as it was. They were off to Connie Millington's, their dance shoes tucked under their arms. 'The time yer've taken gettin' yerselves all dolled up, anyone would think yer were going to a big swanky do.'

'You'd soon have somethin' to say if we went out looking like ragbags, wouldn't yer?' Doreen was smiling up at her mother when she heard the slam of a door. She turned her head and her eyes lit up when she saw Phil. She'd bumped into him a few times over the last week, and each time they'd chatted for a few minutes. It won't be long now, she told herself happily, before he asks me out. 'Hiya, Phil!'

'Hello, Doreen.' Phil crossed the cobbled street. 'All right, Mrs Bennett? And you, Maureen?'

'Me life's full of problems, son.' Molly

grinned. 'If yer've got twenty-four hours to spare, I'll unburden meself'

Standing so near to Doreen, Phil's heart was doing somersaults. He'd give anything to take her somewhere where they could be on their own, where he could hold her hand and tell her the full story from beginning to end. And when it was all out in the open and she knew everything about him and the family he'd left behind, he would ask her to be his girl. They could spend some time together, get to know each other before he went away. And it wasn't as if he was going away for good...from what he'd heard, servicemen got regular home leave.

He glanced at her out of the corner of his eye. She looked so pretty he felt like holding his arms out and waltzing her around, right there in the middle of the street. He sighed inwardly. It was all wishful thinking. Even if he did get the chance to be alone with her, he couldn't tell her his secret...Aunt Vicky had to be the first to know, he owed her that. It was going to be bad enough him telling her, but think how much worse it would be if she heard it from someone else's lips.

'We're off to Millington's,' Mo said, thinking she'd give the course of true love a helping hand. 'D'yer feel like comin' with us?'

'What, like this!' Phil's handsome face wore a grimace as he swept a hand down his overalls. 'I've only just got in from work, I'm in all me muck.'

'We'll wait till yer get changed, won't we, Doreen?' Maureen was doing her utmost to get them together. 'It'll only take yer ten minutes.'

'No, not tonight. I'm just on me way up to the shop to get some sweets for Aunt Vicky.' His eyes locked with Doreen's and it felt like an electric current running through his body. 'I'll come another night if yer'll let me.'

Doreen hid her disappointment well. After all, it was a step in the right direction. 'Yeah, okay!'

Molly had the feeling her presence was restricting the conversation, so she decided to make herself scarce. 'I'll leave yez to it. Nellie came down for a natter, an' she'll be spitting feathers in there, thinkin' she's missing something.'

When she returned to the living room, the smile of satisfaction on Molly's face wasn't lost on her friend. 'Where the 'ell have yer been? Fancy leavin' me sitting here on me own, like someone soft...that's no way to treat a visitor.' Nellie's eyes narrowed to slits. 'An' yer've been up to somethin', I can tell. Yer've got a grin on yer face like someone who's fallen down the lavvy an' come up with a gold watch.'

'I'll tell yer all about it in a minute, so don't be gettin' yer knickers in a twist.' Molly glanced towards the kitchen. 'Where's Jack?'

'He went out the back way to call for George. He said it was such a nice night it would be a shame to sit in the corner pub, so he's goin' to ask my feller if he feels like a stroll along Rice Lane and they can have a drink in one of the pubs down there for a change.' Nellie was fast

471

losing her patience. 'Now will yer sit down, for God's sake. Yer gettin' on me nerves standing there.' She watched as Molly pulled a chair out from under the table. 'Now spit it out.'

'Keep yer hair on! Don't lean out of yer pram, I'll pick yer dummy up!' Molly was smiling as she tutted. 'Yer a nosy beggar, Nellie McDonough. Terrified of missin' anything.'

Nellie gaped. 'Yer cheeky article! How would you feel if yer'd been left sat here like one of Lewis's while yer mate was jangling at the door? In fact,' her chubby fist came down on the table, 'yer wouldn't have sat here like a stuffed duck, yer'd have been out to see for yerself what was goin' on.'

'There was nothing going on.' Molly couldn't help laughing at the expressions Nellie came out with. 'It was just that Phil came on the scene and both him and Doreen took a step nearer to making it up.' Wearing a smug smile, she said, 'I bet they're back together within the next week. An' if they are, no one will be more pleased than me. I think he's a smashin' lad, and I'd be made up if they became serious.'

'That'll be yer two eldest off yer hands, then.'

'Well, hardly off me hands,' Molly laughed. 'It'll be a few years before Jill and Steve get married, and if it does work out with Phil, don't forget our Doreen's only sixteen, far too young to even be thinkin' of getting wed.'

Nellie was thoughtful as her podgy finger made patterns in the plush of the chenille cloth. Her daughter Lily was six months older than

Doreen but so far there was no sign of any boyfriend on the horizon. Still, she couldn't let her friend get away with hogging all the news, so she decided a bit of exaggeration wouldn't do any harm. 'D'yer know there's a new family moved into the Bradleys' old house?'

Molly nodded. 'I haven't seen them yet, but Mr Henry told me he'd let the house. Said they'd had to fumigate the place first.'

'Well from all accounts, they're a nice family. A bit on the posh side, I heard. The neighbours say the furniture that was carried in was lovely, and there's beautiful curtains at the windows. Everyone says they're spotlessly clean, polite, and speak very ooh-la-la posh. Two children they've got, one a big strappin' lad of seventeen.' Nellie didn't pause for breath. The words poured from her mouth as though they'd been fighting with each other to get out. 'An' I believe he's got his eye on our Lily...winks at her every time he sees her.'

'Take a flamin' breath will yer, Nellie!' Molly patted her arm. 'Anyone would think yer were in a competition to see who can talk the fastest.'

'I know I'm going hell for leather, girl.' Nellie dropped her head so Molly couldn't see the telltale glint in her eyes. 'But yer see, I always talk fast when I'm tellin' lies.'

Molly was silent as the words sunk in, then she clicked her tongue on the roof of her mouth. 'An' how much of that was lies?'

'The whole ruddy lot!' Nellie was shaking with laughter. 'I wasn't goin' to sit here quietly

473

and listen' to you braggin' without, stickin' my twopennyworth in.'

'You mean you know nothin' about the new neighbours?'

'Wouldn't know them if I fell over them!' Nellie wiped the back of her hand across her eyes as her huge, shaking tummy rocked the table. 'Mind you, I'd feel sorry for the poor buggers if I did fall over them...they'd stand more chance bein' run over by a steamroller.'

With tears of laughter running down her cheeks, Molly gazed across at her friend. Once again she asked herself what the last twenty years would have been like without Helen Theresa McDonough. And the answer came back quickly...very miserable, empty years.

They were still laughing an hour later when their husbands walked up the yard. 'It never ceases to amaze me what they find to talk about,' Jack said as he opened the kitchen door. 'They see each other every flamin' day!'

'Beats me, too!' George followed him into the house. 'Me an' you must live very dull lives.'

'Holy smoke!' Molly glanced at the clock and was surprised to see it was nearly ten o'clock. 'I had no idea it was that late.'

'Well, yer know what they say, girl? Time flies when yer havin' fun.' Nellie's face creased as she gazed up at her husband. 'Did my beloved enjoy his drink?'

'Yeah, I enjoyed the walk, too. It was a pleasant change to get some fresh air into me lungs.' George cocked his head. 'Me and Jack have been discussing you two.'

'Well now, that must have been excitin' for yez!' Nellie's chins did a quickstep. 'They go out for a pint to get away from their naggin' wives, then spend their time talkin' about them! What a pity yer couldn't find anythin' better to discuss.'

Jack came back from hanging his jacket on the hall stand. 'We were trying to remember whether you two, in all the time yer've known each other, have ever had a row and fallen out.'

The two women looked at each other and burst out laughing. 'We've had at least one row every single day, sometimes two or three, eh, Nellie?'

'Every single day since the children were babies,' Nellie agreed. 'I can even remember our first tiff. Your Jill was in the pram outside, and our Steve had stood on the wheels to reach up and pull her hair. You had a right cob on, came down here roarin' and bawlin'. After that it was a regular thing...rows, slangin' matches, fisticuffs, pullin' each other's hair out, the lot!'

'But have yer ever fallen out?' Jack asked. 'I mean, not speakin' to each other for a few days, or perhaps a week?'

'Don't be daft!' Molly said. 'Of course we've never fallen out.'

'Trust a man to ask a stupid question like that,' Nellie huffed. 'We used to have high ding-dong, with skin an' hair flying, but we never sulked after. In fact, we used to enjoy our tiffs, didn't we, girl? There's nowt better for clearing the air than a bloody good row.

475

Say what yer think, get it off yer chest, then yer can laugh about it.'

'I told yer, didn't I, George?' Jack said, looking smug. 'Didn't I say they'd never fallen out?'

Nellie, her hands on her wide hips and swaying like Mae West, moved towards her husband. Then she opened her arms and pulled him into the softness of her body. Speaking out of the side of her mouth, she drawled, 'Listen to me, big boy! I've fallen out of bed more times than I've fallen out with me mate. Mind you, I've never really fallen out of bed...more like I was pushed when yer passion got the better of yer and yer lost control.'

She turned her head to wink at Molly. 'There's no stoppin' my feller when his passion is roused. He's like a thing possessed.'

His face the colour of beetroot, George groaned, 'Nellie, will yer behave yerself?'

'Ah, bless his little cotton socks, I'm embarrassin' him.' Nellie released her bear-like grip to grab hold of his arm. 'Tell yer what, let's go 'ome an' continue this discussion in the privacy of our bedroom. With me in the bed, if yer please, not on the floor.'

'Nellie McDonough, yer'd make the devil blush.' George could be heard protesting as he was dragged out of the house and down the yard, much to the amusement of Molly and Jack, who fell against each other roaring with laughter.

When Phil got home the following night Victoria

was waiting for him. Without a word, she handed him the letter she'd spent the day wondering and worrying about. He gazed down at the envelope bearing an official stamp, took a deep breath and reached for her arm. 'Let's go an' sit down, Aunt Vicky, I've got a confession to make.'

A hand clutching her throat, her face pale and sad, she sat facing him and listened. When he'd finished, she asked softly, 'But why, Phil? I thought you were happy here.'

'Aunt Vicky, I've been happier here than I've ever been in me life!' The sadness on her face was tearing him apart inside, and once again he questioned the wisdom of his actions. Taking her frail hand in his, he gazed into the lined face he'd grown to love. 'This is me home, the only real one I've ever known, an' I'm hoping it'll always be me home.' He stroked a finger over her hand as he gulped back the tears that were threatening. 'There's goin' to be a war, Aunt Vicky, that's a dead cert. Soon every able-bodied young feller in the country is goin' to be called up to fight, which is only right and proper. So even if I hadn't volunteered, I'd have been conscripted anyway.'

Victoria sighed. 'I'd just got used to having you here, now I'll have to get used to being lonely again.'

'No, yer'll never be lonely again, I'll see to that!' Phil tried to sound more cheerful as he sought for something that would put a smile on her face. 'I hope yer don't mind, but I've put this address on me application form...was that all right? Yer see, I'll always look on this house as my home.'

'And it is your home!' Victoria's voice sounded stronger. 'There'll always be a welcome here for you.'

'I've got another confession to make...promise yer won't get mad at me?' He waited for her nod. 'I hope yer don't mind, but I put yer down as me next of kin.'

The smile that he was hoping for came. 'Oh, Phil, love, of course I don't mind! In fact, I'm delighted!'

'And can I leave all me clothes here for when I come home on leave? If I'm lucky enough to be stationed near, I'll probably be home that often yer'll be fed up looking at me.'

'I'll never get fed up looking at you.' The small hand in his gave a gentle squeeze. 'You know how fond I am of you.' She blushed. 'I feel like you're me own flesh and blood.'

'Aunt Vicky, you mean more to me than me own flesh and blood, an' that's the truth.' Phil let her hand go and squared his shoulders. He'd been dreading this, and now it was over he felt weak with relief. 'I can't tell yer anythin' more because that's all I know. I got chatting to some of the blokes down at the recruitment office, and they said yer get told nothin' until yer get to whichever camp they post yer to. And of course, it all hinges on whether I pass the medical or not.'

Victoria had been saddened and shocked to the core when Phil first broke the news. She'd thought he was happy here, but he couldn't be,

478

otherwise why would he want to leave? But her fears had gradually subsided on hearing all he'd done to prove he had no intention of walking out of her life. Putting her address down as his own, and leaving all his clothes behind for when he came on leave showed he meant what he said.

But the greatest gift he could give, one that she would cherish, was making her his next of kin. The knowledge brought a smile to her face and had her heart bursting with happiness. It meant they were a real family now.

Molly carried all the dinners through, leaving her own until last. Then when she was seated, she gazed around the table. 'Yer'll never guess what I know.'

Jack chuckled. 'It would be easier to guess what yer don't know, love.'

'Aye, well, this will surprise yez. It certainly surprised me.' Her eyes fastened on each one in turn. 'Phil Bradley has joined the army.'

Knives and forks were lowered to plates. 'That certainly is a surprise,' Jack said. 'I'd never have guessed that in a month of Sundays.'

'The lucky beggar!' Tommy said. 'I wish I was old enough.'

'When was this, Mam?' Jill asked, conscious of Doreen sitting beside her as still as a statue. 'He must have done it on the spur of the moment.'

'Apparently he signed up a couple of weeks ago. He's gone for his medical today.' Molly was watching Doreen out of the corner of her eye and noted the pale face and the lips set in a straight line. Perhaps it would have been better to take Doreen on one side and tell her first. But whichever way she'd handled it, the result was going to be the same

'Yer mean he's known for a couple of weeks and not said anythin'?' Anger was the only remedy for the emotions coursing through Doreen's mind. It was either that or bursting into tears. With just a few words, her mother had sent her dreams tumbling. 'I think that's deceitful and dead mean.'

'He had his reasons, sunshine.' Molly's look told Jack she would tell him later. They'd never spoken in front of the children about the night they'd caught the Bradley man in the entry, intent on doing evil. It only needed one person to let the cat out of the bag and it would have been around the street like wildfire, eventually reaching Miss Clegg's ears. So while Molly thought Phil had gone to extremes in joining the army, she sympathised with his reasons, as would Jack when she explained it to him. 'He didn't say anythin', love, 'cos he didn't want to upset Victoria until it was all settled.'

'Well, I think he's sly.' Doreen bent her head and viciously stabbed a sausage with her fork. 'I don't care what yer say, he's sly an' underhanded.'

Jill sighed softly, wishing there was some way she could comfort her sister. She remembered how sad she'd been when she and Steve had fallen out. But in Doreen's present frame of mind, words of comfort would probably make things worse.

Tommy, too young to understand the mysteries of love and romance, rushed to Phil's defence. 'The bloke's joined the army! He's a flippin' hero, so don't you be callin' him fit to burn.'

'You keep yer big nose out of it.' Sparks flew from Doreen's eyes as she glared at her brother. 'I'll call him what I like.'

'That's enough.' Jack banged the end of his knife on the table. 'Let's have some manners while we're eating, shall we?'

'One big happy family,' Molly said drily. But her heart went out to her daughter. Young love could be very painful, and there was no cure for it. But Phil certainly hadn't helped. He'd admitted to Molly that he was too much of a coward to tell Aunt Vicky, and that was why he hadn't mentioned it to his friends. Molly understood and appreciated his honesty, but if he was hoping to win her daughter's hand, he was going about it in the wrong way. He really should have considered her feelings, too.

'I wish I wasn't so helpless,' Victoria complained. 'I get so frustrated not being able to do things.'

'And what things would yer like to be doing?' asked Molly, sitting on the couch next to Nellie. 'Not flyin' through the air with the greatest of ease, like that feller on the flying trapeze?'

'Nothing quite so daring.' Victoria smiled faintly as she rocked back and forth in her chair. 'If I had more strength in me legs, and the use of me two hands, I'd be quite satisfied. At least I'd be able to go to the station with Phil tomorrow night to see him off. All the other lads will have their families with them, but he'll be on his own.'

Molly glanced briefly at Nellie, and when her friend nodded, she smiled across at the old lady. 'He won't be on his own because me an' Nellie are goin' down to Lime Street to see him off. And we're taking a surprise guest with us.'

The rocking chair was still. 'Is Doreen going with you?'

Molly pulled a face. 'There's no joy there, worse luck. I wish there was, but Doreen won't even listen when I try talkin' to her. No, our surprise guest is none other than yerself.'

'Me! But I'd never make it down there!'

'Of course yer would!' Nellie said. 'With me an' Molly either side of yer, it'll be a doddle.'

'Oh, if only I could.' The faded eyes were wistful. 'But I'd be too much of a burden to you.'

'Ay, Tilly Mint! We didn't come over to ask if yer'd like to go,' Molly told her. 'We came to tell yer that yer are! Me an' Nellie have got it all sorted out, so we'll have no arguments if yer don't mind.'

Victoria could feel herself getting excited. 'I feel like Cinderella being told she can go to the ball.'

'Well, there'll be no coach an' horses, sunshine, only the twenty-two tram. But yer will get to see yer Prince Charming off.'

There was a catch in Victoria's voice when she spoke. 'You two are so good to me, I'll never be able to repay you. But I do mention yez in me prayers every night.'

Molly stood up and cupped the lined face in her hands. 'Me an' Nellie don't want any thanks, we do what we can because we think the world of yer. An' we've grown fond of Phil as well, so we wouldn't let him go off without someone there to wave him goodbye.'

Nellie pulled on the back of Molly's coat to hoist herself up from the couch. 'Get yer best clothes out, Victoria, an' I'll pick them up later to iron ready for tomorrow night.' She gave Molly a dig. 'Come on, girl, I want to get to the shops before one.'

'I'll sort a dress and cardi out for meself, Nellie.' Victoria had perked up a lot since they'd sprung the surprise and her eyes were bright with eagerness. 'Phil's gone down to the works to see his mates, but he should be back soon so I'll send him over with them, save yer coming back.' They'd reached the front door when they heard her call, 'You've made an old lady very happy.'

Nellie almost fell down the step. Her voice charged with emotion, she gulped, 'I'm goin' to cry.'

'Don't you dare, Nellie McDonough!' Molly swallowed the lump in her throat, sniffed, then added, 'I'll break yer ruddy neck if yer start me off...so remember, yer've been warned!'

Chapter Twenty-Eight

'I'm blowed if I can make you out,' Maureen said, breaking into a trot to keep abreast of Doreen. 'I got me head bit off when I told yer I thought yer were mean for not saying goodbye to Phil...yer never wanted to see or hear of him again. I even let yer talk me into borrowing a tanner off me mam to go to Millington's with yer, so yer wouldn't be around when he left.' She grabbed her friend's arm to slow her pace down. 'Then, come the interval, yer suddenly change yer mind an' can't get home quick enough.'

'I'm everythin' yer say I am, Mo, bad-tempered, contrary, selfish and childish. But will yer leave it until tomorrow to have a go at me, please? I'd just like to see Phil before he leaves.'

'Some hope you've got! It's a quarter past ten!' Maureen huffed impatiently. 'Oh, come on then, let's start legging it.'

Jack's brows shot up when the two girls ran in, breathless. 'I didn't expect you back so early.'

'Dad, what time is Phil's train?' Doreen's pride had flown out of the window. She didn't care if she made a fool of herself as long as she saw Phil before he left.

'Oh, I couldn't tell yer that, love. All I know is he was told to be on platform two at Lime Street station at ten o'clock.' Jack was sympathetic to his daughter's plight, but why had she left it so late? 'They left here about half eight...there were six of them, because Jill and Steve wanted to go as well.'

Doreen looked at the clock. 'We'll never make it. The trams don't run very often this time of night.'

'The last tram to Lime Street passes the top of the road about a quarter to eleven. After that they only run a skeleton service. So yer need to get yer skates on, lass. It may be too late, but it's worth a try.'

Without a word, Doreen made for the hall, pulling Maureen after her.

The station was crowded and noisy. Groups of people were milling around, their voices raised to compete with the hissing of steam and the shunting of trains. Victoria looked scared and bewildered and Phil was quick to notice her discomfort. 'Steve, will you stand by Aunt Vicky so she doesn't get trampled underfoot? I'll have a dekko where I'm supposed to be, then I'll get platform tickets and you can all come on the platform with me. It won't be so crowded there.'

Once through the ticket barrier, they found that although there was more space, all the seats on the benches set out at intervals along the platform were occupied. 'Come on, Victoria,' Molly said, 'we'll stand by one of those big pillars and yer can lean against it.'

Nellie was glaring at the occupants of the

nearest bench. 'They're young enough to stand...wouldn't yer think they'd have the manners to give up their seat for her?' An evil glint came into her eyes. 'Never mind, one of them's sure to want to go to the lavvy an' as soon as their backside leaves the seat, I'll nab it for yer.'

'I'm all right, Nellie, so don't be worrying.' Victoria's nerves were settling down now as she got used to the noise, and she was beginning to enjoy a feeling of excitement. It was donkey's years since she'd been into town, and the last time she could remember being on Lime Street station was when she was a teenager, going on holiday with her parents. She gazed at the groups of people nearby, mostly women who she guessed had come to see their sons or boyfriends off. One or two of the younger women looked sad, but most of them were laughing and joking.

Phil was standing talking to Steve and Jill, and Victoria feasted her eyes on the boy who had made such an impact on her life. With his height and blond good looks, he stood out from the rest of the crowd. Mind you, she conceded, Steve McDonough, with his dark hair, flashing white teeth and attractive dimples, ran him a close second.

Time passed quickly, with Nellie keeping them amused with her antics. But when it got near to eleven o'clock, Molly voiced her thoughts. 'It's a wonder no one's been around to let yer know what's goin' on! I mean, the train that's in now, is that the one you're going

486

on! An' if it is, what time is it due out, and where's it takin' yer?'

'Yer know as much as me, Mrs Bennett! And listening to these people here, they've no more idea than I have.' Phil's heart and mind were filled with mixed emotions. Apprehension about what lay ahead of him, happiness and gratitude that these people had shown their true friendship by coming along tonight to wish him well, and sadness that the one person he'd give the world to see wasn't here. He'd held on to a glimmer of hope that she wouldn't let him down, glancing at the huge station clock every few seconds and scanning the late arrivals who were crowding on to the platform. But when the hands on the clock turned eleven, his hopes faded completely.

Molly had been watching him and sensed his hopes and, disappointment. She didn't have a magic wand to wave and grant his wish, but perhaps a little pep talk would help. 'Jill, will yer stand here a minute while I have a word with Phil?'

They moved a little way from the group, and it was Phil who spoke first. 'I've been waitin' for a chance to get yer on yer own, Mrs Bennett, to ask a favour. Remember yer told me once that you an' Mrs Mac had met a woman who lives near Tom Bradley's scrapyard?' He waited for Molly's nod before pulling an envelope from his pocket. 'Would yer ask her to pass this into the yard for me? It's addressed to me mam, but I know he'll open it. I want to make sure they know I've joined the army so they'll steer clear of Aunt Vicky.'

Molly crammed the envelope into her pocket before anyone could see it. She'd tell Nellie about it tomorrow and the two of them could go and see Millicent again. 'Your family have got a lot to answer for, son, tryin' to ruin yer life for yer. But don't you let them win, d'yer hear?' She chucked him under the chin. 'You make a good life for yerself and to hell with them.'

'I intend to, Mrs Bennett. I've got it all planned out for when I get out of the army. First of all I'm goin' to have me name changed by deed poll, from Bradley to me real dad's name. Then I'm goin' to see if I can trace his family. I know the area where he lived, so I'll start there.'

'Good thinkin', son!' There was admiration in Molly's voice. Then a gem of an idea formed in her mind. She knew his dad's name and Corker knew the neighbourhood he came from, so what was to stop her and Nellie making some enquiries? That would be right up their street...they were good at detective work. And they'd be doing something to help a nice young lad who'd had to battle against the odds all his life.

'Mam!'

The urgency of the cry caused them both to turn, and there was Jill dancing up and down, clapping her hands, her face aglow. 'What's the matter?' Molly hurried to her side.

'Look who's coming down the platform.'

All eyes followed Jill's pointing finger, and there, rushing towards them, were Doreen and her friend.

Phil was rooted to the spot for a few seconds, then he was pushing people aside in his haste to reach Doreen. He held his arms wide and she ran into them as though it was the most natural thing in the world.

'Well, well, well! Wonders will never cease!' Molly was grinning from ear to ear, her heart warmed by the happiness shining from the two young faces. 'It seems my daughter has pocketed her pride and grown up at last.'

'Better late than never, Mrs B.' Steve smiled, showing his dimples. 'Doreen is stubborn, but she's not stupid. She knows a good thing when she sees one.'

'I'm made up for them.' Jill was too choked to say more.

'They make a lovely couple,' Victoria said, adding softly, 'I hope if they get wed I'm still alive to see it.'

'Bloody hell!' Nellie snorted. 'She hasn't had her first kiss yet, an' you lot have got them married off!'

'Nellie, have yer no romance in yer soul?' Molly asked. 'Think back to when yer were young yerself.'

'Don't remind me of when I was young, girl, or...' Nellie broke off, her face screwed up with laughter. 'No, I'd better keep me mouth shut or I'll have yer all blushing.'

Phil heard the laughter behind him and broke

away from Doreen, but he kept hold of her hand. 'Thanks for coming.'

'Ay, what about me?' Maureen came to stand beside him. 'Don't I get a thank you?'

'Of course yer do.' Phil kissed her cheek. 'Thank you, Mo.'

'Don't you be fluttering yer eyes at him.' Doreen feigned anger. 'He's spoken for.'

Molly saw some uniformed soldiers moving between the groups higher up the platform. They seemed to be checking warrants and Molly guessed the time was nearing to say goodbye. Doreen really had left it very late to come to her senses. But the young couple could still have some time on their own if the rest of the company departed. 'There's a lot of activity goin' on at last, so I think it's time for us to leave. And anyway, I think Victoria's tired, aren't yer, sunshine?'

Taking the hint, the old lady nodded. 'It's way past my bedtime.'

Everyone stood back while Phil held the frail body close. He kissed her and promised to write every day. It would have been a very long and tearful farewell if Molly hadn't stepped in. 'Come on, Victoria, give someone else a chance.'

Taking their cue from Molly, Jill and Steve wasted no time. It was Nellie who grumbled. 'Why can't we stay an' see the lad on to the train?'

''Cos I say so, that's why.' Molly gave Steve the eye and he and Jill took up positions either side of Victoria and led her away, while Molly

490

wrestled with a protesting Nellie and called for Maureen to follow.

Alone at last, Phil gazed down into the vivid blue eyes that had knocked him for six the first time they'd met. 'Yer'll never know how happy I am that yer came. I've got segs on me eyes lookin' out for yer, but when it got to eleven o'clock I'd given up.'

'We only just made it...it was the last tram coming to Lime Street.' Doreen's heart was beating fifteen to the dozen. 'I'd have kicked meself for being so stupid if we'd missed that tram.'

Phil reached for her hands. 'Will you be my girl?'

'I'll have to think about that, Phil Bradley! Yer've kissed everyone else but me! Even Maureen got a peck.'

'I can soon remedy that.' Phil dropped her hands and took her in his arms. 'It reminds me of when we used to dance at Barlows Lane.' He started to sway and crooned softly in her ear, '"I'll see you in my dreams, hold you in my dreams".'

'Phil Bradley, if I don't get that kiss soon, I'll clock yer one.'

When their lips met, Doreen felt as though she was floating in the air. She'd dreamed of this so often, but had never imagined it would do this to her.

And to think she'd waited until he was going away to let him know how much she cared. So much precious time wasted. But he'd be coming home on leave and they could make up for lost time. They could go dancing, sit in the back row of the pictures and hold hands, perhaps sneak a kiss in the darkness. And they could write to each other every day while he was away, put their feelings down on paper. That way, by the time he came home for good they'd know everything there was to know about each other.

Doreen sighed as Phil's lips caressed hers. She knew if she told her mam how she felt, she'd be told she was too young at sixteen to be planning her future. And she'd get a lecture on the uncertain times they were living in, with no one knowing for sure what was going to happen. But Doreen didn't want to think of anything that would mar her happiness. She was in love with Phil, her first sweetheart, and her heart told her that it was with him she would share her future.

Phil lifted his face. 'I've gone all light-headed.'

'Me too,' Doreen answered dreamily.

'Perhaps it's because it's the first time.' Phil's handsome face beamed, This had to be the happiest day of his life. 'Shall we try it again and see what happens?'

'Oh, yes please!'

'Will yer stop pushin' me?' Nellie pulled her arm free as they reached the turnstile. 'All this way an' we don't even stay to see the lad off! I even brought a hankie with me so I could wave to him as the train pulled out.'

'Nellie, the officers are roundin' all the blokes

492

up now, an' I wanted to let Doreen an' Phil have a few minutes to themselves. Surely yer wouldn't begrudge them that?'

Nellie looked sheepish. 'I never gave it a thought, girl! Yer right, I've no romance in me...thick as two short planks, I am.'

'Ay, I'll not let anyone say my mate's as thick as two short planks...not even me mate herself!' Molly glanced across to see that Victoria was being looked after by the youngsters, then said, 'If yer come down to ours in the mornin', I've got a couple of bits of news for yer.'

'Yer can't tell me that then expect me to go 'ome and sleep! Come on, out with it now or I'll never be able to close me eyes!'

Molly shook her head. 'Private and confidential. For your ears only.'

'Oo-er.' Nellie's shoulders moved up and down. 'It sounds excitin', girl, can't yer give us a clue?'

'Just one tiny hint.' Molly winked broadly. 'It's detective work.'

'Ooh, ay, the gear! I'll enjoy that, girl!'

'Yep! Bennett and McDonough are back in business.'

'Yer can forget that!' Nellie puffed her chest out. 'It's McDonough and Bennett...'cos I'm bigger than you.'

Molly chuckled as she took her friend's arm. 'Yer a flamin' headcase, Helen Theresa McDonough, but I love yer just the same. Now, let's go an' join the others.'

This Large Print Book for the Partially sighted, who cannot read normal print, is published under the auspices of

THE ULVERSCROFT FOUNDATION

THE ULVERSCROFT FOUNDATION

. . . we hope that you have enjoyed this Large Print Book. Please think for a moment about those people who have worse eyesight problems than you . . . and are unable to even read or enjoy Large Print, without great difficulty.

You can help them by sending a donation, large or small to:

**The Ulverscroft Foundation,
1, The Green, Bradgate Road,
Anstey, Leicestershire, LE7 7FU,
England.**
or request a copy of our brochure for more details.

The Foundation will use all your help to assist those people who are handicapped by various sight problems and need special attention.

Thank you very much for your help.